I0831704

LITTLE TEXAS COLLEGE

MY SEARCH FOR ANCESTRY AND IDENTITY

Little Texas College

My Search For Ancestry And Identity

A Novel

JAMES R. DAVIS

Santa Fe

Sunstone books may be purchased for educational, business, or sales promotional use.
For information please write: Special Markets Department, Sunstone Press,
P.O. Box 2321, Santa Fe, New Mexico 87504-2321.
Printed on acid-free paper
♾

Library of Congress Cataloging in Publication Data

(On File)

WWW.SUNSTONEPRESS.COM
SUNSTONE PRESS / POST OFFICE BOX 2321 / SANTA FE, NM 87504-2321 /USA
(505) 988-4418

DEDICATION

When I was very young, a genie appeared to me asking my wish. Without thinking, I asked that a lot of women be brought into my life. That included my (now deceased) wife Nancilee Davis, our blind and handicapped daughter, Annalise, (also now deceased), and her older sister Julianne, the mother of my granddaughters Leah, Lindy, and Lauren, who is also the mother of my great granddaughters, Ella and Zoe. Adelaide (now deceased) came from Brazil to marry me and brought her daughter, Marcela, who also has two daughters, Sophia and Olivia. Thank you genie, for this legacy of women—not even one male—sent to me to join and far surpass my legacy of writing. It is to these intelligent, beautiful, and strong women that I dedicate this novel.

ACKNOWLEDGMENTS

During several successive summer visits to the Aspen Music Festival, my wife and I became acquainted with a Mexican woman who was selling handcrafted Zapotec rugs from a cabin near Ashcroft, an old ghost town associated with the early days of gold and silver mining in Colorado. My Brazilian wife Adelaide, now deceased, became close friends with the person selling the rugs, so much so that we were invited to visit her in the weaving village where she lived outside of Oaxaca, Mexico. That experience of visiting and living briefly at Teotitlán, learning about the making of the rugs, and seeing the nearby ancient Zapotec ruins provided the inspiration for key sections of this novel. So, first and foremost, I wish to acknowledge and thank Elena Gonzáles Ruiz for inviting us into her home, her town, and her way of life. Without that invitation and visit, this novel would not have come into being. Without encouragement from Adelaide, I would not have made that trip or started writing about it when I returned home some years ago.

As with all of the characters in this novel, their names and what happened to each of them, are products of the author's imagination, and they are used fictitiously, making any connections with actual people unintended or coincidental. So, it should be noted that the character Juana is entirely fictional and is in no way based on our friend Elena.

I also want to acknowledge and thank Lindy Robinson, my granddaughter from Calgary, Canada, who helped me greatly in providing a carefully edited copy of this novel to the publisher. Lindy spent a year in Spain completing a master's degree and is well prepared in both Spanish and English to serve as informal editorial assistant. She also helped with various technology issues, such as combining individual chapters into a single document with consecutive page numbers and with sending attachments in appropriate formats. Thanks and best wishes to Lindy.

The residue of professor left in me also wants to acknowledge the various novels and texts mentioned in the manuscript as the books that the narrator Carl has been reading and studying. The ideas from those books are important to the story, but none has been quoted directly. Various tourist guidebooks were used to learn about cities or ancient ruins in Mexico, but none is quoted directly. A book on Zapotec customs by Beverly Newbold Chiñas entitled The Ithmus of Zapotecs was very valuable as a guide to Zapotec culture, but was not quoted. For the course Carl took on Texas History, a book entitled History of Texas, published by a group called Captivating History, but with no author named, was also consulted and drawn upon, but not quoted.

Thanks especially to my colleagues at Sunstone Press, James Clois Smith and Carl Condit, for their unmatched competence and friendly working relationship along with their many valuable suggestions. Thanks also to Lindsay Ahl for the creative cover design.

CONTENTS

CONTENTS

PREFACE

In most novels you will find a statement of disclaimer, warning the reader that any similarity between fictional characters and real persons is purely coincidental. A similar statement appears in the Acknowledgements section of this book, but the idea behind disclaimers deserves further exploration.

Many aspiring authors are told by their teachers to "write what you know." Actually, it is difficult for writers *not* to write what they know. The starting point is inevitably some aspect of the author's experience. Much fiction writing, therefore, begins with something familiar to the author that is then transformed by imagination, usually to a point well beyond the reality from which it was drawn. Because much fiction writing is based on something "real," confusion can occur about what is real, what has been transformed by creativity, and that which is purely imaginary.

In this particular novel, the reader will find many things that sound "real." Are they? Consider some examples of descriptions of settings. Do liberal arts colleges exist in Texas? Of course. Are some of them located in small towns near big cities? Yes. Is the college in this novel based on a particular college in Texas? Absolutely not. Even though it seems real, this setting is purely fictional. The layout of the campus and the description of the town are completely invented. They may seem real, but the setting for Little Texas College, including the name, is definitely fictional.

But is there a weaving village outside of Oaxaca, Mexico, named Teotitlán? Yes, there is, and the author visited there as a guest. Are the descriptions of the church, the market, and the plaza, similar to those in this town? Similar, yes, but somewhat changed by imagination, as are the descriptions of the ghost town Ashcroft, outside of Aspen, Colorado. So, sometimes settings are based somewhat on an existing place, while at other times they are completely a work of the imagination. But as they appear in a work of fiction, they are always fictionalized either entirely or to some extent.

The same is true of the creation of characters. For example, the characters in the Zapotec family are not based on real people. There is no "real" person standing behind the character named Juana, or any of the fictional members of her family. Yes, I often stopped at the ghost town called Ashcroft to buy handcrafted rugs. My Brazilian wife became such good friends with the Mexican woman selling rugs there, that we were invited to visit her and stay with her for a few days in Teotitlán. It was through this visit to her home and nearby Zapotec ruins that a credible fictional setting could be created for part of this novel. But the person who invited us to her home provides no basis whatever for the fictional character of Juana. The character from Aspen named Tor is completly fictonal. Likewise, the main character (and narrator) Carl, his parents, and the other students and professors at the college are purely imaginary. Has the author known students and professors like them in his long career in higher education? Perhaps some of them. But there is no direct connection with the fictional characters in this novel.

The interplay of fiction and reality also plays out in the action of the plot. Are the occurences there based on things that have actually happened or are they purely the invention of the author's imagination? This time, the answer is, a little of both. Actual events reported in newspaper articles or on TV, stories that a friend has related, or the author's own experience can stimulate the imagination to create intentional twists and turns in the plot. By the time these occurences make it into the story, however, they are clearly fiction. But in some cases, as in descriptions of Zapotec family customs and traditions, the writing is based on detailed and accurate sholarly research to make the fictional story credible.

It is at the point where the two words *fictional* and *credible* come together that misunderstanding can occur. A writer of "realistic" fiction wants the setting, the characters, and the plot to seem real, to be believeable, but at the same time to be enhanced by imagination. The characters need to look and feel real to the reader, as if they are in actual settings, struggling with plausible problems. But they are not real, they are fictional, and what happens to them is only a story. If you insist on sorting out the mixture of what is imagined and what is real, good luck, but it will be a confusing and unsatisfactory quest. It will be far more rewarding as a reader to look for themes and insights that feel "true to life," keeping in mind that no matter how much a novel is fiction, the author hopes it contains valuable and durable meaning within its created reality.

As you begin to read the first section of the novel called Prelude, note that this is the student Carl speaking, the first-person narrator and main character of the novel, not the author. The narrator tells the story and the views recorded there are his views. The author of the novel should be clearly distinguished from the narrator. Are similarities between the author's views and the narrator's views purely coincidental? Well, not coincidental in the sense of accidental or random. The author has, after all, created the narrator, but the narrator is not the author and the author is not the narrator. Carl is the narrator of his own story. But the author has created the fictional character named Carl and given him the words he speaks and writes.

Writing about college students is daunting because each student generation is different and speaks with its own language. On the other hand, the experience of going to college is not entirely unique for each generation; persistent themes exist and continuities in the "college experience" endure through the years. In this novel, the similarities in the college experience are more important than the differences for student generations. The narrator speaks a relaxed version of standard English, not college slang, and only certain students in the story have a way of speaking that marks them as contemporary. So, don't worry about the language of the narrator and his friends, but focus on the more universal and timeless struggles of coming of age for any student in any generation.

The narrator, Carl, suggests in his Prelude, that the challenge of figuring out the purpose of one's life is not confined to college students. The issues Carl faces—who am I and where did I come from—can be disturbing at any point in life. It is best, therefore, not to think of this as exclusively a story of college life, but rather as a novel about the building of an authentic life now, at the present moment, wherever one might be on life's journey.

Carl's search for ancestry is complicated because the truth eludes him and continues to evolve. Today, knowing one's ancestry has taken on new importance. What does it mean, for example, to be Native American, Hispanic, Jewish, Muslim, or Russian? In defining the self, how important is it to know one's ancestors? In saying "I" is it necessary also to be able to say "we" with some degree of certainty? Or is knowing one's ancestry greatly overrated in the process of determining one's identity? Carl struggles with that difficult question of how ancestry affects identity.

And what is identity? Being able to define one's self by saying confidently and consistently that I am this, but not that. Having a certain amount of justified pride called self-esteem. And knowing what one is capable of doing well or not so well. Carl is trying to build an identity in that sense, and at his age, it is a big challenge . But identity building is seldom a once-and-for-all task, completed, but never revisited. On the contrary, individuals are changed, through the organizations they are associated with, the people they meet, and the unexpected things that happen to them, so that almost every person is faced with building a new identity at some point, perhaps several new identities, sometimes even late in life after losing a loved one. Who am I now? That is the question we ask repeatedly.

If you are interested in the quest for ancestry and identity, and the potential relationship between them, perhaps you will enjoy walking in Carl's shoes, or at least looking over his shoulder, as he tries to figure out where he came from and who he is.

Prelude

While I was at Little Texas College, I had such an odd combination of bizarre and disturbing and wonderful things happen to me, that I decided to re-examine my experience by writing it up, mostly just to make sense out of it, if I could, but also to tell what happened to me and how I reacted, in case some of it might be valuable to someone else who is trying to figure out, as I was, how to live life. Although this may seem like a report on what it is like to go to college, it's much more than that. The things that happened took place at a point in my life when I was particularly vulnerable and extremely confused, and I just happened to be in college at the time. I was running into a lot of new ideas from my courses and all of the reading I was doing, and a really nasty thing happened to my roommate for which I felt responsible. I was uncertain about my ancestry—where I had come from—and my identity—who I was—and I found myself constantly bewildered about the meaning of life. But ancestry and identity are points of puzzlement that can occur at any time in a person's journey through life, to people who go to college and those who don't.

I want you to know that this is not an autobiography or even a memoir—I'm not old enough for those—but just a detailed description of the experience that I had, and many others have, while they are trying to identify their true ancestors and discover their own identity. Along the way, if you read this, you may learn something about small liberal arts colleges, the content of certain courses I took, the peculiar loyalty of professors to their disciplines, communication problems of well-intended families, small town law enforcement, the uncertainty associated with falling in love, and even some intriguing customs and beliefs of a traditional Zapotec weaving community in Mexico. But the main focus of this chronicle is on the intense search that I undertook to find a cure for my nagging sense of nothingness. To put the matter bluntly: In a world that seems not only pointless but absurd, how is a person supposed to live an authentic life?

Now if you are in college, it's normal to ask that question although not everyone does. But if you have just turned age thirty and wonder when you are going to get moving with your life, or if you are entering a mid-life crisis at age forty and you are re-evaluating everything because you don't know who you are or how to live the rest of your life, or if you are in retirement and still have unanswered questions about your ancestors or the meaning of the life you just lived, you may find that you are asking basically the same questions about life that I asked when I was a college student. Of course, you will need to read on to find out whether there is actually any parallel or not between my life of searching and what yours is now. If not, hey, some people just enjoy a good story with plenty of angels and demons, a lot of flips and flops in the plot, and an intriguing romance with an unusual young woman who has the smile of a Zapotec princess. As it turns out, that's what we have here.

Okay, so I had just turned eighteen as I began my first year of college, and now, more than five years later, I'm looking back over that whole experience as I try to tell you what happened. You may wonder, as you read this, how I could describe everything in such detail more than a year after I graduated. I kept a little journal, I have all of my class notes on my laptop along with copies of my term papers on flash drives, and when I traveled to Mexico, I saved the emails I sent back home. Beyond that, I have a nearly photographic memory for people, places, and conversations. I took all of those notes and recollections and put together an initial draft during the first year of the COVID pandemic.

You see, I had just started on a new phase of my life, and I was finally excited about living, but then the "plague" hit, and my dreams were about to be shattered, or at least postponed. But the pandemic provided me with the extra time I needed to tell my story. I've tried to recall, as best I can, what happened to me by revisiting all of my notes and sorting through the fragments of recurring memories. So, if this feels a little disjointed and pasted together to you, it actually is, but, hey, that's life, or at least that was my life. So, let's begin with a conversation I remember having with Brenda.

1

Ending Up At Little Texas College

Conceived as an in vitro baby. Growing up gifted. Being Brenda's boyfriend. Learning how my parents came to Texas. Why I attended LTC. My summer job as grounds assistant. Vacationing in Colorado. A visit from Grandpa Swenson and a lecture on Mendel's peas.

"I was conceived in a petri dish," I reminded Brenda, not quite sure why I was bringing it up again at that moment. But actually, I talked to Brenda a lot about nearly everything.

"Yeah, I remember your telling me something about that when we were in high school. I think you called it in vitro, but I might have been a little young to know what it meant."

"I've been thinking more about it recently."

"Really? Why now?" Brenda glanced up over the top of her psychology text and squinted at me through her stylish, oblong, black-rimmed glasses.

"I've been wondering what difference it made in the way I was raised. My mother—"

"Yes, the biology professor. I should have guessed she would think of in vitro."

"And my father—"

"The astronomer, a star gazer. So, they hooked up in a glass dish," she grinned.

"Have always called me their scientific miracle," I said, finally navigating the speed bumps Brenda had laid down with her interruptions.

"Isn't that an oxymoron: scientific miracle? I thought scientists didn't believe in miracles," she continued.

"They don't. Especially Leon and Elsa." I loved to refer to my parents by their first names at that time. "But for them," I told Brenda, "a chance occurrence itself is sometimes surprising enough to call it a miracle."

"What was their procreation problem?" Brenda looked seriously interested now, put down her textbook, and pushed her glasses up on top of her head. "Do you know?"

"They haven't told me that, nor who was the cause of what. Naturally, I've always thought it was a private matter, so I've never asked them. But lately, it's been on my mind." I paused and felt a sly smile creep across my face. "Why don't you ask them? They'd probably tell you."

"Oh, I can't imagine asking them that," she said, looking a little embarrassed now that she had brought it up.

"I just know that I was one of those really expensive babies to produce and I'm wondering what that means."

"You're always wondering what everything means," she said, drawing out the word means. "Okay, so I'll give you a hypothesis. It means that you may have an overachievement hang-up," she said, her eyes sparkling at the opportunity to provide a psychological explanation. "It is not enough to be the first and only son; you need to make sure that they got their money's worth for producing such an expensive kid."

"There you go again, practicing without a license," I teased, while suspecting she might actually be on to something important.

"Hey, Carl, you asked me what it means, so I'm telling you."

"But wouldn't it be over-achievement only if I did more than was expected? Their expectations are so blasted high, it's hard to over-achieve them. I can barely do what's expected."

"But then again, from their point of view, it's hard for them to know when their gifted son is just coasting." She grinned, put her glasses back in place, and went back to her psychology text, signaling that the discussion was over, at least for now.

If I am remembering correctly, that conversation had taken place in the fall term of our first year of college, and we were studying together in the residence hall lounge, seated next to each other at identical small tables. We preferred the lounge to the library, where everyone was supposed to be quiet but nobody was, because it was the preferred social hub for potentially romantic hook-ups, a buzzing beehive of flirtation. Brenda and I could be found in the lounge most evenings that term, huddled over our books and laptops, serious about our studies. A couple of nerds? Maybe I was more than she. But let me back up a little and explain to you who Brenda is and how we came to be students at Little Texas College.

Brenda and I had been close friends since fifth grade, when we first discovered that we were different from the other students because we always finished our work sooner than they did and had time to talk quietly until the teacher noticed us and brought us extra work. I can still remember the whispered conversations that we had as kids in elementary school that went something like this:

"Are you done?" I asked.

"Of course. It wasn't all that hard," Brenda would reply softly in a matter-of-fact tone, but without bragging.

"Do you think we are smarter or just faster?" I asked.

"A little of both," she said, pushing her little glasses up on her nose.

"Do you think we are gifted?" I persisted.

"My parents hate that word."

"Mine, too. They say it's a label. But the teachers use it."

"And then they bring us more work," Brenda observed.

"Our punishment for being gifted," I said. We both nodded with resignation.

"Only they call it enrichment activities," Brenda added.

"To keep us from being bored, is what they say. But I never get bored just talking to you like this," I told her.

"Me either."

"Neither."

"Either."

Brenda and I continued to be close friends all through junior high and high school, actually closer than close friends, more like brother-sister twins. Although Brenda's family lived on campus and we lived nine miles out in the country, our parents were always willing to transport Brenda to my house or drive me to Brenda's place, or as we grew older to the movies over on Main Street or to a college basketball game on campus. We all met up at her soccer matches or my swim meets, and over the years our parents couldn't help but become well acquainted themselves although they never quite became friends. Brenda and I were comfortable with each other's parents, sometimes telling them things we wouldn't ordinarily tell our own mom and dad. Our parents also ran into each other now and then at the college, because they all had appointments there: Brenda's father, as dean of student life, and her mother as a part-time instructor in women's studies; my mother as a professor in biology and my father in physics although he thought of himself as an astronomer.

Looking back on it now, I would say that my friendship with Brenda and her friendship with me definitely became a problem in high school. We were often seen sitting together in the same classes or standing side by side at our lockers, and the other students assumed that because we were so close to each other, so attached, and so constantly in each other's presence, that we must be boyfriend and girlfriend.

"Everyone just assumes…" Brenda said, shaking her head vigorously to register her dissatisfaction.

"And does that bother you?" I asked.

"What? That it's you? No. If I had a boyfriend, I would pick someone exactly like you. It's not the you part; it's the boyfriend part. I mean, what else are they saying about us?"

"That we kiss, and we…."

"Stop! I don't even want to think about that stuff."

"With me?"

"With anyone."

"They call us 'the A couple,' you know, as in asexual. They're so ACE."

"So what!" Brenda said in a tone reflecting her indifference both to the label and those who were using it.

As a result of our close friendship in high school, no one asked Brenda out, not for smoothies or movies, and certainly not to the school dances, even though she was good-looking. Likewise, the girls never bothered to flirt with me or signal that they were available; they just assumed I was Brenda's boyfriend. I know I wasn't unattractive, and actually I was pretty tall compared to the other guys. My mom gave me stylish haircuts—I had wavy blond hair and light blue eyes—and some of the girls stared at me with what I thought was concealed longing, or at least interest, but hey, they thought I was Brenda's boyfriend. And that's how I began to think of myself.

"Does it bother you when they say 'Brenda's boyfriend'?" she asked.

I had to think about that a minute. Brenda seemed to be much more than 'Carl's girlfriend.' She was editor of the yearbook, a competitive soccer player (but not a star), and eventually the senior class secretary. Her hair was neither blond, brunette, nor red, but a subtle combination of all three, a light oak color like our kitchen cabinets. It flowed to her shoulders with a soft curl and could be worn in just about any style she chose. Her glasses magnified her jade green eyes and she was on her way to becoming an attractive woman now that her braces were off of her teeth. If you saw her once, you would remember her. Brenda had a life. Besides being smart, she seemed to know where she was going and had a clear identity of her own.

"Yes, it bothers me," I said finally. "Of course, it bothers me." Then I had to ask myself why. I played the piano, but I was definitely not a pianist. Mom played the piano as a kid, so she thought I should take lessons, and she had Dad buy a little spinet, the shortest and smallest of the upright pianos, for our living room. I practiced hard without talent. But I was a pretty good swimmer. I began swimming lessons as drowning prevention—Mom and Dad couldn't swim—but it turned out that I was fairly strong and coordinated, so I won a lot of swim meet competitions between local swim clubs. What swimming gave me was a well-developed body, a perfect disguise of normality for the mixed-up dude hiding inside. But our high school didn't have swimming as a sport, and I wasn't known as a swimmer. So you can kind of picture me now, but I really had no identity like Brenda did. I was more like her shadow, and it was natural for everyone at that time just to think of me as 'Brenda's boyfriend."

As nearly as I can recall, that's when I first began thinking seriously about my identity. Who am I really? I remember asking that question a lot in my last year of high school, and it began to bug me that I didn't have a clue about the answer. Simply being Brenda's boyfriend, it seemed to me, was a cop-out, not the right way to think about myself.

Sometimes I considered breaking off my friendship with Brenda. It worried me that we were already mated for life, like geese, only without sex. (I've never been able to imagine geese having sex or even kissing.) But there was no reason or occasion to disturb our friendship. In fact, it grew stronger, no matter what other students thought of us or whispered behind our backs.

We also knew that our friendship was more stable than the precarious relationships of other boyfriends and girlfriends because many of them came to us to share their slights and fights, their break-ups and make-ups, and listening as we did, with sympathetic ears, trying to be helpful where we could, we became convinced that we had the best kind of relationship as just friends. And so, I went through high school without dating a "real girlfriend," and I know I had a confused and diminished self-concept just being 'Brenda's boyfriend.' The question of my identity was definitely starting to plague me. Having an in vitro conception also set me to wondering if there was something kind of artificial about me, you know, like powdered milk.

Like many high school guys, I didn't have a lot to say around my parents. Looking back now, I'm sure I was exasperatingly uncommunicative with them, but they didn't push me out of my comfortable silence; they just let me be. After all, they were a little on the quiet side, too, each respecting the privacy of the other and enjoying their treasured silence for study and thinking. Hey, professional thinkers need solitude. Sometimes there were long periods around our house where nobody said anything to anyone, a pantomime of inscrutable expressions and gestures.

Occasionally, after dinner, while the three of us were sitting around the table in silence, I would ask a question that would get them started talking about something I knew they liked to talk about and that I liked to listen to. Even if we had talked about it before, they appeared to enjoy putting a new spin on the family sagas, and as I grew older, they would begin to add more detail that gave me a better understanding of our odd family and how we came to live where we did.

"Remind me again how you guys met," I ventured. My parents didn't seem to mind my calling them 'you guys.'

"We told you. In graduate school. Remember?" My dad was fiddling with a teaspoon he didn't use at dinner, and he didn't seem to be much in the mood for conversation as he stared out the window.

I was afraid that was going to be the end of it for tonight, so I turned to my mom and said, "I mean exactly where and when."

Mom reached back to the beginning, summoning from somewhere the patience to match my interest, and said, "Well, as you know, I grew up on a farm like the other Swedes and Norwegians in Minnesota, and after four years of studying biology at a small Lutheran liberal arts college, not so very different from this one where we are teaching now, I was awarded a graduate fellowship in botany at New York University."

I didn't ask, but my curious mind wondered why anyone from Minnesota would go to New York City to study botany. Maybe the special attraction of field trips to Central Park?

"If you are smart and study hard like your mother did, you have a good chance of earning a graduate fellowship, too. Don't forget that." Dad often spoke to me like a professor giving advice to one of his students.

Maybe it was his idea of being a good father.

My mother continued, "In graduate school, your father and I had studied in the science building, but on different floors."

"Botany being on the ground floor close to the soil, and astronomy at the top looking out at the stars, so it was unlikely you would meet." They didn't think it was funny, and besides I had interrupted, so I said, "Sorry. Go on."

"We actually met in the library one night, quite by chance," my father continued, sounding a little more interested now. "As you know I grew up in Brooklyn, so it was more natural for me to go to New York University. But my actual reason for going was that I had a graduate fellowship, too, like your mother. At a research university, professors get grants, usually government-funded, and they build into their research proposals the funding for their assistants. That's what you become when you get a graduate fellowship, a teaching assistant or a research assistant."

It always seemed like the same message from Dad: study hard and you can become a successful scholar just like your mother and I are." It's what they wanted for me, but was it what I wanted? "Tell me again about how you met in the library."

"We just happened to be seated at the same table and noticed each other and began to talk," my mother said with an ever-so-slight smile.

"About Darwin and Einstein?" I asked, trying to keep it light.

"More like Mendel and Hawking," my mother said, "but, yes, we talked about our respective fields at first, but we were drawn to each other personally as well. And then…" She glanced over at my dad, and as she hesitated, I sensed they didn't want to go over how they came to live together to save on expenses.

Because I had heard that part before, I helped them skip ahead by changing the subject. "Tell me how it is that you came here to this college, in this town in northern Texas. I don't remember the details on that."

"Oh, my," Mom said. "We both finished our doctoral dissertations at the same time, and we were ready to graduate and look for teaching jobs. We weren't married but agreed that we would get married if we could both land an appointment at the same institution or at least at some place close by. So, we applied to a slew of places and actually received some interesting interview invitations. But if he got an invitation from Maine, the next day I would get one from California; and if I got one from Wisconsin, he would get one from Alabama."

"Until one day…" I led them.

"Yes, we both applied here, stressing our interest in teaching general education science to non-science majors," my mom explained.

"We mentioned in the last line of our application letter that we were looking for appointments at the same institution," my father added.

"And low and behold," Mom said, "they invited us both here for interviews on the same day, and it actually went very well."

"I liked the prospect of being in charge of the telescope here. It's a rather unusual asset for a small college like this," Dad pointed out.

"And we had promised to get married if we could get such an appointment," my mom added with that same slight smile, making me wonder if their marriage was a bit accidental, a promise they needed to keep rather than true love.

"But after New York City," I asked, "how were you two ever going to survive in this little town in Texas? How did you manage?"

They looked at each other with eyebrows raised, as if to wonder whether they actually had managed or not. Then my father said that besides promising to marry, they had also promised each other that they wouldn't stay here very long. It was to be temporary. After one or two years, they would move on.

"But you didn't," I asked, or rather stated, because I obviously knew the answer.

"No, we stayed," my father said with a deep sigh, betraying accumulated distress. "Although we applied elsewhere, we never found appointments together again. We enjoyed our teaching here, we were fairly successful at it, and the academic dean rewarded us with small but regular increases in salary. I suppose you could say that we managed by continuing to remind ourselves that next year we would leave and go elsewhere."

"But you are still here," I said, "transplants from the Big Apple to Texas. And did the transplants ever take root here?" I thought I knew the answer to that, too, but I wanted to hear what they would say.

"Not really," my mom said, glancing at my dad for confirmation.

"Oh, heavens no," Dad said, waving one palm-down hand vigorously from side to side. "Me, a Texan?" I don't think of myself as a Texan." Then he squinted and massaged the round bald spot at the back of his head.

"What then?" I asked.

"To tell the truth I don't think of myself as being from anywhere. I'm just an astronomer in an expanding universe with the good fortune of not having been sucked into a black hole, at least not yet."

"And what about you, Mom? Are you a Texan?"

"No, I'm a botanist. I just happened to land here like a piece of pollen carted in on the leg of a bee."

"And what about me? Am I a Texan? A citizen of the Lone Star State? I was born here, you know. I took Texas history in sixth grade."

They looked at each other again and my dad shrugged and held it, having no answer. Mom said in a very sympathetic voice, "We know it is very difficult for you, dear, but I don't know what to say. You can think whatever you like about who and what you are."

I'm sure they thought that someday I would become an astronomer or botanist or some other kind of scientist, and my academic discipline would help me escape the problem of being or not being a Texan. But right then I had no clear idea of where I came from, who I was, or what I would become.

There is no reason to provide the actual name of the college where my parents taught because it is a fine institution and I would certainly not want to cast aspersions on its good reputation. The college had its pick of qualified students, and US News & World Report put it on its list of "best buys." As my parents taught me, this is a liberal arts college, one of many spread across the US, surviving if not always thriving, still today. Okay, I need to pause here to make sure you know what a liberal arts college is because that's important to understanding my story. The "liberal" part has nothing to do with politics, although some of the town residents think the place is full of woke liberals. The word liberal refers to liberating, as in setting students free to think for themselves, and arts refers to all of the disciplines of the arts and sciences. I didn't go to a big university where they crank out majors in business or engineering who are well prepared to get a first job but don't know much else. I went to a place where everything is focused on helping students discover who they are and where they came from, historically and culturally, which includes knowing something about the science of human origins, art history, anthropology, and literature. For someone as lost as I was, this was a good match.

So, let's just call this place "Little Texas College," which I sometimes refer to as LTC. Now that you know how my parents came to teach here, I will tell you how I came to be a student here. In my eleventh grade of high school, my parents began to talk to me about applying to college, and because my grades were good, there was never any question that I would go to college; there was only the issue of where I would go. As my high school counselors pushed the state universities, University of Texas at Austin and Texas A & M, my parents kept suggesting the names of smaller private colleges across the US, but always with reservations about cost. "Notice how expensive they can be," Mom warned me.

Dad said, "But you can always win a scholarship." I think he wanted to see how well his horse, being me, would run in the scholarship derby. But then he always added, "It will take a full scholarship, you know, or very close to that."

"I'm sure you know, dear," my mother added, "that children of faculty get a ninety percent tuition waiver to attend here, and that's a scholarship that's tough to beat."

So, this little pony applied to some very competitive colleges and universities and won sizable scholarships to some quite notable places, but never more than half-tuition. I didn't know how much my parents could or could not afford to pay for my college, and I didn't think they were necessarily obligated to pay half tuition at some expensive place when they would only need to pay ten percent here. After all, at that point, what did I know about what I deserved or they could pay? So, it became clear as the months passed, after all of the scholarships had rolled in—good, but not good enough—that I would be attending Little Texas College.

"I hope you don't mind, son. It's a good liberal arts college, you know, and besides the education you get mostly depends on what you put into it yourself as a student."

Now isn't that exactly what I would expect my father to say? But, hey, there's a silver lining to this cloudy tale. You already know what happened. I'll bet you can guess what it is. Brenda would also be attending Little Texas College and for exactly the same reasons. At least I would have one friend, but I would need to stop being "Brenda's boyfriend."

The summer before I enrolled as a first-year student, what my parents called a freshman, I worked on campus in the maintenance department as a landscape assistant, which was a pretty fancy title for what my job actually was: moving the sprinkler hoses around and weeding flower beds. During the next year, they put in an automatic sprinkler system and eliminated my job, and then my dad called me landscape assistant emeritus, an academic title, so it seems, that is usually reserved for retired deans and professors. I hauled the hoses out and set up the sprinklers, and while the water sprayed out across the thirsty grass, I weeded the flower beds closest to the stretch of lawn being watered. The best thing about that job is that I became acquainted with every nook and cranny of the sizable campus for our small college. I also cultivated an attractive color—the blond kid with the nice tan—with SPF50 sunscreen.

Little Texas College is in a small town, what my parents spoke of as your typical college town, and I think the Texans were a little ambivalent—they probably wouldn't use that big word—about how they felt about the college, knowing that it was a significant source of revenue for the local economy, but not approving exactly what went on there. The town, which I shall also leave nameless, is situated about thirty miles north of a sizable metropolitan area that you would have no trouble recognizing on a map of Texas. Almost anything a person would desire could be found somewhere in that self-sufficient little town, but if you needed specialized medical attention, some electronics equipment, or an especially fine dinner, you needed to go into the city. Our family never went to the city much.

Stay with me now as I write a couple of paragraphs to describe the campus. Try to picture it, because this is where the stuff that happened to me took place during the first part of my story. LTC was bordered on the west by Alamo Avenue with the sorority and fraternity houses scattered along the campus side of that street, and the tidy bungalows of the residential neighborhood along the opposite side, making a natural face-off between what my parents called "town" and "gown." The college-owned residence for the dean of student life, Brenda's father, was on Alamo Avenue, as if to be strategically positioned to keep an eye on the sororities and frat houses. A formal pedestrian entrance to the campus, marked by a fountain and the name of the college embedded in a stone wall, invited the public to walk in off of Alamo Avenue, but they seldom did.

The east boundary of the campus was marked by a beautiful college-owned park which my mom called the Arboretum and students called the Arb, a carefully-managed grove of trees and shrubs with gravel hiking trails and scattered picnic tables. Beyond that lay the bleak Texas grasslands. In the middle, between the Arb and Alamo Avenue, was the cultivated oasis of our spacious campus. At the south end was the administration building with its two-story columns reminiscent of an old plantation house. Strategically placed around a large central plaza, crisscrossed with wide sidewalks, were the library, the chapel, the student union, and three classroom buildings, one each for the sciences, social sciences, and humanities. These also provided offices for their respective faculties by discipline. The science building was fairly modern, having been built just two years before my parents arrived. Behind it, set back a short distance near the parking lot for the Arboretum, was the astronomical—in function, not size or cost—observatory that my father managed, scheduling it for class use and making sure that on weekends it was open to the public at assigned hours to gaze at the stars.

To the north, on the opposite end of the campus from the administration building, which students called "the wind tunnel," were the residence halls, mostly coed, male and female by floor, and allocated by class. A newly-built set of cluster residence suites that looked like condominiums was reserved for seniors in their last year before graduation. Beyond the residence halls was the field house and a collection of athletic fields for Division III competition in soccer, lacrosse, and baseball. No football at LTC.

Can you picture this swath of campus on the edge of a small town, a mix of old and new buildings, a quiet place where faculty can teach and students can learn? It was actually a rather attractive campus and caught the eye of the visiting parents of prospective students, whose offspring came from thirty states and several foreign countries, including Taiwan, Korea, Canada, and France. How they found Little Texas College is a mystery to me, one of the seven wonders of the Internet. Keeping the campus looking nice, therefore, was not a trivial responsibility, and besides, it provided an opportunity for me to practice my high school Spanish with the jovial maintenance crew, glad to have a steady job at this little college. But who was I to them with their black hair and dark eyes? Blondie? The sprinkler kid with the gangling tan arms covered with short blond hairs? Sometimes I thought I caught them staring at me. On the weekends I also worked as a golf caddy at the country club, and the main thing I learned from that was that I never wanted to be a member of a snooty country club. Besides I saw how golf could become a pathetic obsession for people who don't want to think very hard or long about life. Just hit the little ball.

Toward the end of the summer when my jobs were winding down and my parents had submitted their grades for the summer session courses that they were teaching, we took a family vacation to Colorado, the first such vacation I can remember from my childhood, except for some weekend trips to near-by Diamond Lake to paddle rented canoes. But this was an authentic, full-blown, family vacation outside of Texas, and it opened my eyes to the fact that there actually was something outside of Texas, like snow-capped mountains, sand dunes, and the ruins of ancient civilizations.

On the way to Colorado, we stopped in New Mexico at Santa Fe because Mom wanted to see the art galleries. She had taken an art history course as an undergraduate, as evidenced in her appreciation, but Dad was a little lost with the abstract paintings. I remember his saying at one point, "What the hell is this supposed to be? You did better than that in pre-school, Carl." Mom's explanations didn't help Dad much, but I liked them. Then we went over to Taos and saw the five-story adobe brick complex inhabited by native Americans back through the centuries, now both a National Landmark and World Heritage Site. We kind of sneaked into Colorado the back way on some desolate roads and spent the next night near the Great Sand Dunes National Park at a guest ranch and bison reserve.

The highlight of the trip for the whole family was Mesa Verde National Park with its old ruins left behind by the Anasazi settlers, who built amazing housing structures there, farmed, and then mysteriously disappeared. They left around 1200 CE. My parents taught me to say CE for Common Era instead of AD for the Latin, Anno Domini, Year of our Lord. Dad, especially, didn't like the "our Lord" part.

When we got to Cliff Palace, my dad started his non-stop commentary drawn from the park ranger pamphlets, going on about the amazing scientific understanding of these ancient people. "What they have actually done here," he pointed out, "was to locate their housing under this huge overhanging cliff, so that in the summertime, when the sun is high in the sky, they are in the shade, and in the winter time, when the sun is lower, it shines directly in and provides warmth."

"It is clever, isn't it?" Mom observed.

We walked along among the ruins of old structures that looked like they must have been apartment buildings— Anasazi condos—and crawled down into one of the sacred subterranean rooms where they had their religious meetings. When we came back up, my mom said, "Stop a minute. Listen. Hear the voices down below us in the valley. Close your eyes and imagine the Anasazi are here, real people, homo sapiens like us, laughing, talking to each other. They were here; we are here. It's amazing." I have to admit that my parents were both really good teachers and they were deeply committed to the methods of science, in this case the archeology and dating of the ruins. But…well, we can discuss their defects and shortcomings later.

At the time, I remember being very grateful that they planned this trip and took me along, maybe some kind of high school graduation present or pre-college eye-opener—they never said which—but it definitely had an impact on me and made me promise myself to return to Colorado someday. Naturally, I had no idea at the time of how important Colorado would become for me.

One other interesting thing happened right before my first year of college: my mom's father, Anders Swenson, who I knew as Grandpa Swenson, came to visit us in Texas. I vaguely remember going to Minnesota as a kid once or twice to see my grandparents on their farm when grandma was still alive, but there wasn't much incentive for grandpa to visit us in Texas, and he didn't like traveling alone. That summer, however, Mom somehow persuaded him to fly down, and we had what he said was a jolly old time together. Unlike my dad, he was quite a talker, and he enjoyed telling me what Mom was like growing up as a kid, stuff you just wouldn't expect of the botanist, like being a cheerleader, shearing sheep, and raising a 4H champion pig. What I noticed as I listened to my mom and her dad talking was that there was a lot of family resemblance between them: blue eyes, blondish hair, and fair skin. Naturally, I noticed that I shared all of those traits as well, which were rather different from Dad's dark hair, brown eyes, and swarthy skin that looked perpetually tan. It set me to thinking about why I had so many traits from my mother's side of the family and none from my dad's.

One night after grandpa had retired—he usually went to bed early anyway even if he had no cows to milk the next morning—I asked my mom if she could explain a little bit about family inheritance to me. What I got was a lecture on Mendel's peas.

"I'm sure you learned something about Mendel in your high school biology class," she began.

"I remember reading something about him, but I don't recall much except that he studied peas."

"Yes, he was an Augustinian monk from Austria who grew up on a farm but never lost his scientific curiosity as a monk," she said proudly, as if she herself were an offspring of one of Mendel's peas, blossoming into a botanist.

"What's with the peas?" I asked, hoping to get through the theory part quickly so I could apply it to grandpa and his offspring.

"Peas grow fast and Mendel knew it was possible to study several generations of pea plants within a short period of time."

"Like fruit flies."

"Aha! So you weren't entirely asleep in your biology class. Yes, the same idea, the ability to study efficiently and quickly the mechanism for passing on of certain inherited traits."

"Like blond hair and blue eyes." I was hoping to skip over the rest about the peas, but I should have known better.

"Mendel knew how to mix different types of peas to produce an interesting next generation. What he found was that one trait was always dominant in that generation. You breed peas with white flowers and blue flowers, and you get either white or blue flowers, but not pastel blue, at least not at this point. One trait dominates. No mixing. But in the next generation, even if blue has been dominant, there is one chance in three that there will be some offspring with white blooms. We call those traits recessive. The white blooms, that is. Also, traits are not linked. If they were, tall people would have blue eyes and short people would have brown eyes. No. No. They are independent characteristics, height and eyes. So, there you have it. Mendel's Laws. Independent dominant and recessive traits. The classic foundation of genetics."

Lecture complete, but not answering my questions. I was still curious about why grandpa handed down so many dominant genes. Didn't I get anything from my father? I didn't ask Mom about that directly, but I wanted to. Instead, I said, "If I had kids, they could have my blond hair and Dad's brown eyes."

"Theoretically. Yes, theoretically."

I wondered why it was only theoretically. Mom seemed evasive and a little nervous, like she'd had enough of this discussion. Maybe there was something more important for her to do. But then she asked me if I wanted to go watch the news on TV. We went to the living room, where Dad was already asleep in his recliner, the last thing on his mind being Mendel's peas or his own dominant and recessive genes.

When Grandpa Swenson was visiting, I slept on the living room couch, and we turned my room in the basement back into the guest room, which is what it was supposed to have been originally until I decided in ninth grade that I wanted to sleep down there. Our house is north of town out in the country. Dad was hoping for a better view of the stars and Mom wanted space for a little vegetable and herb garden, but the commute turned out to be a tiresome trade-off, as Dad discovered how cloudy the night sky could be and Mom found out how much water it took for even a small garden to grow in that part of Texas.

We live in the same house my parents bought the day after they received their contracts from LTC, knowing they would be moving from New York to Texas and getting married. The dean made an offer to them both, and they signed their contracts on the spot. He referred them immediately to a real estate agency in town. Just as they never left the college, as they had promised themselves they would do each year, they never moved out of this house either, even though they talked about it a lot. Instead, they remodeled, adding on a sun porch across the back of the house, putting in new oak kitchen cabinets, and creating the guestroom in the basement.

When I expressed interest in living in the guestroom, they didn't object because then they could turn my old bedroom into a home office for the two of them with matching chairs, desks, and computers along opposite walls. They enjoyed their office and I cherished my privacy in the basement. Sometimes I left the basement stairwell door open to see if I could hear things I wasn't really supposed to hear. Looking back on that forlorn living arrangement in the basement guest room, I can see now how it contributed to my feeling of being a long-term guest in my own home, kind of an interested observer and amused bystander, without a full membership in the family or a distinctive identity. Just kind of hanging out with Leon and Elsa.

When I agreed to attend Little Texas College, I told my parents that I wanted to live on campus in a residence hall.

"That's understandable," my dad said.

"Yes, we thought that would be good for you," my mom agreed.

"If possible," I added, "I would like to have a roommate from a foreign country."

That's how I met Ken Lee. He was from Taiwan. Don't get me wrong, Ken became a wonderful friend. But if I had foreseen back then the horrifying disaster that was to take place later, I would never have made such a request.

2

Studying the Origins of Life and Other Timeless Questions

My roommate Ken from Taiwan. Taking my parents' course. Pondering life in the First-Year Seminar. Gloomier than a Thomas Hardy novel. Questioning my co-dependent relationship with Brenda. The picnic for the faculty brats. Holiday break. An invitation from Jolene.

Dad helped me carry my stuff into the residence hall, mom organized my clothes, and I set up the laptop and printer. It didn't take long because I didn't bring everything I owned, just the necessities. After all, I was just down the road from home, and I could have my parents pick up anything I was really missing and bring it in to me when they came to work. I left a lot behind to maintain my tenuous hold on the guest room to make sure they didn't turn it into another office or a lab or something as soon as I was gone. Besides I needed a place to stay between terms.

I was in one of the co-ed residence halls for first-year students, so Brenda lived on the floor below and we could study together in the hall lounge. But it was actually nice to have a roommate, another person to get to know, a guy. He was Ken Lee from Taiwan.

"My name is actually Lee, qing-tian," he explained. "Lee is last name. Qing-tian is first. It spelled q-i-n-g but pronounced Ching and t-i-a-n, like tea and girl's name Ann."

"But does it have a special meaning?" I asked.

"Yes, qing means support and tian means sky. So, think of someone strong enough to support sky. That's me. But most of us from Asian countries take easy-to-pronounce nickname and mine is Ken. Very easy."

His English was pretty good, but he spoke very rapidly and had a lot of missing words and a strong accent, so I had to listen carefully to understand what he was saying. "How did you learn such good English?" I asked, wondering if the phrasing of my question was actually good English.

"My father owns chain of English language schools spread all across Taiwan from Kaohsiung to Taipei. I began study English as little kid as soon as I could pronounce words. Very little kid. Obviously, my father thinks English very important. How about you?"

I didn't know what the heck he was asking, so I said, "I can see how English would be very important in the English language business."

"No, I mean, do you speak any other languages?"

"Oh, a little Spanish from high school."

"No Chinese?"

"No, it's not taught."

"English universal now. We get along just fine."

Yes, I thought, we will get along fine. I liked Ken immediately.

Ken and I attended all of the first week orientation activities together where we learned about the college rules and regulations, the policy of inclusive excellence and harmonious diversity, and the numerous student activities available on campus. A coach tried to recruit me for swimming, but I just said no thanks. The associate academic dean explained the general education curriculum requirements in science, social science, and humanities. Every new student has to take a First-Year Seminar, so I found one among many options called Timeless Questions. Ken and I both signed up to be in it together. He planned to major in business and minor in computer science. When he asked me what I planned to major in, I told him I had no idea.

He frowned. "Why going to college?" he asked.

"To explore. To find myself. Discover something I like to study." The furrows of his frown deepened with each of my explanations. I could tell he couldn't understand this, but being very polite, he didn't say anything more. I gradually learned that Ken and his family had very specific goals for his education as well as general life goals like holding up the sky. I felt kind of lost around him just exploring, like I was slowly hacking my way through a jungle without a compass while he was speeding down a thruway in a Porsche toward his educational goal.

I wanted to start knocking off courses in the general education curriculum and especially to be free of the science requirement, but that posed a problem: my parents taught the course I wanted to take. Origins of Life was identified in the online catalog as 'team-taught,' even though I knew it was just the two of them teaching it together. The course had a really strong reputation on campus and the junior counselors who were our student guides at orientation were all talking it up, saying how interesting it was if you were willing to work hard for a grade from profs with high standards. They didn't know that those profs they were talking about were my parents and I was already accustomed to their high standards.

Naturally, I had already heard a lot about their course at the dinner table while I was in high school, and I remembered how they got the idea for the course and their commitment to teach only what is known through science. I had picked up fragments of the content, like the individual pieces of a jigsaw puzzle, and I wanted to put the puzzle together now. Besides, I was curious about how Elsa and Leon performed in the classroom. But could I really take my parents' class?

My first stop was at the registrar's office where I laid out the problem. They passed me off like a hot potato to the associate academic dean, the same one who explained the requirements at orientation. "It shouldn't be a problem," she said. "There's a precedent. We've had this situation before with the children of faculty."

"I hear they call us faculty brats," I said, just to see what she would say.

"Oh, that's not very nice, is it?" she smiled, running a hand nervously along the side of her auburn hair, as if recalling when she had last used that phrase herself. "But as I spoke to you," she said, I realized that I used the word children and recognized how inappropriate that was. You are certainly not children. My apologies. What should I call you?"

"Maybe homo sapiens? My parents say that we are all descendants of upright apes from Africa, so I'm not really offended by children. I just need to find out how to take this course."

"In the past, we have lined up qualified second readers for the quizzes and the final exam, usually a prof from the same department. How does that sound?"

"Sounds fine to me."

"It avoids any suspicion of favoritism."

"Oh, I don't think my parents would favor me. They would probably grade me harder than the rest."

"Really? I doubt that," she said, looking a little puzzled at why I would say such a thing. "But tell me, why do you want to take it?"

I made something up about not liking the other options and she said it sounded reasonable. So I was able to register for Origins of Life.

That's what started me thinking again about the origins of my own life and brought up the in vitro fertilization bit that I already told you about. After classes started, Brenda and I began studying in the lounge, as we were that night. Ken said he preferred to study in the library hoping to meet "intelligent woman." So there we were together again, continuing the odd couple friendship of Brenda and Carl we had in high school.

A few nights later after that discussion of in vitro, I told Brenda about my mom's lecture on Mendel's peas while Grandpa Swenson was visiting. "I just can't get over the fact that I have no inherited traits from my father."

"I'm pretty much my mother's daughter, too," she said. "I wouldn't worry about it."

"But no traits at all? At least you have your father's big feet."

"I wouldn't call that a trait, but they served me well in soccer."

"Maybe my father isn't really my—"

"Oh, for God's sake, Carl, why are you perseverating on this inheritance stuff?"

"Per...what?"

"Perseverating. The professor uses it a lot in my psych classes. It means repeating something, words or behavior, beyond a useful point."

"Going over and over something again and again?"

"Like a dog chewing a bone after the meat is gone. That's her example, not mine."

"Kind of an obsession?"

"Yes, with a neurotic aspect to it."

"So I should let go?"

"I see that you are still actually having trouble letting go even though you now have the word for it: perseverating. Her voice was loud and she pushed her glasses up on her nose with her middle finger. Did she mean to use that finger?

"Okay. I won't talk to you about it anymore."

"That's not the point," she said, even louder. "You need to let go of it in your head. Stop thinking about it. Drop the bone, Carl."

I should have arrived early for my class in the Science Building, but the popularity of Origins of Life had slipped my mind, so when I got there, the only seats left were in the front row or at the very top of the tiered lecture hall. For sure, I wasn't going to sit in the first row, right under the nose—actually two noses— of my parents, so I hustled up the stairs to the top row and plopped down next to an attractive brunette, whom I later came to know as Jolene. I hoped to blend into the crowd of students as best I could, realizing that the last thing in the world I wanted was to be identified as a faculty brat, particularly the son of the profs who were actually teaching this very course.

Once I settled in, I liked being up high, like a bird perched on a tree limb, looking out over the fifty students that had filled the hall and the two recognizable faces of my parents down below. But then I thought, holy shit, these are my parents. What am I doing here? Maybe this wasn't such a good idea after all. For sure I didn't want to be identified, so I would need to be really careful about what I said to that good-looking student sitting there next to me.

I knew the course had become a campus legend and it was fun to feel the anticipation in the chatter of the students before my parents introduced themselves. But as the class began, I had this weird sensation that the profs were not my parents and I was not really their son. I remembered how some of my high school teachers took on completely different roles in the classroom as compared to when you met them out of class. It seemed that Elsa and Leon had assumed their teacher demeanor, and it was difficult for me to recognize them as my parents. I was wondering if they had a similar feeling when their eyes drifted up to the back row and landed on me, their son. Hey, who let in the Neanderthal? Did I look as strange to them as they did to me?

The professors passed out the course outline and began to talk about the two textbooks, five quizzes, and the final exam. I can't resist saying they started off with a bang: the Big Bang Theory on the origin of the universe. Students began taking notes like crazy on their laptops, a few scribbled furiously by hand in notebooks, and I had to remind myself to pay attention to the subject as I watched the stocky, clean-shaven astronomer, Professor Wallace, stalking back and forth behind the lectern, pausing only long enough for a quick glance at his lecture notes. There was a certain shyness in his manner, as if he was not completely comfortable with so many students staring down at him. A few moments later, Professor Swenson—she had maintained her unmarried name for professional reasons— began to describe how life as an event in the history of the universe came much later, and that she would be making further contributions in a few days as the subject unfolded. She looked out and up at the students, running her fingers through her short blond hair laced with streaks of gray, her blue eyes flashing with excitement about the subject.

Let me tell you a little more about this course as it was presented over several weeks because it became an important aspect of my confusion about myself. Stay with me through the details and remember that I still have all of the facts in the notes on my computer. It was established on the first day that the Big Bang took place around 13.8 billion years ago, setting in motion the outward movement of everything from a singularity, an infinitely dense space of incomprehensible tininess. The Big Bang was not so much an explosion as a dramatically forceful expansion of everything outward. We know about this because astronomers today can observe and describe this continuing pattern of expansion by measuring the changing distances between stars over time. They have been deeply absorbed in studying what happened from the first billionth of a second to the present day, now billions of years later.

From an intense inferno, many, many stars were created, and they formed into huge galaxies. Back in 1924, Edwin Hubble, was able to observe that our galaxy is but one of many moving outwards from that single point of origin. Everything is on the move in what appears to be an expanding universe. All of this was explained in detail by Professor Wallace in the first week.

In the weeks following, we learned about how our solar system, the sun and its planets, formed around 4.5 billion years ago, all of them having about the same birthdate. Our earth, originally a rotating disc of dust, eventually came together in a more solid mass. But then an accident occurred. Dad dramatized this with strong slashing movements of the red marker he held as he constructed a diagram on the whiteboard. A planet almost the size of Mars crashed into the Earth, knocking off a piece that became the moon and tipping the earth's axis of rotation to create different amounts of summer and winter daylight in temperate regions of the globe.

The students were definitely attentive and interested. One student asked if everything would just keep expanding outward forever and ever.

"You are asking about the fate of the universe, which we will get to at the end of the course, if we don't run out of time, that is." I could tell that this was one of Dad's subtle attempts at humor, but very few students seemed to get it. "Actually," he continued, "astronomers have wrestled with this question for years. Although they once thought the universe would draw back into itself, like a ball thrown into the air that reaches a point where it reverses direction and falls back down again. Today, astronomers believe that expansion will continue, with everything getting farther and farther apart, not just things in space, but space itself, before an eventual termination."

Students glanced at each other with a puzzled look, some registering shock. Termination? The world will actually end? How soon? It was easy to see that many students, who were encountering a new idea, were frightened by this prospect. As for me, I had been hearing about the end of the world since I was old enough to stand on my tiptoes and look through Dad's telescope out behind the science building. But now, as a college student, along with other students I am sure, I was asking what it implies for the meaning of life in general if the universe will eventually terminate.

When Professor Swenson began to lecture in the following weeks, I noticed that she did not use notes, but instead worked off of PowerPoint slides, using a laser pointer to emphasize key points in each slide, while expanding upon this base of information with detailed descriptions and elaborations, a deep fund of knowledge that she must have simply stored in her brain. She explained how the earth itself had evolved, prior to the existence of living creatures, by cooling from a searing fireball into a place more hospitable for life, with floating plates of granite continents, basalt ocean bottoms, and huge liquid oceans, unique in this solar system and possibly in the universes. Yes, plural. Astronomers now have proof of many universes. Eventually, methane-producing microbes evolved some 3.8 to 4.1 billion years ago and every living thing thereafter descended from these earliest life forms.

Then, for almost three billion years, the planet was ruled by singleton cells and microbial slime. It was a little boring, Mom added, looking up with a slight smile. Then, 2.7 billion years ago, an amazing thing happened: microbes developed the capacity to draw energy from sunlight through photosynthesis, a process for making food from carbon dioxide and water while giving off oxygen. All of that new oxygen plunged the earth into a cooling crisis and the earth froze, at least many parts of it did. You might think of it as the opposite of the global warming we face today. I remember how she closed that lecture by saying that after photosynthesis, things start to get really interesting, leaving the whole class waiting for the next lecture. Yes, Elsa and Leon were very good at what they did as science professors.

~

Jolene and I used to chat a little before and after class, and one day she asked me where I was from. "Microbial slime," I said. "Oh, you must mean something else. I'm from here. I went to high school here."

"So did I," she said.

"Then why didn't we meet?" I asked, knowing the answer as soon as I asked the question.

"I went to Sacred Heart."

"The Catholic school for girls," I said. Then hoping to put the focus on her so she didn't ask any more about me, I said, "This must be a little difficult for you to reconcile religious beliefs with all this science."

"Not really," she said. "I'm not Catholic. My parents thought it was an outstanding high school and worth the tuition to keep me out of trouble."

"Away from the boys?" I teased.

"Men," she replied with a sly grin. "And other things." She nodded her head slowly.

Jolene had certainly given me an opening to get better acquainted, and I should have jumped on it, but I didn't want to take any chances about revealing who I was until this class was over.

My mother's approach to evolution was simply to describe it, eliminating the idea that it was debatable. After stating that it was a well-established, comprehensive theory based on accumulated evidence, and not a hypothesis yet to be proved, she flashed onto the screen several magnificent fossil-based drawings of odd sea creatures from the Cambrian Era explosion of life forms around 370 million years ago. After describing the mechanisms of evolution as a chance mutation that becomes useful to the organism, she moved on to the complicated story of the evolution of humans.

"I'm sure you have all seen these cartoons of human evolution, starting on the left with some subhuman form and gradually evolving through several figures until arriving on the right as a modern human—usually a white, European-looking male." She flashed several of these cartoons on the screen that day one after the other, including one of a grasshopper on the left and an NBA basketball player on the right, another one being a frog on the left and a Photo-Shopped picture of my father on the right. For an otherwise serious class, the students were all laughing hysterically now. "It was not a straight, linear process," she shouted above the din.

"It was complicated and unpredictable. A mutation occurs by chance and if it is beneficial, the organism uses it to thrive." She switched to a new set of slides and waited for the class to settle down. "Okay. Here's what I want you to remember about our origins." The classroom was hushed but bustling as the students started taking notes furiously again, certain that this would be on the next quiz. I still have my notes:

> Six million years ago: apes split into two separate species, one leading to humans, the other to chimpanzees.
>
> Four million years ago: a species on the human path stood up. Scientists grouped them into a pre-human genus, Australopithecus.
>
> Two million years ago: a large, brainy biped started using tools and was given the genus name homo.
>
> Between 100 thousand to 200 thousand years ago: a new type within the genus homo, emerged, less heavily built, more mobile, with better cognitive flexibility. It was given the name homo sapiens.

"That's us?" one of the students asked.

"Yes," Professor Swenson observed. "And anyone alive today has come down from our ancient African origins."

"Tell us about Lucy," one of the students in the back shouted out. "I learned something about her in our natural history museum at home."

"Thank you for reminding me. Yes, Lucy is one of the more amazing recent scientific discoveries. She is an Australopithicus aferensis, a young woman from what time period?" Mom looked up and opened her hands to indicate she was expecting an answer.

Students checked their notes for the name and date. Someone shouted out, "Four million years ago."

"Good," Professor Swenson shouted back. "They have actually dated her remains at 3.2 million years through argon-argon radiometric methods. She was short, fully mature, and they think she died young, about your age," she said, sweeping one outstretched hand across the class. Some students frowned; others squirmed. "And yes, the story is true: That night at basecamp near the discovery, they were playing a song popular at the time called 'Lucy in the Sky with Diamonds.' She is one of our oldest known ancestors."

The class ended and Jolene said, "I've heard that song was a code for LSD. But that's literally awesome stuff about Lucy. I know some of the students find it disturbing. We're a long way from Sacred Heart High with God creating heaven and earth in six days."

"And resting on the seventh." As I raised my eyebrows, I noticed how thick hers were. Perhaps a direct descendant of Lucy?

The following week something happened in class that I will never forget. It was right before reading week, and the professors were conducting a review. Little Texas College schedules something called 'reading week' the week before final exams, suspending class meetings so that students can study, although I need to tell you that not all students actually used that week for reading. The frat houses scattered along Alamo Avenue were blasting out their live music and holding boisterous parties on their front lawns for most of the week.

It was toward the end of class and a student raised his hand and began by saying, "Maybe this isn't the right time for this question, but this is something that has been bugging me through this whole course."

"Out with it," my father said. "The perfect moment is now."

"Well, if the universe is so vast, with so many galaxies and stars and planets and black holes out there, and if our development through evolution is so chancy and accidental, and if the eventual doom of the universe is certain, then what's the point of an individual life? All of these Australopithicuses and standing upright homos, and now billions of us walking the face of the earth, it seems that we as individuals are literally nothing. So my question is: How do we cope with our nothingness? I mean, not to get personal or anything, but how do you cope with it?"

From my perch in the top row, I could see the heads of many students nodding up and down, as if this question was long overdue and being asked on their behalf. A hush came over the classroom in anticipation of the answer. I could see the professors looking at each other to see who would attempt to respond. After a slight pause, my father said, "It is not within our expertise to speak of life's meaning, only of its development. Our task as scientists is to describe what is known."

A silence hung over the class after his answer, which to the students was really no answer at all. Recognizing this, my mother added, "This is why we have courses in the humanities and social sciences, to help you in your search for meaning. But quite seriously, it would not be appropriate for us as scientists to speak about matters that lie outside the boundaries of our disciplines."

The same student started to speak again, "But I'm not asking for a scientific…" He cleared his throat and spoke up in a strong voice, "I'm just wondering…" and then he threw his hands up into the air, signaling that he had given up. The professors didn't say any more. My dad gathered up his lecture notes; my mother unplugged her laptop. Class was over.

Jolene leaned over to me and whispered, "Oh, geez, he's over it. Giving up." Her ponytail swished back and forth as she shook her head and pursed her lips. "That was not good. They could have been more sympathetic. It leaves an unbelievably bad impression."

"Who was the guy that asked the question?" I asked.

"Nick. His name's Nick. He's president of the Student Senate and popular AF." I have to interrupt here to tell you that being as naive and nerdy as I was at the time, I didn't know what the heck Jolene meant. So I remember going back to my room after class to Google AF and found out she was saying that Nick was popular as fuck (AF). Was that just a cool way to say very? Anyway, I also remember her saying that she thought Nick was literally speaking for the whole class that day by asking his question about nothingness.

"And I have that question, too, about my nothingness," I said, "but the refusal to answer is justified. This is a science class. It would just be speculation and who knows where that discussion would go."

"So," Jolene looked directly at me with her penetrating brown eyes, "you're defending the position of your parents?"

"Who?" I was so shocked I couldn't make a sensible response. How the hell could she know?

"They are your parents, are they not? Fess up. Your last name is Wallace, right?"

"But I have been trying to remain anonymous in this class. I'm sure you understand why."

"Not really. It's pretty hard to be anonymous on this campus. I mean, actually, there's no place to hide."

"How did you find out about me?"

"Oh, I have my spies. And eyes. I noticed your name on the quizzes. Carl Wallace. But my question is this: Why does Brenda have exclusive access to your attention?"

"Brenda?" How the hell did she know about Brenda? "Did Brenda tell you?" I asked to make sure, but I was certain that Brenda wouldn't do that.

"No, not Brenda. But she's a faculty brat, too."

"Are you?"

"Of course."

"What department?"

"Art history."

"Your mom or your dad?"

"My mother."

"Does she know my father?"

Hardly anyone really knows Professor Wallace, or for that matter, Professor Swenson either."

By now the classroom was empty. My parents had left long ago, and the students who had lingered to try to generate their own answers to Nick's burning question about nothingness, had disappeared. Jolene and I were alone in the back row, still chatting.

"Are you coming to the picnic?" she asked with a flirtatious smile.

"What picnic?" I didn't know what she meant.

"Next week is reading week. I'm sure you know what that is, right, and the faculty brats and their parents are having a little picnic. Didn't your parents tell you?"

"No. I don't think they know about it, but if they do, they didn't mention it."

"Didn't Brenda tell you? She's invited."

"Are there many of us?" I was dodging the mention of Brenda.

"Considering all four years, each class, I'd say around a dozen."

"Wow! And you know who we all are?"

"Actually, there's an announcement for the picnic with all the names posted on a bulletin board in the Union. It's not a secret society, you know. There's a place to sign up to bring food if you plan to attend. So now that you are aware, will you?"

"Will I what?" I was still a little dazed from learning that she knew about my parents.

"Attend the picnic, man."

"Where is it?"

"At the Arb. Wednesday at noon."

"Aren't you supposed to attend with your parents?"

"That's the point, yes, but you can come by yourself, you know. So, are you?"

"I need to check with my parents."

"Oh, give me a break."

The next time I saw Brenda, I asked her about the picnic, but she said her parents weren't going.

"Why not?" I asked. "It sounds like fun."

"They call it the B and C Club."

"Meaning?"

"Bitchers and Complainers."

"About what?"

"Faculty salaries. A number of them have told my dad that if faculty salaries were adequate, they could send their kids to the college of their choice, instead of here."

"Hey, my parents think of the tuition waiver as a generous employment benefit," I told her.

"So do mine, and besides, this is really a pretty cool school."

"We could go to the picnic together," I suggested.

"That would not please my parents."

"Hey, aren't we beyond pleasing our parents?"

"True," Brenda observed, "but I don't go out of my way to piss them off either."

"You've got a point, but I don't think my parents care, if they even know."

"How did you hear about the picnic?" Brenda asked.

"From a student who sits next to me in Origins of Life, named Jolene."

"Oh."

"Oh?"

"Yes, oh." She pushed her black glasses back up on her nose and I could tell that the conversation with Brenda was over. But I wondered if she knew something about Jolene that I didn't know. Was she jealous?

I asked my parents if they would go with me to the picnic, but Dad said he had a department meeting and Mom was planning a day trip to the city to do some shopping. "But you can go," they both said, as if speaking with the same set of vocal cords, like they were relieved to be previously committed that day.

So, I went to the picnic alone. The other parents parked in the lot that serves both my dad's telescope and the Arboretum. I walked over from the residence hall with a family size bag of potato chips I had picked up at the Union. I opened it and plunked my contribution down on the picnic table where all the dishes of fancy food were laid out. People were helping themselves, loading up their bright red plastic plates, and standing around talking small talk. For some reason, the students had drifted off into a small circle by themselves and the parents were left in their own little groups. I didn't like that separation thing, and even though I knew I was supposed to join the student group, I went over to meet some of the parents.

I need to confess that I have always felt more at home with adults than people my own age. Hey, I've been an adult since around age six. My parents taught me to say please and thank you and to speak up. I had no siblings, only my adult parents. So, I learned how to smile, shake hands, ask how things were going, and enter in where I could to the subject being discussed by the adults. Besides I wanted to meet some more professors and see if they were really bitchers and complainers.

I entered a faculty group of two couples and introduced myself as Carl Wallace.

"Oh, yes, we know your parents," the woman explained with a touch of accent. I teach French and a course on Comparative World Literature. My name is Jacqueline Bouchardet and this is my husband, Pierre."

He reached out to shake my hand as he remarked, "I'm a cook."

"Actually, he's the chef at Le Grande Hotel in the city," she said proudly.

"And your student?" I asked.

"Oh, yes. Suzette. She's right over there." She pointed at a petite blonde, well dressed like her mother.

"And you are?" I asked, turning to a tall athletic-looking man and his physically-fit wife. "I'm Carl," I said.

"Richardsons here. Kevin and Louise. I teach American history and a summer course for teachers on Texas history. It's required in all the schools here, you know."

"Yes, I took it in sixth grade. All I remember is the Alamo." It was a bad joke, you know, 'Remember the Alamo,' but he laughed anyway.

"That course is a big deal here in Texas. Oh, and this is my wife, Louise. She teaches high school over at Sacred Heart."

"Then maybe you know Jolene."

"Oh, yes, she was a handful. She's right over there talking to our daughter Olivia."

I glanced over to see Olivia and noticed Jolene frowning at me, like, what the hell are you doing over there with the parents? That inspired me to meet some more parents and chat with them a little longer, so I drifted over to another cluster, hoping to meet hers. "Nice to meet you all," I said as I turned to leave the Bouchardets and the Richardsons.

Jacqueline winked as she said, "Thanks for bringing the chips for Pierre's gourmet artichoke dip."

I walked over to introduce myself to more parents, hoping not to interrupt the conversations they were having. "I'm Carl Wallace."

"So, you're the Carl we've been hearing so much about," remarked a tall slender woman, wearing a bright, patterned blouse and laden with silver jewelry. "I'm Jolene's mother."

"You must be in art history."

"Indeed, I'm Vanessa Winter. And this is Frank."

"Hi. It's nice to finally meet you," Frank said.

Finally? It sounds like they've been talking about me. "Do you work here, too?" I asked Jolene's father.

"No, in the city. I'm an architect."

"Nice," I said. "Nice." I was nodding my head too long as I realized that I didn't know what to say to an architect.

Jolene's mother asked me, "And how are you getting along here? I've been wondering what it must be like to be the son of those two scientists. Jolene says they are awesome teachers."

Naturally I wondered what else Jolene had said about me and my parents. "They give me a lot of freedom to be who I am," I said, but I didn't tell them that I had absolutely no idea who I was. "We go our own ways, and sometimes I have to remind myself that they are my parents." I just made that up on the spot, and I didn't realize until the words were out of my mouth how true they sounded to me.

"And this is Professor Schmidt," Jolene's father said as he introduced me to a tall distinguished-looking man.

"Ya, ya, Hans Schmidt here," he said with a strong German accent as he shook my hand up and down firmly. "Hans Junior is right over there." As he pointed, I saw the son they called Junior, who looked like his father's clone, not so tall, but a clear likeness. Jolene was talking to Hans Junior now and smiling this way.

"What do you teach?" I asked.

"Religious studies. The Bible. I specialize in the Hebrew Scriptures. I also teach Modern Religious Thought. And this is Frau Schmidt." She was half the size of her husband and very fragile looking.

"She makes ceramic pottery and paints lovely folk designs on it," Jolene's mother said. "We have our love of art in common."

"Well, yeah, I can see that." We chatted a little more and then I left that group to join the students. But I really must tell you, in case you may be wondering how I am able to provide all of the names and detailed descriptions now as I write this years later, that I became well acquainted with those professors by taking a course from each one of them, not because they were the parents of faculty brats like myself, but because I got interested in their subjects. And you know what—I never heard a word of bitching and complaining, either then or later.

As I wandered over to the group of students, I felt all of their heads turn as their eyes watched me approaching. Had I broken some rule, some unspoken social norm, by going to meet their parents?

"Well, look who's here," Jolene shouted out, the first to speak. "Did you have trouble figuring out which group was the students?" She was definitely attractive in that lowcut tank top, but kind of sarcastic.

"Trouble? No. I just wanted to meet some faculty. I'm new here, you know."

"Well, what did you think of our parents? Did they pass your test?"

"I'm just hoping I can pass their tests if I take some of their courses. They teach some really interesting stuff. You've probably noticed," I said, smiling at the others, "Jolene and I have met."

"We've been taking a course together," she said.

Thank God she didn't say 'the one his parents teach,' but by the way the others nodded silently and smiled, I figured she had already filled them in. "Let me see here," I ventured "you must be Hans." He was the clone. "And this is Suzette" I remembered the blond Frenchie. "And…and…help me out here."

"I'm Olivia."

"Oh, yeah, of course, Olivia Richardson.

"So, you've been talking about us," Jolene persisted, doing whatever she could, it appeared, to get my attention even if it made me feel uncomfortable.

"Not really. As your parents introduced themselves, they proudly pointed at each of you." I saw an opportunity to get back a Jolene a bit, so

I turned to the others and said, "Jolene invited me here. I didn't even know about this picnic until Jolene just begged me to come to it." Now the eyes were on Jolene and there were a few smirks.

"She keeps a lookout for the good-looking guys," Hans said, without his father's accent, but with a touch of warning in his voice.

We talked on, joking around, being cool, and I gradually got everybody figured out. Hans Junior had moved here from Connecticut with is parents a few years ago and was studying in the School of Music. Olivia, the daughter of the Texas history prof, had also gone to Sacred Heart, where her mom taught. Suzette was in her second year and planning to study in France. I started to like them.

Jolene didn't want the picnic to end and seemed to be organizing something at a restaurant in town, but I think it fizzled. I said that I had to go study. After all, it was reading week. I really couldn't figure out Jolene. I guess she was attracted to me, but then she would make these snide remarks to make me feel uncomfortable. It seemed like she wasn't able to control herself, saying stuff without thinking about how it made people feel. Was she a little messed up?

I need to fill you in on the rest of what happened during my first term at Little Texas College. While I was in my parents' course, The Origins of Life, I was also taking the First Year Seminar, Timeless Questions. Ken Lee and I registered for that together, you may recall, during orientation week, and it was scheduled for eight o'clock in the morning, not really a problem for either of us as long as we allowed enough time to walk from the residence hall over to the Humanities Building. It was on Monday, Wednesday, and Friday, and neither of us had a class right after that, so we usually stopped at the Student Union after Timeless Questions to grab something to eat before going our separate ways for the day. We had a good opportunity to exchange our thoughts about what was discussed in class, and we often did that.

The seminar was a small class, twelve of us, and we sat around a large square table in a paneled room on the top floor of what was actually the oldest building on campus. Professor Adams was from the Religious Studies Department, and he had a preppy look about him, dressed as he always was in khaki pants and a short-sleeved shirt with a button-down collar open at the neck. He explained that the First Year Seminars were designed to introduce students to the methods of scholarship within a particular field of study. If students became "hooked" on this field and decided to major, that was okay, but it was not the main purpose of the course, which was to introduce students to ways of thinking and writing at the college level. What better way to learn than by exploring difficult questions and writing what you think about them?

He also wanted to make sure that we understood that he was not there to convert us to or away from any particular faith and that non-believers could also enjoy studying religion. I found that refreshing, especially since I came from a home of unrelenting atheists. I was intrigued by the format of the course. He had assembled a series of what he called 'timeless questions' and then brought in ideas from the world's great religious traditions, not so much as answers, but as a means of framing and thinking more carefully about these questions. Along the way, we were to learn about some of the modern-day methods that scholars use in the field of religious studies.

The syllabus included questions such as: Is there a god? Was the world created? What is human nature? Why is there suffering? What happens to us when we die? As you might guess, we never discussed such matters at the family dinner table at my house, and I quickly discovered that the questions on the syllabus were very interesting to me. I was impressed that they could be analyzed and talked about in sophisticated ways. At the same time, the seminar was also an introduction to the world religions, which I knew nothing about but was eager to explore. It felt really good to be in college learning new stuff not covered in high school.

One day Ken and I went over to the Union after class to get doughnuts and coffee, and it was then that I noticed that Ken always preferred tea to coffee. He carried an extra tea bag in his wallet—like the frat guys carry a condom—and he told me that his parents had sent him off to the US with a small box of select Chinese teas. So we picked up two hot waters, and he shared his teabag with me. It didn't take long for me to cultivate an appreciation for fine Chinese teas.

Professor Adams had opened up the discussion of God very gently the first week of class by introducing the idea of "something more." He explained that some people believe that there is something more beyond the observable universe, and conversely, some people do not believe that there is. He asked for a show of hands. "How many believe there is something more? How many do not?" I didn't put my hand up either time and he looked at me sympathetically and said, "Of course there are those who honestly don't know, and that's okay. They are called agnostics—the

I-don't-knowers."

Adams went on to introduce the Jewish and Christian ideas of God, the Muslim view of the one God and unity of everything, as well as the Hindu idea of many gods. Then he surprised me by saying that the Confucian idea of God wasn't very well developed. When a student asked how there could be a religion without God, he said that both Buddhism and Confucianism in the earliest forms might qualify as religions with no god.

One day when Ken and I were munching doughnuts and sipping tea in the Union, I asked if he had grown up in the Confucian religious tradition, and he said 'yes' and 'no.'

"It is not like it is here where people say 'I'm Catholic' or 'I'm Baptist.' Chinese culture very much influenced by Confucianism and Buddhism, so you be Confucian without choosing to be. It's everywhere, and you are Confucian whether know it or not. And we don't go to church like people do here. We go to temple at special times to give thanks for something or ask for help."

"Professor Adams said that people began to worship Confucius like a god," I said.

"Yes, it's true, but I don't think Confucius be very happy about that. Maybe Jesus not so happy being worshipped either. Today, many people go to temple, but not to worship Confucius as god. They are only expressing reverence for him as first scholar. That's how my family see it. First scholar. What about you?"

Was he asking about me or my family? "Oh, my family…they…I don't know what to say, Ken. They are scientists and not interested in religion. I'm just…I don't know what I am. I'm trying to figure that out. But I like learning new things and talking to you about them over tea." I think Ken liked that, too. He was all involved with accounting and computer science courses, and this gave him "different topic" as he called it.

Another day, he told me that his father was grooming him to take over the family business, and they were sending him to the US for training and to develop his English. He had a younger sister and she would join him in the business, but he would be CEO and board chairman. "Not minute to waste in college," he said over and over. We became very good friends, and it made what happened later extremely painful for me. But I don't want to get ahead of my story.

As the course on Timeless Questions progressed, I got more and more involved in the study of religion. I have to admit that my parents' course on Human Origins left me with the same questions asked by that guy Nick. By the end of the course, I also had an overwhelming sense of my nothingness—a mere accident in a cosmos of accidents—and I had no idea about how to make sense of an individual life, particularly with my own, chancy, in vitro start in life. I had certainly had enough science drummed into me to know I wasn't going to find the answers to my timeless questions by studying more science, and I began to think seriously of taking more courses in religious studies next term. Why not, if they could help me to start making some sense out of my confused life.

I was also taking a course on The Nineteenth Century English Novel. It was restricted to English because there were a lot of novels written during that century in other countries, too, especially France and Russia, so I got a taste of reading literature in that course although I was already a pretty good reader. I was exempt from English 101, the writing course, because I transferred in two Advanced Placement English courses from high school. They call them AP and they also help to reduce the overall credit hours needed for graduation, which became important to me later on, as you will see.

Professor Eliot lectured a lot to give us background on each author and the development of the novel in general, but she also distributed a reading list from which we could choose what we wanted to read. I bought some paperbacks on Amazon and checked out several books from the library to read just because I found them interesting. She described how it all began with Thackery, with Vanity Fair, but then she explained how George Eliot (the male name of Mary Ann Evans) had written Middlemarch, the novel that provided the example of what a novel really could be. She urged us to scan a few chapters, but I read the whole thing; I just couldn't put it down. Wonderful lessons there on what happens when people make stupid decisions. Naturally, we studied Charlotte Bronte's Jane Eyre and Emily Bronte's Wuthering Heights. When we read Dickens, Professor Eliot told us to think of cartoon characters like caricatures of different types of people, but I never really got off on Charles Dickens.

For some reason, I was drawn to Thomas Hardy, and I couldn't believe how skilled he was in developing twists and turns in his gloomy plots. One day, I was in Professor Eliot's office discussing Hardy—I had learned that professors at this college actually liked it when students stopped by to chat—and she suggested I write my term paper on Hardy.

"Here's a topic for you," she said. "Are Thomas Hardy's plots too highly constructed so that they appear to be artificial, or is life like that, full of chance occurrences and ironic events. You need to take a stand and provide examples."

I took up her challenge and carried it one step further: I argued that real life was actually worse than the plot of a Thomas Hardy novel. Professor Eliot apparently liked it because she gave me an A+. What I didn't know at the time was that the point I was making about life in general was about to be demonstrated in the events of my own life—worse than the plot of a Thomas Hardy novel.

I enjoyed my studies in literature, particularly the enlightenment I gained through the concept of irony, but I found that the emphasis was on the writing itself as the aesthetic vehicle for ideas, rather than the interesting ideas themselves. I began to realize that I was searching rather desperately for my own identity, purpose, and meaning in life and it was the ideas that were useful in whatever form they came. I was beginning to feel that I would find those ideas better in religious studies than in literature. I just knew I had more searching to do and a lot more to read before I would find the real Carl.

My friendship with my roommate Ken grew stronger as we continued to talk seriously with each other, not only about Timeless Questions at breakfast three mornings a week, but at night when we were finished with studying, sometimes even as we were falling asleep. I had never had a deep friendship with a guy like that, American or otherwise, and it seemed odd that two people who were assigned to a room by someone in the housing office who knew neither of us, should become so attached.

One night I asked Ken, "Why do you think we became such good friends?"

He didn't hesitate in his reply, "Serious guys. We both serious. Like study. Eager to learn. I'm surprised at what I see in other American students. Not to criticize, but… So much emphasis on drinking in those frat houses. But it's more than drinking."

"What do you notice?"

"Much joking around. Teasing. Like contest. Who can tell best joke about other guy. Sometimes quite cruel. Waste a lot of time—how do you say—horsing around. Missing college. Not serious. You not like that."

As I was falling asleep that night, I began to think about what Ken had said. They were simple observations that he had made, but true. And I realized how alienated I was from my supposedly fellow American students. I was different, and I don't mean that in any snobbish way, like feeling superior. Just different. The black sheep, or is it a blond sheep? A cloned Norwegian sheep. And besides being different, I was indifferent. I didn't really care that they were the way they were. They could do what they wanted. I just knew I wasn't one of them.

It's strange how you can be really tired and almost falling asleep and then your mind suddenly grabs on to something—wham—that you didn't mean to be thinking about at all, and after that there's no possibility that you're going to fall asleep soon with so much anxious shit bouncing around in your head so that you can't stop going over and over it, even when you tell your mind to shut up. Professor Adams said the essence of Buddhism was learning how to tell your mind to be still. Because I didn't know how to do that, I went on thinking about being different. Even the good students, those who appear to be serious, seem to be missing out on their education because they are so focused on grades and credits and their grade point average. They seem to study hard but without applying anything to their life. They look like they are holding their college experience at arm's length, repeating and repeating what other people think, without ever asking themselves what they think. Maybe that's why Professor Eliot liked my paper on Thomas Hardy because I told her what I thought about Hardy, instead of regurgitating what all the critics thought about him.

So here I was at Little Texas College, feeling different from most of the other students, like the king of nerds, loving to learn and applying everything to myself. I knew who I was not; I was not like the others. If only I knew who I was. How can you know what you have to contribute if you don't know who you are? How can you know if contributing is even the point? And how could I pay tribute to my ancestors, as Confucius taught, if I was uncertain about who they were? It isn't easy being king of the nerds in an empty castle, contemplating your nothingness from the ramparts. Thank God for my serious buddy, Ken Lee. I looked over and he was already asleep, maybe dreaming about computer chips. I wondered if he dreamed in English or Chinese.

Ken had met a cute Chinese-American student from San Diego named Susie, and he often went to the library to study with her after dinner.

I didn't study with Brenda every night; sometimes I went to the library or just stayed in my room. One night, two weeks before reading week, I went down to the lounge in the residence hall to see if Brenda was there. I was going to ask her something, but when I got there, I forgot what it was. She was buried in her psychology text and hardly took notice of me when I sat down beside her.

Finally, she looked over at me and said, "I learned a new term in psych yesterday: co-dependent. It refers to relationships where both members, in their own way, have a neurotic need for the relationship with the other person." She slipped her glasses up to the top of her head.

I expected her to say more, but I saw she was waiting for my reaction. "And you think that applies to us?" I said, sounding a little defensive.

"Well, it could. Let's say that I don't want a boyfriend with all that goes with that boyfriend crap. So, I maintain my friendship with you as a kind of defense against having to face my hang-ups about having a real boyfriend."

"Could be, I suppose. And what about my neurosis? Do you have that diagnosed?"

"Well, one hypothesis would be that you are shy and don't like making new friends. So by holding on to your relationship with me, you don't have to initiate new friendships because you already have a close friend."

"But I made friends with my roommate Ken."

"That doesn't count. You didn't have to go out and find and cultivate a new friendship. He was already right there under your nose. Besides, Ken's a guy, and friendships with girls are different."

I thought of Jolene and had to agree with that. "So, you think I'm neurotic."

"We are both neurotic. That's what co-dependent means."

"Well, it's a good theory, I guess. But isn't it possible just to have a normal close friendship? What about love? Can't there be happy marriages that aren't co-dependent? Besides, how do you know when something is neurotic or not?"

"That's why people study psychology: to learn about defense mechanisms, like rationalization, and projection, and displacement. That's how we learn to identify the neurotic aspects of our behavior."

"Your behavior," I said, just to test if it would piss her off, but she was unperturbed and just bulldozed straight ahead.

"Everyone has little neuroses running around that they aren't aware of and psychologists call that 'unconsciously-motivated behavior.'"

I paused for a moment to absorb what she was saying. I noticed how she was enjoying slinging around the jargon. Then I asked, "What do you think we should do? If we were boyfriend and girlfriend, we would break up. Are you suggesting that's for us? Break up? Just because we have a few neurotic goblins, our friendship should end?"

Brenda could not hide the series of expressions that crossed her face as her thoughts moved back and forth across the alternatives. Finally, she said "End? No."

"That's it? Just, no?"

"Not yet. I'm not ready for it to end now. Maybe later."

"But you're the one who started talking about all this co-dependency horseshit. Why did you bring it up?"

"I said I'm not ready to end it yet." She slipped her glasses back in place.

"Well, so as not to perseverate on the possibility of our neurotic, co-dependent relationship, maybe we need to stop talking about it. Just forget it."

It didn't come up again, but being me, I couldn't stop thinking about it. Maybe we could overcome the more neurotic aspects of our friendship without having to 'unfriend' completely. But I had a strange premonition that sometime in the near or distant future, our friendship would crash.

I finished up with two grades of A+ and one of A, the grade of A being in Origins of Life. The professor who graded my exams called me in to his office to tell me that even though he regarded the numbers as warranting an A+, it would not be appropriate, given that my parents were the professors, to assign an A+. In other words, it would look bad. So there went my grade point average. Just kidding.

As soon as the term ended in early December, Ken flew back to Taiwan to be with his family until school resumed in mid-January. I returned to the guest room in the basement at home to brood about what to take next term. I was really getting interested in religious studies and I knew my parents weren't going to be happy about that. What I could do was register for the courses I wanted to take and tell them about it later, but I knew I would have some explaining to do.

Professor Adams was offering a course on East Asian Religions, which included Confucianism, Buddhism, and Daoism, and it really looked interesting. Professor Schmidt, whom I met at the picnic, the father of Hans Junior, was teaching a section of Introduction to the Hebrew Scriptures. I also signed up for Anthropology. Brenda had taken it and said she really liked the teacher. Maybe I could write something on Mesa Verde in Colorado.

During the break, Brenda and I stayed in touch by phone, but otherwise the holidays were really uneventful. My parents talked politics a lot at the dinner table. The front runner for the Democrats was a woman and a sure thing, but there was a former TV star gaining in popularity for the Republicans, who the Texans were all excited about although he trashed their senator, who was also a candidate. I listened, but I found it confusing and really couldn't get interested in politics. It was all just talk to me—talk, talk, talk— and I thought it was a waste of time.

When I was a kid, my parents limited my screen time, so I've never been very interested in TV or social media. I mean, I know about Twitter, Reddit, LinkedIn, TikTok, and Facebook, but I'm just not into it. I use my phone to call and text my parents and Brenda, but that's about it. Oh, yeah, and they wouldn't let me use slang. I had my schoolwork and piano lessons when I was growing up, so when I returned to our house during break, I fell back into my old pattern of reading books and playing the piano. I read more of the novels on my reading list for Nineteenth Century English Novel, some good ones that I didn't have time for during the term. I also rediscovered the piano and worked up some of the pieces I could play when I quit formal lessons in tenth grade. They came back fairly fast and I even memorized two of them, short pieces by Beethoven and Mozart. So, I really was a special kind of out-of-it nerd. I just didn't look like one.

I need to tell you, though, about one surprising experience I had during break. Somehow—don't ask me how—Jolene got my phone number and started calling me as soon as the term ended. Just to talk, she said. Okay, so we talked. That's harmless enough. Then she said she was trying to pull together a party of the faculty brats. That seemed odd to me since we had just had the picnic, but she said this was for students only. I wasn't up for a party of just students, but then I began to think about how limited my social life was: just my roommate Ken and old co-dependent Brenda, really. Maybe I was getting too serious, too distant from my peers, so that I was missing out on that fabled 'college life.' So I said okay. She looked at the weather forecast and picked a nice day. We have some of those in Texas in early January. The students were all to meet at the parking lot for the Arb.

When I got there at four o'clock, I noticed there weren't any cars. Maybe I was early. But it was already starting to get dark. Had Jolene forgotten about the sundown time in January? A few minutes later, when Jolene arrived, she pulled in right beside me, and I jumped out to meet her. We talked for a few minutes, supposedly waiting for the others, and then she said, "Oh, by the way, the others can't come."

"What? None of them?"

"They said they would, and then one by one they canceled. Excuses, excuses. So I guess it's just you and me."

The tone of her voice made me realize that this was what she had planned all along. Just the two of us. She lied. How romantic. "Well, this is a surprise," I said, although it wasn't really. "So what will we do?"

"Well, we are at the Arb, Carl, so we might literally go for an actual walk as long as we're here."

A walk sounded okay, but she wasn't dressed for a walk in that short black dress and platform sandals. Why was I suspicious of Jolene? Maybe because she gave me good reasons to be? We picked up the path at the corner of the parking lot and started our stroll. I didn't know what to say, so I began, "My mom is on the committee that oversees this place."

"That figures."

"She says they've planted a lot of new things in the last five years and it's looking a lot better."

"A forest planned out by a committee."

"Well, sort of, but with everything still natural. They've labeled all the trees and shrubs with their Latin names. Here's one right here. Ulmaceae. See. From the family of elm trees. Jolene ignored my nerdy remarks. I noticed that it was cloudy and getting really dark. No moonlight. I wondered where the heck this little hike was going. I needed to find out some stuff, so I asked her directly, "Do you have a boyfriend?"

"Actually, no. I tend to go out with a lot of different guys without settling in with just one."

"Are they okay with that?"

"Well, that way we don't stay together long enough to make breaking up difficult."

"Going from one to the next like a serial killer."

"Carl. No. What a thing to say. I don't kill anyone. I just gently drop them. If they get hurt, it's not from the fall."

"So, why did you invite me here tonight?"

"You seriously think I did that?"

"Well, that would be a lot of last-minute cancellations now, wouldn't it?" I smiled at her and she looked away. "But tell me, Jolene. Why me?"

"I like you. Besides, you're a spectacular challenge. I mean, sitting next to you in class for a whole term, I really got attracted to you."

"Well, attracted is one thing."

"The first thing. But I literally care about you, too. I do. Really. I'm worried about you." She frowned and put a hand on my forearm. "Wow! Growing up with those parents. I mean, they're awesome teachers and all, but I can't imagine them as your parents."

I retrieved my arm. "Well, yeah, they have high expectations, but they're good to me, especially my mom."

With a steady gaze into my eyes, Jolene said, "I really want to help you with your nothingness."

"That's nice of you, but if I remember my math, zero plus zero is still zero." She didn't seem insulted, maybe because she didn't realize she had been. We came to a big boulder and Jolene sat down on it. "I brought some repellent," I said, taking a bottle from my pocket.

"Oh, that's funny. You must mean insect repellent. Actually, I could use some. Can you rub it on me?"

That's not what I had intended, but I said, "Where?"

"You could start with my arms. Maybe the back of my neck."

"I was sorry I had asked. I just started to pour it on her and rub it back and forth energetically like an athletic trainer.

"Really though, Carl, I do worry about you. You're so unbelievably serious. I never see you where people hang out and have fun."

"Maybe because I don't think that what they are having is fun."

"See, that's the problem. You need to relax. Chill." She reached into a little leather purse she was carrying and pulled out two small objects that looked like old-fashioned fountain pens.

"What's this?" I asked.

"Vape pens. You ever smoked these?"

"No. What are they?"

"This little cartridge here has some dabs of THC."

"THC?"

"Marijuana concentrate. Geez, Carl, don't you know about this?"

"Where'd you get those? Isn't that stuff illegal here? It's certainly against the rules for the Arboretum."

"Oh, don't worry about your mama's precious Arboretum. I'm asking you if you've ever used one of these."

"No. And I'm not—"

"Oh, come on. A little dab won't hurt you. Like I said, you need to chill. This will help."

The next thing I knew, she had handed me one of her vape pens and was expecting me to inhale that stuff. I wasn't going to do that. So I had to figure out how to fake it.

"Come on," she said, as if to compel me, "we'll do it together. On three. One…two…"

No way. I was driving. So, I touched it to my lips, but I held my breath.

"Like it?" she asked.

"Well, I don't notice much," I said.

"Be patient." She inhaled a deep draft. "Like this," she said.

So, here we were back in the Arb, the sun down, Jolene getting high, and me faking it the best I could. She seemed to be enjoying it a lot. "Got any more of that insect repellent?" she asked. "I could sure use some on my legs." Then she let out a long roll of giggles.

While she was enticing me to rub her beautiful legs, all I could think about was getting Mom's car home safely. Was this how Jolene dealt with her nothingness? Vape pens? Look at her. "How are you going to drive home?" I asked.

"You think of everything, don't you, Carl?"

"But really."

"I drive okay high. Literally. No problem. I just slow down and enjoy the ride." Another roll of giggles escaped her.

It took a while, but when she finished, she asked me to help her back to the parking lot. It was pitch-black now, but we found our way, stumbling along hand-in-hand, as I tried to keep her on the path in those wobbly shoes. When we got back to the cars, I asked her if she wanted me to take her home. She looked really stoned.

"Home? No, that would be a bad idea right now. I'll just sit here for a while and enjoy life."

"Do you want me to sit with you?" I didn't want to but thought I should offer.

"Well, that would be nice, but you don't have to." She leaned back against her car and looked up at me with half-closed eyes. "But you could give me a little goodnight kiss, if you will."

I didn't really want to do that here in the middle of the parking lot. What if someone saw us? Maybe that's what she wanted. I could just imagine all of the faculty brats jumping out of the bushes and suddenly yelling 'Surprise!' Unlikely. I obliged her with a little kiss on the cheek. She used the moment to settle her hands around the back of my neck and pull me toward her.

"Oh, man, that was everything," she said with a smirk, and then laughed some more.

"I'd better go," I told her, wiggling loose from her giggling, eager to escape.

"It's okay, but don't forget," she spoke slowly, over-pronouncing each word, "I'm completely worried about you. You totally need to have some fun." Her head bobbed from side to side slowly as she spoke, and her ponytail wagged back and forth like...well...a pony's tail.

I didn't tell anybody about Jolene. I might have told Ken if he was around, but I couldn't tell Brenda and certainly not my parents—or hers. Jolene had a strange way of liking me that I didn't understand. I worried about what was going to happen to her. And me, if I encouraged her.

As I look back on it now, I'm still confused about that encounter with Jolene in the Arb, even though I know now what actually happened to her. I'll tell you about that later.

against her [illegible] looked up at me with half-closed eyes. "Hey, you could get me a little something, huh? [illegible] you will?"

I didn't really want to do that here in the middle of the parking lot. What if someone saw us? Maybe that's what she wanted. I couldn't imagine [illegible] of the faculty [illegible] out of the [illegible] and suddenly [illegible] Chapel [illegible]. I [illegible] her [illegible]. She used the moment to [illegible] her hand around the back of my neck and [illegible] me toward her.

"Oh, man, that was [illegible]," she said, with a smirk, and then laughed out loud.

"I'd better go," I told her, wriggling loose from her grappling, eager to escape.

"It's okay, [illegible]," she said, [illegible] "[illegible] completely [illegible] you [illegible] to have [illegible]." Her head [illegible] from [illegible] to [illegible] and [illegible] convey [illegible].

[illegible] I [illegible] might have [illegible] through [illegible] her, a strange sort of [illegible] and didn't [illegible] going to [illegible].

[illegible] I [illegible] about [illegible] and [illegible] never [illegible] actually happened [illegible] I'd [illegible] later.

3

Building a Friendship, Then Coping With Tragedy

Returning from holiday break. Anthropology and cultural norms. Ken comes to Sunday dinner. Myth and the Hebrew Scriptures. Confucius, Siddhartha Gautama, and Dao. Suzette's tough questions. Why I was named Carl. The black truck. Dad shows up. Ken's family.

Ken returned to the campus just in time for the start of the second term. "How were the holidays?" I asked, realizing after I'd said it, that these weren't his holidays. I think Chinese New Year was yet to come.

"Holidays good," he said. "Parents and sister meet me at airport. Good fright. Happy to see me. Worry about me."

"I'm sure." Was he trying to pronounce the word flight?

"We had many good meals. Was missing Chinese food, especially Dim-Sung. Comes in a little wood basket." He pressed the thumbs and forefingers of both hands together to show me the size of the basket. "Thin dough stuffed with many good things. Shrimp. Pork. Steamed or fried. You know these?"

I admitted that I didn't, but that it sounded delicious.

"I have large family. They all come to see me. Grandmother and grandfather, both sides. Many aunts and uncles, several cousins. They all want to know about my study in US."

"What did you tell them?"

"Going well. Good courses in business and computers. Then I told them about you. How we took deep course together and talk about it. They thought it was nice. Good to have a friend."

"And what about your girlfriend. Did you tell them?"

"Amy? No, Amy just friend. Nothing serious, so nothing to tell.

What about you?"

I assumed he was asking about the holiday break, not Brenda. "Actually, a little boring, but I caught up on my sleep." I considered telling him about the strange walk in the Arb with Jolene, but decided not to. "Did you go to the Confucian Temple?"

"In Taipei? Yes, twice. Once with grandparents to pay respect to ancestors, and another time with my parents to ask blessing and protection while studying in US."

It was good to have Ken back, and I told him that. I could see that he knew all about the members of his large family, those who were still alive, and the deceased. There was no doubt about his ancestry: he had Chinese genes going back centuries. I was a little envious of Ken's family, all working together as needed to help Lee, qing-tian support the sky. I knew I had grandparents, but they lived far away and I didn't see them very often. Did they even think about me?

I realized at that moment how much I liked Ken and that I wanted my parents to get to know him. I would ask them if we could invite him to a Sunday dinner.

Okay, so it's second term and I was liking the anthropology course that Brenda had recommended to me. You don't have to worry; I won't describe every course I took at Little Texas College, just those that had a particularly strong impact on me and are important to my story. Like this anthro course inspired me to want to travel to see more ruins of ancient civilizations. The professor, Maria Martinez, had researched and visited the archaeological sites in Mexico, and after listening to her, everyone wanted to make a visit to Mexico City to see the Temple of the Sun and Temple of the Moon. I was shocked by the practice of human sacrifice, cutting out a person's heart as they lay on a slab of stone on top of one of those huge pyramid temples, and I wondered what it would be like to stand on that very spot and imagine how it was done.

But the main point I took away from that course was about the importance of culture in shaping human behavior. Professor Martinez came up with amazing examples of cultures with what she called "strong cultural norms." She presented some of the early studies by Margaret Meade of Samoan island dwellers and Ruth Benedict's studies of Native American cultures. People set some rules that shape the patterns for how to act in marriage, sex, work, and recreation. These norms that she presented to us as examples, were completely different from ours and seemed kind of strange. Most people in our culture take the cultural rules for granted, Professor Martinez said, or they treat them as absolutes, failing to recognize that these norms are "socially constructed," meaning they are built up over time by the people themselves. Different cultures simply have different norms. She told us to take a step backward and examine closely the norms shaping our own behavior.

As you might guess, her encouragement sent me into another tailspin of self-examination. In my case, it was not so much that I was a captive of unidentified cultural norms, but that I was alienated from them; I didn't embrace them and I didn't feel that they shaped my behavior. I wasn't exactly sure about the difference between US and Texas norms, but from what I could gather about the people around me in this town, outside of the college, I was pretty sure that these were not the rules I could follow for everyday living. And they couldn't provide me with a basis for my cultural identity. Why?

Well, let's take a look. I made a list of the cultural norms of our society as I understood them. (I still have that list.) Sorry to be so negative, but this was what I came up with at the time.

My Cultural Norms List:

Every man for himself, even if it means taking advantage of women.
Isolate yourself from everyone not like you and stick together with your own kind.
Oppose the federal government and its regulations that strangle freedom.
Think of America first and of other countries as third world failures.
Support the military and realize that war isn't so bad as long as it's fought on foreign soil.
If priests molest little kids or if kids are shot at school, probably it won't happen to yours.
TV teaches us that violence is just part of life and life is cheap.
You'll be safer if you carry your own gun, and it's your right to do that.

I have to admit that there is another set of norms, too, such as be kind to those in need, strive for fairness and justice, don't scam or cheat, obey the laws. But I wasn't sure if they were cultural norms that govern behavior or just talk. So, I knew what I would write about for my term paper and it wouldn't be Mesa Verde. I would describe how I felt alienated from the cultural norms of my society. Then I would express how I longed to be part of a culture with clear and acceptable norms that I could value, letting them be a guide to my behavior, even if it meant I might end up on the top of a pyramid some day with my heart cut out. Let's see what Professor Martinez would say about that: an A, or a "red alert" memo sent to the Director of Counseling Services about a student she would probably call El Sicko?

I borrowed my mom's old Honda to pick up Ken at the residence hall and bring him out to our house for Sunday dinner, a lingering cultural artifact of Mom's upbringing in small-town Minnesota. As a kid, she went to church with her family on Sunday morning, and after church, the Swenson's had a big Sunday dinner, sometimes a pot roast of beef left cooking on low in the oven while everyone was at church singing hymns. Well, needless to say, there was no church-going by anyone in our household, but Mom still knew how to make an awesome Sunday dinner. I asked her for something really American, so she was assembling the ingredients for fried chicken, mashed potatoes with gravy, creamed corn from a packet she had frozen in September, and jellied cranberry sauce.

"Ken will love it," I said as I headed out the door to go get him. Ken was dressed in black pants and a short-sleeve sport shirt with a pattern that looked Chinese to me. He was handsome and his hair always looked like he had just stepped out of a barber shop. When we arrived, my parents welcomed him graciously, thanking him profusely for being such a good friend to their son.

When we sat down at the table, my mother explained to him about growing up among Swedes and Norwegians in Minnesota and how she had learned to cook standing at her mother's side. Ken was interested in how everything was prepared, and as he sampled each different dish, Mom explained how it was made.

Not to be outdone in finding a topic of conversation, my father asked him, "Do you know about TSMC?"

"Oh, yes, of course. One of Taiwan's largest companies. Very good. Still growing. Many people learning English."

When I asked what TSMC was, they had to explain to me that

it stood for Taiwan Semiconductor Manufacturing Company, which produced silicone computer chips for other companies all over the world.

"We use computers extensively in the field of astronomy," my father pointed out. "We are worried there will be a shortage of chips."

"Shortage coming," Ken predicted. "More demand than supply. Computer chips used everywhere now. Cars, phones, appliances. Chips control global economy now. Good for TSMC as supplier. Not so good for consumer."

"Are you ahead of China in production capacity?" my father asked.

"Yes, Doctor Wallace. Five years. But we work with China, too. Developing site in Nanjing. Try not to make China upset."

I was amazed at what my parents knew about China, the revolution, the migration of nationalists to Taiwan in 1949 to establish the Republic of China, and the awkward politics of Taiwan's trying to be a friend both to the US and China. As I sat there listening to them talking so freely, I wondered why my parents never talked to me like that. Well, not never, but seldom. What was the hesitation and awkwardness they felt talking to their own child? I remembered being jealous of Brenda as a kid because my parents were always especially nice to her, and I wondered if they liked her better than me. For an instant, I had that same sensation of jealousy with Ken, but then I told myself to grow up and be glad that they liked him so much.

Ken bowed slightly when he thanked them as we were leaving, and my mother returned a slight bow with her palms together, fingers up. A sign of respect. Definitely not praying. He was surely not the first international student she had encountered. Actually, I was kind of proud of my parents that day.

I need to make clear to you that I never once doubted the scientific conclusions presented by my parents in Origins of Life. I was not one to doubt science, and I can probably still recite the story of how the universes came to be, the way the earth was formed, and the process of photosynthesis that became the foundation of life. I am still fascinated by the story of my ancestor Lucy. I have no reason to doubt evolution as the explanation of human origins, and I wonder about people who claim to be anti-science, but who still go to a doctor when they are sick. No, I've never had a quarrel with science.

What I discovered was that science was just not capable of answering my questions about the meaning and purpose of life. Those timeless questions were raised systematically by Professor Adams in the First Year Seminar, and sparked a quest which ran parallel to my studies in my parents' course. Maybe those timeless questions really couldn't be answered, but I surely enjoyed the search for answers in the world's religions. But I was so steeped in the language and methods of science from being raised in a house of skeptics who doubted everything not based on hard facts, that I couldn't project an alternative way of looking at the world. Was there another respected form of scholarship that would help me examine the timeless questions that were simply out of bounds for science?

I began to discover what that might be in the course I was taking on Hebrew Scriptures taught by Professor Hans Schmidt. Doctor Schmidt had been educated in a German university and he knew just about all there was to know about Biblical scholarship. He was also a dynamic teacher with a great sense of humor and he "acted out" the Garden of Eden scene in a way that made the whole class laugh: Adam blaming Eve, Eve blaming the snake, both of them trying to conceal their nakedness, and the anthropomorphic God, Jahweh, calling after them "Where are you?" when they were trying to hide in the garden. It was a great show. Professor Schmidt simply referred to the story as the creation myth. Then he went on to describe myth, and that's when I started to catch on.

Myth is a profound story, he told us, religion's way to explain why things are the way they are. If you read a myth literally, of course it's not true. It even sounds ridiculous. A talking snake? Come on. But if you look for the metaphorical meaning beyond the words, if you search for what it may be saying about human nature, the mystery of our being and non-being, our alienation from God and each other, then you may stumble upon some significant interpretations of human existence. Myth, Herr Schmidt said, is profound storytelling, not just a story that entertains, but an account that tries to explain the most unexplainable mysteries of life. Where science throws up its hands, myth says, 'well, let's take another look at this.' Without providing definitive answers, myth suggests explanations worthy of consideration. Whether you believe the answers or not, Professor Schmidt told us, at least you will have thought deeply about the question and can decide what you will believe. Let me tell you, this was exactly the academic ride I wanted to take because it seemed relevant to my search for the meaning of my life.

The ride started out on Noah's ark, took us through the saga of Father

Abraham, and on to the legend of Moses parting the waters of the Red Sea to guide his people over to the Promised Land. We encountered not one, but three versions of the Ten Commandments, we met the powerful King David and wise King Solomon, and we explored the Psalms, the prophets, and the wisdom literature of Job, Proverbs, and Ecclesiastes. All the time, Herr Schmidt was teaching us about the manuscripts, the multiple sources of the texts, the historical situation out of which they grew, and the reasons why they were collected, saved, and valued as guides to the mysteries of life. It was a trip.

One of the highlights of the course on Hebrew Scriptures, which itself was one of the highlights of my first year in college, was Professor Schmidt's interpretation of the book of Job. Like before, he dramatized the story, and when Job got out of line and God had to reprimand him, Herr Schmidt read those stunning passages of poetry in that German accent like he was God himself speaking from the whirlwind. Oh, my, what a discussion we had of why innocent people suffer.

I really liked that section of the Hebrew Scriptures that Herr Schmidt called the Wisdom Literature. That stuff is very philosophical and full of skeptical questioning. I remember how I went home that night, and after our discussion of Job I started to read Ecclesiastes. When I came to the passage about vanity, I screamed out loud "All is vanity." Then I stood up and shook my fist in the air. "Yes, all is vanity. It says so right here in the Bible." Fortunately, I was studying alone in my room that night, so no one else could hear me shouting "Vanity." I had to find out if I had the right interpretation of that word, so the next day I stopped in at Herr Schmidt's office and he gave me a private tutoring session on Ecclesiastes.

The book's Hebrew title is Koheleth, and except for short passages at the beginning and end, it appears to be written by one person, but not King Solomon as claimed. The main message is that human effort is merely chasing after wind. Oh, right on. It seemed to me that's exactly what most people were doing. So I said to Professor Schmidt, "Tell me about this word vanity. Does it mean all effort is self-centered, or does it mean vain as in pointless?"

"The Hebrew word hebel literally means vapor, like the steam coming from a teakettle. Modern commentators offer the word absurd as an equivalent. But a key meaning of the word hebel is transitoriness. Nothing lasts."

"Like the teaching of Buddha."

"Ya, that's a good comparison. Are you taking East Asian Religions with Professor Adams?"

"Yes, and I love it."

"Well, the reason everything is hebel is the finality of death. All is vanity in the sense of pointless because no matter how much effort we put forth, we all die. Right? So the writer seems to get obsessed with death and wants to be sure that even the true believers, the followers of Yahweh, won't forget how death can make life seem completely absurd." He let those words sink in, and then he asked me, "And what will you write your paper on for this course?"

"Ecclesiastes," I replied without hesitation. I want to learn more about this weird book."

"Well, here's a clue. Besides the doom and gloom about death, there are some thoughts, scattered throughout, about how to lead a good life and enjoy a happy life."

"I'll look for those. I need some wisdom about that." I nodded several times, and then I said, "Well, there's a time for talking and a time for writing, but no time for procrastination. I'd better get going."

"Ya, ya, like a time to keep silence and a time to speak. You need to speak out in your paper. Tell me what you think about life."

I brought Ken to our house again for Sunday dinner, and after dinner he noticed the piano in our living room.

"Who play piano?" he asked.

"I do, a little. Nothing great."

"I want hear you."

So, I sat down at the spinet and played him the little Beethoven piece I had memorized over the break. Then it occurred to me to ask if he played.

"Yes, but very different music."

"Will you play something for me?" We had roomed together for several months, and here we were just discovering that we both played the piano.

Yes, his music was very different: quite romantic sounding with sweet melodies and sweeping arpeggios of harmonious chords. Not much rhythm, but full of emotion. And soothing. It sounded good and my parents clapped, encouraging him to play another. So he did. I can't remember my parents ever applauding when I played the piano.

I thought I knew Ken well, but then I wondered if he had other talents I didn't know about. He was not "foreign" to me anymore, but there was something reserved about Ken, something about his humility, that made me wonder what else there was to learn about this guy. Had he played sports? Could he draw or paint? Had he or his family ever experienced a tragedy? We were good friends already, but I felt like I was just getting to know him, so maybe we could share a room again next year. Well, so much for those shattered dreams.

I need to tell you a little about the course on East Asian Religions. Professor Adams had introduced these religions in the First Year Seminar, of course, and this was a chance to go deeper into them, and as we did, each one became my favorite religion until we moved on to the next one.

The way he introduced Confucius, I could actually picture a humble, bearded philosopher of good government walking on dusty roads from town to town in ancient China to try to find a ruler who understood his principles well enough that he could feel comfortable working with him. But it never happened; he always felt compromised. I could relate to that. So, he became well-known as a teacher and had numerous students as followers although they couldn't always agree on what Confucius was saying.

Confucius was himself pretty positive about human nature, believing that people in general were born with good intentions and a natural capacity for virtue. But some of his followers believed that people weren't really born good; but like the sprouts of young plants, their goodness could grow with proper cultivation. But sometimes it took a huge amount of cultivation. I hadn't made up my mind yet about whether people were basically good or basically bad, and as for myself, I wasn't sure whether I was a good person or not. I didn't feel like a sinner, but for sure not a saint either. Maybe I hadn't been tested yet. Is that how you find out who you are? When life tests you?

Confucius had very little to say about God, but he provided a full description of the characteristics needed to be a good leader. The criteria he gave sound really modern: wisdom, honesty, humility, and acceptance by the people. Would I ever be a leader? Probably not. But then, maybe not a very good follower either.

To explain Buddhism, Professor Adams began with the early life of the young Buddha, an actual person named Siddhartha Gautama, and his awakening to suffering. Apparently, he was a rich kid who had led a sheltered life, and as he ventured outside the family compound, he ran into people who were old, sick, or dying. He couldn't comprehend the suffering he saw, and it sent him on a search for a way to live a balanced life and for answers to the meaning of suffering. I really identified with the search of this Siddhartha person, the original Buddha.

Professor Adams explained how Buddha came to believe that a lot of human suffering is the result of attachment, not only to things but to people, our loved ones, and even our own self. So, we need to let go of everything because nothing is permanent; everything will change. Suffering comes from clinging to things that are for sure going to change. Buddha spent his life trying to teach people to let go, to calm the mind, and to find a place beyond the self, called nirvana.

We studied Daoism, too, and although it wasn't exactly a religion at first, or even an "ism," there were philosophers and their followers, who tried to describe an essentially indescribable Dao, sometimes spelled with a T as Tao, and roughly translated as Way. Dao was a spiritual force found in nature, a Way, and elusive though it was, it provided guidance for how to live a simple and happy life. Its chief book, The Tao Te Ching was full of nearly incomprehensible sayings, but I loved them. Like this one describing Tao:

If one looks for Tao, there is nothing solid to see;
If one listens for it, there is nothing to hear.
Yet if one uses it, it is inexhaustible.

My parents would want to know how the heck you could use something you can't see or hear. Also, this Daoist plea to curtail our desire for more and more things rings true for me:

No lure is greater than to possess what others want,
No disaster greater than not to be content with what one has.

This is not a monk's vow of poverty. Having things is okay, you just need to know when to say 'enough is enough.' And I love this next one, but at Little Texas College, where there's so much emphasis on talking—everybody talking all the time— this one would probably not be very popular:

Those who know do not speak.
Those who speak do not know.

As I was studying Daoism, I began to think that there was a side of me that could really enjoy a simple, quiet life, close to nature.

It was in this class on East Asian Religions that I became well acquainted with Suzette, having sat down next to her on the first day and every day after. I remembered her from the faculty brats' picnic, her mother being very French, her father a chef. I asked Suzette what it was like to have such a beautiful name as Suzette Bouchardet, being careful to pronounce the det to sound like day.

"I've never thought about it much," she said.

"You might think about it more if your name was Carl Wallace." That's how I reintroduced myself, but she said she remembered me from the picnic and how rude Jolene had been to me about visiting with the parents first. This mention of Jolene reminded me that I hadn't seen her around much this term, only passing her a few times walking across campus.

Another day, after class, I asked Suzette "What's it like to have a chef for a father?"

"I really don't know," she said with a slight grin, "because he's usually gone at dinner time."

"Oh," I said, trying to hide the embarrassment in my voice for having asked kind of a dumb question, "I guess that would be so, wouldn't it. Does he ever cook breakfast?"

"He's usually sleeping. But sometimes he brings us leftovers." Her grin grew wider.

It occurred to me that there were leftovers available because it wasn't his most popular dish, but I decided not to go there. Suzette was always well-dressed. Even her jeans had a designer-look to them, and she had a lot of different ways to fix her blonde hair, but what I liked most about her was the way she asked questions. It was a small class, and we were graded on participation in the discussion. Suzette often asked a question that got the rest of us talking. When we were in the unit on Confucius, she asked, "Is there any way to resolve this Confucian confusion about human nature?" Wow! I thought that was a good way to put it, and the hands shot up in response. And for Daoism she asked, "If Dao is embedded in nature for everyone to see, why is it that only some people see it and follow the Way?"

Suzette was a real thinker; I could see it in her questions. I was beginning to discover that not all of my peers were shallow hedonists; some were serious and thought about life like I did. "Will you really be gone all of next year?" I asked her.

"That's the plan," she said.

"Where in France will you be? The Sorbonne?" It was the only French University I'd ever heard my parents mention.

"Aix-Marseille in Provence. My mother studied there. It's huge, but

Mom says everything is divided up into little units and I will be in my own area of French language and literature."

"Aren't you scared?"

"No, I'm terrified. From this little prairie dog mound to a big French University? But they have some courses taught in English, too, and lots of international students."

I could sense the nervousness in her voice, but also her strength. She was going to take on a big challenge and figure out how to survive. Maybe I needed a challenge like that. Something to test me. Suzette was really cute, someone I could get interested in as a "real" girlfriend, and it made me sad that she was going to be gone next year. I decided that it would be kind of a waste of time though for me to begin a relationship with a young woman who is going to be away in France for a whole year. I wondered if her father had taught her to cook, but I didn't ask her. No more dumb questions.

I became intrigued with studying those aspects of religion that didn't seem to have much to do with God, like human nature in Confucianism and suffering in Buddhism. One day Professor Adams was explaining the Buddhist concept of the impermanent self, and I knew then that I wanted to write my paper on that, so I checked with him and he gave me some good references.

In our culture we are taught to believe that we have a permanent identity, and no matter how we develop and grow, we have this essence of a self that stays with us through life and maybe into an afterlife. That's how Professor Adams introduced it. Then he said that the Buddhist view was that there was no such thing as a permanent self. I found that very interesting, perhaps even relieving. Maybe that meant that I didn't have to work so hard at finding out who I was now because another self might appear spontaneously later, like a genie out of a bottle, and I would feel more comfortable with that self. 'Hello, new self. Welcome. You're not at all like my old self. Much calmer. I like you better.' But which one of these many selves was the real me? Maybe none.

I found a story in some ancient Buddhist scriptures where the master had asked his young student if the light coming from a candle burning at the beginning of the evening was the same light as at the end of the evening. Well, it is and it is not—they call that a paradox. And so it is with us: we're in some sense the same person within that ever-changing body, but not necessarily the same self. We surely are not the same self we were as a baby or high school student, even though it appears that we exist as some sort of continuing entity in our maturing body. Buddha himself tended to emphasize the idea of no permanent self because everything changes and passes on.

I reviewed all of that in my paper, and then I confessed that I wasn't even able to describe my present self very well. My self-concept—my identity— is not very strong or well-defined at this point, I wrote, and I am hoping to develop a clearer sense of self soon, recognizing that I will need to develop other selves, and revise my self-concept as I go through life.

Well, guess what, my confession earned me an A. Professor Adams wrote me a long note at the end of my paper praising me for the thinking I had done with such a difficult and somewhat foreign idea, and then he used a lot of kind words to reassure me that it was normal and acceptable not to have a very well-defined idea of myself at this point in life as a first-year college student. He ended with a question: Are you having trouble deciding on a major?

Brenda and I were studying together during reading week, and I didn't want to interrupt her because she seemed completely absorbed in her text for developmental psych, the second required foundational course for majors. But I had to share something with her because it was about to drive me crazy. "I've been thinking about my major," I said quietly to acknowledge that I was interrupting her.

"We don't have to declare until the second year as sophomores," she said without looking up.

"Unless you are in the sciences."

"And will you be?"

"See that's the problem. Probably not."

She shrugged. "Then you can wait until next year." She continued to pour over her text, underlining nearly every word with a yellow marker.

After a few seconds, I asked her, "What are you going to major in?" As if I didn't know.

"Probably psych."

"Will your parents be happy about that?"

"They told me I could major in whatever I want, but yeah, I think they'll be pleased." She finally looked up from her text. "Why are you asking me if my parents will be happy about my major?"

"Because I don't think mine will be happy at all. In fact, my dad will have a huge conniption fit."

"Why?" Brenda let her book drop, but didn't close it, acknowledging my questions as an interruption, with study to be resumed soon. "What are you considering for a major?"

"I'm not sure, but not science."

"Not science? They expect you to major in a science discipline?"

"Didn't I tell you how I got my first name?"

"Your first name? Carl? If you did, I don't remember."

"Well, there was this famous astronomer, and he gave a lecture at NYU when my parents were graduate students there. He put together this TV mini-series called 'Cosmos.' Well, my dad had a serious intellectual crush on this guy."

"What is his name?" Brenda asked, looking curious now.

"Carl Sagan."

"Oh, yeah, I think I've read about him." She frowned. "So they named you Carl after Carl Sagan? Are you sure?" Her voice rang with disbelief.

"They've repeated that story to me of how I got my name several times, not just once."

"So, you're thinking they gave you that name because they wanted you to grow up to be a famous astronomer?"

"And still do. They had big plans for me, high expectations, even while I was still in vitro."

"Oh, come on."

"No, really. You know how they are. And it's going to break their beating little ventricles if I tell them I don't want to major in science after taking their course."

"But you can tell them you adored their course, only you've just found other interests."

"That's the problem."

Brenda looked like she was figuring it out, but she waited to hear me say it. "Other interests in…"

"Religious studies."

"Oh, my God, Carl, yes, I can see how that might be a problem." She removed her black-rimmed glasses and folded them in front of her on the table, then crossed her arms.

"As you know, they follow the scientific method of empirical observation as the only means of establishing the truth."

"And that truth is limited to what goes on in the Science Building?"

"Exactly."

"Well, yeah, but what about the Social Sciences Building, you know, where the psych department is?"

"The Castle of Half-Truths and Pseudo-Science, the Land of Correlations and Probabilities. But not truth."

"And what about the Humanities Building? Home to music, art history, literature. Should I even ask?"

"The Hall of Nonsense. The Poet's Water Closet. The House of Horseshit. And home to—you guessed it—the Department of Religious Studies."

"You're exaggerating," Brenda said, frowning and shaking her head.

"Not at all. I've grown up with it, Brenda. I've heard them refer to those buildings in exactly those words. I never knew what they were talking about exactly until I began to study here at LTC and learned what goes on in those buildings."

"And they don't expect their son Carl, the embryo of an astronomer, to stray into the Humanities Building and start studying that horseshit religion stuff."

"My dad especially. He might get pretty hysterical."

You know what? You can perseverate over this one all you want. I think you've got a real problem this time."

By the end of reading week at the end of the term, I had my papers written and turned in, and I was free to study for my exam in anthropology. Ken had his work done, too, as expected, so I invited him over for one last Sunday dinner before he took off for Taiwan. I had travelled from our house to the college and back many times in Mom's old Honda sedan, and it was an easy drive, a straight shot, on one two-lane road with only three intersections with other roads, none requiring a stop from me. I always slowed down at those crossings to give a glance to make sure that nothing was coming. Dad called it 'defensive driving.' I had picked Ken up at the residence hall, and we were on our way out to our house for that final Sunday dinner.

I slowed down for the second intersection and glanced to my right, just in time to see a big pickup truck slam into the passenger side of our car, with all of that horrible grinding sound of metal being crunched in a car crash. I was horrified, but I remembered my childhood training from Dad: "Keep your wits about you." That meant think, but also monitor your thinking to make sure you are doing everything you should be doing. Don't panic. So I grabbed my phone, called 911, and gave them our location. I noticed that Ken was out cold and bleeding, so I mentioned that calmly to the dispatcher, but I was really starting to panic. I checked myself to see if my legs were okay, at least not broken, so that I could stand. I opened the door, slid my feet to the ground, and started over to see if the other driver was hurt. As I came around the back of the Honda, I saw him slam his crew-cab truck into reverse and then pull away, spinning his wheels, as he continued on in the same direction he had been going. He was gone before I could get his license plate number, but I noted the color of the truck as black and with some sort of symbol that I didn't recognize on the tail gate. I noticed a girl's face looking back at me through the rear window.

I heard the sirens. It wouldn't be long. I tried to check on Ken, but the door was so badly caved in, it wouldn't open. I went through the driver's side, but it was hard to get to him because the airbags were activated. I could see that Ken was badly smashed up and bleeding through the head. Oh, man, don't die on me out here. I reached over to his left arm and found a pulse. At least he was still alive.

I started to feel nauseous, seeing Ken like that, and then I noticed that I had a pounding headache that was making me dizzy. I made a call to home to tell Dad that I was in an accident and that it was a hit-and-run and not my fault, but that Ken was badly injured and bleeding from his head. I told him where I thought I was and told him to come quickly. I needed to sit down before I fainted. I had done all I could think of to do. Due diligence. Then I must have passed out, because they said they found me on the ground leaning up against the open car door on the driver's side.

I woke up in the hospital because they woke me up, the nurse telling me that it wasn't good to sleep straight through with a concussion. She checked a bunch of vital signs, as she called them, and then Mom came up to the side of the bed.

"Are you okay?" she asked, a look of relief on her face, seeing that I was awake.

"I think I took a blow to the head somewhere, or maybe it was just the airbag. Otherwise, I'm fine. But how's Ken? Where is he?" I looked around, as if he should be here. He was my roommate after all. "And where am I?"

"At University Hospital."

"In the city?"

"Yes. Ken is in intensive care. Your father is up there now, trying to get a report on him."

"I feel so bad," I said.

"Are you injured?"

"No, I mean I feel so bad for Ken."

"It wasn't your fault."

"As near as I can remember, it wasn't, but I still feel bad for Ken.

"Of course, you do. We all do." Mom's voice was soft and sympathetic.

"Where's Dad?" I asked, forgetting that she had just told me.

"With Ken."

"On a different floor? I want to see Ken."

"Maybe tomorrow."

"Did they examine me, too?"

"As soon as you arrived in the ER, but Ken required most of their attention. That's why I'm asking if you have any other injuries."

"Not that I know of. Just this headache."

Just then my father returned and I sat up straighter to ask him questions about Ken. "What's happened to him? Tell me what you know."

"I had trouble getting information out of them, but when I told them that he had no kin here in the US and that I was a professor acting as his father at this point, a nurse told me he had a broken collar bone and right wrist, and that he had a broken leg, the right femur near the hip joint, and that would require pins. He'll probably have that surgery tomorrow."

"What about his head? All that bleeding?"

"He had a bad cut and bled a lot, but they stitched that cut up and gave him a transfusion, so he's okay there. Maybe a concussion, too, like you."

"Will Ken live?" All I could think of was vanity of vanities, his life evaporating like steam before the age of twenty.

"Unless there is something going on internally or within the brain, he will live. But he's going to have a long rehabilitation."

I didn't say anything for a while, trying to absorb each new detail, feeling really sorry for Ken and more and more responsible. My parents gave me a few moments to get calm, then Dad asked me, "What do you remember from the accident?"

As I searched my memory, trying to give the details he wanted, I realized I was having a memory problem, a kind of black-out around the crash. I vaguely remembered a black truck hitting the passenger side. I didn't answer him.

"Okay, it was at the Teller Road intersection, right?"

"I guess. That must be what I told 911."

"And me."

"I phoned you?"

"Yes." He frowned and nodded.

"Did you see the driver of the truck take off?" Dad asked.

"I heard some tires squeal."

"The cops are calling it hit-and-run."

"That seems right. Did you go to the accident scene?" I asked him.

"As quickly as I could get there after you phoned to work with the police. I took a lot of pictures and so did they. Then I came directly here."

"I feel responsible."

"You might feel that way," he said, "but please don't say that around the police, or any lawyers, or members of Ken's family if they come."

"Have his parents been notified?"

"We found a phone number and email in Ken's wallet."

"Are they coming?"

"It would be logical that they would. Soon."

It was nice to have Dad's scientific mind working on this. He could be detached and objective. I was just a mess of whirling emotions, ready to go straight to the top of the Temple of the Sun and ask them to cut out my heart. Actually, I felt like they already had.

I was released from the hospital the next day during Ken's surgery to put screws in his femur. Mom drove me home in a rental car while Dad stayed to be with Ken to make sure he was getting the care he deserved. For the next few days, it seemed that my phone rang without stopping. Some people were curious and wanted more details on what happened, but mostly, people were genuinely concerned. Suzette called, full of sympathy and understanding of how terrible I must be feeling. I heard from Professor Adams and Herr Schmidt and they both said that if I needed to talk, that their door was always open.

Naturally, Brenda called and then drove over to our house with her father. It was good to talk to him. I hadn't done that in a while. He's a good listener. Then he said that he recommended I see the director of the counseling center, a person named Marvin Cohen, who reported to him. Good man. When he and Brenda left, on the way out, I overheard my mom say that she was worried about me. She had reason to be, hey, I was worried about myself. I was really gloomy—Brenda called it traumatic depression—and even though it was nice to have people concerned about me, I just wanted to be left alone.

I kept having this recurrent image—both a night dream and a daydream—of my body floating face down about ten feet above the accident scene, my arms stretched out, like I was a drone just hovering there, as I watched that truck pull away. Looking in through the smashed car window, I could see Ken bleeding, and I had this sensation of being really helpless up there floating around, feeling responsible for arriving in the wrong place at the wrong time, crashing, and not even being able to help Ken get out of the car. But I realized that brooding about the accident in the basement guest room probably wasn't good for me. I needed to break through the gloom.

Jolene called twice, but she was a different person: no sarcasm, no flirting, no teasing. She showed surprising empathy for the situation I was in, and she told me that her parents kept asking about me, and of course about Ken. She asked me what kind of truck it was, and I had to say I didn't know. Ford? GMC? She told me I should try to remember.

The toughest call to take came from Amy, Ken's non-girlfriend friend, and she wanted all of the details about what happened and information on Ken's injuries. She was really broken up and said she was longing to see him. I told her I would try to work something out. So, I asked Mom if we could take her with us the next time we went to the hospital to see Ken, and she said that would be fine. What we hadn't anticipated was that Ken's parents were there, having already flown in from Taiwan.

We picked up Amy and mom drove us into University Hospital—I wasn't even driving to our nearby Seven Eleven—where we found Ken just coming out of a physical therapy session to join his parents. Ken was walking very slowly, but the PT nurse said he was making good progress, especially having those other injuries, so that he couldn't use crutches or a walker very well. It would be a long time before he would be holding up the sky.

Ken was surprised to see Amy. He introduced her as his classmate, a friend from accounting class. His parents greeted her politely, but didn't take much notice of her. Then Ken introduced me and my mom, and they were polite to us, too, but rather cool. I mean, how would you feel meeting the guy who had mangled your son's body and totally upset his future? Would you be able to say "pleased to meet you" or "my pleasure"?

I said to them, "I want you to know that I'm really sorry that this happened. It was the fault of the driver who hit us, but we don't know who that is."

"Yes, we understand. Bad to leave accident like that. Irresponsible," Ken's father said.

"Our son could have been killed," his mother said, shaking her head back and forth.

"I've thought about that a lot," I said. "I hope that Ken told you what good friends we have become, and that you will understand how much this upsets me."

They nodded, but I was not sure they could understand anyone's feelings but their own right then. How could they, seeing their son in such condition?

"First year over," Ken's father said. "Ken good student. But we are making arrangements to take him home as soon as he can get on airplane and handle long fright."

Flight? Yes, that made sense taking him home, I had to admit, but I would miss seeing Ken, not being able to track his progress or give him encouragement. I could see that Amy was also having trouble processing that announcement. Ken would leave. Would he come back? Would either of us ever see him again?

Mom tried to describe to his parents what my father had done to see that Ken was getting the proper medical attention. They thanked her, but they didn't seem to understand how much my dad had actually done to care for Ken. In their eyes, we were the American family that got their son into a situation where he nearly lost his life. Now he is suffering and his plans, and their plans for him, are on hold with no one knowing how soon Ken will recover or in what condition he will be in when he does.

That was the only visit Amy made to the hospital. She said to me on the phone later that she felt rejected, and she started to cry. Soon we were both sobbing. Hey, this was tough for both of us because Ken was our best friend. His parents would fly his mutilated body back to Taiwan and our friendship with Ken would probably be finished. I told her that I would not forget her and would look for her on campus.

Within five days, Ken's parents had booked a first-class flight to Taipei to take him home. I saw him just once more. Mom left us alone in his room so that we had the privacy we needed to try to say good-bye. "Let me tell you one more time how sorry I am that this happened," I said.

"Not your fault. We know that. Just keep looking for hit-run driver."

"Will you come back here to finish college?"

"Hard to say. Depends on what parents think. They were worried before this happen. Now bad accident. Probably not."

"You know I would like you to return to be my roommate again. I feel like I am losing a good friend, in fact the only guy friend I've ever had."

"Me, too. Good friends. You will make other friends. I will, too. I will recover. Family will help. Don't worry. Just little delay in plans."

On the drive home with Mom, I was thinking about fathers and how important they can be. I was impressed with how my father jumped into the situation and began to work with the police, care for Ken, give me guidance on what not to say, and then stay with Ken through his surgery. Whatever Dad had on his schedule those days, he cleared it to do what he needed to do. Professor Adams said in class one day that leading a good life sometimes just involves showing up at the time you are needed. Dad showed up. But what about me? Did my true self show up, or was I mostly absent? Was this life's first big test for me, and had I failed it? Was I flunking out of life? Oh, my God, what a mess I had made.

I remember thinking that Ken looked just like his dad; he not only had an amazing family resemblance, same eyes, same dark hair, but his mannerisms and his way of speaking English were all like his dad. His father had made plans for him in the family business, raised him with every advantage, and brought him this far. He was not happy with having his son hurt badly and his plans disrupted. There were no tears, as with Ken's mom, but I could tell that he was at this point a very frustrated and angry man. Ken had told me that in Taiwan his father was a powerful and respected person. I worried about what he might do.

4

TRYING OUT THE TALKING CURE

Checking on Ken's credits. Notorious and legendary. Getting out of the house. Registration for two summer workshops. Meeting Marv for counseling. Putting the blame where the blame belongs. Learning Texas history. Studying for the real estate exam. Illusory lives as a cure for nothingness. Discovering art at Carlsbad Caverns.

After Ken left for Taiwan, my life collapsed and I found myself thinking about him constantly. I warned you that something terrible would happen to Ken, but I had no warning myself, and it left me traumatized and in an unimaginable state of shock. But first off, I had things to take care of for him. The term was over and my work was turned in, and I was fairly certain Ken's was, too, but I wanted to make sure. I had his schedule of classes and made it a point to check with each of the professors to be certain that he would receive a grade and credit for all of his courses. They assured me, most sympathetically, that he would. I emailed the news to Ken and he sent a short note back thanking me. Nothing more. I was starting to think our friendship would totally fall apart.

It was as I was making the rounds to check on his credits, and mine as well, that I discovered how widely-known I had become as the driver in the car wreck that had badly injured Ken Lee. Everyone I met, from departmental assistants to staff in the registrar's office, to his professors and mine, all knew who I was and just kind of stared at me like I was some kind of yellow-plumed exotic bird from the local zoo that had flown its coop. I had to look up in the dictionary the subtle distinctions between famous, infamous, and notorious. I discovered that I was well known for a bad deed, so infamous fit me best, as well as notorious, being widely and unfavorably known, but I was not prominent or renowned, that is, well known in a favorable sense of being honored; and as more and more people repeated my story, not always getting the facts straight, I discovered I was becoming legendary.

The article in the local Herald got the details of the accident generally correct, emphasizing the search for the hit-and-run driver who ran the stop sign. But people, being what they are, for sure must have added their own speculations about me. Perhaps he had been high, under the influence, or distracted on his phone. Could they consider how disturbing it might be to have been the unharmed driver in an accident that nearly killed his best friend? I never welcomed, and certainly never sought, being so well known across campus. It only made my sense of alienation from everyone and everything around me grow stronger, like I didn't belong here, but as Jolene had told me, there was no place to hide.

I had been living at home while Ken was in the hospital, and when I eventually returned to the residence hall to retrieve my belongings, I found the room cold and barren, like the inside of an empty refrigerator. Ken's things had been removed by his parents, and my stuff, left behind, was unfamiliar and alien. I even had trouble thinking of it as mine, like maybe I should give everything to the Salvation Army.

I was really silent and distant around home, just going through the motions of being Carl, the son of Elsa and Leon. Naturally, my parents, who were watching me closely anyway, grew concerned. My dad asked me, "Don't you think it would be a good idea to take one or two summer session courses?"

"It may be too late to register," I replied.

"There are always exceptions," my mother pointed out.

"It would at least get you out of the house for a few hours each day," Dad said.

"That would be a relief for both of you, I'm sure." Knowing that was not what they meant, I said it anyway. They looked at each other, unsure how to deal with my anger and sarcasm. So I said, "Sorry."

"There's always the intensive workshop for teachers on Texas history," my dad said, a little half-joking tone in his voice. "There's open enrollment in those workshops."

"Or what about the real estate workshop offered by the business school," my mother suggested, her voice, like my father's, betraying a lack of seriousness.

No wonder it shocked the hell out of Mom and Dad when I told them I was able to get into both workshops and was registered for them. They frowned simultaneously, like someone had clicked on an emoji. It was clear to me that I really needed to get out of that house, not for my sake, but for theirs. I was driving them crazy. Even a lonely single room in the only residence hall left open for summer session students seemed better to me than languishing in the downstairs guest room under the worried and watchful eyes of the astronomer and botanist.

"Are you serious about those courses?" my dad asked.

"Yes, I need to get back to campus. Face it. Work it through. Stop brooding. Earn some credits toward my degree. That won't happen if I stay here."

"Okay," my dad said, drawing out the word for expressing reluctant agreement. "We can cover the cost of your room."

"But there is one condition," my mom said. "Well, not really a condition, just a suggestion," she said, nervously correcting herself. "I hope you will seek out Marv Cohen at the Counseling Center."

"Well," I said, not resisting, "why not? I admit I could use some help. If it would make everyone happy, who knows, it might even make me happy, too."

I'll tell you about these two intensive summer workshops shortly, because like everything else I studied at Little Texas College, I had to relate to each one personally, sucking the last bit of meaning out of the experience even when on the surface, they seemed like an irrelevant waste of time. I actually surprised myself by liking both courses in an odd sort of way, and they set something in motion that later proved very useful. But I had a difficult time studying, paying attention in class and reading the textbooks, because images of Ken's bloodied head kept flashing before my eyes. As I was soon to discover, my emotional life was a disaster.

The Counseling Center is in the Student Union, around the corner and down the hall from the office of the dean of student life, located well to afford appropriate privacy. I'd never been down that way. On Monday, when I stopped by to make an appointment with Marvin Cohen, I discovered that one had already been made for me on Wednesday afternoon at three o'clock. No schedule conflict, so I told them I'd be there. Then I started to get nervous. Did I really want to discover more about myself when what I had discovered at college so far was not all that great? After the horrible accident with Ken, how many sessions of picking and poking would it take to get me back to anything like a normal human being? Maybe I would be a complete waste of time as a client for this Marvin Cohen guy.

What I dreaded most, was having to recount the gory details of the accident all over again, using up the whole hour of the first session with the facts. I remember Brenda telling me one night last term while we were studying together in the lounge how Sigmund Freud had invented "the talking cure," but I didn't understand how a person could get cured by just talking. The people I knew who talked a lot didn't seem very cured. And who was this Marvin Cohen? I hoped he would at least do some of the talking.

When I went for my appointment, an older woman, his administrative assistant, greeted me, smiled, and showed me into a private counseling room, separate from the director's office. She invited me to have a seat in a soft tan leather chair that actually had a full-length window view of the leafy green Arboretum. The room seemed soundproofed, like a recording studio, the only noise being the ticking of the clock high on the wall opposite me. I sat there alone, untying and tying the shoelaces of my sneakers.

A few minutes later, to my surprise, Doctor Cohen came wheeling himself through the door in a wheelchair. What was this? My counselor was disabled? It looked permanent, both legs dysfunctional, definitely not a sprained ankle. He wore a light blue, short-sleeve polo shirt. Muscular arms to compensate for withered legs. Younger than my parents, dark hair, swarthy complexion, clean-shaven. A serious but friendly look, like he was already on my side even though we were just meeting. His brown eyes were focused on mine.

"Hi, Carl. I go by Marv, not Doctor Cohen, so just call me Marv if you're comfortable with that."

"Probably not comfortable, Doctor Cohen, but I'll try." These were my first confused words of the talking cure.

"I know what happened to you from the newspaper and the dean of students, so we won't make you go through the unpleasant details of the accident again if that's okay."

"It's pretty much all over campus now." I said, noting that Marv didn't speak with the drawl of a three-generation Texan.

"Yes, one version or another, but try not to let that bother you." Without further explanation, no mention of his reason for being in a wheelchair, Marv—excuse the expression—jumped right in, not wasting a moment of the ticking clock with chit-chat. "Tell me how you are feeling about the loss of your roommate, Ken Lee."

"Well, he lived. At least it's not that kind of loss. But I miss him a lot as a friend and I feel terrible about what happened to him."

"Feel terrible? How?"

Why did Marv pick out those two words, feel terrible, and why did I say them? What did I mean? "I feel terrible that he was injured so bad," I began, and then noticed how sad I really was feeling, swallowing hard to hold it back. "And I wonder why it happened. I mean why did we invite him for dinner that day? Why did I pick him up right at that time? Why were we in that intersection at that particular moment?"

"Well, there are no answers to those questions, that's for sure," Marv said. "It sounds like you feel responsible even though you weren't."

"It's one thing to tell yourself it wasn't your fault, it's another thing to believe it," I said.

"Well put. So that even though you know you were not responsible for the accident, it feels like you were?" Marv asked.

Geez. How does he get to the basic problem so fast? I mean, that is the problem. "The rational part of me tells me that it's not my fault. I've been over that again and again with my parents. But I still feel responsible somehow." I could feel small tears forming at the corners of my eyes.

"Whose fault was it?" Marv asked, drawing a little closer in his wheelchair to hear my reply.

"Well, the driver of the truck, but we don't know who that is."

"A person without a name at this point, but another person, not you. How do you feel about that person?"

"Well, I'm upset, naturally…"

"Upset? Just upset?"

"Well, yeah, a little angry."

"A little? How about totally pissed off at the son-of-a-bitch for wrecking the life of your good friend?"

Wow! I didn't expect to hear that from my counselor, but he was expressing exactly how I felt. I just didn't know how to say it. I needed to respond but couldn't come up with anything.

"I'll let you borrow some of my words if you don't have any of your own," Marv said.

"Yeah. Pissed. Definitely." I pictured Ken trying to walk during his physical therapy session at the hospital. "How can somebody do something like that and just drive away? Only a real asshole."

"It's a start," Marv said, nodding. "We need to take this responsibility crap off of you and move it over onto the guy who deserves the blame. Don't you think?"

"I do." All at once, it was like there was a bright spotlight shining down on the accident scene, and I could see clearly that it was not my fault at all. "So then, I'm really not guilty, am I?"

"Beyond a reasonable doubt." Marv wheeled his chair back a little, and in the remaining time we chatted more informally about Ken Lee, how we had taken First Year Seminar together and had a chance to talk about the deep stuff most students don't discuss. "He was my first real guy friend."

"But just friends?"

"Definitely. I mean, the truth is, as you will discover, I don't really know who I am and I've never had a real girlfriend. But one thing I know about myself is that Ken and I were just good friends."

"So this was a true friendship, not a closeted romance?"

"For sure. Hey, Ken had a really cute girlfriend." Marv nodded his head and smiled a little like he knew Amy. Maybe he was counseling her, too, but of course, he couldn't say. We talked some more, and I'd never felt so relaxed, like the big burden I had been carrying around was being lifted off of my back. I stared out the window at the trees gently blowing in the wind over at the Arboretum, and it gave me a nice calming sensation. I probably shouldn't have asked, but I did, feeling so comfortable already with Marv. "What happened to you?"

"Oh, this?" He pounded the side of his wheelchair. "I was in Iraq, at the wrong place at the wrong time. A mine. I was wearing a protective jacket that saved my upper body. I had good care, but only half of me came back alive." He nodded and swallowed hard, then came back to me. "Look, you made a good start today, but we're just getting going. Stop at the desk and confirm an appointment for next week at this time if it works for you."

"I'll do that." As I stood up, I became acutely aware of my legs and my ability to stand, and as I looked down, I noticed my sneakers taking steps toward the door. Holy shit, when I came in here, I thought I had this horrible unresolvable problem. It turns out that my counselor has the problem and it has already been resolved—spending the rest of his life in a wheelchair.

"See you next week, Carl," Marv said as he wheeled out after me.

As I walked past the office of the dean of student life, I remembered that I hadn't seen Brenda around. Maybe she was living at home for the summer. I wanted to tell her what Marv called the driver of the truck.

The workshop on Texas history was open to the public and priced lower, which meant you didn't have to be a student enrolled at Little Texas College to register. It drew in teachers from the surrounding school districts, including some from the city, because the course had built a strong reputation there, coming highly recommended through the years by school principals. The students in that class were mostly those teachers seeking recertification or professional advancement credits, and the handful of students from the college were all in teacher education, except for me, who had just landed there by accident after the accident.

I arrived early on the first day to get a seat at the top in the back row, my preferred perch now for surveying the dynamics in a large class. Shortly, a student who I recognized as being from the college, sat down next to me. I say recognized, because he was one of maybe eight or ten black students at Little Texas College. "I'm Carl," I said, reaching out a hand, which he shook as he smiled, exposing a gorgeous set of white teeth. Was it prejudiced of me to notice his teeth? I never noticed anyone else's teeth.

"You can call me Alex, although I'm really Alexisius Jefferson, Junior.

"Alexis?" I tried to repeat it.

"Alexisius," he said. "It's that extra 'isi' that throws everyone." He smiled again. "And don't ask me where it comes from, except that I'm junior, and my dad, wherever he may be, has that name, too."

"You're going to be a teacher?" I asked, to get away from his name as the only topic of conversation.

"That's the plan, man. Otherwise, I wouldn't be taking this course."

"Are you from Texas? I asked.

"Austin. But I've never felt much like a Texan."

"Me either, although I grew up right here in this town."

Alex looked at me straight on for a second, started to speak as if to ask a question, and then said, "Sorry about the accident."

"I guess I'm pretty well known around campus now," I said, surprised that he was so sure about who I was.

"That must have been tough."

"It still is. Hard to forget. But not as tough for me as for my roommate."

"Ken? I knew Ken a little. Nice guy. He went back home?"

"His parents took him back to Taiwan as soon as he could travel."

Alex shook his head. "And they never found the driver of the truck?"

"Not yet." I was surprised a second time at how much Alex knew about the accident.

Just then, Doctor Richardson started the class. His tone of voice and manner were exactly what I remembered from meeting him at the picnic for faculty brats: no teacher demeanor here. Kevin Richardson, his wife Susie, and daughter Olivia. An ordinary family man who just happens to study and teach American history.

After he distributed the course outline and reviewed the requirements, he asked, "How many of you are from Texas?" Most of the hands shot up. "And who among us are from elsewhere?" A few hands went up, scattered across the classroom. It was a clever way to identify the students regularly enrolled in the college year-round. "And how many of you all—he gave it just the right drawl—think of yourselves as Texans?" A smaller number of hands went up, but by far the majority of the class. "Where did you get that name Texan?" he asked. "Where did that name come from?"

Students glanced at each other but no one seemed to know or venture a guess, so Professor Richardson told us, "It comes from an Indian language. You've probably heard of Apache and Comanche tribes, but there was another tribe from this region called Caddo. They used a word for friend, tshya, that got translated into the Spanish, tejas or texas, pronounced tay-hass." He printed all of this quickly on the whiteboard with a red marker. "So if you think of yourself as Texan, which is what it became in English, you need to remember that the term comes originally from the people who lived here first, and they used the Caddo word to call the settlers 'friends.' Texans. That's the first irony. I'll explain irony later."

I could tell right then that I was going to like this course, and I was going to get more out of it than I had imagined. After an hour, we took a short break. I'd heard my parents talk about the intensive summer session workshops: two hours a day and five days a week for four weeks. That's what this was. My real estate class was scheduled like that, too, only in the early afternoons. Lots of butt-sitting that summer.

I sat down next to Alex, or he sat down next to me, each morning in the Texas history class and we began to grow a friendship. After two weeks with a mid-term exam coming up, we decided to go over to the union after class, as we had been doing for several days for lunch, but this time for an hour of intensive study while we ate our cheese sandwiches and chips.

Between the two of us we quickly pieced together the history of Texas, which went something like this. Indian tribes were the original owners of that land. The Spanish colonists, looking for get-rich-quick gold and finding very little, were poor settlers. The land, all of Mexico and the present-day states of the Southwest, belonged to the Spanish, who had encouraged westward pioneers from the US to settle on their lands to help populate them and shove off the Indians. But there were conditions that went with this very cheap land deal from the Spanish, such as no slaves, convert to Catholic, and become citizens.

"The seeds of conflict," Alex observed.

The Mexicans were busy fighting a war of independence from Spain, and eventually won, and when they did, they were willing to continue the land contracts with the US settlers, but they expected to enforce the rules of the agreements now, which the settlers had never intended to keep. No slaves? Catholic? Are you kidding me? As the settlers grew impatient with their Mexican owners, particularly over the issue of keeping their slaves, the seeds of revolt began to sprout. One of the leaders of the settlers, who had always been supportive of the terms of the agreements, was Stephen Austin, but the Mexican government made a huge mistake by throwing him in jail, apparently to make an example of him for trying to negotiate those agreements when all he was doing was seeking a peaceful resolution to avoid conflict. When he got out of jail, angry and upset, he returned to his lands and became a leader of the revolt to break away from Mexico.

"Okay, we've got that part covered," I said.

"What about the Alamo?" Alex asked.

"We can't forget that part of the story, so let's continue," I said. The Mexicans sent an armed band to retrieve a stolen canon, but the settlers were also well armed and the Mexicans were outnumbered, so they retreated. The rebels concluded from this that it would be easy to win battles against these Mexican guys. They replaced Austin with Sam Houston, more of a military leader, and drafted a Texas Declaration of Independence. As the settlers turned to the US for support, they discovered that the US didn't want to get into a war with Mexico over their land, at least not yet. So, the War of Texas Independence had no US support or assistance.

"They did this on their own," Alex observed.

To put down the rebellion, a large band of Mexican soldiers under the leadership of the Mexican general Santa Anna attacked the Alamo, an old fort, actually more of a Catholic mission outpost than a fort, and the

US rebels were badly defeated, not killing every last one, as legend has it, but all but fifteen. At a second battle called the Goliad Massacre, around three hundred fifty rebels were killed.

"It's not going well," Alex noted.

But then the tide turned, and the rebels caught up with General Santa Anna, also Mexico's president, and captured him and negotiated their independence with him. So the rebels got this big chunk of Mexican land, which was now called the Republic of Texas, and because the US was not ready to annex it as a state, it became an independent country.

"And I remember this," Alex said. "Professor Richardson told us that some Texans are still proud of having once been a country all on their own, and they dream about becoming independent from the US again someday."

What the Texans didn't comprehend was that there was a civil war brewing in the US over slavery, and Texas couldn't be annexed as a slave state. So Texas was left hanging as an independent country with its own one-star flag. And that's how we were left hanging at the end of the first half of the course.

"But help me understand this concept of irony that Professor Richardson lectured on for a whole hour that one day," Alex said.

"Yes, that's important and I'll bet it will show up on the exam," I said. "Let's see if we can explain it to ourselves."

"I'll take a shot at it," Alex said. "Somebody takes some action, but then there are unintended consequences. Something unexpected happens."

"Yes, and not only unexpected, but exactly opposite to what was hoped for or planned," I said, remembering what Richardson had said.

"An ironic twist," I think he called it," Alex said, twisting his hand like he was holding a knife.

"So when the Spanish settlers invited the US settlers to solve a problem, they became a problem." I tried out an example.

"Oh, yeah, man, that's good." Alex thought for a minute and then came up with another. "Mexico takes Stephen Austin, who was actually a good friend, and turns him into a bad enemy. Just the opposite of what was intended."

'Perfect example," I agreed. "So now the Mexicans are fighting to hold on to their lands in battles with people they had invited to settle on their lands."

"And how about this one?" Alex asked. "The Texans fought with

Mexico to keep their slaves, but it was the issue of slavery that kept the rebels from becoming a new US state."

"Perfect. And can we add that probably nobody in the long history of Texas ever intended that a black guy and a white guy would be sitting here in an integrated student union helping each other study for a test on Texas history."

Alex laughed loud and long at that, as if a little surprised by my frankness, but then he turned serious. "And that's still an unintended consequence for a lot of people today."

Well, that opened the door for Alex and me to talk about race and just about anything else we wanted to, and our friendship, as you will see, grew even closer. For now, let's just say that we both got an A on the mid-term exam.

I won't bore you with all of the details of the real estate course, but it was the same open enrollment deal, only sponsored by the business school. The workshop I signed up for was designed to help students pass the Texas real estate licensing exam, which had a reputation for being tough. Actually, there were tons of online tutoring resources available to anyone trying to obtain the license, but this was billed as a workshop that would not only walk students through the exam preparation, but also provide a broad overview of the field of real estate.

I forgot to mention that the School of Business has its own building separate from the other three, and business was viewed by the traditional faculty as a sellout of the basic liberal arts mission of LTC. The business program, they said, was started by the college for financial reasons to attract cash-paying students interested in a business major. The business faculty was always quick to point out that Little Texas College would have closed thirty years ago without the College of Business. I'd heard my parents discuss this, and I knew that they disliked the study of business almost as much as the study of religion.

I felt like the proverbial fish out of water in that real estate class at first because of the terminology, but I caught on okay once I began to learn business speak and the language of acronyms. I had no interest in selling property at that point and couldn't imagine myself becoming a real estate agent, but here I was registered for the course with my parents paying their share, and my grade point average at stake if I screwed up, so why not do my best? An older woman sitting beside me was using the course as a prep for actually taking the exam, so she made it her mission to get me to try the exam. "You can do it, kid," she urged. I usually did well on tests, so why not?

There I was learning about exclusive right and agency listing, the difference between foreclosure, forfeiture, and adverse possession, along with fiduciary responsibilities of an agent. It didn't look all that hard to learn the definitions of the jargon and pass the test, so I decided to use the class like the others were using it: to prepare for the Texas licensing exam. I found out from the lady beside me that I needed an agency sponsor, so the professor hooked me up with a local real estate agency in town and the receptionist there said they were always happy to help students. I hoped that she didn't recognize me as the infamous driver. I sent an email to Ken to tell him I was taking a business course, thinking he would be pleased, but all I got back was a note of good luck, nothing more, no news.

The licensing exam was harder than I expected, but I passed with a high score, and later on I would pass that exam in Colorado, but let's not get ahead of my story because there is a lot that happens before I end up in Colorado.

When the course on Texas history was complete, Alex and I put our heads together again to study for the final exam. As we went over the material, we talked about it, too, and that's how we became even better acquainted. We made another summary.

The United States watched with interest for ten years while the new country of Texas, under the leadership of President Houston, struggled without US support to define its boundaries and its relationship to Mexico. Mexico was ready for a peace treaty, but only with Texas as a separate nation. Texas was ready for annexation to the US, and by the end of 1845 received it, through a proclamation signed by President Polk. With the US behind Texas now, Mexico began to worry about losing more land. Neither the US nor Mexico wanted war. What the US was hoping for was buying cheap land, as was the case with the Louisiana Purchase from France, but Mexico had no desire to sell. So Polk sent troops to some of the disputed land south of Texas, hoping Mexican soldiers would fire on them, and they did. Then he claimed Mexico had killed an American soldier on US lands.

"Hold on a minute here, "Alex said. "Polk provoked a war by invading Mexican lands and then spun the story to make it look like the US was attacked?"

"You got that right," I said, "and it started the war that enabled the

US to pick on Mexico—"

"Like a bully. So then there's a full-scale war, an actual invasion, with the US marching all the way to Mexico City," Alex added.

"Exactly. And the peace treaty, along with less than half the money originally offered for purchase, gave the US what is essentially most of the rest of the American Southwest: California, Nevada, Arizona, Utah, New Mexico, and half of Colorado. So in 1848 with the Treaty of Guadalupe Hidalgo, Mexico had to give up approximately half of its country to the US."

"And here's the part I don't understand," Alex said, a puzzled frown on his face. "Manifest Destiny. Okay, it was the belief that the spread of the US from the Atlantic Ocean to the Pacific was inevitable. It was America's destiny. Is that it?"

"And not only that, it was manifest, meaning it's what God wanted for America," I explained, tilting my head and widening my eyes to register disbelief in such an extraordinary claim.

"What God wanted? How completely arrogant that was, not to mention blasphemous to the name God." Alex was shaking his head back and forth, while I was shaking mine up and down.

"Exactly," I said. "But as we both know, there's more."

"And it has to do with slavery," Alex said.

"When the civil war came, the new state of Texas, no surprise, fell firmly on the slavery side."

"Seceding from the United States which they had begged to join less than twenty years earlier. More irony," Alex noted.

"Good example." I scrolled through some of the notes on my laptop to make sure we were getting it all straight. "To his credit, Governor Sam Houston was opposed to secession, but a lot of people wanted it and found a way."

"Sure," Alex said, "because they wanted to hang on to their precious slaves."

"Over the years of the Civil War some 70,000 to 90,000 Texans joined the Confederate Army. They fought just about everywhere until Robert E. Lee signed the Confederate surrender on April 9, 1865. And the aftermath was a mess as the Union gradually took back control of each state one at a time."

"And in Texas, slavery continued for two years after Lee's surrender, until it was eventually abolished on June Nineteenth, which we black people still celebrate as Juneteenth, the real end to slavery, Texas being the last to eliminate it."

"Yeah, Texas had trouble returning to the Union as a state but eventually did, even though they failed to ratify the thirteenth and fourteenth amendments to the Constitution. Then the pattern was set for Jim Crow laws and racial segregation as it developed elsewhere in the South."

"As they say," Alex pointed out, "the rest is history." But then his face took on a really serious expression and he surprised me. "You know what's going to happen to this course? Professor Richardson is going to be criticized and eventually attacked because he's too honest about the past. People from the schools will start slamming him for being so negative about Texas and America. They'll stop recommending this course to their teachers. I predict an honest man will be brought to his knees for teaching the truth."

"Wow! Seriously? You think that could happen?"

"You watch."

Then Alex surprised me again. He asked if Ken was coming back to study at LTC, and I told him I hadn't heard, but probably not.

"Then you need a roommate," he said.

"I do. Yes, actually I do."

"I'd be interested," Alex said.

"Me, too," I replied, surprised but pleased. "But what about the brothers and the sisters in the Black Student Alliance? Won't they be upset with you?"

"Probably. But if I really cared about that I should have gone to a historically-black college. My momma thought I should get a taste of integration."

"Then let's do it," I said. Wow! Maybe I could learn about how black people really felt. I knew we would talk on and on into the dark night.

I went back to the Counseling Center each week on Wednesday at three o'clock, right after real estate class, and although I had stopped blaming myself for what happened to Ken, that senseless accident had become one more proof that life is random, pointless, and absurd. The issue was starting to move beyond my life to the pointlessness of life in general. That made me depressed and anxious, and I was starting to have trouble going to sleep at night and then when I did, I had bad dreams. I hadn't gotten a haircut all summer, so with long hair my appearance must have changed, and not for the better. On the day when I told Marv about the loss of sleep and how depressed I was feeling, I think I startled him, looking so disheveled and distraught.

He sat up straight in his wheelchair. "How bad is it? Are you having suicidal thoughts?" he asked, rolling his chair in a little closer as if to peer inside my skull looking for suicidal thoughts with those piercing eyes of his.

"Let's say that I think about suicide, but mostly in an intellectual sense, like it's really the logical outcome of knowing that life is pointless, the one honest action a person can take. But I don't sit around planning on how to get my hands on enough meth for an overdose or how to hang myself with the residence hall window drapes."

"That's good, because if you were, we'd need to institutionalize you at a place where they can keep an eye on you for a while. So, are you sure?"

"I'm sure. For now. I don't want to quit yet, but I'm pretty confused and I'd like to figure life out. I've been raised in this family, you know, with all these facts about how insignificant we are on our lonely little planet in an expanding universe, how chancy our evolution has been, how random our personal existence—"

"Yes, yes, I know. I see the refugees from The Origins of Life quite regularly in this office, trying to cope with their nothingness. But for you it has been more than a one-term course. You have known from an early age of your nothingness." Marv held a sardonic smile in place. "Is this not so?"

"It is. But I believe my parents are right. Those are the facts. We are nothing, and they do a good job of waking up the students at LTC who take their course."

"No need to defend them. They are highly respected professors and the course has a strong reputation." He paused for a moment, then nodded a single nod. "What's the issue?"

"What keeps me awake at night is that I have no idea about who I am or how to build a credible life, a way out of my nothingness."

"Your nothingness. Hmm." Marv pursed his lips as if to kiss the air. "Why is it so hard to build a life?"

"Because most of the things that people do to build their life are completely ridiculous. They grab on to some illusion to provide a little short-term meaning as a cure for their long-term nothingness."

"Like what? I need concrete examples."

"Okay. Golf. I worked at the local country club during high school as a caddy, watering greens, stuff like that, and I can tell you there are people who build their entire life around that little white ball. Golf clubs. Golf shoes, Golf shirts. They go on golf vacations to famous golf resorts. When they die, they hope to go to a heavenly condo on a green to play golf eternally."

"Maybe a pleasure fixation for them, but to you it's an illusion."

"Self-deception," I said confidently in a loud voice.

"And you think these people are deluding themselves about life." Marv seemed to be restating my point to make sure he wasn't misunderstanding me. Or was it to make me own what I had just said?

"Yeah, to me they are deluding themselves. Using some ridiculous obsession to cure their nothingness."

"What else?" Marv probed.

"Well, everything else. Political fanatics. Abortion crusaders—both sides. Evangelical fundamentalists with their folksy obsession with holding hands with Jesus. Catholic priest pedophiles. Conspiracy theorists. And don't get me started on football, the ultimate vanity of vanities."

"Life is vanity?"

"Yes, as in Ecclesiastes. I just did a paper on it last term."

"So you are studying the Hebrew Scriptures. That's interesting. What did you conclude?"

"That because of death, which gets us all, life is vanity, a striving after wind. The Hebrew word means something like water vapor, you know, like evaporating steam, which makes life absurd."

"But aren't there some suggestions in Koheleth about how to live the life you have? Some wisdom?"

Did Marv know about this, too? How the hell could this guy know so much? I needed to reply. "Yes, actually that's what I found. Work hard and enjoy your work. Take pleasure in what you eat and drink. Don't be greedy. Live a simple life. Oh, yeah, and two people are better than one. Stuff like that. But just remember, in the face of death, it's all absurd."

"You believe that?" Marv asked, looking straight at me with a kind of grim scowl on his face.

"Well, it seems to me that most people are grasping for any illusion they can concoct to put a little meaning in their ridiculous lives just to keep from falling off the edge of a pointless universe." I liked the sound of that sentence.

Marv nodded his head several times, but I was pretty sure it wasn't in agreement. He looked like he was about to come up with one of his jolting observations. Then he did. "Who's to say," he began slowly, "what is illusion and what is not? It sounds like you are making some pretty big value judgments, calling someone else's interests and passions illusions.

Okay, so Marv was challenging me to look at this in another way. Maybe it was a little arrogant of me to use the word illusion to criticize someone else's interests. But still, people do so many completely ridiculous things. Before I could respond, Marv was speaking again.

"To tell the truth, it's easy to agree with you about many of your examples. I really do agree, Carl. People do stupid things. But don't you think some things are less illusory than others, like caring for the sick or providing meals for the homeless? Donating a kidney? Tutoring disadvantaged children in a poor country? Do you really mean to write off everything that people do as vanity?

"That's a good point. Maybe I should be trying to make a distinction between those things that are a little less stupid and stuff that is totally ridiculous."

"Here's the problem, my friend. If everything you consider to do to build a life is an illusion, some ill-considered self-justification, then how will you ever overcome your nothingness? It seems like you have caught yourself in your own trap."

"I feel trapped. That's my problem."

"Well, if everything people do is pointless, and we are all truly nothing, then suicide is the logical conclusion. But you say you're not considering it. Is your heart telling you something else?"

"Yes. That I'd like an authentic life, not a delusional life."

"Ah, ha, nicely put!" Marv let a long silence settle over the room as he nodded his head, apparently thinking how to respond. Finally, he blew out a long breath, puffing his cheeks. "Look, a lot of what people do may seem ridiculous, some things being more ridiculous than others. I agree. The challenge is for you to find a genuine passion you can believe in."

"Even if I think it's an illusion?"

"Well, if that's where you need to begin, let's call it an acceptable illusion for the time being, but a possible source of meaning. Someday it may seem authentic to you, enough at least to make you feel you have some actual purpose in your life, some legitimate cure to your nothingness." Marv wheeled a little closer to me and leaned forward from his wheelchair.

I could see his withered legs and it made me realize that he must have struggled like hell to find an authentic life after his military service. Then he whispered to me, almost like he was sharing a secret with me. "Maybe it is your nothingness that is the illusion." He raised his eyebrows and widened his eyes, looking directly at me. Then he continued. "We shape ourselves day by day with our choices and commitments, like a sculptor chisels a beautiful figure from a rough block of marble, one chip at a time. Why don't you have a shot at being something instead of nothing?" He paused for a moment, as if to let his words sink in, and then he asked, "Next week? Here?"

"Yeah, of course."

"Sweet dreams."

After my summer workshops were complete and my parents had turned in the grades for their courses, my dad suggested we take another vacation together. Getting out of town sounded like a good diversion to me. I needed a break from counseling, and Marv probably needed a break from me. Hey, I could cancel my appointments. I remembered how much I had enjoyed our trip to Colorado. "Where?" I asked, not disguising my enthusiasm.

"Carlsbad Caverns," Dad replied.

"Caves? That sounds cool."

"They will be. A good place to go to escape the heat. And we can also try out the air conditioning in the new CRV getting over there." With the old Honda totaled, my parents used the insurance money as a down payment for a new one. An upgrade.

"Where are these caves?" I asked.

"Southeastern New Mexico," Mom replied. She was usually the navigator on trips, making sure that Dad didn't make any wrong turns. And what was I? The back seat historian in residence? Should I remind them that most of this land belonged to Mexico, and before that to the Apache, Comanche, and Caddo tribes? Until their "friends" settled on it.

On the long drive across Route 180, I gave them a quick summary of my Texas history course. Mom was impressed with how much I remembered just reciting it without notes, and Dad admitted that he only knew some of it but wasn't surprised at the rest. He kept repeating over and over: Manifest Destiny…Manifest Destiny…America's greed becomes God's will. Such bullshit."

It turned out that Carlsbad Caverns was another national park complete with informative pamphlets and a guide standing at the entryway to the cave to send us on our way. "What's that horrible smell?" I asked.

"Bat poop," the guide said. "The bats love to hang out at the entry of the cave. Literally."

"Are there bats in the caves?" Mom asked, an unusual concern showing in her voice.

"No, just at the beginning here," the guide said. "Ignore them and start down the path. It's all downhill."

And to get back out?" Mom asked.

"Take the elevator, ma'am. That's what it's for."

Dad took on the role of tour guide from there onward and read us the important facts about the stalactites and stalagmites.

"Remember that stalactites come down from above and are hanging on tight to the ceiling," Mom reminded me.

She was full of useful memory devices, and I had always been taught to remember every little detail. Now, after a whole year of college, I began to wonder if my brain would fill up and spill over with so much memorizing to do before graduation, but Brenda had told me that it doesn't work that way, that the memory has infinite capacity and we only use a small portion of the billions of brain cells that we have. So, I listened closely to Dad and tried to remember the stuff he was saying as we worked our way down into the caves. "Two hundred fifty million years ago..." Dad started to give us what he called the speliogenesis. "On the edge of an inland sea. Turned into a reef. Lifted up by tectonic plate movement during Cenozoic period." Dad had a way of reading the pamphlets and distilling them down to the basic facts, and they came out of his mouth, one after the other, like little droplets from a dripping faucet. I guess he thought I was understanding everything he was saying. "Hydrogen sulfide seeps up from deep underground. Mixes with oxygen. Produces sulfuric acid. The H2SO4 continues upward aggressively. Dissolves the limestone. Makes the caves."

Mom asked me, "Do you remember the rhyme I taught you about sulfuric acid when you were in junior high?"

"I doubt it," I said, "but let me hear it again."

"Alas, for poor little Johnny/ For now he is now more/ What he thought was H2O/ Was H2SO4."

I did remember it vaguely, and wondered if Johnny was having suicidal thoughts or if he just made an honest mistake. Maybe Johnny had read Ecclesiastes. In any case, my brain was automatically recording H2SO4 as a suicide elixir. I didn't respond and the far-off look on my face must have scared Mom a little.

"Carl, where are you, son? It's just a silly joke," she said, tapping me on the shoulder.

"Oh, sorry. Yeah, when you told it, I realized I'd heard it before, but then I started wondering how H2SO4 was able to carve out such beautiful limestone deposits." I thought I had recovered nicely and smiled at her.

My father continued as tour guide. "We're in the Big Room now. Four thousand feet long. Longest cave in North America. Explored by a teen-age boy in 1898. He gave most of the cave rooms the names we use today: Bat Cave, Green Lake Room, Queen Anne's Chamber. Imagine that," he turned to me, "making your mark at such a young age."

"Impressive," I said, not sure I would make my mark at any age, at least not boldly enough to impress my father.

As we walked through the Big Room and the Queen's Chamber, I was taken by the exquisite beauty of the shapes and colors of the various formations. It was as if an expert sculptor had worked on each one, shaping it in a unique way and adding just the right tint of color to make it absolutely beautiful. I remembered Marv telling me to chip away at making a life like a sculptor, and I tried to imagine how to make not just a life, but a beautiful life. Could I do that?

While my parents were enjoying the science of it all—still another example of the continuing evolution of the earth itself—I was caught up in the aesthetics. How could the erosion and dripping and building up of calcium carbonate deposits produce such a gorgeous visual fairyland? Soft curves, tall pinnacles, deep overhangs. Father was reading the words that were used in the pamphlet to describe the various structures, but for me, there were no words, certainly not those words, to describe the beauty spreading out before me wherever I turned. Naturally, I had to ask myself why I perceived it as beautiful. How did I know it was beautiful? What was transpiring in my brain to produce this unparalleled visual sensation of color and form? I wanted to talk to my parents about this experience of beauty, but I didn't know how. I was wondering if they were having it, too, but I wasn't so sure about that.

The trip to "Charles' Bath Caves," as Dad began to call them, could not have been more enjoyable for the astronomer and the botanist. There was an amphitheater for lectures, seventeen species of bats to get acquainted with in the early evening, night-time viewing of the stars (Dad had brought along his portable telescope), above ground hikes in the wilderness area ecosystems, three hundred species of birds to spot (Mom had brought her binoculars), and a desert wetland called Rattlesnake Springs. A gigantic outdoor laboratory.

As for me, I couldn't get the multitude of shapes and colors out of my mind. The caves seemed to have awakened a dormant aesthetic sense in me, something I didn't realize I possessed. I would definitely need to take an art history course next term and maybe a class in painting to see if I could create something beautiful based on what I had seen in these caves.

My mind kept drifting back to the first-year seminar with Professor Adams, who spoke about "something more." What created the awesome beauty of the caves? Was it simply a natural process or was it that "something more" that we don't apprehend fully because it works so mysteriously? Can nature produce art without an artist? If it is only a process of nature, the work of H2SO4, then, it seemed to me, that process itself was also pretty miraculous. For me, there was something holy about these caves. Sacred space.

On the way back, Mom and Dad listened to the news on their new satellite car radio and they liked the radio but not the news it brought about the coming election in November.

"Of, course, he could never win," my mother said.

"Don't be so sure," Dad pointed out, "and if he does, it will be a disaster."

Politics seemed very distant to me. It was like I was up on that satellite orbiting the earth, looking down from far, far away, not caring about those political creatures down below, slinging lies, slamming each other with attack ads, and arousing old hatreds among their followers. Mostly, I found politics to be ugly and grotesque. But my parents took it very seriously. I heard snippets of the newscasts and bits and pieces of my parents' outrage as I dozed, half asleep and half awake, with images of stalactites and stalagmites floating somewhere behind my closed eyelids.

5

Deciding How Much Ancestry Really Matters

Classes in art history and studio art. Meeting Rachael Katzenbaum. Lessons in blackness from Alexisius. The lawsuit from Ken's parents. Grandpa Lawenski dies. Was I maybe Jewish? Inspecting the crash site. Yoga meditation in the Arb.

In the fall term of my second year, I took Art History 101, the introductory course to the study of art. It was held in a small lecture hall on the ground floor of the Humanities Building, and because Mom told me to expect to see a lot of projected slides, I sat in the middle, neither so close as to be in the face of Jolene's mother, but not in my bird perch in the back row either. I was surrounded by women, which made me feel good— maybe I was especially hot that day— but then I glanced around and counted only three guys in the whole class, also surrounded by women.

"I'm Vanessa Winter," the professor began, letting the bracelets on her arm jangle as she gestured toward the class. "You have come to learn about art history, and of course we will do that."

Her face was thin and her hair was black as a crow, and I was having difficulty convincing myself that she was Jolene's mother. There seemed to be no family resemblance, and as I remembered her architect husband from the faculty brats picnic, I began to wonder if Jolene was adopted. She didn't look like her parents at all.

"But I have another goal for this course," Professor Winter continued, "and that is to help you see, in a more sophisticated, differentiated, and elaborated way, so that when you look at a work of art, you will see more things than you did before you took this course. And by extension, this more sophisticated seeing should apply to anything that comes within your view." The goal was written in a simpler form on a projected slide.

THIS COURSE WILL HELP YOU SEE

She passed around the syllabus and explained how each unit had an out-of-class project attached to it involving the creation of our own little work of art, using pencil, crayon, watercolor, or all three. Beginning with the Egyptians, for example, we had to present a figure in profile. She projected some Egyptian art, and sure enough, all of the figures were in profile, not only the faces, but feet as well. "When we get to Rembrandt, you will do a self-portrait." She projected several slides of a sad-looking old dude all in shades of brown. "And in the modern period, you may try your hand at a cubist abstraction." She showed us a slide called 'Nude Descending a Staircase' and when the students frowned, she said some critics had called it 'Cyclone in a Shingle Factory.'

The student on my right provided only one-word responses to my efforts to get acquainted, so I gave up on her, but the young woman on my left was talkative and lively, and in a few days, we had become good friends. It turned out she was from Brooklyn, and I told her my dad was from there. "How did you ever find Little Texas College?" I asked.

"My mom went here, so I'm an alumna brat."

"And I'm a faculty brat." So we laughed and joked about being different kinds of brats and which was the brat worst. My joke, my bad.

"My parents lived in Texas and moved back to New York," she said.

"And mine moved from New York to Texas, but I don't think they view themselves as Texans."

"Mine either. They're much more comfortable in the neighborhood where we live now in Brooklyn."

When she told me her name, Rachael Katzenbaum, I must have paused without responding, and she looked over with a smile and said, "Of course, I'm a Jewish princess."

I told her, "I'm Carl Wallace."

She must have put two and two together immediately, and when she said, "OMG" I knew she was taking my parents' course.

"This term?" I asked.

"This morning." she said with a frown. "They said the world was coming to an end."

I thought Rachael was really cute, and I noticed that she had a straight nose. Maybe she had it fixed. Was I prejudiced for examining the nose of a Jewish princess who lives in what must be a Jewish neighborhood in Brooklyn? Like noticing the white teeth of my black roommate? I remembered coming across a passage in my study of the novels of Thomas Hardy where he said something like, "If a woman has a straight nose, everything else can be forgiven." Did he have nasal prejudice? Actually, there wasn't much to forgive about Rachel. The next day I leaned over to her and whispered that if she needed therapy after taking my parents' course, she should look up a guy named Marv Cohen in the counseling center, and she exploded into laughter. "I'm already seeing him," she said.

Two days a week in the afternoons, I went to the top floor of the Humanities building to a small art studio with floor to ceiling windows, like a penthouse, overlooking the residence halls and athletic fields out at the north end of the campus. I remembered how I watered lawns out that way, the summer before I came to college here, what seemed like centuries ago at the time and eons ago as I am writing this now. The studio art professor had reddish brown hair that stuck up like a sable brush and he was as skinny as the handle. He spoke in a whisper as he floated around the room like a ghost, making confidential comments about each student's painting. We paid a fee for brushes, acrylic paint, a pallet knife, and canvas, and we just stood there at our easels, about six feet apart, supposedly creating our own little masterpiece. I started painting the shapes and colors I could remember from the Carlsbad Caverns stalactites and stalagmites. When the prof came around to me, he would fold his arms across his chest and say "hmm" and "interesting." I kind of liked having my long hair and hanging out in the art department, but it only took me a few weeks to discover that I had about the same amount of talent for painting that I had for the piano. It would be a challenge even to get a B in that course.

Rooming with Alexisius was like taking another course, maybe like The Black Experience in America, and it was definitely 101 for me, not having known anyone like Alex in high school. Our little town was still mostly segregated by neighborhood housing, and the two high schools, North High and South High, had attendance areas that followed the housing boundaries, so hardly anyone from the black neighborhoods ended up in my school. As I had hoped, Alex and I talked about everything, including school segregation. Depending on the issue, he would suggest some book to read, and I did usually read it, at least some chapters. One night, I asked Alex if he was sure he was descended from slaves.

"I'm pretty sure my parents were not offspring of the Nigerian ambassador."

"Meaning?"

"Unless there was some more recent lineage, we were all descended from slaves, man, there ain't no other way."

It was interesting to me how he was so sure of his ancestry, and I was so uncertain about mine. "It's hard for me to think of people owning other people as slaves, actually owning them and bossing them around," I told him. "I've seen some pretty raw films portraying that, you know, humiliation and whippings."

"Many white people have not bothered to learn what slavery actually was."

"Or don't want to know about their ancestors," I added.

"You mean the owners? Good point." He was nodding his head and went over to a little collection of books he kept in his bookcase and pulled off a novel. "Let me recommend to you, if you haven't read it already, Uncle Tom's Cabin."

"I've heard of it."

"Written by Harriet Beecher Stowe, the daughter of a famous abolitionist. A book that made a big impact at the time and began to energize the anti-slavery movement in the Northern states."

"I've heard of Uncle Toms," I said, somehow unable to keep my mouth shut when I didn't know what I was talking about.

"Oh, yes, white folks take the main character and turn him into someone who sells out and betrays his race. But you read it and tell me if Uncle Tom is an actual 'Uncle Tom' or if he is just doing what he has to do to stay alive, protect his family as best he can, and keep body and soul together. Read it. Tell me."

Another night, when we were getting ready to sleep, I asked Alex if he had ever been called the N-word.

"You mean other than affectionately by the brothers and the sisters?"

"It's used affectionately?" I asked. That was surprising.

"Not so much anymore, but, yes, as a kind of insider's term of affection, turning it around, you know, like sometimes 'bad' means 'good.' But that's not what you are asking."

"No, I mean—"

"Of course I've been called the N-word, as you refer to it so politely. It really wouldn't be so bad if it was just name-calling, but it goes way beyond that." Then he started telling me his story, gesturing, kind of acting it out. "I will never forget the first time it happened. I was just a little kid, eight years old. I was only walking down the street, minding my own business, when I heard the N-word shouted at me, followed by the clattering of stones on the pavement around me. Then I felt the sharp sting of a rock that got me in the shoulder. And I said to myself that these people, white kids, who were older and bigger, didn't even know me. I hadn't done anything to them. So it must be only one thing: the color of my skin, just like my momma told me would happen someday. I couldn't believe that these words and rocks were being aimed at me, a total stranger, because of my skin color and nothing more. You know what I'm sayin'? And, yes, it would be nice if the humiliation only involved name-callin' and not rock-throwin'. Not to mention being spit on, shoved around, tripped, and oh, yes, being lynched by the KKK and shot by the police."

I knew some of this, of course, but not really, and when Alex described it, it shook me up because Alex was my friend now. How can some people think those things, say those things, and do stuff like that to people they don't even know? To a nice guy like Alex. I shook my head back and forth, wishing somehow to find the words for an apology.

Alex noticed that I wasn't able to speak. "It's okay, man, he said. There's really nothing to say. But there's plenty to do."

That stuck with me.

Mom sent me a text message and asked me to stop by her office, neither of which was common because both parents understood my need for privacy as I was going to college where they were both on the faculty. Besides, they were busy. Mom's office was on the first floor of the Science Building, at the end of a long hall among the zoologists and the other botanists. Naturally, I had been in her office many times before, but it looked different to me now that I was a student, more like the offices of other professors although neater and more organized. The only thing to identify her as a mother was a small, framed picture, wedged among the science books on the bookshelf behind her desk, a snapshot of me when I was ten. I knew she must have some urgent business or she wouldn't have called me in like this.

She was sitting behind her desk and motioned me toward an empty chair like she would have, I supposed, to a biology major. She looked nervous but spoke in a calm voice. "Everything good?" she asked.

I nodded and returned the question, "What about you?"

"Well, it was good until your father and I received these papers." She held up a large Manila envelope and pulled out the papers.

"What's this?" I asked, completely unaware of what was coming.

"This is a summons to appear in court. We've been sued by Ken's parents for damages associated with the car accident."

"But it wasn't my fault," I protested. Was this why Ken had been so uncommunicative? His parents were suing and they told him to stop emailing me? Mom let me sit for a few seconds to absorb the shock.

"You weren't at fault. But who was?"

"The driver of the truck," I replied, firm in that belief now.

"Whom we can't identify. But from his parents' point of view, someone was responsible for their son's suffering, and, of course, his medical bills. As a legal case, you were the driver and there were no witnesses."

"But the police report provides the evidence to show it was a hit-and-run," I complained.

"Yes, and they have pictures and so do we. Ken's family isn't likely to win this, but they are aggrieved, perhaps lashing out."

"How much are they asking for?"

"One million, two hundred fifty thousand."

"Dollars?

"Dollars. Our insurance stops at five hundred thousand."

"How's Dad handling this?"

"He's wondering why this is the thanks he gets after taking such good care of their son."

"I can't blame him for that. But tell me, does he have any ideas, any strategies?" As much as I might have disagreed with my father on certain things, I had a deep respect for his ability to think things through rationally and solve problems.

"He says it would be a lot better if we knew who the driver of the truck was so that the law suit could be redirected to the person actually responsible. He's not sure why the local police investigation isn't turning up suspects. He wants you to try to remember everything you can about the accident, perhaps revisit the scene with him."

"We do that every time we drive home. Isn't that painful enough?"

"He means to get out, walk around, and let the recollections come back."

"Just as I'm finally getting rid of them? But he's right, Mom. I agree.

We need to find the son-of-a-bitch who hit us."

"Carl."

"That's what my counselor called him."

Do you recall the conversation I had had with Brenda about my first name: how I had been named Carl for the famous astronomer Carl Sagan? I was supposed to be a famous astronomer myself, only it really wasn't going that way now with all of those courses in religion, literature, and most recently, art. Well, after that exchange with Brenda, I was telling her one day about how I had started to think about what I could have been called besides Carl. I was recounting how my dad made a big deal out of his Polish ancestry, poor but very hard-working people, and she mentioned that she had heard some of that family saga herself directly from my dad.

I told her that I had done a Google search for Polish first names and, of course, she wanted to know what I had found. I told her, "Albin, Jakub, Wiktor, and Igor." We had a big laugh over that, and she said that I must really be relieved now to be named Carl. We laughed again, and that was it, but that started me to wondering about my last name, Wallace. It didn't sound very Polish to me. Wallace? Carl Wallace? I filed that away in the back of my brain and promised myself not to perseverate.

This past weekend, more of the truth came out. Two weeks after I got the call from Mom about the lawsuit being filed by Ken's parents, I got another call from her telling me that Dad's father had died. Could I come over to her office? Yes, of course.

"When I entered, I said, "Grandpa Wallace died? Back in New York?"

"Yes," she said, "your father wanted me to tell you."

"Are we going to fly back to the funeral?"

"I wasn't invited. Nor were you. Your father has already left."

That seemed strange to me. Mom seemed a little edgy. It was a Friday afternoon, so I asked her if she would like some company for the weekend and she said yes.

At home, Mom was unusually quiet, and I wasn't sure why. I didn't think she knew grandpa all that well, so it probably wasn't grief. Maybe she didn't like the idea of being left behind to answer all the questions she was sure I would ask.

While she was putting together some salad and salmon for dinner, I was in the guest room downstairs with the basement door open. I heard her take a phone call on the land line. Sounded like it was Dad. So I listened. I heard her ask Dad what she should tell me about Grandpa Walenski. Holy shit, I could have been named Igor Walenski. That's all the information I needed to inspire a little after-dinner conversation with Mom.

I asked her, very gently of course, if Dad's name was originally Wallace or if he might have changed it from Walenski. She knew immediately that I had overheard her conversation, and she was probably wondering what else I had heard. Maybe everything. So she was fairly forthcoming.

"Yes, he changed it in graduate school right before we started looking for jobs."

"To Wallace from Walenski?"

"He was afraid he would experience discrimination during the job search," she said in a matter-of-fact tone, as if we were discussing the name for a species of birds.

"Is this why we weren't invited to the funeral, because Dad didn't want to explain to us and to everyone else why his father was named Walenski and everyone in our family was named Wallace?"

"Yes, I'm sure he would have found some embarrassment in that. Your father is very sensitive about his name. There was a time when people told bad jokes about Polish people."

"I've heard about that. But tell me, is that why we never went back to visit grandpa, after I was old enough to remember? Because Dad didn't want me to know that his last name was Walenski?"

"That's part of it, I'm sure, but unlike my side of the family, your father did not embrace his family heritage. It wasn't something he valued, and he certainly didn't want to cultivate it in you. In fact, he spent a lot of energy trying to shelter you and distance himself from it."

"But I have another question. Grandpa Walenski lived in Brooklyn, right? I know someone in my art class from Brooklyn, and she's Jewish. I think she lives in a Jewish neighborhood." I just threw that out and let it land on the dining room table to see what Mom would say. I hated to put her on the hot seat because she really wasn't responsible for my dad's artful dodges about his heritage and sly coverups through his name change.

"Are you asking if grandpa was Jewish?"

"Well, weren't there a lot of Polish Jews? Don't I remember reading something about a Warsaw ghetto from World War II? I mean grandpa could be—I should say could have been—Polish and Jewish. It's not uncommon.

"That's true."

"And somewhere along here maybe there was a Jewish grandmother Walenski, whose maiden name was not Walenski but something else, and I could have a Jewish grandmother." I had read somewhere that having a Jewish grandmother was important.

"Well, that's a possibility," Mom said in a non-comital voice, without answering my questions or addressing what I was implying. My mom is a very quick thinker, and after a brief silence she asked, "Does it bother you that you could be Jewish?" dodging my question about whether I actually was.

"Bother me? No. There would be things to adjust to like maybe my grandparents were Holocaust survivors or something, but I think I would be proud, like proud of the gray matter I had inherited in my gifted brain. But don't you think it would at least be nice for me to know?"

"But, Carl, as you do know, these matters are not really important to your father in the way that they are to other people. He and his father, your grandpa, were not close. And you know how he feels about religion, so maybe it's not surprising that he hasn't discussed your ancestors with you. My guess is that he just doesn't think it's important."

"Except that he was always bragging about his Polish heritage, but then he thought the name Walenski was embarrassing enough as a name to have it changed to Wallace."

"Maybe just for practical reasons while we were seeking jobs." Mom heaved a big sigh, indicating that perhaps she had had more than enough of this conversation with me. Then she said something that shocked me even more. "I understand how things like this are of concern to you right now, dear, but maybe there will come a point later as you mature, that none of this will matter to you."

"Perhaps," I said, taking my dishes to the kitchen and then withdrawing to the sunporch, not to view the night sky, but to ponder seriously what my mother had just said. There were two different ways to interpret that ambiguous remark. One explanation was developmental. As you mature—man, how I hated that word mature—you will put away your childish preoccupations about your heritage and discover how exaggerated and unimportant they were. The other interpretation was that your fixation on your ancestry is inconsequential because you will discover one day that your father is not actually your father at all. Thus, questions about paternal ancestry would become irrelevant.

On Monday, I would make an appointment with my counselor Marvin Cohen.

Except for the smoldering hot and horribly humid summers, the weather in this part of Texas was mostly good, more warm than cold, more dry than wet, but every so often we got a rainy day when it rains most of the day, and the expansive campus lawns recover their green. Mom said the grass profits nutritionally from the moisture, and Dad said the appearance of a deeper tone of green is from the altered refraction of light from the water-covered blades of grass. The day I went to see Marv it was rainy like that, a low-hanging cloud of drizzle covering the whole campus, so that I had to stomp the water off of my sneakers and shake the drops off of my hooded nylon jacket at the doorway before entering the Student Union.

I told Marv as succinctly as I could the details surrounding the death of Grandpa Walenski and then explained what I thought were the ambiguous meanings of my mother's remark.

Marvin smiled and began, "If I were a judge, I would need to recuse myself from this case, but instead, let me do something we counselors are trained to do: disclose aspects of our own background that might affect our impartiality in counseling the client on certain issues. Would that be okay?"

"Better than making me start all over again with someone else." I grinned.

"In the interests of full disclosure, then, let me mention that I am Jewish, which you may have guessed from the name Cohen."

So that's why he knew all about the Hebrew Scriptures. I should have figured that out.

"I was raised in an Orthodox family," he continued, "which includes aunts and uncles and my own brother, all living in Israel, some temporarily, some permanently. When I signed up for duty in Iraq, I thought I was doing a good thing for Zionism early in my military service, but when I got there, and learned later of the pretext that brought the US there, the orders to disqualify Bath Party members, and disband the Iraq army, I became disillusioned with the war in Iraq, and many other things as well. You know the rest of what happened to me."

I thought I could see where this was going, but I just said, "And…"

"And I grew less attached to my faith, becoming what is called 'non-observant.' I'm telling you this to reveal a possible bias in favor of your father on this matter. In other words, I'm not completely neutral. No doubt your dad not only wanted to change his name, but also to disentangle himself from his Jewish roots. Apparently, he wanted to spare you what he had experienced growing up in a conservative religious household."

"So to spare me, he hasn't always been able to come out with the plain truth about the family tree. He'd prefer to cover up his own roots."

"The way he has done it may not have been the best, but we can say his intentions were good."

"He lied to me."

Like I say, not the best."

"But what about Mom? She lied, too."

"Until this weekend when she seemed to make some attempt to straighten out some of the story for you, treading a narrow path of loyalty to her son and her husband."

"But what about the remark?"

"I agree with you about the ambiguity in what she said about 'there will come a day,' which makes it hard to interpret what she meant."

"They could still be lying to me, this time an even bigger lie."

"That he is not your father?"

"Exactly."

"Well, we don't know that, do we? It's only a possibility. You could ask him directly, I suppose, but now you may not trust his answers. Being lied to one time doesn't build trust for the next, does it?"

"Right."

Marvin paused for a moment and then wheeled a little closer to me. "Let's get back to counseling now. Why do you feel this is so important?"

"Being lied to by my own parents?"

"No, no. Having to know for certain about your ancestry."

I had to stop and think for a minute about what he was saying about my unsatisfied craving for the roots of my family tree. "Well, doesn't our ancestry shape who we are?"

"To some extent perhaps, but how much? How important is it for you to know and why?"

"I think it would help me know who I am."

"And if you don't know who you are at this point because you are still mixed up and searching, then knowing your ancestry becomes really important to you. Maybe too important."

"So, I'm perseverating."

"Nice word. You could be letting it get in the way of the main goal which is…"

Marv paused for me to recollect the goal and I could see he expected a reply. "To build an authentic life, like a sculptor chipping away at a block of marble."

"You've got it. Very good. Knowing your ancestry may help, like knowing if you are dealing with marble or granite, but roots can also get in the way, as they did for me, and seem to have for your father. Sometimes not knowing your ancestry is a blessing. It's nice to know you are a little bit of this and a little bit of that, but how much, really, do you need to know to build your life?"

As I walked out of the building, I noticed that the rain had stopped and the sun was trying to build a sunset out of the clouds left behind after the storm. Was that the message today? Cut the drizzle and go build something beautiful? Then I wondered what it was like for Marv to wheel his way through a rainstorm. Did he ever go wheeling in the rain just for the fun of it?

That night I told Alex about everything that had happened over the weekend and what my counselor had said about weighing the importance of knowing your heritage as you build your own identity.

Alex listened, a little impatiently it seemed, and then said, "White man's privilege."

"What?" I asked, not sure what he meant.

"All this searching. Wanting to know if you are Polish or Jewish or both or none of the above. Me? I don't have a choice and I don't have to do much searching. If I want to know my identity, I just look in the mirror. Black Male. No escaping it. My ancestors? Well, I told you about them. Slaves. Oh, you and your dad can deny that you are Polish or Jewish or whatever, but I can't deny I'm Afro-American. No, sir, I see it every morning when I wake up and stretch my arms. If I found out that my dad wasn't really my dad, I'd still be black. Even if my dad was white, I'd still be black 'cause of my mom. Those are the rules. It must be nice to have a choice, Carl, but if I were you, I wouldn't get too agonized over it."

"Wow! I'd never thought about it that way. You're right You know your ancestry for certain, and there's no running from it."

The next day I invited Rachael for coffee after class at the Student Union.

"Coffee?" she said.

I loved the way she said "coffee" with that New York accent. "Or whatever you like. I need to talk to you about being Jewish."

She frowned. "You or me?"

"I'll explain."

So we found two plastic chairs at a secluded table where we could talk, after picking up a couple of mango smoothies. I told her about my dad's name change.

"Not uncommon," she said. "Happens all the time although more in the past when the immigrants first landed at Ellis Island."

Then I explained about how my dad may have been concealing his Jewishness, hiding it from me."

"Sparing you?" Her eyebrows went up.

"But I don't necessarily think of it as sparing. I mean, I know there's anti-Semitism and all, but there's a lot to be proud of, too."

She hesitated and then smiled. "It's complicated, Carl. Really complicated, but you can join us if you want. We can probably get you a circumcision exemption if that would help." We both laughed and I hoped I wasn't blushing.

"But tell me," I continued, "does it feel good to know that you have a heritage?"

"For me, yes. I know I belong to a community of Jewish people, and not only a community that exists today, but one that goes back over the centuries. My parents and aunts and uncles speak of being part of the Jewish people and they remind me of the years of suffering and struggle. Even Jews who have become non-observant in matters of faith still remind themselves of their Jewishness."

"And for you?"

"I'm telling you about me. Yes, it's important."

I decided to go visit Brenda and see what she thought about this mess. She and I were both in different residence halls, different from last year, and different from each other this year, although next to each other. I didn't see her around campus much because she was in the Social Sciences Building most of the time for her psych classes, while I was in the Humanities Building, but we still studied together once in a while in the evenings. I would slip over to her building, walk up two flights to the lounge, and see if she was there. We weren't so "co-dependent" as we were in high school, but we were still good friends, and when something was troubling me, I would seek her out. For example, I had told her about the lawsuit as soon as I found out about it, and she agreed with my dad that we needed to find the driver of the truck. But how?

Tonight, I wanted to tell her about what had happened the weekend that Grandpa Walenski died. I could hardly get the whole story out because she kept interrupting with her infernal questions and observations as I went through it.

"Maybe your dad always made a big deal of his Polish ancestry as a kind of denial of his Jewish heritage. It doesn't surprise me, but lying to you about it does, because he's always focused on getting to the truth with facts and empirical evidence."

"We might say he has very strong commitments to his version of the truth."

"And your mom, too. But she's kind of been trapped here, don't you think, having to cover for him?"

"That may be so, but now I'm worried that she's got her own lies."

"Like maybe your dad is not really your father? That's a biggie."

"For sure she has to know the truth about that," I said emphatically.

"Yes, but you don't know that he's not your father. You're just speculating based on one remark, maybe jumping to conclusions."

"You're right. I need to be careful about that. But don't forget, I'm an in vitro fertilization baby—they call it IVF now—and a lot of things could have happened in that petri dish. You never know."

"And you may never know for sure," Brenda said, nodding her head several times.

"Do you think about stuff like this?" I asked her.

"Like if my parents are really my parents?" She paused to think it over, but not for long. "Not really." I would trust them to tell me about anything irregular."

"That must be a good feeling: trusting your parents."

On the way back to my room in the other residence hall, I began to realize that I was really confused. Rachael thinks having a heritage is important and enjoys belonging to the Jewish people. Alex thinks that all of this talk about my ancestry is a white luxury, but for him his ancestry is a burden he can't escape. Brenda says I may never know my ancestry for sure. Marv shows that it is possible to disengage with one's heritage, but he also suggested that I may be placing way too much importance on knowing my ancestry.

I took the stairwell steps up to my room two at a time. Maybe it was time for me to get my mind back on Michelangelo, Rembrandt, and Picasso and start figuring out who the hell was driving whatever kind of black truck that was.

~

A few days later, as I was walking across campus, I went past the Science Building and noticed my father coming toward me from the entrance. I hadn't seen him since Grandpa Walenski had died, and I was nervous about how this unplanned encounter would go, but Dad was very warm and friendly. I told him that I was sorry to hear about his father's passing, and he said it was a difficult weekend. But then he asked me how it was going with my studies this term and how were Alex and Brenda. He wanted to know if I ever heard from Ken. My dad really could be nice to me at times, and then I felt bad that I had become so agitated about his last name.

Then Dad invited me to come home for a visit some weekend. We both exercised our thumbs on our phones to access our calendars, and the date we found free was the second weekend in November. It seemed odd, having to make an appointment with my own father. Dad acted like there was nothing to explain about his solo flight to Brooklyn and nothing to clarify for me about the family names of Wallace and Walenski. Just pick up and go on from where we were—that seemed to be his attitude. But for me, I became more suspicious about whether Grandpa Walenski was really my grandfather. Anyway, I agreed to ride home with him in a couple of weeks on a Friday afternoon.

On that afternoon as we were heading home, when we came to the intersection where the crash occurred, Dad asked if I minded revisiting the scene. I wasn't eager, of course, but if we could pick up some new details, some small piece of evidence, why not stop? We walked around a bit before Dad asked if I was remembering anything new. I told him not yet. I noticed the stop sign, the probable point of impact, and the place where Mom's Honda had come to rest.

"I know you took a lot of pictures," I said. "But did you do anything else?"

"I scoured the place for physical evidence without much luck. The city police quickly gathered up what little there was."

"Were there paint marks on our car?"

"A few. I took pictures of those, and I even went to the junk yard and took some more. Some of the metal from the door was loose and I bent off a piece with black paint on it. I have that piece of scrap at home."

"I vaguely remember now how the truck knocked us to the far side of the intersection, over there." I pointed toward the shoulder of the road, now mostly covered with faded wildflowers that had already bloomed.

"Want to take a look?' he asked.

"Sure, why not?" So, we crossed the asphalt intersection and searched through the brush beyond the shoulder of the road without much success until I saw something shiny reflecting the late afternoon sun. I picked it up and showed it to Dad. "What do you think?"

"Maybe a piece of headlight. Hard to tell. Pretty small, but perhaps big enough to corroborate the make and year if we ever identify the vehicle. Yeah, let's keep it." We searched for something more, but found nothing.

"What do you remember most? What stands out for you?" Dad asked.

"After Ken's bloody face? Well, a truck backing up and then taking off. I was so shocked, it's kind of a blur. Somehow the back of the truck as it pulled away sticks in my mind. Oh, yeah, and a face looking out the rear window of the cab from the passenger side, a kind of terrified looking young woman."

"Do you think that you could recognize that face if a photo was put before you?"

"I could now. It's getting clearer." We glanced around the site one more time, got back into his car, and drove the remaining four miles to home.

That weekend at home, to me at least, it seemed like there was only one topic of conversation: the national election. I thought we might have some discussion of Polishness and Jewishness, contrasting lifestyles in Brooklyn and Texas, and the merits and drawbacks of knowing one's ancestors. Earlier that week, on Tuesday night, my parents watched the election results come in state by state and were apparently totally flabbergasted by the returns. The man who could never win beat the woman who could never lose. I had never seen my parents so upset and so engaged in a non-scientific subject before, as if the world was about to end, which come to think of it, is a scientific subject of high priority for astronomers. But this was different. The ranting and raving of my parents was horrendous, and I just kept my head down as the conversation bounced back and forth, remark after remark, about how the country was going to hell.

"I just don't know what happened," my mother said. "Our one chance, finally, to have a woman president."

"The country is very divided now, and in each state, whether Republican or Democrat, there are still significant divisions, like each state is on the verge of its own internal civil war."

"Texas liked him," Mom said.

"But even Texas is divided. There are many people who don't.

They asked me if I had voted. I knew they would get around to asking me that eventually. "I was registered," I told them, "but it's not easy for college students to vote in this state. I knew there would be a long line, and I had class and a paper to finish."

"It's true, dear," my mother said, directing the 'dear' to my father. "It's not easy."

"It's disappointing that you didn't vote," my father said flatly, looking directly at me one of the few times all weekend, "but I guess it wouldn't have mattered much here in Texas."

Then they started making predictions. "The free press won't be so free," my mother said.

"The rich will get richer and the poor will be poorer," Dad said.

"Foreign relations will be a disaster," Mom said. "America first? What about our allies?"

Then my father started in on what could happen to colleges and universities. "The whole concept of truth will be upended by this guy who tells lies and gets away with it. This college will be a struggling oasis of truth trying to survive in a desert of alternative facts and conspiracy theories."

"We may even lose our freedom to teach about evolution," my mom said, a worried look on her face.

"Or race. The old ethnic and racial hatreds are being aroused. Imagine wanting to build a wall across the whole southern boundary of Texas."

"Of the entire US, and make the Mexicans pay for it,' Mom added. "What a joke."

Actually, I agreed with most of what my parents said; I just didn't feel involved. I knew in my mind that it was important, but I had my own agenda of personal problems. And now as everything was going the wrong way in the country, I felt more alienated than ever. Was this my country? Did I belong here? Could I call myself an American? It didn't seem to be a very big factor in defining who I was. Red? Blue? Red, white, and blue? More like black and blue as in hematoma.

We desperately needed a change of subject, so I asked my parents if they had heard anything about the picnic for faculty whose children attend college here, carefully avoiding the word brats. They looked at each other a little puzzled and then back at me. Finally, my mother said, "I'm not sure they're still doing that, but you may go if you wish."

"I'll check it out," I said. But then I realized that all of those parents and their kids knew about my accident with Ken and probably the lawsuit, too, and I didn't want to stand there with them looking at me with that look. Besides, I had taken courses from some of those people. They were my professors now, which reminded me of Professor Winter, which got me thinking about Jolene. Where was she? I hadn't seen her at all this fall. Had she dropped out?

I was taking another course in the religious studies department, slowly accumulating enough credits for a major without actually declaring one. This term it was Hinduism, taught once again by Professor Adams, who I was getting to know quite well and liked as a person. He was taking an interest in me and told me to stop by if I wanted to chat, which I did from time to time.

For class we were reading selections from the Vedas and portions of the great epic, the Mahabharata. I decided to write my term paper on the belief in reincarnation, more accurately known as rebirth, which also involves an understanding of karma. The basic idea of karma is that every deed has good or bad consequences, and these consequences accumulate in you—I'm not exactly sure where—but they stick with you for life and beyond this life to other lives. I didn't know whether or not there really was an accumulating karma, but I liked the idea that there are consequences for actions, that people can't just get away with stuff. As Grandpa Swenson used to say, "the chickens will come home to roost." I was imagining all the bad karma accumulated by the driver of the black truck, and I was hoping the chickens would come flying at him and he would get what he deserved in this life, not the next.

I also decided to do my paper on reincarnation to show how it wasn't just about what happens after death, but how it tries to answer a lot of other questions, too, like: Why is there so much inequality when we arrive in existence at birth, and what happens to the unfairness and injustices that are still unresolved by the time we die? Like what if we never find the son-of-a-bitch? The Hindus probably wouldn't say it like that.

One of the interesting aspects of Hinduism is meditation and all of the different kinds of yoga that grew out of it. Professor Adams, being the dedicated teacher he was, wanted us to actually experience, and if possible, practice some yoga. Hindus think of it as the path to God-realization, so it is serious stuff for them. Toward the end of the term, for three of our classes, we met over at the gym and an experienced yoga instructor taught us to meditate. I thought that was cool.

Yoga is actually quite difficult to do, not so much the postures, but the meditation part to settle the mind. The goal is to focus on something beyond the general garbage that fills up our chaotic consciousness almost every minute of every hour of the day. I was liking the instruction in meditation, and I wondered if everyone had a mind as badly cluttered as mine, or if I was exceptionally loaded with meaningless random thoughts. I took the practice of yoga to heart and began to meditate.

I need to interrupt here and tell you about my hair. When I discovered that I really wasn't cut out to be an artist, I grew tired of my long hair and decided to walk into town to get a haircut at a barbershop. Mom had still been cutting my hair when I asked her to—maybe it was time to outgrow that little habit—so I didn't quite know what to say when the barber asked me how I wanted it.

"Short," I said.

"Yes, lad, but how short?" he asked.

"Pretty short," I said, forgetting that this was a small town in rural Texas. So he proceeded to shave off my blond hair, and as I saw it falling in my lap, I realized I was getting a military-style buzz cut. But what could I say? You can't really change your mind in the middle of a haircut. Oh, well, maybe fewer people would recognize me on campus as the driver of the car that almost killed Ken. As I left the barbershop and began to walk back to campus, I caught a glimpse of myself reflected in a store window and saw what looked like a Buddhist monk. I just needed an orange robe.

One evening, shortly after the haircut episode, I decided to go to the Arboretum to meditate. I had discovered a winding path—not the one I went down with Jolene, but another—that led to one of those picnic tables, and I climbed up on top of it and set myself up there on the table part, not the bench, for some serious meditation, crossing my legs beneath me, putting together the forefinger and thumb of each hand, and straightening my spine. I did my deep breathing and became mindful of my cluttered consciousness, emptying out as much of it to the trash as I could. But I needed a point of focus so that I could concentrate only on that and obliterate all other thoughts. I don't know exactly why, but I chose the rear of the black truck that had totaled the Honda and crushed Ken's body. Let's just focus on that, the back of the truck as it was speeding away. It must have worked because I totally lost all track of time, and when I stopped focusing on the back of the truck, I noticed that it was dark in the Arb. Was I mastering meditation? At least I hadn't fallen off the picnic table. Had the haircut helped?

I retraced my steps back to the parking lot, and as I emerged from the Arboretum, I was met by an officer of the campus police.

"You're not supposed to be in there after dark," he said in a stern voice. Then he looked at me with a quizzical expression and said, "Geez, is that you, Carl? What are you doing back in there?"

He calls me by name? The police know me and even recognize me with this haircut? I was sure that students went back in there for many illicit purposes, so I needed to sound credible. Well, there's nothing like the truth, so I said, "Meditating. It's part of a course I'm taking on Hinduism. We're supposed to meditate."

"Okay," the campus police guy said, "I'm just trying to keep the campus safe after dark. Let me walk you back to the residence halls if you're going that way."

"Sure. That would be fine," I said although I didn't really need a police escort to my dorm room. I'd seen campus police around, but never talked to one, so here was my chance. Sure enough, like everybody else, he knew all about the crash.

"I'd been hoping to bump into you," he began. "Excuse me, that's not a good expression, but it is the topic. I've been wondering, now that you have some distance on the accident, if you've had any more memories of what happened. Sometimes when you've had a concussion, everything goes blank for a while, but then later on, your power of recall comes back."

"Interesting that you should ask," I said. I wondered how I could ever explain that I was meditating on the rear end of a black truck and make him believe it. I had to try. "I know it seems odd," I told him, "but back there in the Arb, where I was meditating, I was focusing on the back of the black pickup that hit us and drove away. When you are meditating, you're supposed to have something really unique to focus on to take your mind off of everything else, and weird though it seems, I picked the truck."

"And what did you see? Any recollections.?

"Well, with my eyes closed like that, I kept seeing what I thought was a sheep. You know, the head of a sheep with big curved horns."

The campus policeman, who I later learned was Officer O'Reilly, stopped dead in his tracks, grabbed me by the shoulder and said, "Geez, Carl, that's really important. Do you know what that is?"

"Probably some sort of trademark or something, but I don't follow that kind of stuff."

"It's the logo for the Dodge Ram. This could be an important breakthrough. May I turn this in as new evidence?"

"Sure, if it will help find the son-of-a…the guy who was driving it." I assumed that if the officer knew this much, he was aware of the lawsuit as well.

"Is the memory of the logo clear enough that you could testify under oath that you recall the symbol of the Ram?"

"Oh yeah, I just didn't know what it stood for. You want me to draw it, sketch it out for you? I could do that."

We were standing there outside the Humanities Building, smack in the middle of the campus. Finally, Officer O'Reilly said, "Okay, you can take it from here. I need to get back to the office to report this."

We shook hands and I felt like I should salute or something. Maybe the military haircut. I was slowly awakening to how important this could be for catching the creep.

6

First Steps Toward Finding My Identity

Dinner with Amy. The case against the hit-and-run driver. Fighting the plague with Camus. Planning for a service term in Mexico. The Black Experience 101. Pop music lessons. The indictment. An invitation to Alex. The vote of confidence from Professor Adams.

While my hair was still short during last term, I started to grow a beard to compensate, like a lot of bald guys do, you know, for hair loss. But a beard on a blond dude doesn't amount to much, and it gave me a kind of ghostly look, like a Viking lost at sea. I don't think my parents even noticed I had one. At least they didn't comment. Had they begun to accept the idea that I wasn't going to be the son they had hoped for? I let the beard grow anyway and promised myself that when my hair grew in, I'd shave it off, and I could get back to my normal look, although being me, I wasn't sure what looked normal.

Over the summer and during the fall term, I had seen Amy, Ken's non-girlfriend friend, several times in the common cafeteria for our residence halls, sometimes chatting with her for a few minutes before or after lunch or dinner. At first, she was very emotional about what had happened to Ken and wasn't very friendly with me, scowling at me with her Asian eyes, but gradually she drew a little closer and one night in mid-January, at the beginning of spring term, she invited me to sit down with her at dinner. I was surprised she even recognized me.

During the conversation she said, "I just want you to know that I don't blame you for the accident. I talked to one of the counselors about what happened to Ken, you know, my feelings about losing him, and I gradually learned to put the blame in the right place."

I hoped that if it was Marv, he didn't use the same language with this proper young woman as he did with me. "That's okay," I said. "We were all pretty upset at the time."

"I also want to say," she continued, "I'm sorry about the lawsuit."

She must have seen it in the newspapers or heard it from a friend, like everyone else. "Nothing to be sorry about. We're just trying to get it directed at the responsible party."

"The driver of the black truck," she said.

"Exactly. We all agree on that, but it's been tough to identify that truck and driver, and we don't seem to be getting much help from the local police. I think we are making progress though." We both nodded. "Do you ever hear from Ken?"

"Not a word."

"What a pity. You two were on your way to becoming the perfect couple."

"Thanks, but I'm not what Ken's parents will pick out for him when the time comes."

"Do you think he will come back here to study?" I asked her.

"I hope, but I think the chances are slimmer than a sesame wafer."

"We won't ever see him again?"

"Not likely."

Soon after that conversation with Amy, Officer O'Reilly called me and asked me to come over to the offices of the campus police, also in the Student Union, on the second floor with other student services. I wondered why he was calling and hoped he had some news about the driver.

"Sit down," he said. "We need to talk strategy."

I noticed that we were in a conference room, not an office, and there were no pictures on the walls, just eight straight chairs around a table. I wondered if the Student Misconduct Board met in here. "What have you found out?" I asked.

"There are three black Dodge Ram trucks in this county. Two belong to farmers. One belongs to the son of the mayor."

"The mayor of this town right here?" I asked. "Well, if it turns out he's the driver, that won't be very good publicity for his old man."

"Which may be the reason why the investigation has stalled in the local police department," he said.

"Oh. Because they're too busy covering up to find the hit-and-run driver? Who just happens to be the mayor's son."

"That could be exactly what's been going on," Officer O'Reilly said. "That's why we have a strategy now. We've drawn the sheriff into this. He's elected by the people of the whole county, and he doesn't report to the mayor like the local police do."

"And what does the sheriff say?"

"That the mayor's son was at the top of his list after we identified the truck as a Dodge Ram."

"Top of his list? Why?"

"The young man has other arrests on his record, including a DUI. The sheriff has sought an investigative warrant to examine that truck, along with the two others, of course."

"And it's been denied?" I don't know why I was so quick to see the dark side of everything."

"No, the judge has granted permission, and the county prosecutor is all over the case now."

"Well, that's good news. How can I help?"

"I think you said there might have been someone with him."

"Yes, a woman who turned around and stared at me out of the back window of the truck."

"You remember her?"

"More clearly now."

"Could you identify her?" he asked.

"You mean like from a lineup?"

"From photos we might be able to provide. Could you select her, say, from among five?"

"I think so. I'll for sure try."

In three weeks, I was sitting with my parents and their lawyer in the county prosecutor's office along with the sheriff. They had contacted my dad about his photos of the vehicles, and he mentioned the piece of scrap metal he had pulled off of the wrecked Honda. The paint samples and pictures—the sheriff had his own—matched up exactly. Dad had also given them the small piece of headlight we picked up at the intersection that day we revisited the scene, and it checked out as part of a Dodge Ram. Now it was up to me to identify the face in the back window of the truck. They were to show me five images of women comparable in estimated age to the girlfriend of the mayor's son. When they laid them out side-by-side like that—the photos, not the son and his girlfriend—I had no doubt. To me, the one I pointed to was unmistakable.

"That's the one," the D.A. said as the sheriff swallowed a smile. "Looks like we have a case." My dad breathed a sigh of relief as my mother clutched his forearm.

Much of my time and energy as well as my mental concentration was taken up that term with the case of the hit-and-run driver, but I still took a heavier load of four courses to increase my total number of credits toward graduation. I surely didn't want to fall behind and take more than four years to earn my degree at Little Texas College.

I need to tell you about my favorite course that term: Comparative World Literature taught by Suzette's mother, Jaqueline Bouchardet. She usually dressed up in fashionable bright-patterned clothes and often looked like she had just stepped out of an Impressionist painting, maybe a Renoir. She had just a hint of French accent and the fragrance that trailed after her for sure must have been French perfume. The annotated reading list, some students said, was worth the tuition for that course itself. It contained most of the notable nineteenth and twentieth century authors from all over the world: Europeans, of course, but also examples from Japan, Brazil, Mexico, and South Africa. Most of them were new to me.

Professor Bouchardet's lectures introduced key works of these authors for us, and the theme that ran through her lectures was "disintegration," the gradual breakdown of what had become classical styles of sequential storytelling into more fragmented methods, moving back and forth in time and in and out of the character's consciousness. Also, the use of more metaphors and symbolic forms. At the same time, she was describing the disintegration of the modern worldview, or Weltanschauung, as she called it, demonstrating how there was no longer a tidy view of a world imbued with meaning by the Creator God of Judaism and Christianity, but rather a God-is-dead world in which each individual is trying to make sense of human existence independently, as were these authors she had selected for the course. We had quizzes and a final exam on the selected authors and their works, as well as an essay question on the themes in her lectures, but we were free to roam widely in selecting works to read and authors to explore for our paper.

When Professor Bouchardet lectured on Albert Camus, a Frenchman (actually Algerian) writing at the time of World War II and after, I knew I wanted to learn more about his philosophy of the absurd. What he seemed to be saying was that life is not just pointless in a neutral sense, but actually absurd, meaning ridiculous, crazy, stupid, ludicrous, preposterous, and absolutely asinine. Professor Bouchardet had dug out a long list of synonyms for absurd and wrote each word on the board as students patiently copied them down. I remembered telling Marv about the stupid things people do during one of our first counseling sessions when I was ranting about golf and stuff like that, but I didn't have the word *absurd* on my tongue at the time. Absurd has a nice cynical ring to it, like: Isn't that just absurd?

Camus wrote a novel called The Stranger—in French it is L'Etranger—in which the main character, Monsieur Meursault, is overcome with a sense of the absurd and ends up killing an Arab on a hot and sunny beach for no reason at all. I read that book and it made me wonder if the author, Camus, had ever figured out how to live in an absurd world or if he just ran around killing Arabs. So, I had to start digging into his other writings.

Camus sticks to his atheist guns and insists that we accept the absurdity of this closed universe. He doesn't want us to make a big leap of faith to believe in a divine being or even a reasonable universe. Instead, if we truly embrace absurdity, we will want to rebel against it and begin to fight back. That is his message in The Rebel. But Camus goes a step further in a novel he calls The Plague. The plague, in this novel, has aspects of an actual bubonic plague, complete with rats, but the plague is much more than that, perhaps a symbol of all the absurdities of life. The central character, Doctor Rieux, fights the plague—that is his mission in life—and he does so without understanding exactly how to fight it and without knowing if he will succeed or die in the process. He just knows that he has to resist, rebel, and fight against absurdity on behalf of humanity. Professor Bouchardet told us that Camus was an underground French resistance fighter during World War II.

So I did my paper on Camus, relating his ideas, as I always did, to my own confusion. It turned out to be kind of a turning point for me, because I began to see, for the first time, a way to build a life by doing a little good in the face of absurdity. I didn't need to withdraw from life completely, basking in my alienation, nor did I have to join some big cause; I just needed to do what I could do, in a humble way when an opportunity presented itself, as Camus would say, on behalf of humanity. Or as Doctor Rieux would do, one rat at a time.

Another turning point that ended up being a huge life-changer for me grew out of a conversation I had with Brenda on a boating trip. Her parents had bought kayaks, two of them, and a big rack to hold them on top of their SUV, and they were going to try them out on a short, day trip up to Diamond Lake, a half-hour drive just north of here. You know, that same place I used to go with my parents to rent canoes. Brenda said she needed a second person to help paddle her kayak. I hadn't seen Brenda in a while so it sounded like a nice spring outing to me and I was eager to go.

Everything around this part of Texas is pretty flat, and the setting for Diamond Lake is flat, too, although the lake itself is surrounded by green trees and shrubs, a welcome break from the dry grassy prairie. Brenda and I, as you might expect, caught on quickly to the stroke for paddling a kayak together (a co-dependent's dream boat) and took off in a straight line. We circled back to her parents who seemed to be struggling a bit over who was supposed to do what when. Brenda told them we were going to head over to a little sandy area that people called Outlook Beach if that would be okay with them. Her dad said sure, it would be fine, if we would be back in an hour and watch out for them a little to make sure they hadn't capsized.

Brenda and I fell into a coordinated smooth stroke and took off. We reached the sandy shore quickly and found no one there, so we beached the kayak, took out some towels that Brenda had brought along, and found a spot in the warm sun. I stretched out hoping to soak up a few rays, but as soon as we sat down, Brenda began to explode. I wasn't ready for that.

"I've got to get the hell out of here," she began.

"Out of where?" I sat up and looked around. "You don't mean here." I pointed to the sand.

"This town. Little Texas College. My god, Carl, it's all I know. There's a world out there. And here we sit."

"Well, yeah, I can relate to that. I've learned a lot at LTC. I've read about a lot of places, but I've never gone to any of them or seen anything. Is that what you mean?" I asked.

"Exactly. Other students, most of them anyway, are from somewhere else. They have another home, and a lot of them have traveled all over the place. We're from here. We went to grade school here and high school here and now college here. All we know is here."

"It's true. I know what you mean. So where do you want to go?" I asked.

"Anywhere. Just away from here to see a different place, meet different people, experience a different culture. I'm telling you it's time, or I'm going to suffocate breathing nothing but this Texas air."

"You know Suzette, right? Professor Bouchardet's daughter? She's in France this year. The whole year."

"Sounds fantastic although I'm not so sure about France or the whole year. But yeah, away from here. Away from parents."

"Speaking of which, where are they?" I stood up, shaded my eyes with one hand, and searched for them. I hoped they weren't hanging upside down in their kayak. No, they were headed this way, going slowly and staying close to shore. "There they are." I pointed to them. "They're doing fine." I sat down on my towel again and asked Brenda, "What's the plan? Do you have one?"

"Well, we can take an overseas service term and get credit, you know. We just need to sign up. The people in that office report to my dad. I'm sure we can arrange a good placement."

"I think I heard you say the word we—three times actually. Are you suggesting that we go together somewhere?"

"Well, not necessarily, but maybe. I mean, it could be nice, but of course we could go separately, but then again…"

It was like she kept interrupting herself. "Hold on a sec. You want to get out of here but you're scared to go alone."

"Not scared, Carl, come on. I just need some support."

I remembered her lecturing me on co-dependent relationships in our first year here, and I couldn't hold back a smile.

"I know what you're thinking," she said. "Co-dependent. Here we go again. No, it's not that. I'm a woman, and in some countries, they treat women even worse than they do here. It would be nice to have a guy along."

"Someone you could depend on."

"Stop it. Forget I mentioned it." She yelled in a loud voice, then flopped back on her towel.

"Sorry. I was just kidding. Actually, I think it's a great idea, Brenda, and I'd love to go with you."

"You would?" She sat up and her eyes grew suddenly big. "Really?" Then she stood up and made some moves like to dance or something, spinning around and shaking her booty.

"What do we need to do?" I asked, looking up at her, surprised to see her acting like that.

"Start planning now for next year. But not the whole year. Maybe spring term." She sat down next to me again.

"Where?" I asked.

"I'm open. Maybe Mexico?"

"Exactly what I was thinking. Maybe we can see some of those ruins we studied in anthro."

"This is really exciting," she said. "Thank you for still being my friend." She nodded a few times and then continued, always ready to take charge and follow through. "Let's meet at the union on Monday. You know where that office is. Second floor. It's called International Studies and Service Learning. We can go together."

"Together, but not co-dependent."

"Oh, shut up."

Alexisius and I became close friends but in a different way from my friendship with Ken Lee, so Alex wasn't replacing Ken, just being himself as my roommate. I had become relaxed around him, and I think it was a good experience for Alex as well. Perhaps he was a little surprised to find this compatibility with a fair-skinned Nordic, white non-supremacist like me.

"You can become a close friend with a guy without being gay," he said, not just once but often, as if to reassure not only me, but himself. He continued his informal lectures with me on The Black Experience 101, and he was always recommending some book to me. "You've never read James Baldwin? Well, come on, man, here's the place to get started." Then he pulled a book out of his collection and handed it to me. "'Giovanni's Room.'" he said. "On loan to you alone." I glanced at it and began to thumb through the pages. "The main characters are gay," Alex said. "But that's not the point. It's just great writing. Not a great black author, but a great author who happens to be black. There's a difference. It's quite sad, actually, how those poor gay guys in the story agonize over who they are."

"Do I detect just a bit of—"

"Prejudice against gays? Absolutely not, but like everything else, it's complicated for us. We have our share of gays in the black community, everyone knows that. And sometimes they are made fun of because straight black men are already working like crazy at being men, and they get pretty uncomfortable around some effeminate guy casting doubts on the masculinity of black males, you know, with people ready to humiliate us or tear us to shreds anyway. So there's some teasing and joking within the black community, inappropriate now, of course, very inappropriate, but

I've grown up with that teasing. Underneath it all, most black people know that it's really difficult being both black and gay."

"Some of those politicians say that gays choose to be that way. It's a choice. What do you think about that?"

"Oh, come on, man, if it's a choice, who the hell would choose to be gay, you know, with all that goes along with that? And to choose to be gay when you're already black, Jesus, that's really insane."

We both laughed at that, and then I said, "You've got a point there, but let me ask you a really tough question now." I was a little nervous asking this, but I wanted to see what Alex would say. "If you could choose, now that you know what you know, would you choose to be black?"

Alex smiled, nodded his head thoughtfully, and said, "Before I answer, let me just ask: Would you?" Before I could respond, he added, "Most black people ask your would-I-choose question a lot, knowing there is no such choice. It's purely hypothetical. But I've never met any white people who said they would choose to be black. Maybe there would be a little more understanding of us if white people began to ask this question of yours."

"But back to my question: If you had a choice, would you choose to be black?"

"Well, my momma did a good job instilling in me some racial pride, like black is beautiful, and pointing out all the prominent black movie stars, singers, and sports heroes, so that I would be able to live with who I am, comfortable in my own skin. But would I choose to be black? Hell, no, man, do you think I'm crazy?" We laughed some more. Then, growing serious, Alex said, "Just to press the point a little, let me ask you a question. You took that course in the fall on Hinduism, and we talked some about karma and reincarnation, or being reborn, I guess you prefer to call it. I didn't say anything at the time because I didn't know you so well then, but when people talk so glibly about being reborn, do they ever think about being reborn black? All those upper-class white people sitting there in their yoga classes, thinking that reincarnation is such a cool and fashionable idea, do they ever consider that they might come back black?

"I don't think they do, Alex, and I hate to admit it, but the idea never occurred to me either until just now when you brought it up. I guess we don't think much about not being white."

"See. That's exactly my point. Something you never have to think of, something you take for granted, I have to consider every day. Black? Why me? Oh, but don't worry, man, there's always reincarnation. Oh, yeah, I almost forgot. I could be reborn as a white person. See, I can say that and it's okay. But if you said, 'Geez, Alex, maybe you could be reborn as a white man,' to me that would really be arrogant, superior, condescending, insulting, and offensive. Do you see what I'm saying?"

"Got it."

Alex was really into music, usually plugged in even while he studied, downloading music from his computer or phone, but he was careful not to disturb me. Sometimes he would start to talk about his music, but I couldn't follow him very well because I didn't know anything at all about that kind of music. You see, there wasn't any music in our house except the noise I made when I was practicing the piano. Hardly music. In high school, I was such a nerd and so bound up with Brenda, that I didn't have other acquaintances who might have drawn me into the music of "our generation." I say generation because I noticed that with the exception of my parents, each generation seems to have its own music. Even Grandpa Swenson, mom's dad, when he came to visit, had his songs that he would hum or whistle. Once I asked him what he was singing, and he went all in telling me about a singer named Bob Dylan and a group called Peter, Paul, and somebody—I can't remember who—and he loved that music.

Alex was shocked that I didn't have any music of my own that I really liked, not even that popular country music stuff that everyone in Texas seemed to listen to all the time. So, spotting an opening, he began to teach me about his music. Remember, Alex was preparing to be a teacher, and he never missed an opportunity to teach someone something he knew.

He began with the so-called Negro spirituals and showed me how they have a double meaning, like the chariot in "Swing Low, Sweet Chariot" might also be a hay wagon and the band of angels could be abolitionists coming to take slaves to their freedom across the Ohio River, not the Jordan. Everything was disguised so the masters wouldn't know what the slaves were singing about. Cool. He sang the verse that begins 'I looked over Jordan and what did I see.' Wow! I never knew Alex had a voice like that. Impressive.

Then he started teaching me about jazz, with its off-beat African rhythms and solo riffs. He described some of the black singers and played examples of their work, like Perl Bailey, Dorothy Dandridge, Aretha Franklin and Ella Fitzgerald, and those who came later like Smokey Robinson, the Supremes, and Stevie Wonder. He knew right where to source the examples he played for me. Then he explained how Blues grew out of jazz and produced the basic movement called Rhythm and Blues, known as R&B, out of which came hip hop, rap, soul, and disco. I asked him about rap and he said it was like a chant over a pre-recorded accompaniment, full of street language from black culture. It was really fast and he said I might have trouble catching it as he played me an example. He was right about that. "And don't forget funk, and punk, and reggae, man. We just getting you started here." I didn't comprehend everything he tried to teach me, but I did understand that there was a whole world of music out there that I knew nothing about.

Alex needed to take the course American History for his social studies concentration required for secondary education certification in teacher education, so when he registered, he persuaded me to take it, too. Professor Richardson was the teacher, the one we had for Texas History, and we both liked him a lot. So we studied together again for that course and sat next to each other in class. Alex began to notice what he called "moments of truth" when Doctor Richardson would explain certain historical events that weren't all that favorable to the American image of "liberty and justice for all." When those moments came, Alex would whisper "uh-huh" or "oh, oh" under his breath and would give me a nudge with his elbow. One night when we were studying, he said something that kind of shocked me.

"I'm really worried about Richardson now," he said.

"Why?"

"Because he says stuff that makes a lot of white students uncomfortable. You can see them wiggle, like it's their grandparents and great grandparents he is talking about."

"But he's just doing what a professor does, he's reporting the best research available, the facts as they are laid out in edited books and articles in refereed journals. He's not only free to do that, he's supposed to do it. It's his job." O, good God, I sounded exactly like my father.

"I know that. I'm on his side. I'm just saying that he's very open and direct, and he may be sorry someday. It starts with threats on social media, then someone else is assigned to his courses, eventually he gets fired.

"Really?"

"I'm just saying that criticisms of the United States of America or its leaders are out of fashion right now and are seen as unpatriotic."

"You think that stuff like that could happen right here at Little Texas College?"

"Especially here, man. Hey, I'm not predicting when, I'm just thinking it could happen. You know what I'm sayin'?"

It made me uneasy to hear this from Alex and I started to wonder if my mom and dad would lose their freedom to teach about evolution in Origins of Life.

Brenda and I had met at the Student Union as planned to go to the Office of International Studies and Service Learning. I had asked Mom to pick me up for Sunday dinner, and while I was there, I asked her for one of her normal haircuts. I'd already shaved off my beard that morning, so when I met Brenda on Monday, I was looking like my old self again, at least that's what she told me.

Naturally, the woman in charge, the director of the office, knew who Brenda was, and me as well, but she treated us, I thought, like any other students. She asked us a lot of questions about what we hoped to get out of the experience, and we had to come up with some better answers than just "get the hell outta this damn town." I was interested in the service part of the experience, finding a way to make some contribution to the place where we were staying. Some way to fight the plague, although I didn't tell her that. We both mentioned our great anthropology course with Professor Martinez and our interest in exploring some aspects of an ancient civilization. We suggested Mexico as our preference.

In two weeks, we both received a call to come in and talk with the director some more. She had just received a request for two native English speakers for a language school in Oaxaca. "Where?" we both asked together, having to learn how to pronounce "wa-ha-ka," and being even more unsure about how to spell it, until Brenda came up with, "Look at how each letter is followed by an 'a': o-a-x-a-c-a, so all you have to remember is o-x-c." I guess she's still gifted, I reminded myself.

The placement would start right after the holidays as soon as possible in January of the coming academic year, which would be our third. We would receive ten credits for our service learning projects by keeping a log and writing up a final assessment of what we had learned. We were also informed that many students arranged for one or more online courses or independent study projects in their major or with professors who knew their work. I liked that idea.

So, this academic year, our second, came to an end with big plans for our appointments the following year at the English Language Center at the university in Oaxaca. We were really pumped at the prospect of getting out of town and into another country with an ancient culture. Brenda looked it up on Google and discovered that there really was an established university in Oaxaca and some ancient Zapotec ruins known as Mt. Alban, but pronounced like one word, Mountalban. Was this really happening to us? A family in a small weaving community with some ties to the Language Center had already made housing arrangements for us to stay with them. How cool would that be?

I decided to take an intensive Spanish workshop, along with Brenda of course, during the summer session, and I registered for a marketing course with the College of Business. What the hell, someday I might need to earn a living.

As soon as I knew that I would be going to Mexico during spring term of next year, I told Alex he would be without a roommate in January.

"Oh, I've been meaning to tell you." he began, looking a little embarrassed. "The Black Student Alliance has petitioned for and received permission to live together in one residence hall next year, and they are putting pressure on me to join in with them. Because I'd be the only one not living with them, it has become, let's say, an issue."

"It's okay. You don't need to explain. You need to do what you need to do. Are you comfortable with that arrangement, all living together?"

"We'll find out, won't we?" I just can't be the only one not to do it," he said.

The expression on his face told me he wasn't all that enthusiastic about the high-pressure invitation to join his brothers and sisters. I remembered when Alex and I had heard Richardson lecture on Martin Luther King's leadership in the Civil Rights Movement, about his efforts to break up segregation in order to integrate. "Now you will be segregated again in your own residence hall," I said. I wasn't sure if I should have said that, but that's how it seemed to me.

"Yeah, but there's an important difference: we're choosing to do this," Alex said.

"I understand," I said, but wasn't sure I really did.

Naturally, there was a hearing for the indictment of the driver of the truck, and I had to appear in court along with my parents, but it wasn't as bad as I had thought it would be. Officer O'Reilly met with us beforehand to brief us on what to expect, and what he advised proved easy to carry out:

respond with brief, but truthful answers, preferably yes or no. They wanted to know if I was the driver of the Honda and if anyone was with me, but I didn't have to elaborate on Ken's injuries because those would be described by medical personnel from the hospital. When they asked me if these were my parents, I almost said "I think so," but then I remembered to keep it short and answer yes. I had to describe the accident, my recollection of the Dodge Ram logo, and the process used to identify the face looking out through the rear window.

It was the first time I had seen or heard the name of the accused, Billy Bob Wilson, the alleged hit-and-run driver. He had a clean white shirt and a striped tie, but no jacket. He was wearing jeans, let's say not the cleanest. His brown hair was hanging long over his ears and it curled up at the back of his neck. In general, he looked kind of scraggly and unkempt. But the girlfriend was another matter, well dressed and made up in tones matching her outfit. Nothing shabby about her. They called her Mary Jane Jones. Now I had a body to associate with that face, and I was surprised to find her a little pudgy. They both seemed to be in their late twenties, older than I, enough that I wouldn't have known them in high school.

Mayor Wilson, on the other hand, Billy Bob's father, was in a short sleeve blue sport shirt and dark blue pants, well-groomed and ready, it seemed, for a TV appearance, smiling confidently and greeting everyone as if he were campaigning. He seemed to be no longer embarrassed by those aspects of his son that couldn't be covered up with a clean shirt and tie. Some things, like attitude, are hard to hide.

The county prosecutor proceeded in a low-key, systematic way, methodically assembling and presenting the forensic evidence from the scene: paint sample analyses, the dents, the scrap piece from the door, and the headlight fragment, all of which supported the indictment. The defendant's prior police record was also entered into the proceedings. A trial date was set for late September. In spite of this, the mayor seemed confident that nothing serious would come of it. But then the judge notified the defendant that in light of the evidence, the family in Taiwan bringing the civil lawsuit for damages—that would be Ken Lee's parents—would be notified and advised, thus encouraging them to rename the persons to whom their suit was addressed. He reminded everyone that there were two cases, one criminal and one civil. The defendant's drivers license was revoked, pending outcome of the criminal case. In lieu of jail or bail, Billy Bob would remain under confinement at home, a huge concession we thought, but then, maybe it was nice for Mayor Wilson to have his scraggly son right there for breakfast every morning so he could keep an eye on him, now that he was becoming a campaign issue.

Anyway, it all came out like we had hoped, and my parents were relieved to have the financial pressure lifted. That was the main goal, besides justice for their son and his friend Ken. The prosecutors and attorneys conferred, and in a quiet way we thanked Officer O'Reilly of the campus police. But as I look back on it now, this indictment seemed like a tipping point in the so-called town-gown relations, which had been at least calm, but never cordial. The mayor had somehow arranged to keep the little piece of news about his son out of the newspapers, and who knows what might be going on behind the scenes with his supervision of the police? Maybe the friendly working relationship of the campus police and town cops wasn't going to be so friendly anymore. People from the surrounding community began to find fault with the college. All because a hit-and-run driver was justly charged?

Brenda and I studied hard in the summer workshop on Conversational Spanish, and we found it difficult at first with our not-so-advanced second year of high school Spanish, but we were highly motivated, knowing that in a few months we would need to speak Spanish just to get through the airports, find something to eat, and deal with the pesos, which we learned to count and use.

As a break from the study of Spanish and my course on marketing, I stopped by at the office of Professor Adams, my world religions prof, to tell him that I would be heading for Mexico next January. He thought it was a great opportunity and the right thing for me at this point. Then the conversation drifted to my major.

"I notice that you are accumulating enough credits to be close to a major in religious studies, already having more than enough for a minor. What are your plans?"

"Well, yes, I'm getting the feeling that this will be my major. I just haven't declared."

"Is there a reason for that?" he asked.

"My parents were hoping I would be in science. I don't mean to reveal their personal views, but they are not all that enthused about religion. I'm sure they don't see how it can be a legitimate academic subject."

"I would suspect that might be the case. But many students disappoint their parents when they major in religion," he said with a slight smile. "You're not alone."

"And then some students tell me that I'll never get a job with a major in religious studies."

"Get a job? Is that why they came to college? There are a lot of ways to support yourself, to earn a living comfortable enough to take care of the needs of a simple life. Most college graduates work at something quite unrelated to their major. What I've also noticed is that some people who do succeed in the employment world don't have much grasp of the mysteries of life. Sometimes, in a crisis, things fall apart for them and then they begin to suffer and get confused. Others go on through life glibly without asking serious questions or thinking deeply about life. Sometimes they wake up at the end of their life wondering what the hell happened. You, Carl, on the other hand, are a thinker. You've already pondered the timeless questions. You are already well along the way in your quest to understand life. I have no doubt whatsoever that you will find a way to make a living. That would be the least of my worries."

"Wow! Thank you for those kind words and your confidence in me. That's really reassuring. Actually, a great relief." I glanced around the office of Professor Adams and noticed how neat and tidy everything appeared. "It helps to be organized, too," I said, pointing randomly to indicate his office.

"Yes, just not too organized. But back to your major. I would be happy to sponsor one or two independent studies while you are in Mexico. We could outline the project before you leave, identify resources, give you a book or two to take along, and you can work away at your studies as time permits. We can exchange emails as you progress, and you can complete your paper when you get back next summer. You don't need to announce your major with a trumpet fanfare; you just need to complete it."

"That would be good. I'd like to do that," I said, feeling like my whole body was smiling at him.

"Where are you going to be in Mexico? Do you know that yet?"

"Yes, in Oaxaca," I told him.

"Really? How fortunate. The center of the old Zapotec culture. It will be an excellent place to do some thinking about the religious traditions of the ancient Americas. If I am remembering correctly, you will find there some ancient Zapotec ruins."

"Yes, I'm already hearing about those." We were both quiet for a moment, and I suddenly felt very comfortable with Professor Adams, as though he wasn't a prof, but a friend, maybe even the dad I always wished I had. So I told him I had been getting some counseling from Marv Cohen over at the Counseling Center. "What started out as exploring my feelings about that horrible accident with Ken, has turned into a much bigger project: helping me to build an authentic life."

"You couldn't be in better hands. What a fine person Marv is. We are so fortunate to have him here."

"He's even fortunate to be alive. You know his story?"

"Yes, most of it. I was on the student life search committee that found him and recommended that he be hired."

"You did us all a favor there," I said. "A big favor."

"An authentic life, you said. Hmm. Interesting phrase. Do you know the work of Henry David Thoreau?" he asked.

"The Walden Pond guy? I've heard of him, but that's about all I know."

"Yes, the environmentalists love him today because he went off to live in the woods. But that's not why he left town."

I suspected that Professor Adams was about to share something profound with me about building an authentic life, so I wanted him to continue. "Then why did he go?" I asked.

Professor Adams stood for a moment, scratched his head, walked straight toward one of three packed bookcases, and pulled out a small paperback. How could he know exactly where every book was in his office library? Was the inside of his brain like that, too, with shelves for every book he had ever read? Did his memory come equipped with flash drives? He came back to the chair behind his desk, sat down, and held up the book as he said, Walden. He looked inside. "Originally published in 1854." He started leafing through it, but when he found the familiar passage that he seemed to be looking for, he stuck his thumb in to hold the place while he started to give me some background. "Thoreau is known for many things and one of them is the quotation 'The mass of men lead lives of quiet desperation.' Of course, we would not exclude women from that opportunity today, some of whom may end up even more desperate than men. But we need to be careful not to take the quotation out of contest. When Thoreau looked around, he saw a lot of conformity, people doing what everyone else was doing without giving much thought to it. Resigned to their routines. Going through the motions. Not thinking about life."

"Yeah, I see a lot of people doing that," I said.

"Exactly. Which leads to the quiet desperation of their not really having chosen their life."

"Is that why he went out to the pond? To think about life?"

"Yes, we might say so. But here, let me read you the exact passage in Thoreau's own words. He says, 'I went to the woods because I wished to live deliberately, to front only the essential facts of life, and see if I could not learn what it had to teach, and not, when I came to die, discover that I had not lived.'"

"Dying without living. Oh, my God, how perfect. That's my fear, Professor Adams."

"That's why I read it to you. You're a searcher. I think I know you well enough to be sure that you will continue your deliberate search for an authentic life until you find it."

"Maybe I will find it in Mexico."

"We never know where we will find it. Remember, the challenge is not to make a living but to make a life." He paused to let that sink in. Then he smiled and said, "I'm sure you will learn to live a beautiful life, to cherish it, and maybe even grow fond of someone to love."

Wow! What a vote of confidence from Professor Adams. I needed that.

7

Learning About My Father As I Was Leaving For Mexico

Brenda's dad shares his worries. Modern ideas about God. Dad's lunchtime revelation. What Brenda's parents told her. Sorting out ancestry with Marv. DNA research. Holiday in Mexico City.

I lived alone in a residence hall room without Alex during fall term of my third year at Little Texas College, knowing that in January I would be heading for Mexico. I actually liked the privacy of a single room, and although my parents worried about my being lonely—something they never seemed to care about while I was alone in their basement guest room—I definitely enjoyed it. No depression, no suicidal thoughts, if that was what they were concerned about, because I was beyond that and totally psyched about going to Mexico. Now I had a concrete goal: to build an authentic life through deliberate choice, here, there, or anywhere. Was I at last beginning to come to terms with my nothingness?

Two weeks into the term, I was leaving a counseling session with Marv and feeling really positive about everything when I ran into Brenda's father outside his office. He was talking to another student, but he motioned to me to stop, so I stood a little distance away, trying not to overhear them, while they finished their conversation. I've mentioned him before as Brenda's father and Dean of Student Life, but I don't think I've ever described him. He is a nicely-dressed, well-built guy, just over six feet tall, but not exceptionally muscular, not having much time, I'm sure, to be lifting weights in a gym. His hair is still mostly dark brown with a few streaks of gray. Quite handsome actually. He wears glasses that sit most of the time on the top of his head, as they were at that moment, while he was talking to the student. I have to say, that he comes across as genuinely interested and sincerely engaged with anyone with whom he speaks. He surely has the right personality for that job, which I'm sure is really challenging. But from what I've heard, most of the students like him.

When he was finished talking with the student, he motioned at me to come inside his office saying, "Do you have a minute? I'd love to talk to you about Mexico." I'd never been in his office before although I knew their home quite well because of my friendship with Brenda, so this was a new experience seeing his books, his computer, and the spindle-back chairs gathered in front of his desk, not just one, but four, arranged in a small circle, so that when he talked to students, he was sitting with them, not behind his massive desk. Cool. So that's how we sat down together, in two of those black chairs with the college name and seal on them. "Congratulations to you two," he began, "for getting those placements teaching English at the university in Oaxaca. I wish I could go, too."

I hoped he was just joshing because I remembered that one of Brenda's goals was to ditch her parents for a while. "Yeah, I'm really looking forward to it. I'm glad Brenda brought it up."

"Oh, I understood her to say it was your idea."

I was surprised to hear him say that, but I covered for her. "Let's just say it was something we both thought of together and the director of your international studies office upstairs here was able to suggest an interesting placement for us together in Mexico."

"We do get some good service opportunities at this little college, especially in Mexico." Then he went straight to his purpose in calling me in. "I just wanted to tell you that although I'm excited about this opportunity for Brenda, I'm a little worried, too."

"Really? Why?"

"Oh, just the normal parental concerns, I suppose. She's our only child, first time away from home, going to a country that can be dangerous."

"It may turn out to be harder for you than Brenda." I tried to lighten things up a little, but I don't think it worked.

"I'm sure we will adjust to her being gone, but I'm worried because Brenda has seemed a little, how shall I say, unsettled lately, not exactly rebellious, but not completely happy either."

Oh, jeez, just as I'm calming down Brenda is getting all agitated. I saw that when she exploded on the kayak trip. "I think she's just eager to get out of this little town and see more of the world," I said, hoping that was all there was to it.

"I expect that's the case." He removed the glasses on the top of his head and started to chew on one of the pieces that curves back over the ear, when he wears them, that is. Does he ever do that? "I hope you can keep an eye on her," he said. "She listens to you."

Since when? I wasn't so sure about that, but I did remember agreeing to be someone she could depend on. I needed to make sure I wasn't promising to be her guardian. "Well, I can make suggestions if she asks me, but I can't be responsible for what she chooses to do. We're actually trying not to be so dependent on each other as friends, but I did promise to be there for her like a brother if she needed help." A good counselor would ask him why he was feeling so concerned, but, hey, it wasn't my job to be counseling the dean of student life, so I just told him not to worry and that Brenda would be okay on her own.

"I'm not asking you to be responsible for her and ruin your good time in Mexico or anything like that," he said. "I'm just hoping you'll keep an eye out for her because she's been so..."

"Unsettled."

"Yes."

"But she's a college student and unsettled is our trademark. Nobody knows college students better than you."

"Well, yes, I suppose I do, but her mother and I are worried."

"Don't you think that the parents of all of your students are worried? That's why you are here, providing these services, doing your job, and from what I hear, doing it very well."

"Oh, thank you. It's good to hear that. I feel better." He put his glasses back on the top of his head.

As I stood to leave, I remembered to say, "Thanks for getting me started with Marv Cohen. He's been…well, a great help to me."

As I walked across campus to my class, I hoped I hadn't backed myself into a situation with Brenda. I couldn't take responsibility for her actions. It was hard to tell what the hell she might do if she was "unsettled" and free as a bird in Mexico.

I took another heavy course load that term because I didn't want to fall behind while I was on service-learning term in Mexico, so I filled in my schedule with a sociology course, where the prof used a unit on adoption practices to show how race, class, and ethnicity affected decisions and policies. I even surprised myself by taking a course in botany from one of my mom's colleagues and surprised myself a second time by liking it and doing well. Science has lots of answers about flowers, shrubs, and trees, yes, just not my life.

I was also taking the upper-level course in religious studies that Professor Adams had recommended to me called Modern Religious Thought. It really gave me some new ways to think about God, so I have to tell you about it. It was taught by Herr Schmidt, who not only knew everything about the Hebrew scriptures but was apparently an expert in a field he called philosophical theology, part religion and part philosophy, it seems. We studied Kierkegaard and learned about feminist and liberation theology, but my favorites were Buber and Tillich. You might recall that it was a big discovery for me to learn that some religions like Confucianism and Buddhism didn't have much to say about God. Well, this course had a lot to say about God, and it drew mostly on the modern religious thought of the Jewish and Christian traditions.

We started out with some philosophical ideas from Kant and Hegel, and I really had to scramble to understand them. Sometimes, I would read a sentence over and over, really slow, and still wouldn't understand it. I had a rule: three times and out. If you can't understand it after three careful readings, either fall asleep or turn the page. Reading all that philosophy was killing my reading speed for novels.

I especially liked a Jewish philosopher called Martin Buber who invented this terminology, I-It and I-Thou to describe different kinds of human relationships. The former, I-It, is very impersonal and routine, like the communication with the check-out person at the supermarket, and the latter, I-Thou, is used to describe deep personal relations, as with a close friend or counselor. Naturally, I thought of Marv, and how special it had been to share my deepest feelings with him. Marv is definitely an I-Thou guy. Professor Schmidt explained that I-It relations were okay and even necessary because you wouldn't want the person in line in front of you at the supermarket to start having an I-Thou relationship with the check-out clerk. Everyone laughed at that and then we started building a list of necessary I-It relationships, like the pharmacist, the airplane pilot, and the dentist. I liked the dentist example; I mean, how could you have an I-Thou relationship with all of that equipment jammed into your numbed-up mouth.

But here's the thing. Buber suggested that in deep, authentic interpersonal relationships, there is a bit of God present: the Thou is present in the I-Thou exchange. In other words, there is something sacred about communication when it is filled with concern and empathy. Wow! What an interesting way to think about God, the invisible third party in a serious conversation, the something more in deep dialogue. Was God in the room when I talked to Marv?

I also became interested in a twentieth century theologian named Paul Tillich and wrote my paper on one of his many books called The Courage to Be. I was drawn to the book by the title, which made me wonder if my problem was that I really lacked the courage to be. Maybe all this searching around crap I was doing was because I was such a chickenshit about embracing my own life. The book turns out to be about God, and Tillich suggests that believing in God can help us live with courage, but what an amazing concept of God this man had.

First, Professor Schmidt had to teach us a little about ontology, a branch of philosophy concerned with the nature of being. Some of the German scholars, particularly a guy named Heidegger, got off on thinking about being. How is it that things exist? Where do they get their being? What makes the difference between being and non-being? Well, Tillich picks up on this and says that God is that force that enables being. God is not one more being in this universe of beings; God is the ground of being, which Tillich calls Being-Itself. God is the underlying force of being itself, which makes God different from all other beings and not actually a being. Herr Schmidt told us that Tillich's idea of Being-Itself is kind of a God beyond God, or at least beyond the traditional theistic descriptions of God, you know, like Michelangelo's cloud-floating God on the ceiling of the Sistine Chapel. Ya, ya, very different.

Then Herr Schmidt said something that really caught my attention. If this kind of God, the ground of all being, brings us personally into being, then we are also sustained in our being as well by the ground of being day by day. This is why, Tillich says, we can live with courage, knowing that our life has importance because it is being is sustained by this ground of being. I decided right then and there that if I ever believed in God, this is the God I would believe in. Seriously, I even found the courage to officially declare my major in religious studies.

I never went into town much because there was almost no reason to go there. One haircut in town was one haircut too many. The campus dining halls and Student Union provided sufficient, if not always nutritious, meals and snacks and the student bookstore in the union sold incidentals like dental floss, deodorant, and nail clippers, just about everything a person needed to get through college. Naturally, I was surprised then when Dad called and invited me to go into town with him for lunch. Did he have something so private to tell me that we needed to go off-campus? No need for a car; I would meet him at his office and we would walk over together from the Science Building.

We went past the fountain and out through the main entrance to the campus, heading south on Alamo Avenue past the fraternities, sororities, and the home of Brenda's family, strolling along for two blocks until we came to the intersection with Main Street, one of three stoplights in town. As we crossed the street, turning west on Main, I thought I was seeing things in that town that I had never noticed before—maybe because my art class really had taught me to see. Like what? Well, the gothic revival Catholic church on the corner, the simple brick and white-steepled Southern Baptist colonial-style church across from it, and the neo-classical design of the county courthouse with its tall Doric columns, already visible at the end of town behind the small, landscaped park in front of it.

That was where Billy Bob, the driver of the Black Dodge Ram had finally been convicted and sentenced in late October. The fine was light and the prison term short, my family thought, considering the amount of damage he had done. A lot of people on campus called it Texas justice. But, hey, he did go to prison. I learned that the mayor was trying to settle the suit with Ken's family quietly out of court. But I digress. Let's keep walking.

A few modern glass and concrete buildings on Main Street were mixed in with a slew of old shops looking to be straight out of Texas history, their wooden facades forming a nearly continuous cowboy movie set along a wide street that must have been unpaved and trodden by horses at the beginning of the last century. Were there gunfights right here on this street? Will there be more?

As we walked along, we passed the old hardware store with an antique butter churn in the window, a women's clothing store with dowdy housedresses, and a small bookstore with a sign that read "Students Welcome." Really? You need a sign for that? The movie theater where Brenda and I had watched the latest films in high school appeared to be closed, either for remodeling or permanently, hard to say which. Two doors down we passed a Victorian gabled house in good repair, serving as the real estate office that sponsored me for my licensing exam. And, of course, across the street was the barber shop, complete with striped pole out front, where I got the buzz cut.

We finally arrived at the place where I guessed we were heading, a small restaurant called "Biscuits and Brisket," the undisputed source for the best Texas barbecue for miles around. We found a booth at the back, away from the din and clatter of the counter and the shouting in the kitchen. My side of the booth had a big rip in the plastic seat, and I squirmed around to get comfortable although I soon learned there would be a lot of squirming and no getting comfortable during that lunch.

I asked Dad how his work was going at the college, and he told me he was the department chair of physics and astronomy now. "Congratulations," I said, wondering if this was the purpose of the lunch: to celebrate his appointment. Was it a promotion?

"Well, thanks," he said, "but I need to confess that it's more of a burden than an honor. We rotate the chairmanship every three years, and there comes a time when you run out of excuses for refusing your colleagues' unanimous nomination.

"It was your turn?"

"Way past."

"And what does it involve?"

"Saying no to almost every request because there's no money in the budget for that."

"Do you deal with students?" I asked.

"Some. More than before, so the other faculty tell me. Students seem to want to be involved in everything now. Some want to see more minority representation, but others complain that there are already too many minority students on campus. Students want to have their say on what to teach and how to teach it. Some prefer less lecture, while others want more lecture. For me, it's basically a no-win situation, damned if you do and damned if you don't. It's really rather frustrating."

As we ate our barbecue sandwiches with our side dishes of coleslaw and baked beans, I thought about Dad's situation, dealing with that stuff he couldn't do anything about and that took his attention from the discipline of astronomy, to which he seemed to be still deeply devoted as a scholar and teacher. When we were finished eating, he began to tell why he had brought me here. Yes, I squirmed. The news was shocking.

"As you may have guessed," he began, "I didn't ask you to join me just for the Texas barbecue although mine was very good. What about yours?"

"Outstanding." I was silent for a second, and then I said, "But what, then?"

"You're going to be gone next term and I'm really quite excited about this opportunity in Mexico for you. You're going to be fine. You've really matured a lot in college here, and I'm proud of you. I just thought that this would be a good time to tell you this now, knowing that you'll be gone for a while, and who knows what could happen to us."

"What, Dad. Just tell me."

He took a deep breath before he said, "I'm not your biological father."

"You're what?"

"I'm not your actual father." His voice had lowered to almost a whisper. "Your mom wanted a child very badly and we were having problems conceiving, or I guess I should say I was having problems."

"And that's why you did the in vitro..."

"That's what we told you because we didn't want to disturb you with the complete story."

"Which is?" I knew they had been lying to me. Damn. I sensed it all along.

"We used a sperm bank at a clinic in the city."

He stopped talking and looked at me intently to see how I was taking it. Actually, even though I suspected something drastic like that, I wasn't taking it very well, but I didn't want to lose my Texas barbecue all over the table in front of us, so I took a couple of deep breaths, swallowed hard, and said, "Aren't sperm donors anonymous?"

"That's correct."

"Now I don't know and can't ever know my biological father."

"Those are the arrangements, and we signed legal papers to that effect," he said in a lawyer's flat voice.

We were both quiet for a moment until I said, "So I'm neither Wallace nor Walenski."

"You are neither Polish nor Jewish, not through my family ancestry anyway, even though I am both."

"But I could be, depending on the sperm donor."

"Correct. But unlikely, a very low probability. We know you are not black or Chicano, and you seem to take after your mother's Scandinavian side of the family very strongly anyway. It was her egg, after all."

I remembered Mom's lecture on Mendel's peas, and then her evasiveness about my lack of inheritable traits from my father. I also recalled vividly at that moment the night when Mom told me that there would come a point in my life when this Polish or Jewish ancestry question wouldn't matter. That time was now, and I saw why: Dad wasn't really my father. I sat there, kind of stunned, not moving a muscle, and he just let me have my time to think about it. At first, I didn't want to say anything because I was so pissed, but I knew I should respond politely. Now was a time for true maturity. I began slowly, making sure to control my anger. "First, I wish you had told me sooner because I'm really struggling with who I am."

"We've noticed, and that was the reason we didn't tell you sooner, a judgment call on our part, and probably wrong. We are sorry."

"It's okay. You were trying to do what you thought was best. Thanks, at least, for telling me now." Then as I thought about what I wanted to express next, I felt my eyes begin to water and I was determined to control my feelings so that I could say what I wanted to say as a man. What was happening is that I was wondering what this must have been like for my dad: being sterile, trying to please my mother, agreeing to the sperm bank, lying about it all these years. I don't know why, but I was suddenly walking in his shoes. So I said, "Thank you for raising me as your son. I mean, that really takes dedication to raise a kid that's not your own, and I want you to know that I recognize it."

Now it was his turn for the eyes to tear up as he said, "I've always thought of you as our son, our child, and your mother and I as your parents. I may not have done the best job as a father, so busy being an astronomer, but I've tried."

"And done very well." My mind was flashing with memories of all he actually had done for me: attending my swim meets, taking Brenda and me to the movies, caring for Ken at the hospital after the crash, revisiting the accident site, and being focused and calm in court through the trial. I was also having fragments of images from family vacations at Mesa Verde and Carlsbad Caverns running through my head. "I mean it. You've done a lot for me, Dad. Oh, geez, can I still call you Dad?"

"I certainly hope you will. Your mom knows I am telling you now, but no one else on campus knows."

"Or needs to know. It's none of their damn business."

"If you will, please keep calling me Dad, and I will always refer to you as my son. That's important to me."

"There's just one person I need to tell."

"Brenda?"

"Well, yeah, I tell her everything, but I'll warn her not to repeat a word of it. But actually, I was thinking of Marv."

"Of course, you need to tell your counselor. In fact, I encourage you to go see him again soon. This must be a shock to you."

Oddly enough, at this moment when I learned that I had no identifiable paternal ancestor, I felt closer than ever to the father who had raised me as his son.

Yes, I needed to tell Brenda what I had learned at lunch with Dad, so I arranged to meet her in the Student Union for smoothies and we found a secluded table where we couldn't be overheard. She swore she wouldn't repeat a word of it. When I had finished telling her the abbreviated version, namely, that my father wasn't my biological father, she said something that surprised me.

"I was wrong," she said.

I don't remember ever hearing those words from Brenda before, so I asked, "How?"

"I told you that you were perseverating about your ancestors and that you should just let go of it. I was definitely wrong. There was something in your soul that told you otherwise."

I'd never heard her use the word soul either. "No need to apologize. I'm sure I was sounding a little crazy at the time with my ancestor mania. Actually, many times. But at last, the truth has come out. I don't know my paternal ancestry and probably never will."

"Why probably?"

"Only if the sperm donor is identified, and that's highly unlikely since it's illegal to do that here. My parents thought they were protecting me, I guess, waiting until I was mature enough to handle it."

Brenda took her hand and placed it on my forearm, registering a look of shock, apparently from the thought that had just passed through that active mind of hers. "Good God, Carl. I wonder if my parents are hiding some tidbit of astounding information from me until I am mature enough to handle it. What if I'm adopted?"

"Slim chance of that. But you know what? You are mature, and if you ask them directly, telling them that you are mature enough to hear anything, they will find it difficult not to tell you, if there is anything to tell, which there probably isn't."

A few days passed and then I got a text from her asking me to meet her in the Union that day at three o'clock. Same place. I was already at the table waiting for her with the smoothies.

"Well, you won't believe it," she began. "I asked them and just like you said, they had no excuse now not to tell me."

"Not to tell you what? You're adopted?"

"No, not adopted. They are my parents."

"What then? Tell me."

"I had a twin sister born dead."

"What?" I thought I saw some tears collecting in her eyes, whether of anger or grief, I wasn't sure.

"I was born alive; she was born dead." The tears began to flow.

"Jesus, Brenda, an identical twin?" It was hard to imagine another person exactly like Brenda. Was I her substitute sibling all of these years for a deceased sister? Well, not really if she didn't know. "But why didn't they tell you?"

"They were afraid I would spend my childhood wondering why I was alive and my sister was dead. It might create an emotional problem for me. They thought I could handle it better when I was more mature." She was wiping away the tears furiously now with the back of her hand. "Well, I can't." She sniffed deep sniffs and swallowed hard.

"There's our favorite word again: mature. Now you can spend your adulthood asking why your twin didn't make it and you did." I found some tissues in my rear pocket and handed them to her. "Marv says there are no answers to questions like that and it's best to stop asking them." The tears had turned to sobs. "When do you think they should have told you?" I asked.

"At least by high school, damn it. Maybe before. I was already on the road to being their perfect little gifted only child. I could have handled it," she said, pounding her fist on the table firmly but softly.

"It's strange, isn't it, how our own parents lie to us because they think it's in our best interest not to know. They get to decide what we know, when we know it, and whether we are ready to handle it or not."

"Yeah, instead of teaching us to cope, they are training us to lie and deny."

"Not to mention what all of this lying, or lack of full disclosure, does to our relationship with them. So much for basic trust."

"My God, Carl, I had a twin sister." Some tears were still running down her cheeks and she slowly brushed them away with a fist. "It certainly makes me wonder what other skeletons are in the closet."

"Me, too," I said, beginning to picture the skeleton of an unidentified sperm donor, dead and gone beyond my reach. Or was he still alive? If so, where was he? Here in Texas? Whose closet was he hiding in? Did I even want to know?

Naturally, I went to see Marv to talk to him about the lunch with my non-biological father. I didn't say anything about Brenda's situation because Marv reports to her father. She would have to decide if she wanted help and where to get it. When I told Marv about my dad's disclosure to me, he said, "The ancestor researchers today call this an NPE, a non-paternity event. It's happening more frequently now with DNA testing becoming popular. For some people, learning about their non-paternity is pretty shocking. I'm guessing you weren't totally surprised." But then he asked, as I knew he would, "How did that make you feel, finding that out?"

I told him that I had suspected something irregular like that, and I was angry about its being concealed for so long, but then I told him what I said to my dad about raising me and being a good father.

"That's very generous of you, and you can take pride in accepting the news graciously that way."

Marv never uses the word mature, thank God. "So, I guess I will never know my paternal ancestry."

"Well," he said, "on your dad's side, you don't know if there's anything to be proud of or ashamed of, so you can try to forget about it if you can. You do have some sense of your mother's side of the family, don't you?"

"Unless I'm adopted."

"I really think your father would have told you that, and preferred it to the truth about the sperm donor, but you can always test your DNA to see if it matches your mother's. To me, it seems fairly obvious that you are your mother's son. I recognize her, you know, as she passes me while I'm wheeling across campus. I wave and she smiles. You have her smile although neither one of you seems to smile a whole lot."

That made me smile, and I told him, "I'm working on that, Marv, I really am." Then I started to laugh.

~

"Why are you laughing?"

"Because you know everything about me and unlike my parents you tell me the truth, straight in the face—blam—whether it hurts or not." That made Marv smile. "Yes," I told him, "the Swensons are Scandinavians, there's no doubt about it. Blond hair, blue eyes. I suppose I could have a kid like that."

Unless you marry a Mexican." We laughed out loud over that, and then he said, "Oh, wow, I shouldn't have said that, Carl, but sometimes I have to break the rules. You know, my life has been full of rules, Jewish rules, military rules, the rules of my profession." Then he turned serious. "It looks like the search for your ancestry is at a dead end now. But you can still build a good life just knowing what you know."

"Exactly. Professor Adams introduced me to Thoreau and his idea of living deliberately."

"Ah, yes, Thoreau. I like that word deliberately. Choosing the life you want to live."

"That's my hope." We both nodded and fell silent. Was the I-Thou God in the room? "I'm going to miss these sessions while I'm in Mexico," I said, a little undisguised sadness in my voice.

"I'm learning to use this thing called Zoom. We can try that if you get in a jam, but I think you will be terrific on your own now. You understand the process well. Stay in touch with your feelings. Face reality, however painful. Solve the problems you can solve and let go of the rest."

"Live deliberately."

"Well, yes, but don't forget about responding positively to the unexpected."

Did Marv suspect that something unexpected was going to happen to me?

I told Brenda what Marv had said about DNA testing and she got online and became an instant expert about the ancestry search sites—AncestryDNA, 23andMe, MyHeritage DNA, FamilyTree DNA—and the methods used by each of them for DNA testing. A few days before reading week, we sat down together in the cafeteria for dinner. Tacos, enchiladas, and burritos were the choices for what they were calling Mexican Night. Was this what it would be like in Mexico? When we were seated, I asked Brenda, "How do they do this DNA testing?"

"They swab the inside of your cheek, you know, in your mouth, or have you spit in a vial."

"That sounds vile. Just kidding. My bad. I mean that sounds easy enough. Maybe we should do it."

"Tell you what," Brenda suggested, "let's ask our mothers to test along with us to reassure us that they really are our mothers, you know, that we weren't adopted. At a minimum, we both deserve to know that."

"For sure."

"And while they are at it," she continued, "they can check their own ancestry. My mom has said she would like to do that but never has."

"Maybe our parents could reassure themselves that their families are not full of hidden secrets. Do you think they could tell my mom how much Swedish and how much Norwegian she has?"

"Probably not, but maybe they could rule out Slovenian."

"Hey, she just might get really curious about her ancestors with all of that scientific knowledge she has about Mendel's peas."

"It could be their Christmas present to us this year," Brenda suggested.

"Except my parents don't do Christmas," I said. "Besides, I thought we were going to hit them up for a little trip to Mexico City."

"I almost forgot about that. So let's make the trip their holiday gift to us, and just ask them straight out to do this ancestry stuff. They owe us."

"When do you think we would get the results?"

"Probably not before we leave. They can email them to us in Oaxaca."

"What if there's some unanticipated outcome?" I asked.

"Oh, you mean like you're Vietnamese?"

"More likely that you are Austrian, a direct descendent of Sigmund Freud."

"Like I'm genetically determined to be a psychologist? Is that what you're saying? That's called 'essentialism,' and it is well-documented bullshit. The genes only go so far."

I noticed that Brenda's glasses were on the top of her head. Was there a gene for spectacle behavior? Do genes go that far? Maybe she could test for that on her father's side. Did her grandfather wear his little wire-rim glasses up there like that? We were chowing down our food, and after a while I asked, "What do you think of this Mexican food?"

"It's okay."

"Tell me honestly, if you closed your eyes, could you tell the difference between tacos, enchiladas, and burritos?"

"Tacos are crunchy."

"No, I mean the taste."

"Oh, I don't think we'll be eating this crap in Oaxaca."

We bussed our dishes and walked back to our residence halls in silence, each in our own world. I didn't know what Brenda was thinking, but I know I had had just about enough of this ancestry stuff. What difference does it make that I don't know my patrilineal ancestry? Or my matrilineal, for that matter? I need to move on. Build a good life. Live deliberately and get ready for the unexpected. Really? How do you do that?

Only a few weeks remained until we were to fly to Mexico, both of us trying to recover from the long-delayed news we found upsetting: Dad was not my biological father and Brenda would have grown up with a twin sister, had she lived. It was good that we had plans, jobs, and a destination to occupy our troubled minds. We asked our mothers to do our DNA testing and they were surprisingly enthusiastic about it. Then Brenda and I had to figure out how to request our parents to fund a brief stay in Mexico City, so that we could see the city—the ruins, the galleries, the cultural center—before we were due in Oaxaca. We had to fly through Mexico City anyway, so why not stop for a few days to see the place and get acclimated to the language, customs, and food? But how could we assure our parents that we would be safe?

I told Brenda we needed to write it up in detail like a research proposal, identifying everything we would do each day as well as the costs. Before we presented the idea to them, Brenda had located online a private tour guide, a hotel near El Zocolo plaza, and a nearby restaurant. Both sets of parents, perhaps feeling a bit guilty for their long silence and deception with us, agreed to fund our request. So, we flew to Mexico City on Christmas Day, not exactly an observed holiday in either family, and began our life in Mexico as tourists. Our parting from our parents was a little sad and awkward, and their words "be careful, be careful" were still ringing in my ears at 30,000 feet as I looked down at a thick layer of dark clouds, hoping the pilots were being careful.

Brenda and I were really overwhelmed, as you might expect, when we arrived in Mexico City, and saw the size, the crowds, the street traffic, and the miles and miles of crowded slums, poverty like we had never experienced before. But what a glorious time we had seeing the sites, even as we were budgeting our pesos and trying not to use our credit cards any more than necessary. After breakfast on the first morning, the guide met us at our designated restaurant and took us directly to his car for a day trip north of the city to the ruins of an ancient capital called Teotihuacan, the site of the Temple of the Sun and Temple of the Moon.

In our anthropology class, Professor Martinez had presented these ruins in great detail through her lectures and slides, so we were acquainted with them, but being there, walking through them, was a totally unique experience.

"It's not just the pyramids, there was a whole city here, right?" Brenda said to the guide, seeking more information.

"Mexico's biggest ancient city," the guide replied, "around two hundred thousand people. In the sixth century, it was the world's sixth largest city."

"But the pyramids are earlier?" I asked, remembering an older date.

"They think the Temple of the Sun, the larger one over there, is from 150 A.D. Most of the rest of the city came later. If you want to climb one of them, I suggest the Temple of the Moon here."

So, we began our climb, up the irregular stone steps, until we reached the top, sweaty and winded, where we found an open area with what seemed like a high table, a wide slab of rock held up by other rocks, all carefully balanced. It was here, I recognized, that the human sacrifices were made by cutting out the heart. "Here?" I asked the guide, pointing, and he nodded his head yes, but said nothing more. I knew that ancient peoples worshipped the sun and the moon, the great mysterious powers that nourished their world and held everything together in its place, providing night and day, and the right amount of rain to grow crops. And so it became necessary to worship and satisfy these gods by sacrificing a human. Did it mean that they placed no value on human life, as is often said, or that they placed a very high value on it, offering a person, not a goat or a sheep, to keep the universe running smoothly? Even though I thought I understood it, it gave me a creepy feeling.

I turned away from the slab of rock and looked out over the vast expanse of ruins, over to the Temple of the Sun and beyond, to the smaller ruins scattered around the town's main street, called the Way of the Dead. Then I did what Mom had taught me to do at Mesa Verde: pretend that the voices I heard and the movements I saw were of the ancient people who lived here, as if I could be transported back into their time and imagine what it was like when they were here. I created that sensation in my head and must have looked kind of far off because Brenda said, "Where are you, Carl? Time traveling?"

"Yes," I said. "And going back over so many generations and centuries like that, I'm starting to have those old feelings of nothingness I used to have."

"Well, get over it," she said, "because I need you to take a picture of me here, so I can send it to Professor Martinez."

"Happy to help," I said. "Will you be standing, or do you want to lie down on the table over there?"

"Carl!" Brenda's voice had that familiar tone of reprimand.

Of course, we went to the popular Palacio de Belles Artes to see the folk ballet and a famous mural by Diego Rivera, and to the amazing but overwhelming Anthropology Museum one afternoon, where we checked out displays from the Oaxaca region. But the highlight for us both was the Blue House Museum of Frida Kahlo. I told Brenda a lot about my art course while I was taking it, and she registered for it last term, so we both knew about Frida, the famous off-beat Mexican woman painter. When we told the guide of our interest in Frida, he said he would take us straight to her house.

"What? To her house?" Brenda asked.

"Her house is a museum, but it's also where she actually lived," the guide said.

"Didn't she have some physical problems?" I asked, as we drove through the back streets, trying to remember my class notes.

"Besides polio at age six?" the guide responded. "Well, yes, she was also in a horrible bus accident that left her with broken bones in the back and right leg, plus broken ribs, collarbone, and pelvis."

I couldn't help thinking about Ken and wondering if he was walking okay now. "She suffered," I said.

"Physical suffering as well as the mental suffering of living with Diego Rivera."

"The mural guy?" Brenda asked.

"That's the one," the guide replied.

I recalled Buddha's descriptions of so many kinds of suffering. Frida had them all, it seems.

While our guide navigated the narrow streets in his old car, I felt a little sleepy, and may have dozed off for a while, awakening when I heard him say, "Here we are. Let me take you inside."

As we wandered through, I was struck by the beauty and simplicity of this small house painted a light blue, the lush courtyard gardens, and little rooms converted into galleries for some of her paintings.

"Let me take you up to her room," the guide said.

"Her room?" Brenda asked.

"Yes, of course, Right up this stairway here. See."

There before us was Frida Kahlo's room, her paints, an easel, some of her self-portraits, her wheelchair. The chills went straight up my spine. This was not a course with projected slides in a tiered lecture hall. I mean, I was standing on the spot where Frida Kahlo lived and painted and suffered.

"It's one thing to study her," Brenda said, "It's really different to step into her home, her life, the place where she painted. It's so sad but so amazing, I want to cry."

"I knew you would like it," the guide said, noticing her tears. "It's one of our national treasures."

On the way out, Brenda said to me, "She was quite the non-conformist for her times, you know. A friend of that Marxist, Leon Trotsky. She drank a lot, told dirty jokes, traveled in spite of her injuries, and was bisexual. I did my paper on her."

Had Brenda found a role model she would try to emulate while she was in Mexico? While I was supposed to look out for her? Oh, please, dear Ground of Being, keep her out of trouble.

8

ENJOYING THE CULTURE OF A ZAPOTEC WEAVING VILLAGE

The door in the wall. Juana's smile. Meeting the family. English class tutors. Learning about weaving. The market, the church, and the plaza. Brenda's acquaintance. Working the farm with Francisco. The ruins at Monte Albán. The news about Grandpa Osvaldo.

Brenda and I were met at the Oaxaca airport by a young man who introduced himself as Francisco's amigo. We learned later that Francisco was the oldest son in the family where we were staying, and that his friend Guillermo Ortiz had been asked to pick us up in his stylish Ford Focus, saving Francisco the embarrassment of greeting us in his dilapidated Volkswagen van. Guillermo, Spanish for William, skirted downtown Oaxaca and drove us out to Teotitlán del Valle, the little town where we were to stay. I was glad our plane had arrived on time and that there was still enough daylight to be able to see the surrounding landscape as we drove along: rolling hills dotted with upright branching cactus, valleys of open fields and grazing sheep, small trees covered in bright pink blossoms, and what appeared to be several streambeds without any flowing water. An unusual landscape for a dry climate and very beautiful to me.

We took a left where a narrow, paved road began to wind upward into the foothills, eventually reaching a small town with a network of cobblestone streets. "Almost here," Guillermo told us in his limited English. But the street appeared to be lined with walls, as were several other streets. A town of walls?

I looked over at Brenda and she frowned, whispering, "Where are the houses?"

Eventually Guillermo pulled up to an entryway into one of the walls, a beautiful large door of dark natural wood with big black metal hinges. And I wondered what new life I would discover as I entered that door in the wall.

As we unloaded our suitcases and backpacks, the door opened, and through it came a handsome, strongly-built, black-haired young Mexican man. He introduced himself as Francisco, and he and Guillermo began to gesture and speak in a language we couldn't understand. Brenda and I exchanged glances. Had we studied the wrong language? But then we heard bienvenida from Francisco and buenos tardes from Guillermo and we knew they had switched to Spanish. They insisted that we not touch our luggage, gesturing firmly with outstretched palms, and they quickly gathered it up to carry through the door. We thanked Guillermo and he smiled at us and started to give both of us hugs, then hesitated, and got into this Ford and drove away.

As we stepped through the door, we entered a large open courtyard formed by three wings of a two-story, U-shaped dwelling, the wall where we entered being the fourth side of this broad enclosure. So this is where the houses were: behind the walls. At our right was a small tree, which we later learned produced mango fruit, and under it was a large round wooden table with a collection of several unmatched old wooden chairs. "Be comfortable," Francisco said in Spanish, gesturing toward the chairs. "Welcome to our community. I'll let the family know you are here." He slipped away, leaving us there alone.

But we couldn't sit down, awe-struck as we were with this magnificent courtyard, now bathed in the orange and gold of the setting sun. Under red tile roofing, the tan stucco walls seemed to have numerous arches and doorways leading into secluded rooms and work areas. To one side of the courtyard were several buckets that appeared to be for soaking wool, perhaps the dyes used for weaving different colors? In one corner was a sizable pile of gray wool, looking as if it had come directly from recently shorn sheep. Through one archway we glimpsed what appeared to be two weaving looms. We kept meandering around, curious about everything we saw.

At the far end of the courtyard, stood another mango tree, and beside it was an open stairway to the second floor, a sturdy structure with polished wood railings and brightly-colored decorative tile risers and treads, a work of art in itself. I was examining the artistry of the tiles, when I looked up to see a young woman hurrying down those stairs, neatly dressed in a simple white cotton skirt and turquoise blouse, her dark eyes flashing, one black pigtail bouncing on her back, and the cutest smile in the world consuming her whole face.

"Hi. I'm Juana," she said. "Sometimes they call me Juanita so Juana is just like the Juan in Juanita. You must be our guests from the United States."

"I'm Brenda."

"I'm Carl." We both reached out our hands to shake, but Juana ignored the hands and gave us warm hugs instead.

"Please sit," she said, "while I fix you something to drink." She moved through an archway part way down the right side of the courtyard that must have led to the kitchen.

Sit? Yes, I needed to sit down. Catch my breath. I felt like I had just completed a hundred-meter free style sprint in an Olympic pool. I remembered that feeling as a swimmer, but why was I having it now? I had never seen anyone quite like Juana, and the impression of her coming down that stairway for the first time was rattling my brain. The fraternity guys at LTC would call her "bad-ass beautiful," but I could never use words like that to describe this gorgeous little creature with such amazingly unusual features. Perhaps it was because she was different from any young woman I had ever seen, being not just Mexican, but Zapotec, with ancestors going back, as I was about to learn, to some of the original people who lived on this land centuries ago. Was it the dark eyes? Her slender form? The shiny raven black hair? Maybe it was the smile that seemed to lift every burden I had been carrying for the last three years. In any case, my heart was doing some serious pounding. What the heck was going on with me?

Brenda looked over at me and said, "Where are you, Carl?' But I think she must have known.

"It's so…so different here," I said, sounding elusive.

"But pleasant and secluded in this courtyard behind that wall," Brenda said, still looking around at everything.

Francisco came back into the courtyard wearing tight fitting jeans, a black short sleeve shirt, and leather boots. I noticed that his hair was cut short on the sides but left longer on top. Now it was Brenda's turn to be absorbed in his presence. He sat down beside her and began to speak some simple Spanish, as if to test her out. Apparently, she passed the test, because they were soon talking and laughing together like old friends.

Juana came back with two cans of something that looked like ginger ale, but wasn't. "A local favorite," she said. There was that smile again. Dang. How beautiful.

Just then an older man and woman, who appeared to be around the age of my parents, entered from the other side of the courtyard and came over to us. We jumped to our feet as Juana made the introductions. "This is my mother Magdalena and my father Sebastian." We gave our names and bowed slightly, not knowing what else to say or do until Brenda remembered 'my pleasure' in Spanish and I repeated it after her. Twice. Had they understood? They seated themselves in two chairs, and I began to wonder if those unmatched chairs belonged by tradition to each family member because there seemed to be no hesitation about where they would sit. Were we sitting in someone's chair?

After they were seated, and before we could speak further, a much older woman came tottering across the courtyard pushing a wheelchair. "This is Abuela Paulina, and Abuelo Osvaldo, my grandfather," Juana said, putting a loving hand on the shoulder of the old man in the wheelchair. We jumped to our feet again, bowing even more deeply this time out of respect for their age. Bowing? Did we think we were in Japan? "Abuelo is not doing so well these days. It's hard for him to hear and speak," Juana said in an intimate whisper.

We were all quiet for a moment, but the quiet was natural not uncomfortable, as we sipped our whatever-it-was. I noticed that Juana's mother, Magdalena, had a rather stern look, perhaps the keeper of the family rules, while Juana's father had the appearance of an artist, more of a free spirit. Abuela Paulina gave the impression of an ancient sage, full of wrinkles and wisdom, and poor Abuelo Osvaldo looked like he was not going to be long in this world. Those were my first impressions anyway.

"I need to tell you," Juana said, "That abuelo and abuela speak only Zapotec, the language of our ancient ancestors. It's all they know. My parents speak Zapotec and Spanish, but only a few words of English. I speak all three, and my older brother here, Francisco, he sticks mostly with Spanish although he understands Zapotec and some English. Somehow, all of us in the Hernandez family communicate one way or another. Well, most of the time."

"And speaking of English," I said, "yours is very good. Almost no accent. Big vocabulary." Brenda nodded vigorously in agreement.

"Oh, thank you. I'll talk to you about that later. Not everyone in this family thinks I should be learning English."

Just then another person came across the courtyard, a young woman perhaps a few years younger that Juana, but she had an odd look on her face, more like a scowl than a welcoming smile.

"This is my younger sister Cecelia. She has a few problems, but we all love her very much and she is an expert weaver." Cecelia did not come over for greetings or hugs, but quickly took her place in the only chair left at the round table.

I thought we had met everyone, but then two young boys came creeping up like alley cats, from where, I don't know. They just arrived.

"These are my younger brothers Naxeli and Naconda." Juana then switched to Spanish, and I had the sense that she was reprimanding Naxeli for wearing a lady's silk scarf around his neck, perhaps his grandmother's, because as Juana spoke, he clung to it with both hands and made a face at her.

I had heard about the extended families in Mexico, but now I was seeing one—all three generations—before my eyes. And we hadn't even begun to meet the aunts and uncles and cousins, many of whom, I discovered later, lived nearby in other courtyards behind other walls. If family resemblance was any indicator of ancestry, everyone in the Hernandez family was obviously related. No DNA tests needed here. Generations of Zapotec ancestors had passed on dark eyes, black hair, a straight nose, and copper-colored skin. Did it matter that they were Zapotec? I would find out that it mattered deeply for some, but that for Juana it was mainly problematic and confusing. As I was mulling over my thoughts about ancestry, her father, Sebastian, stood up abruptly, ready to deliver a short welcome speech, and speak he did, but in Zapotec. Juana translated into English for her father, phrase by phrase.

"As head of this household, I want to welcome you as our guests. We take our responsibilities seriously. We did not all agree as a family when the university made its housing offer to us, and we discussed it carefully. But it was my mother here, Dona Paulina, who spoke up to remind us that hospitality is one of the strongest Zapotec values. We are glad you are here. We will feed you well and make certain that you are comfortable and happy as we welcome you into our family and traditions."

He smiled at us directly in a kindly way, and I thought I saw part of the source of Juana's smile; the rest, I was sure, came from her lively personality.

After a while, as the sun had set and the courtyard had become dark, Juana said, "I hate to break up this gathering of the Hernandez family, but our guests need to be at the downtown campus of the university by nine o'clock tomorrow morning. We need to allow them time to get settled and sleep after their long trip from the United States." She followed with one sentence in Zapotec, and without anyone saying a word, the sons, with guidance from the eldest son Francisco, took our luggage up to our separate rooms.

I followed my luggage up that marvelous stairway and down a little hallway into a room, which I later learned was one of two rooms reserved for occasional tourists who wanted to learn more about Zapotec weaving, the other room next door being Brenda's. The tidy little space was plain and spotless. I was sure that Juana had cleaned it herself, arranged everything in order, and even provided a fresh tube of sunscreen. I soon had my belongings unpacked and placed in the old hand-painted chest of drawers and small free-standing wooden closet. The bed, covered with one of their colorful hand-woven blankets, was comfortable and firm, the way I liked it, as mine was at home in the basement guest room. Now I was the guest in an actual guest room with this Zapotec family. They were definitely something different to my eyes and ears, but then I began to think about how strange Brenda and I must appear to them, maybe even a little scary, with Brenda's light wood-colored hair and green eyes, and me with my blue eyes and blond hair. I remembered reading somewhere that the native Americans on the upper east coast were absolutely terrified of the liquid blue eyes of the Scandinavian Vikings.

I wondered if Juana was as fascinated with me as I was with her. I hoped she wasn't frightened by my uncontrolled constant observations of her. I went next door to check on Brenda, but when I knocked, she said she was asleep. Now how could that be? So, I returned to my room and opened the window on the exterior wall. I knew only that I was in a small village somewhere in the foothills on the outskirts of Oaxaca, but I must have felt completely secure because I fell asleep immediately.

I awoke at seven to the tolling of a deep-toned bell that seemed nearby, but I discovered that I was definitely not the first one up. Juana was already in the kitchen fixing breakfast for us as I came down the stairway.

After a buenos días in Spanish she asked, "Have you ever tasted the world-famous chocolate from Oaxaca?"

"No, I don't think so."

"Well, I'm starting you off right with cups of cocoa made from our Oaxacan chocolate. Here. Sit. That and some home-baked bread with guava jelly. I hope it's enough."

"Maybe you think we Americans all eat bacon and eggs every morning?"

"I've heard that. And Tigre Antonio,"

"What?"

"Tony the Tiger cornflakes cereal. That's my rough Spanish translation." She smiled that smile again and I just about fell off my chair.

Brenda joined us and when we had finished, Francisco was waiting out front in the VW van to take us into the city.

"I'll show you our little town here later," Juana said. "Right now, we need to get to class."

The ride down into town was bumpy and jerky, and the engine of the van was loud, even going downhill, so we didn't talk much and just looked out the windows. Francisco dropped us off at the Zócalo, the main plaza near the big cathedral, and drove off waving one hand out of the window. We had only a short walk to the branch campus of the university, where English language courses were offered through the School of Languages. The downtown campus, actually just one building mainly for classrooms, was convenient for the students, most of whom were already employed and were just trying to polish their English skills. Some students were studying Spanish, and a few older students were studying Zapotec.

As Juana introduced us to her professor, Ruben Valdez, she explained that he was also the supervisor of the interns, and when the intern program was approved, he turned to her to see if her family would consider an offer from the university to pay for housing them. Juana appeared to be a special favorite of Señor Valdez, as they called him, and I could tell that she was not just another student but had become his amiga.

Brenda and I attended the class taught by Señor Valdez in the morning and after a short break, the students broke into three smaller tutoring groups, one led by the teacher and the others by us, the two interns, to practice speaking and listening. Señor Valdez was an excellent teacher and provided stimulating materials for the students. Our job was to improvise short conversations in English based on the lesson materials of the day. We had no advanced preparation for the day's topic, and needed none really, because of our language fluency in our native language. We just jumped right in, even on our first day, getting our students to speak English and offering gentle corrections to their mistakes while modeling correct pronunciation. It was a comfortable set up for us and appeared to work for them. Señor Valdez left his students with Juana for a few minutes to observe our groups, and he smiled, nodding his head and mumbling with satisfaction, "It's working, just as I knew it would."

We learned that classes were on Monday, Wednesday, and Friday, one in the morning and another in the afternoon, with a little free time after the second class to be downtown until Francisco picked us up in the van, fitting us into his busy schedule as soon as he could. The sound of the van's arrival was unmistakable and we named it "the green bean machine" for its color and noise. On Tuesdays and Thursdays, Señor Valdez served as a tour guide at Monte Albán, so he not only knew English, Spanish, and Zapotec, but a lot about Mexican history. That gave us our Tuesdays, Thursdays, and Saturdays free to use as we wished in Teotitlán del Valle, the weaving village where we lived.

The next morning, Tuesday, I went down to the breakfast that Juana was preparing for us and found Francisco and his father Sebastian getting up from the table to leave. Francisco looked like he had already done a day's work and he and his father were chattering in Zapotec about something that sounded very important. They gave us a buenos días in Spanish and Francisco threw Brenda a charming smile. But then he and his father went out through the door in the wall, still speaking with great animation, apparently about some project for the day.

Juana's mother, Magdalena, was in the kitchen, too, cutting up fruit, and Brenda, instead of asking if she could help, picked up a knife and joined in with the peeling and slicing to assist Magdalena, who seemed to enjoy this unsolicited help.

After breakfast, Juana took us around the open courtyard to introduce us quickly to the home-based weaving business in a way that she must have used with other foreign guests who had visited and stayed in the guest rooms. First, she showed us how her brother Aconda was carding wool by combing through it to remove impurities. Then she sat down at the spinning wheel for a short lesson. Brenda asked if she could try. The challenge is to turn the crank with one hand while gently pulling on the wool with a subtle touch. Brenda seemed surprised at how quickly she caught on, producing in no time at all a thick, strong piece of yarn. I tried it, too, but I wasn't so good at it and felt pretty clumsy. Juana pointed out, "It used to be just the women who did the spinning and weaving, but that changed a few years ago." As we moved away from the wheel, Naxeli, the oldest of the younger brothers, took his place there and began spinning, as if to prove Juana's point. "Hey, you guys, aren't you supposed to be in school?" she asked. But Naxeli told her it was a holiday.

From the courtyard we entered through an archway into a work area where one of the two-pedal looms was set up. Juana sat down to demonstrate, but this time the process was not so simple with lots of coordinated movements of the feet and arms. "How does the weaver know how to follow the pattern and change colors?" I asked.

"Like this," Juana said, demonstrating, but I didn't catch the this, and she just said, "It takes time to develop the skill."

I also noticed it was a demanding physical activity as well, requiring stamina and coordination. "This family works hard to make these beautiful rugs and blankets," I noted.

"Oh, yes," she said, returning everything to its place before sliding off of the bench. "And we don't make a good price selling them here in Mexico." Out in the courtyard where birds were chirping in the mango trees, she showed us the buckets of dyes, but said, "I'll give you a lesson on colors another day. I want to get to the market before it closes."

Juana led the way, out through the door in the wall where we found Francisco finishing up his discussion in Zapotec with his father, whom he left behind as he joined us, starting up a new conversation in Spanish with Brenda. We walked up the cobblestone street together toward the broad, open plaza in front of the church. Just as we arrived, a bell in one of the tall church towers chimed, and I suddenly realized where my alarm clock was located, though it was much louder now with my standing right there under it, and I could feel the reverberations run through my bones. It tolled nine o'clock for everyone near and far in this community to hear. With the church telling the time of day, were clocks even necessary? No one seemed to have a wristwatch or carry a phone.

As we were walking along up the slight cobblestone incline, Francisco had explained that this was Avenida Benito Juárez, one of the many in the area so named for the famous Mexican President from Oaxaca. Brenda wanted to know more about Juárez, so I had to listen closely to Francisco's explanation in Spanish. From what I could gather, Juárez was governor of Oaxaca and President of Mexico more than once in the 1860s. I guess that made him a contemporary of Abraham Lincoln, well, at least until Lincoln was assassinated. Juárez was a sponsor of the Reform Laws and helped make primary education free and compulsory. So, he was a famous Zapotec from Oaxaca, and Francisco knew his Mexican history.

I noticed as we walked along, that many people recognized and seemed to know Juanita and Francisco and were forever saying hola as a greeting, with a half-smile for me and Brenda, the strangers, obviously from the US. There were many different kinds of shops scattered around the plaza and on the streets leading into it, but the whole town was so small, I felt like I could hold it all in my two cupped hands. As we passed the church, Juana paused in an archway on our right leading to an indoor enclosure that housed the market.

"Come on guys," Juana called to me and Francisco, "you can come in, too, although it's mostly women." She was right about that, women of all ages, selling as well as buying, definitely managing the commerce related to food. Okay, so the women dominate the market, but men are welcome.

And what a market it turned out to be! Corn, beans, tomatoes, and several vegetables I didn't recognize. Many fresh fruits were spread across the tables: bananas, oranges, mangos, pineapples, and plums. Vanilla beans and chocolate were prominently displayed, as well as every type of pepper, red and green, hot and mild, that a cook could ever want. And limes, lots of green limes. As we moved along, we came upon cuts of pork, chickens cut up or whole, and a separate table for fish, many different kinds displayed over ice, the head still on. At the center of the market at a low brick table with a stone slab sat a wrinkled old lady with a brown and black headband that looked like a turban. What was she selling? A variety of seeds, nuts, and fresh cut herbs. She answered questions, took orders, and scooped her products into small paper bags, very much in charge of her operation. We passed two women dressed in bright, boldly-patterned long dresses, standing face to face and toe to toe, speaking Zapotec while underscoring the spoken words with bold gestures, expressing strong feelings, so it seemed, but apparently agreeing with each other.

Brenda was taking pictures of everything with her phone. I was just trying to take it all in, banking direct deposits to my brain. "What are the hours here?" Brenda asked Juana.

"It's usually open from seven to ten," she replied, "but that's just in the morning when people shop for breakfast and the midday meal. Then it's open again from four to ten when you will find more prepared foods such as empanadas, tamales, and enchiladas."

Fast food, like Taco Bell, I thought, but wouldn't dare say it. Not a fair comparison, but they do have the idea of take-out, it seems. Then it dawned on me that maybe we got the idea from them, not the other way around.

"Do you shop here?" Brenda asked Juana.

"My mother usually does the shopping early in the morning, but sometimes we will pick up prepared food in the late afternoon. The women of the village make delicious food."

"The women of the village cook it?" Brenda asked. "In their homes? Maybe I could learn how."

"If you are interested, Abuela Paulina taught us all. She doesn't cook much anymore, but when she does, it's terrific. She has all of the traditional recipes in her head." Juana tapped the side of her head with a forefinger and said, "She's a walking around cookbook." It was one of her few errors in English and I let it pass because she was so darn cute saying it. Why was I listening so closely to each word she spoke and watching her every move?

"Do the women like cooking?" Brenda asked.

"It's not really a choice," Francisco said, after what had been a long silence of observing. "So I guess most women learn to like it. It's another one of our traditions."

"Cooking?" Brenda asked, surprised again. "A tradition?"

"Food is important to our people," Juana replied, "so we take time to prepare it and enjoy it while we eat."

Quite a contrast from Little Texas College, as I remembered it, where you fill your plate with whatever slop is in the steamer that night and stuff it down as fast as you can without thinking about what it tastes like.

As we left the market, I looked straight ahead and noticed a sign for a clinic. It was good to know they had some medical services right here in town. I found myself squinting from the bright sun as we stepped back into the plaza. I hadn't noticed how massive the church appeared until I stood in front of it and looked up.

"This plaza is really big," Brenda observed, then asked, "What's it used for?"

"Special celebrations of the church and community gatherings," Juana said.

"Fiestas," Francisco added with a broad smile. "We have fiestas for everything, but especially weddings."

"And the church. It looks like there are some other buildings here associated with the church," Brenda observed.

"Yes, many useful spaces. There is a small private pre-school in that building over there." Juana pointed at it and said, "It used to be a cloister for nuns."

I stepped back a bit and shaded my eyes with one hand to get a better view of the church. I remembered something about Spanish Colonial architecture from what the tour guide told us in Mexico City. The church had a symmetrical design, with two bell towers, not exactly the same but matching, on each side of the large front entrance. At the curved top of the façade, there were painted-in architectural features—columns, moldings, a shelf, vases—all actually flat, but providing convincing three-dimensional representations in blue, gold, and a deep maroon red. Above the main entry was a large, clear glass octagonal window with stone and brick decoration around it. Further back, partly hidden from view, there appeared to be a big dome. There was a lot to take in for those of us who had learned to see.

"Is the church open?" Brenda asked. We had seen several churches in Mexico City but had never had time to go inside.

"Almost always," Juana replied. "Would you like to see it?"

At the entry was a simple wood sign with painted letters that displayed the name, Templo de la Virgen de la Natividad. As we walked through the massive front door, the church looked even bigger, the long nave stretching ahead under curved arches. No pointed Gothic arches here, but sure enough, as we took several steps down the aisle, there was a huge dome overhead, painted with what appeared to be scenes from the life of Jesus, his birth, baptism, hillside teaching, and crucifixion. As we continued to walk further down the main aisle, past the pews, toward the altar at the front, I noticed at my left a small, sculpted figure with an actual red cloth robe around the hips. What is this? A Jesus of reduced proportion in flashy dress at the side of the church? At the front behind the altar and surrounded with intricate gold work was a huge painted representation of the Virgin Mary, for whom the church was named. Jesus on the side with Mary front and center? Hey, it's Mexico, I told myself.

I remembered my readings about Hindu temples, Muslim mosques, and Buddhist stupes, and I could imagine the work and expense that must have gone into this place centuries ago. It was effective, too, because I still felt that sense of reverence in the space that they had created.

Pointing to the many vases of cut flowers lined up near the altar railing, Brenda asked, "Where do all of these flowers come from?"

"Each Sunday we have fresh flowers provided by a—what's the word, not a cancer?"

"Sponsor?" Brenda suggested.

"Yes, sponsor. An important person from the community provides flowers, not always so many or so beautiful as these, but that's how it works. There is a florist just around the corner from here."

"And do people come to this church on Sunday?" Brenda asked.

"Yes, but also at other times during the week, just to be close to God, perhaps to pray."

"Like, does your family attend on Sunday?"

"Well, not everyone." Juana glanced at Francisco and smiled. "But we try to follow the teachings. The Zapotecs became Catholic, not having much choice, and some Zapotec traditions continue."

"And the priest," I asked, "is he here?"

"Padre Paulo? Usually he is out in the town, visiting somewhere, attending meetings, or supporting some cause. He's very active."

Like a good liberation priest should be, I thought, but didn't say. We came back up the aisle and out into the bright sunlit plaza, now busy with the activity of many townspeople. I walked with Juana, and Brenda chattered with Francisco, as we retraced our steps down Avenida Benito Juárez, but we passed our entrance through the wall to continue on.

"I want to show you where we went to school," Juana said. "Over there is the elementary school, and that smaller building is the high school. Francisco went to high school, and—how do I say it?—me, too."

"Yes, me, too, is good," I told her, not bothering to explain that it is the name of a women's movement in the US.

"It was a little unusual for a girl to go on with her studies, but I did it. My parents have wanted all of us to go to high school, but not the university. I just go there to study English. How am I doing?"

"You are doing fantastic. And if you keep talking to me in English every day like this, you will be completely fluent."

"It helps to be best friends with the tutor, right?" The smile was accompanied by a wink that time.

We went back into the courtyard of the Hernandez household and I asked Juana if they had an internet connection.

"Oh, yes, we need that for the business. And you probably want to get on, right? Come over here and I will show you.

She took me into a room that looked like a business office and explained that this was where Francisco and her father coordinated the sales and shipments of the rugs and blankets to shops in Mexican resort towns, a service they provided to several of the families in the neighborhood, mostly relatives, but not all.

I went up to my room and brought down my laptop, and in a short time, working side by side with Juana and identifying a password, I was all set to send emails home, or to Marv, or Professor Adams. Juana left and I sat down out in the courtyard and typed notes on everything I had seen and learned about that morning. Of course, I still have those notes.

Then I sent an email to my mom and dad, thanking them again for our trip to Mexico City and letting them know about our work as tutors at the university and the arrangements here with this lovely host family whose ancestors are Zapotec Indians. I reminded Mom to let me know as soon as she had found out anything about her ancestry search.

We went to the university in the green bean machine on Wednesday and again on Friday. Everything was going well, and I loved the tutoring. The students, besides being polite and respectful, were curious about the United States and quizzed us about everything. Sometimes it felt like they knew more than I did about what was going on there. At other times, I felt a little embarrassed, trying to explain something that was unexplainable, like why they should be expected to pay for a wall between our countries.

Juana and I sat outside on a bench in a park near the cathedral after the tutoring session was finished, and Brenda said she was going to explore downtown Oaxaca a little.

"Alone?" I asked.

"You got a problem with that?" Her ponytail bounced as she shook her head back and forth.

"Not really. I just have some reservations."

"Well, save them for dinner when we get home."

I was a little surprised and Juana frowned. Brenda seldom spoke to me like that. "You were right," Juana said after Brenda left. It's not always safe around here."

Francisco was tied up with his responsibilities with the business, so he was late in picking us up. That provided some time for me to get better acquainted with Juana that day.

"Everyone in the family is talking about me," Juana began.

"Why?"

"Because I'm studying English and actually learning it."

"They don't want you to learn English? Why?"

"My brother Francisco thinks I will leave, go to Mexico City, or even the US, and if I do that, it will be a big loss for the business. My mother is worried that I will go away and come home with some strange guy who is not Zapotec. My father is concerned about my safety in a big city. With all of these people worrying about me, I am beginning to think I should drop my English and try to forget what I've learned. Francisco says I have created a small tornado in our family."

"And what about you? Why are you studying English?" I asked. "How did you get started?"

"It is the universal language of business and commerce. I know, I sound like Señor Valdez, but it's true. I started in high school and loved it. I heard about the courses at the university and begged my parents to let me take them. As I improved, I had to persuade them to let me take more each term."

"But they are allowing you."

"Yes, but it was Abuela Paulina who encouraged the head of the family, my father, to permit it. I love her."

"But you haven't told me: Are you planning to leave?"

"Well, there is a side of me that really wants to see the world, leap over all of these walls and see what's out there. I would like to live on my own and work in one of those high-rise towers in Mexico City. But then, I know that if I did that, it would cause big problems at home. Every family member is needed in the weaving business, and if one leaves or dies—I'm not planning on dying—it is very unfair."

"Disruptive. Do you know this word?"

"Yes, that's it, disruptive. But do I have to give up my future for a rug? It doesn't seem fair." Juana nods her head slowly. "On the other hand, I have to admit that I love my home, my family, our community, our way of life."

"It's very traditional, and from what I've seen in this short time, it's really wonderful. I enjoy being a part of it."

"See. That's the problem. There is a lot to like, but sometimes I get tired of the rules and customs and routines, and I want to break away and experience something different." Her arms were spreading out in sweeping gestures.

"Should your family be worried about you?"

"My safety? No. I can take care of myself. I don't do stupid things. Leaving? Probably I wouldn't stay forever. Marrying someone who is not Zapotec? Well, that's not really a crime, you know. Besides, we are kind of inbred, marrying all our own cousins."

I had to smile at that, wondering what a little DNA testing would turn up in Teotitlán del Valle.

Juana continued. "Sometimes I dream about making a lot of money so that my parents could retire, but then I know that they wouldn't retire even if they could. It's not just a business; it's a way of life."

"That's what appeals to me; the way of life you have here." We stood up and walked around the little park behind the cathedral for a while and it reminded me of walking in the Arboretum with my mom. When we returned to our little bench, I said, "Tell me about the Zapotecs. What should I know?"

"It's difficult to explain. You've heard some of the language at our home. It's very important to the people who think of themselves as Zapotec to speak the language. It defines us as a people."

"But who are these people?'

"Well, we are indios, as you can see." She held out one sun-tanned copper-colored arm. We are part of an ancient civilization that was here long before the Spanish arrived. In a few days, we will go on a field trip to see some of the most famous ancient ruins, and Señor Valdez will be our tour guide. He'll explain everything then. Those ruins are Zapotec, and, of course, so is the weaving, even the designs and colors. We have pottery, too, and Zapotec carvings with decorative painting. Each village around Oaxaca has its specialty craft."

"But how old are these traditions?"

"The ancient civilization goes back to 500 B.C. Some say further. When the Spanish arrived, we were about three hundred fifty thousand people, but we were almost wiped out. Then the numbers grew back again, and now we are up to around that same number again. We are a very proud people once again with strong traditions. But sometimes it seems like all we have is our traditions, no future."

"But it is a very stable way of life."

"That's the advantage."

"And what's the disadvantage?"

"This is not five hundred B.C. Or fifteen nineteen, when Cortez invaded. This is the twenty-first century and Señor Valdez says the world is flat, without boundaries or limitations. English, it seems to me, is the key to the future. Zapotec is a mirror for looking back."

"Like in a car. We call that a rear-view mirror."

"I'll remember that, because that's us, always looking back." She looked down at her feet for a moment, as if suddenly ashamed about something before she said, "There's another disadvantage, and I probably should tell you before you discover it on your own."

"What's that?"

"Prejudice. We are pre-colonial people you know. Indios. Our skin is darker and we are short, shorter than most other people who live in Mexico, both men and women. Sometimes the tall, light-skinned Mexicans, so proud of their pure Spanish heritage call us Oaxacitos, which is a nasty way of referring to our being short."

I didn't know what to say. I thought of Alex. It seemed like every people has a nasty word for other people they don't like. I actually loved the way Juana looked, being short like that, although I began to think about how far down I would have to bend to kiss her.

Brenda returned and just then Francisco drove up in the van. I asked Brenda about her walk in the city, and she said she met an interesting guy at a café. Oh, oh, here we go.

As the days passed, we fell into our routines for tutoring on Monday, Wednesday, and Friday, and I'll tell you in a moment how I worked with Francisco at the farm on Tuesday, Thursday, and Saturday. Sunday was a free day for study or writing emails home. But for me, a strange thing happened to time: it had slowed down. Back at Little Texas College, every minute was filled with some responsibility: a paper, a quiz, an urgent deadline, class attendance, a counseling appointment. Time flew by, and there was never enough of it. Here, time crept slowly, if it was noticed at all. Even though everyone in the Hernandez household worked hard, there was time to enjoy meals, listen to the birds chirping in the mango trees in the courtyard, and watch the sun set and the moon rise. Time had lost its importance, and its only reminder was the resonant gong of the church bell every hour. Life was serene.

So you may have noticed that I've changed the pace of my story, and even though everything occurs during what is the spring term at Little Texas College, I have broken the experience here in Oaxaca into three different chapters that I have numbered eight, nine, and ten although what happened to me was mostly, with a few exceptions, a slow steady flow of enjoyment. I'll try to share that with you.

Each time we went down into the city of Oaxaca, I learned something more about it, noticing the contrast between the busy life of the city and our peaceful home at Teotitlán del Valle. We discovered that the name of the university is Universidad Autónoma Benito Juárez (same guy our street is named for), and that in addition to the main campus to the south of the city, there are several programs besides languages offered right here in the downtown facility, including business and education. Juana told me that the Aztecs had a city here, and that the Spanish laid out a town around this same Zócalo by the cathedral, and by 1529 Oaxaca had grown into the most important city in southern Mexico. But there were also earthquakes, she said, one in the mid-nineteenth century and another in 1931 that destroyed seventy percent of the city, requiring a lot of rebuilding. I don't know which I enjoyed more, the history of Oaxaca or Juana telling me about it.

One day, after our afternoon tutoring session, Brenda wandered off into the city again—she admitted later that she got lost—and came walking back to the park by the cathedral with her amigo, whom she introduced as Ismael. Just as she walked into the Zócalo, Francisco came toward us from the opposite direction, walking away from the street where he had parked the van, and I thought there was going to be a serious confrontation on the very spot where they met. Ismael was well dressed with an expensive gold watch on his wrist and three big gemstone rings on his fingers, and to Francisco, I learned, that signaled something bad. There was no greeting, only unfriendly stares, as Francisco said, "Let's go, Brenda. I'm parked over there." He pointed and then motioned with his head to me and Juana, as Ismael was left standing alone. When I looked back, he was still standing there watching Brenda with a worried look on his face.

The ride back home was quiet, if riding in the green bean machine could ever be called quiet, meaning there was no conversation until Francisco spoke up in a loud voice, directing his comments to Brenda in Spanish. We had developed the habit of Brenda riding up front with Francisco while

Juana and I took seats in the back to chatter away in English. From what I could gather of their conversation in Spanish, Francisco was reprimanding Brenda for going into the city alone. I thought I heard him say something like "I know American women are much more independent, but here a woman of your age and with your…your beauty, should not wander into the city alone." I heard him ask Brenda several questions about Ismael, and she tried to tell him that Ismael was very unhappy and wanted to escape from his sad life. She felt sorry for him. He needed help.

During the silence that followed, I understood why Brenda, with her interest in psychology, wanted to help a desperate Mexican, but I also understood Francisco's concern for Brenda's safety. The silence was broken when Francisco spoke again in a strong voice, saying something like, "I can't forbid you. I can only warn you. I am quite sure that Ismael deals in drugs."

"How can you tell?" Juana asked her brother. I suspected she asked because she knew what his answer would be.

"The way he was dressed. He is really young to have so much money for clothes, a fancy watch and those rings." Then he asked Brenda, "What is his last name? In Mexico, a last name can be important."

"I didn't ask him," she replied.

"I don't mean to be critical," Francisco continued, "But I'm concerned about keeping you safe while you are here with us." He paused and then looked over at her. "You are a beautiful young woman and I care about you," he said, and as he did, Brenda looked out the window to hide a smile. I thought that would end it with Ismael, but it didn't. It was going to be hard to separate the psychologist from her first client.

On Tuesdays, Thursdays, and Saturdays, if Francisco went to work on the ejido, the farm on the communal property, I went with him to help with weeding, trimming, and harvesting, and with repairing the fencing that contained the pasture for the sheep. Jobs like that. At first, Francisco was reluctant to accept my help. "It's not necessary," he would say. "You are an English teacher. This is not expected. Doing common labor is certainly not part of the university's contract with the host family."

But I enjoyed the physical labor, fresh air, and sunshine, and in spite of what Francisco said, he appeared to welcome me as an extra hand once that I had proven I was strong and could work hard. I pitched in where I could to become a part of whatever Francisco was working on at the moment. That day we were clearing and reinforcing an irrigation ditch that supplied a pathetic little stream of water to a communal vegetable garden. It reminded me of that summer I worked on campus with the Mexican maintenance crew.

"Do you live on a farm?" Francisco asked me.

"No. My parents are professors. My mother is a botanist and she knows a lot about plants. She grew up on a farm, but not me." I was having trouble explaining that in Spanish, but then I realized I'd probably have trouble explaining it in English, too. "My father is an astronomer. He looks at the stars." That was even harder to explain. Just then I wondered if my parents could earn a living at something besides being professors. Maybe something a little easier to describe.

At the point where the irrigation ditch joined the vegetable garden, Francisco found an extra hoe and we started digging out the weeds between the rows. "When did you meet Brenda?" he asked. I explained to him about our long friendship since elementary school and how the other students in high school thought we were boyfriend and girlfriend. "Yeah, at first I thought that, too," he said. "But you aren't actually?"

"No, just good friends."

He smiled and I thought I could see that he was relieved when I said that. Then he observed, "You and Juana are becoming good friends."

"Yes," I said, "like you and Brenda. I hope we aren't creating problems for your family with our friendships."

"Problems? No. But people are beginning to talk about us."

"Your family?"

"Yes, of course, my family, but in town as well."

"Really? Why?"

"Because I'm always walking with Brenda and speaking Spanish, and Juana is always walking with you and speaking English."

"People notice things like that?"

"They also notice that no one is speaking Zapotec." He grinned.

In the following week on Thursday, Señor Valdez scheduled a field trip open to all of the language students, not required, but free to any of the students who could fit it into their schedule. As I mentioned, he worked as a tour guide on Tuesdays and Thursdays at the old Zapotec ruins called Monte Albán. He told Brenda and me to pronounce it as one word, like Montalban, saying that we once had a famous movie actor in the US named Ricardo Montalban, but that we were probably too young to have heard of him. Anyway, that's the spelling and local pronunciation.

Francisco drove us there directly to join the others at ten o'clock, and then he stayed on and walked around with Brenda during the tour, who apparently fancied herself capable now of translating English into Spanish for him. Juana told me that her sister Cecelia had heard about the field trip and begged to go along, but Juana told her it was impossible and inappropriate because it was for the language students. Juana said that Cecelia was getting very jealous of the attention the interns were receiving and hoped her sister wouldn't do something crazy. She said that we needed to keep an eye on Cecelia.

Francisco coaxed the old van up the long road to the ruins, shifting down, then up, as the hills and turns required, until we finally reached the parking lot where we met Señor Valdez and our group of university students. As we were standing there, he told them to look at the flat plateau of the ruins and be ready to comment on what they observed about the location. On the short trail up from the parking lot, I noticed a huge tree in full bloom with lavender blossoms. In February? Mom would love this place with all of these flowering trees. I missed her.

As we reached the ruins, we began to see the remains of several stone structures stretching across a broad plain of short grass, like a huge dried up golf course. "What do you notice?" Señor Valdez asked the group. "Reply in English, please."

"It's high."

"It's flat."

"But it's the top of a mountain."

Señor Valdez smiled and nodded. "Exactly right. It's the top of a mountain, but flat. So how did it get flat?"

"Bulldozers?" someone said, and those who knew the word laughed. The others asked, "What's a bulldozer?"

Señor Valdez said, "But in three hundred B.C.?"

'A lot of shoveling," someone else said.

"Could be," Señor Valdez resumed. "But the truth is, no one knows. There are many theories, but no solid proof. Somehow, they leveled off the whole top of this mountain. And the location is strategic, because from here, you can see all three valleys." He pointed them out, and I tried to imagine living here in one of these stone buildings, standing out crisply against the blue sky that morning, with this scenic view down into those valleys.

By then, some of the tourists, mostly Americans and Canadians, had joined the group. We walked a short distance over to the first structure, big stones arranged in tiers for what looked like seating, two sides parallel, with an oblong field between them. Something like a high school gym for basketball games, only outdoors. "Yes, it's a small stadium," Señor Valdez pointed out, called Juego de Pelota. It was used for some game, we're not sure exactly what."

"Maybe for lacrosse?" an American shouted, and then a Canadian wearing a Calgary Flames cap added, "For sure it's not hockey."

"It probably involved a ball and some sort of rackets," Señor Valdez explained. "We're not sure if these are even seats. Maybe a part of the field. But now I'm going to tell you what we do know about it, and I don't want you to be shocked. We don't have the rules of the game, but there is strong evidence that the winners were sometimes sacrificed to the gods."

"The winners?" some guy from the tourists blurted out. "Who the hell would want to win?"

"Yeah, we've got some players like that on our team back home," the guy next to him joked.

"Better to sacrifice the losers, I'd say," a curly red-haired lady next to him added, making the "L" sign with her forefinger and thumb at her forehead.

Señor Valdez smiled, as if he had heard these observations before, many times. "But think like a Zapotec for a moment," he suggested. "The sacrifice is to the great god who brings you the sun, the rain, fruitful harvests, and fertility for Zapotec babies. Wouldn't you want to offer your very best to this god?"

I was having great fun observing this exchange, almost as much as if I were seated there watching the game in the centuries-old stadium. Here was that idea of human sacrifice again, and this time it seemed not so different from what we do today with our young military men and women when we send them off to war in a foreign land. Human sacrifices in a godless age. Then I remembered Marv rolling toward me in his wheelchair, a living sacrifice.

Señor Valdez led the group onto what he called the Gran Plaza, and again I could see that, like the Temples of the Sun and the Moon, this was once a whole city, nearly the length of three football fields. He pointed to the pyramids at either end of the Plaza and mentioned that the tombs hidden under the structures we were passing had contained many relics that could be seen in the onsite local museum or in the Museo Nacional de Antropología in Mexico City. Then he took us to the ruins of a building that stood on a forty-five-degree angle to the other buildings, as if deliberately positioned that way.

"This is believed to have been an observatory for astronomers," Señor Valdez said, pointing out its twisted location for celestial alignment. "The leveling of the mountain top, as I mentioned, dates from around three hundred B.C. The city built here was developed between two hundred B.C. and three hundred A.D. Most of what we see here as ruins comes from that time. These are some of the oldest—some say the oldest—in Mesoamerica. Picture a city of twenty-five thousand people, a culture dominated by priests, with a strong interest in the natural world, including the stars. From their observations, without telescopes, the Zapotecs developed a celestial calendar, the first of its kind in the Americas.

My dad would have loved this place. Now I was missing him, too. Professor Valdez led the group across the Plaza, and along the way a tourist asked., "Why are the people called Zapotec?"

"Good question. The Spanish called them Zapotecatl, from the fruit zapote, which is common in the region, but before the Spanish arrived the people called themselves in their own language Ben 'Zaa, meaning cloud people, or just Za, meaning the people. Their creation myth suggests that they came from the clouds."

Wow! I was impressed with how much Señor Valdez knew about his people. I also wondered what it felt like to be part of a people like that with known ancestors going back that far in history. He led the group past a temple and a tomb, and after brief explanations at each, moved on to the site of the Danzante Stone. Was the terrain so uneven that Brenda and Francisco had to hold hands the whole way?

"The Danzantes, or dancers, are seen around the lower part of what's left of this structure." Señor Valdez pointed to the figures. "Note the open mouths and closed eyes."

"I have some friends like that back home," the red-haired woman said.

Without acknowledging her comment, Señor Valdez continued, "And here you can see the depiction of blood where their genitals have been cut off."

"No free speech here," someone observed.

Professor Valdez was pointing at the letters now. "And here we have the famous writing. Dates and names accompany what is thought to be the earliest writing in North America."

"What were they writing?" an elderly gentleman asked in a sincere voice.

"Probably a to-do list," his wife said.

"Actually," Señor Valdez commented, "that's not a bad guess. Archeologists think they may have been compiling a list of which soldiers had been captured or taken away, perhaps a type of prisoner exchange list."

Our tour continued on, ending at a small museum, where Brenda became completely fascinated with the large collection of ancient artifacts from the adjacent ruins. "Wouldn't it be cool to work here?" she said.

I told Juana how impressed I was with how much Zapotec history Señor Valdez knew.

"Well, he is Zapotec," she said with a wink. "He probably learned half of it from his grandmother."

When we returned home to Teotitlán del Valle in the late afternoon, I went straight to my room and pulled out my laptop to make notes. Time passed, and the bell of the church told me it was past five o'clock. I heard a lot of commotion in the courtyard and I stood up to leave my room and go see what was happening below. Lots of activity, the whole family in motion. As I started down the tile steps, Juana was rushing up them, apparently to find me. She laid her small hand on my forearm and squeezed. "What is it, Juana? What's happening?"

"Abuelo Oswaldo has died."

"Grandpa? He's passed away?"

"No, death came to him. Within this hour. I thought you should know. It will be busy here for a while, but join us if you wish. I hope you won't mind our customs."

"Mind? I'm just sorry about your grandpa, Juana. I barely got to know him."

9

My Near-Death Experience

Osvaldo's funeral and fiesta. Searching for Ismael. Messed up rooms. Discussing friendship and romance. Cecelia's gift. A high fever. Pre-school teaching. Learning about Montessori. Father and son murdered.

From the stairs, I could see the family beginning to scurry around the courtyard, each member engaged in some important task, with no one appearing to be in charge but everything going smoothly without panic. I stood there observing, not sure whether to go down those stairs or not, until Juana signaled me to join her.

"I hope you won't think we are completely loco with all of these traditional customs," she said. "Of course, we knew that Osvaldo would die soon, and we are ready, but it is still difficult to do all we need to do so quickly."

"Well, I don't want to be in the way. I just want to understand and observe quietly, so tell me, if you have time, what is going on and what it means. Like what's this?" I had pointed to what looked like a pile of sand recently dumped in the middle of the courtyard. We walked over to it.

"This is fresh, clean sand from an old riverbed. Francisco found a good source several weeks ago and stored it in a special place, knowing we would need it soon."

"What is it for?" I asked.

"They are preparing a bed of sand right here in the center of the courtyard for grandpa to lie on. The sand absorbs any sins he may have had left, and our people believe it is important to place the deceased in an open space so that the sins can go out with the heat of the body."

It was a warm day, and naturally I was wondering how long he might be lying there. "What are these bricks for?" I asked.

Francisco and his father Sebastian were smoothing out the sand into a flat bed and had placed upon it a palm leaf mat. "They will place Osvaldo here on top of the mat covering the sand and will rest his head comfortably on these bricks." I must have frowned because Juana said, "I know it doesn't sound comfortable, but it is our custom." She looked up and pointed across the courtyard toward the room of her grandparents. "Oh, look. Here he comes now. They are bringing him."

Francisco and Sebastian were carrying Osvaldo in their arms and Naxhali and Naconda tried to help with the legs and feet, all three generations together. "The women here have already washed him and dressed him for burial," Juana said. A white handkerchief was placed over his face after they laid his head to rest gently against the bricks.

Maybe I looked a little shocked at the way family members were handling his body like this. "I don't understand much about your customs in the US," Juana said. "One day Señor Valdez was trying to tell us how you call in the professionals to pump some fluid into the body to preserve it."

"Yes, it's called embalming."

"Or you burn it."

"Yes, it's called cremation. We do both. I mean, one or the other." I hoped I hadn't confused her. "This seems more natural to me what you are doing here. More personal, keeping it within the family." Then I looked down at Osvaldo. "I see that he is wearing a white shirt and some black trousers," I observed.

"Yes, many people from our village will come to visit him tonight and tomorrow morning. He would want to look nice. As you can see, they are already arriving."

Just then, Brenda started down the tile stairs, but she stopped halfway, perhaps sensing that she might be intruding on some family occasion. As she started to turn to go back up, Francisco caught her eye and signaled for her to come down and join him. She hesitated, then finished her descent and stood beside him as he began to explain to her what had happened.

Noticing Brenda, Juana said, "This must seem so strange to both of you."

"Not strange, just different," I replied. "It's okay. Do what you need to do."

~

"Oh, my," Juana said, "just stand here for a moment. I need to join the women."

Juana, her sister Cecelia, her mother Magdalena, and some neighbor ladies were distributing pink bougainvillea petals around the edge of the sand where Osvaldo was lying. They brought in tall candles to place at his side and at his feet. Abuela Paulina used her cane to shuffle over to the mat where Osvaldo was lying. She seemed composed, like she had things she knew she needed to do. Juana provided her with a small cushion and helped her sit down carefully to be at Osvaldo's side. Then Juana returned to be with me.

"Well, I got her down, but I don't know if we will get her back up," she said. There was a moment of silence, a time of prayer for Osvaldo's soul. I thought I could see Paulina's lips moving as she prayed. Gradually, more people came into the courtyard and began talking softly, and I felt I needed to speak to Juana in a whisper. "I don't see a lot of crying and grieving. It's almost like he hasn't really died, that he's still with us."

"His body is but his soul has already started on its journey," Juana said. "It will take eight days to get wherever it is going."

"He just slips away quietly over time so as not to create a disturbance?"

"You can think of it that way," she said. "But Osvaldo has been dying for a long time, gradually leaving us over the past months. But even more than this, Carl, you need to understand that in Mexico, and especially among us Zapotecs, death is a natural thing. We believe that our life is on loan, not really ours. Death is a part of life, not something to be hidden away or feared."

"I noticed even your younger brothers participating."

"What is there to hide? It will happen to all of us. The boys need to know what is done and be prepared to help their mother and father on their journey when the time comes."

Later that evening, after the church bell had tolled nine, there was a knock on the door in the wall. Some ladies from the village entered. Juana told me, "They have come to be with Abuela Paulina through the night. See, they are lighting the candles. The family can go to bed now, and you and Brenda can go to your rooms. I will help Abuela Paulina get up now and go back to her room."

I had been sleeping much better in Mexico, but that night was an exception. I'd never seen a family caring for a dead body like that—Texans would say a corpse— and I wondered how anyone in the family could sleep, except for Osvaldo, of course, in his sleep of death on that layer of sand. In the US, that body would have been carried straight off to the undertaker long ago; here there is a more leisurely good-bye, like an honored guest lingering at a party reluctant to say adios to the host and the other guests. This dying stuff was all new to me, except for the death of the grandmother on my mother's side when I was still a child, but I had no clue then. Naturally, my over-stimulated brain was pondering death itself, perhaps for the first time seriously. Osvaldo woke up alive this morning. Now he is gone. Where? Like the evaporating steam of Ecclesiastes? Just gone?

I remembered my father saying that death is merely going to sleep without waking up. You don't know that you didn't wake up because your brain has ceased to function. That rather scientific explanation held by my father was fairly reasonable while I was in high school, but after taking all of those courses on religion and encountering so many conflicting views of what happens after death, I was badly confused, and didn't know what to think. I was impressed, though, with the confident faith of the Zapotecs as expressed through their customs. I know that my mind wandered back and forth over the terrain of death for several hours that night, considering the Islamic paradise, the Hindu notion of rebirth, and the Christian concept of bodily resurrection, not just as answers for an exam, but as plausible possibilities for my life after death. Did I resist falling asleep because I was spooked that I wouldn't wake up? I had a terrible time getting to sleep, and just as I did, that resonant church bell would wake me up.

Except, that is, the next morning when I was supposed to awaken and get up. When I opened my eyes, I knew I must be alive. I could see and hear. My brain must be functioning. But what was all that noise? It sounded like a live Mexican band. But where was it? Was Osvaldo still asleep down there on his little mat? I must have overslept.

I jumped up, put on a clean short-sleeve shirt and a pair of khaki pants, slipped on my one pair of actual shoes, and went out to the stairway. From the top I could see a small group of musicians playing a lively tune not far from where Osvaldo was lying on his bed of sand. I raced down the stairs to find Juana. "What is all of this?" I asked her, gesturing at the crowd and the musicians. "Did I miss something?"

"Just breakfast," she said with a twinkle in her eye. "People from the village have come to be with Osvaldo and to celebrate his life."

"They all knew him?"

"Yes, some of them very well through the years. Many remember him as the handsome young man who married beautiful Paulina. He was the head of our household. He sponsored many fiestas."

"I wish I had known him like that."

"He was a different person then. Very lively. Most people here remember him that way."

"How long will these festivities continue?" I asked, not sure about what might come next.

"Until we bury him."

"When will that be?" I expected her to say that it would be in a few days, but she surprised me by saying, "This afternoon. They are digging the grave and finishing the wood coffin now."

I gazed around at the lively party, feeling a little out of place. Or was it the party that was out of place? How could you have a party with a dead person lying right there in the middle of it? Maybe at a fraternity house?

"Get yourself something to eat and drink," Juana said. "The women of the village have brought in some wonderful tamales. Don't miss them." She wandered off to greet some neighbors.

Just then, Brenda came up, nicely dressed and her hair down on her shoulders. "Have you ever seen anything like this?" she whispered. "If this is a funeral, can you imagine what New Year's Eve must be like?"

"It's fascinating, isn't it?"

"A different world. Get some tamales," she urged.

The party continued to a certain point when everyone seemed to understand that it was time to leave. The music stopped, and slowly people made their way out through the door in the front wall. The family was left alone. One by one each family member knelt down next to Osvaldo to say a little prayer and a good-bye. At Brenda's urging, we both participated in this observance as well, as if we were family.

In a few minutes, Francisco, Sabastian, Naxali, and Nacanda came in through the door with the coffin. They stationed themselves at the four corners of the mat and used it to lift Osvaldo gently into the coffin. I found myself holding open the door as they passed out onto the street. Outside, I noticed that the people at the party had never left; they were just standing around outside while the family had its private last moments with Osvaldo.

The men of the family led the way, carrying the coffin at the head of the procession down the Avenida to the cemetery, which lay just beyond the schools. Other members of the extended family followed, then the neighbors, then others from the town who had known Osvaldo. Many of the women were in traditional dress and were carrying flowers. Always flowers, everywhere. The band had assembled again behind the family and was augmented now by additional instruments—several more guitars and trumpets—playing softly now, a mournful tune, but not really a dirge. I noticed how this Mexican music could make me feel sad as well as happy. Brenda and I walked with the family, blending into another culture, not knowing exactly what to do or where we were supposed to be, but trying to fit in without asking or being told.

When we reached the cemetery. The band stopped playing and the crowd coiled around the graveside like a long friendly band of angels. The priest said a few words in Zapotec, and offered a prayer, but others spoke, too. Then the band started playing again and the procession reversed itself, stopping at the door in the wall to enter the courtyard of the deceased. Another party was about to begin.

While others were at the cemetery, some women from the town, a different group of ladies this time, had prepared a grand fiesta. How does all of this happen, unspoken, without direction, without a catering service? Brenda asked if she could help, and with a little guidance from Juana, she found her place.

That night, when we went to our rooms, the party was still continuing down below, and I pulled out my laptop to write down my observations and comments:

Field Notes
Zapotec Society

The formal structure of current Zapotec society, at least in this weaving community, favors men, fathers and sons, as the head of the household and in certain community roles, but the informal structure is definitely dominated by women. Professor Martinez, my anthropology professor, made the distinction between the terms matriarchal and matrifocal, but I realize now that I didn't understand it very well at the time. It appears that this society is matrifocal, where the women are not in charge of a hierarchical system but are communicating behind the scenes to make plans and get things done, not really secretly, but with minimal conversation, and great influence. In Grandpa Osvaldo's funeral, if I can call it that, it was definitely the women who made things happen. The men are brought in for the heavy lifting, to be sure, and they maintain their status and position, but it is the women who do the work and get results.

When social roles are clear and fixed, everyone seems to know what to do. There is very little telling or directing, so Brenda and I were able to blend in or just watch. The children are expected to participate and learn the customs. Learning seems to take place primarily through observation and imitation. Formal instruction by parents appears to be almost entirely replaced by modeling and participation, to the point that there are hardly ever any explanations or directions. I believe we call that learning by doing.

Looking in from outside, as an anthropologist would, I can see the socially-constructed norms and customs, but to this family these are firm beliefs, held over the centuries as true and observed carefully and respectfully. Their beliefs give them order and hope. Does it matter where they come from or if they are actually true? I don't know the answers to those questions; I just know that I am very impressed with how things work here.

The social behavior around Osvaldo's death provides a stark contrast to what I know of the American way of death. In Mexico, death is neither feared nor hidden, but is viewed as a natural process. Maybe this Zapotec community is not only a pleasant place to live, but a good place to die. I hope it will be many years before my parents die.

I slept well that night, perhaps catching up on lost sleep from the night before and resting with greater assurance that I would wake up alive. When I went down into the courtyard, I noticed that no one had swept up the sand. I heard words coming from the kitchen that suggested a strong disagreement in Zapotec between Juana and her mother Magdalena. Juana told me later that the sand was still there to remind everyone of the eight-day journey of Osvaldo's soul to its destination. The sand helped us to remember that he was still traveling. I knew then not to clean up the sacred sand, and I asked Juana if she and her mother were having some disagreement.

"It was about my observance of the eight-day period of mourning after Osvaldo's death. I told her I had responsibilities, and that Francisco and I needed to get you and Brenda downtown to class."

"How did it come out?"

"Well, we compromised. It would only be for this week, Monday and Wednesday, and Guillermo Ortiz would drive you to your classes in his car on those days."

The guy who picked us up at the airport?"

"That's the one." She rolled her eyes in a way that made me think she didn't like him very well.

On Monday morning, after our breakfast, Guillermo was waiting outside the wall for us in his Ford to take us downtown to class. Everyone asked about where Juana was, and Señor Valdez was especially concerned because he wanted to talk to her about something. "Perhaps on Friday," I said and then explained what had happened to her grandfather.

Brenda and I met with our tutoring groups and structured the discussion around Zapotec culture because the students were still talking about the field trip to Monte Albán. Afterward we went out into the Zócalo to kill some time before Guillermo picked us up. It just wasn't the same without Juana, Francisco, and the green bean machine.

"I have an idea," Brenda said. "Let's walk into town to see if we can find Ismael. If you go with me, I wouldn't be unaccompanied."

"Ismael? I thought you had given up on him."

"Well, I have, but not completely. You know, the psychologist in me wants to help. He's so upset."

"Well, okay, I'll go with you, but you know that Francisco thinks the guy is dangerous.

We strolled through some cobblestone streets that were closed to auto traffic but filled with pedestrians peering into shop windows. Along the way, I asked Brenda if she was more interested in psychology or anthropology.

"Both equally. I almost have enough credits of each for a double major. That's what I'm shooting for.

"Tell me what you know about this Ismael. How many times have you seen him?

"Honest? Three. Each time I have met him at the Coffee Beans Café."

"And that's where we are headed now?"

"Straight ahead."

"What's the attraction?"

"Come on, Carl, I'm not really attracted to him," she said, shaking her head vigorously from side to side. "It's his problem that interests me."

"Which is what?"

"He's trapped. He seems caught in some situation, and he really wants to get out. I don't know why he was pouring his heart out to me, but he was."

"Does he live here in Oaxaca?"

"He says he is on an assignment here. His family lives in Jalisco."

"Have you asked him directly about his work?"

"He says it's a business. International commerce. He looks around a lot, as if he's being watched. He just seems very anxious and really wants out. He says it's very dangerous."

I didn't say anything more to Brenda about Ismael, but for sure he sounded like a drug dealer to me. I agreed with Francisco on that.

When we arrived at the Coffee Beans Café, Brenda spotted a waiter who smiled at her, as if he recognized her. "May I help you?" he asked in Spanish.

"I am wondering if Ismael is here."

"Ismael? Ismael who? Oh, Ismael Guzman. No, I haven't seen Ismael all week. Sorry."

We ordered two lattes and sat outside chattering about the funeral, Monte Albán, and how nice the weather was in Mexico. But Ismael never showed. We got back to the plaza just in time to see Guillermo pulling up. Nice enough guy, but without a subject. Silence all the way home.

When I returned to my room that afternoon, I noticed that things were out of place, like someone had been in the room checking things out. I looked for my laptop and it was there, but turned around backwards. I looked in the chest of drawers and nothing was missing, but things were rearranged. A shirt that I remembered hanging over the back of my desk chair, was thrown across the bed. And the blanket, which I pulled up and smoothed out each morning, had wrinkles in it, like someone had been lying there. I went next door to check with Brenda and she was having the same perception: nothing missing, but a lot of things disturbed. We decided to mention this to Juana.

"I'm sure it was Cecelia," Juana said.

"Maybe Naxali or Naconda?" I asked, not wanting to jump to conclusions about Cecelia.

"They would never enter your rooms. No, it was Cecelia. It's part of a pattern."

"What pattern?" Brenda asked.

"Well, I hate to mention this, but last night Cecelia went to our parents and told them that there was romance going on in this house behind their backs. And not just one romance, but two: Juana and Carl and Brenda and Francisco."

"How do you know that she did that?" I asked.

"Because my parents sat me and Francisco down at the round table by the mango tree and asked us."

"Oh, my God," Brenda said. "What did you say?"

"We told them that we had all become very good friends, but that friendship is different from romance."

"In other words," Brenda said, "you lied."

We all laughed at that, taking Brenda's words as joking, until Juana said, "Friendship or romance. I guess that's what we have to figure out." Then she punctuated it with one of her smiles. "But that's why I know it was Cecelia messing with your rooms. Cecelia is a little strange. I guess you know that. But she is my sister. Recently, she has been doing some weird things. Is that the right word, weird?

Brenda and I looked at each other and nodded. Then I said, "From what you have been telling us, yes, I think we would say it's a little weird."

"My parents think that she feels left out and they asked if we could find ways to include her more."

"That could be a challenge," Brenda observed.

"Maybe not," I said.

Brenda and I returned to our rooms, but in a short time I heard a soft knock on my door. I opened it as Brenda said, "Can we talk?"

"Of course, always. Come in."

"What did you think about what Cecelia said to Sebastian and Magdalena?"

"Looks like she is a bit of a troublemaker."

"For sure. And Juana's observation that we have to figure out whether it's friendship or romance?" she asked looking puzzled and uncomfortable.

I didn't respond right away because I knew it was a sensitive issue and Brenda could get badly upset if I said the wrong thing.

"I'm asking, Carl, if you are falling in love with Juana?"

"Well, we have become very close friends. As for love, I don't know very much about it, so I'm not sure that I would recognize it if it was happening." Was I being truthful to her, to myself? "How about you?" I asked.

"How about me what?" Brenda said.

"Are you falling in love with Francisco?"

It was her turn to be silent. Then she said, "I don't know. I like him a lot as a person."

"It's probably not too cool having the two interns fall in love with…"

"I didn't say I was in love."

"Neither did I. But if it were to happen—remember the conditional subjunctive mode—it could cause some complications for the university, for the host family, and…and even for Little Texas College, including your dad."

"Oh, geez, you're right about that," she said, but she seemed to be pondering something else. "Francisco is just so nice to me. He really cares about me."

"I think he really does," I noted.

"And Juana is so cute. I wouldn't blame you if you did."

"Did what?"

"Fell in love."

We both stared off into space for a moment, and then Brenda said, "I just don't know what kind of a girlfriend I'll make." We were both quiet again until finally Brenda said. "If this thing gets serious for either one of us, we can't get all jealous," she said.

"Agreed. Maybe now's the time for us to let go of each other," I said.

She nodded and left the room without a smile. That conversation was supposed to make it easier for us to talk about friendship and romance, but I was pretty sure it wouldn't. Were Brenda's old hang-ups about boyfriends still with her? She seemed pretty confused about Francisco.

I have to admit that Osvaldo's death shook me up a bit. The abstract idea of dying was made very concrete for me with the corpse in the courtyard on a bed of sand. I still wasn't sure what to think about the big philosophical question of life's meaning, but I did remember that I was on an international service term sponsored by Little Texas Collee, and although Brenda and I were definitely being of service as tutors, I needed more to do on Tuesdays and Thursdays than pull weeds with Francisco. Maybe help fight the plague in some way? I had finally met Padre Paulo from the church at Osvaldo's funeral fiesta, and he invited me to stop by sometime, so I did. I told Juana that I wanted to do something that would be of service to the community and took her along with me to help explain that to Padre Paulo in Spanish.

The priest, it turned out, spoke Zapotec and Spanish, read Latin and Greek, and knew a little English, so we settled on speaking Spanish, and Juana helped me out by translating to English what I was missing in Spanish. The priest was a short guy with a round body and round face to match, held together by a clerical collar. He understood immediately that my request was sincere, and I could see him flipping through a mental catalogue of community needs, no doubt something the clergy are well-acquainted with in the rural towns surrounding Oaxaca. After some consideration, he said, "Our greatest need is right here at the pre-school sponsored by the church. It may not be the best use of your talents as a college student from the United States, but we have so many little children, and they need more attention than we can provide. Perhaps you could also work with the volunteer teachers to help them be more creative with the children."

I had never worked with children, and the word teacher made me think of my parents lecturing in the Origins of Life class. It must have another meaning, too. Where was this innocent request for a service opportunity taking me? Into something I knew nothing about? "I'll try," I said. But then I wondered what in the world I was going to do with four- and five-year-old kids. "I mean, I will be happy to help if someone will guide me."

"No, you guide us," Padre Paulo said. "Work here for a few weeks and then come and tell me what we could be doing better."

So, I would be consulting on something I knew nothing about. It happens, I guess.

"Next Tuesday?" Padre Paulo asked.

"Yes, that's fine," I replied, wondering if there really was a God of destiny, who at that moment was guiding me through this priest into a career as a teacher—me who had no idea of what I should become.

On Saturday of that week, having promised myself to spend a little extra time with Juana's sister Cecelia, I slipped a few extra pesos in my pocket and invited her to walk up the Avenida to the Oxxo, a kind of Mexican convenience store, like a US 7-Eleven.

"Without Juana?" she asked.

"Yes, just with you."

"Alone?"

"Is it a problem?"

"No, just a surprise."

Apparently, it was a surprise that made her happy because she had a rare ear-to-ear grin. Had I even seen her smile before that? We passed through the door in the wall and started our walk up to the plaza area. At least I had a chance to practice my Spanish, asking her how many years she had.

"Seventeen," she said, then corrected herself with "in November."

That was six months away and it told me she was sixteen and still in high school. "And how are your studies?" I asked. "How's school?"

"Okay, but I don't care for school," she said. "My parents make me go."

"Do you like weaving?"

"It's my family's work."

"But do you enjoy it?"

"Not really."

"What do you enjoy?" I asked.

"Tamales," she said, and laughed a long, loud silly laugh. "Actually," she said, when she had recovered from her laughing, "I like coloring the wool to get the shades just right from the dye."

"What's your favorite color?" I asked, feeling like I was talking to a pre-school child,

"Cochineal."

Now I felt like the child. What's that?"

"Red."

"Red? You like red?"

"Yes, I like mixing the wool in that deep red color of blood. I like that."

I didn't know what the heck to make of that, so I let it pass. I had never had so much trouble sizing up anyone as I did with Cecelia. Her features weren't bad, and she had a few that reminded me of Juana. But her attitude was so negative that it totally ruined her countenance. She was a teen, but she often spoke with the voice of a little girl. Did she have what they call "developmental delay?" If so, it's getting late for her to be catching up, which makes it more than a delay. As we walked along, I kept waiting for her to initiate some topic of conversation, but she didn't. What was her problem? I was puzzled.

The clerk at the store was dressed in a tan uniform and he seemed to recognize Cecelia right off. He was watching her closely as she moved through the shop, and he gave me some odd glances, too. I found a lot of things that I thought I could use in the pre-school—crayons, colored pencils, paper clips, glue, three by five cards—and I bought some without any real plan for what I was going to do with them. Then I asked Cecelia, "Would you like something?" She shook her head no, but then I asked again, "I would like to buy you something. What will it be?"

She started scurrying through the narrow aisles of the store like a rat in a maze looking for the cheese. The shopkeeper watched her closely. Was she a chronic shoplifter? She returned and stood by my side, holding up an old-fashioned, tall, skinny, blond Barbie Doll. I wondered if this was what Brenda looked like to her. I hoped she wouldn't stick pins in it. "Your parents won't mind?" I asked.

"My parents won't know. I'll hide it." She seemed pleased that she had come up with a present that no one else would buy for her.

I paid for everything and we started out into the plaza where Cecelia spotted a street vendor selling drinks from a small metal cart that had been wheeled over the cobblestone street to this particular spot in front of the church. Cecelia took me by the elbow and pulled me over to the stand. "You must have one of these. It's called horchata, and it's a specialty of this region. They are delicious."

"I'm okay," I said, "but I'll get one for you if you'd like one."

"No, for you. I have my own money. See." She pulled some pesos from her pocket. Bills and coins. "I want to buy something for you now. I insist."

Before I knew what had happened, Cecelia had completed the transaction with exact change and in fluent Zapotec. She insisted on carrying my sack of purchases from the Oxxo so that I could hold my drink and enjoy it. I tasted it and she was right: it was delicious. It tasted good because the sun was hot and the afternoon was warm, so a cool drink was refreshing that day. Suddenly, Cecelia took my free hand. Had she seen Juana holding my hand like that? Or did she just want to see what it was like to hold an American hand? It seemed inappropriate, but I let her continue until we came to the door in the wall. Without noticing, I had finished the entire drink, including the melting ice.

In my room, an hour later, I was fighting nausea. I lost that fight quickly and in fifteen minutes, I was also losing the battle with diarrhea. The attacks at both ends were more severe and frequent than any I had ever had in my short life. Brenda must have heard me puking and pooping and knocked on my door, but I shot out past her in a desperate flight toward the bathroom. I took some Imodium, and she stayed with me until the diarrhea attacks subsided, but then she noticed me sweating. She felt my forehead and said, "You're burning up. I'll get Juana."

When Juana arrived, she asked me how I felt, and when I told her, she said, "We need to move you to the courtyard."

"Why?" I asked, nearly screaming, freaking out as I pictured that pile of sand.

"For fresh air. Sunshine. Where we can give you the proper attention."

I had always thought that intestinal sickness was a private matter, even a little shameful and embarrassing, but if that's where she wanted me, out there in front of the whole family, that's what I would need to do. I felt a little dizzy going down the stairs, but she and Brenda steadied me, and soon I found myself lying on a portable cot, not far from—you guessed it—Osvaldo's bed of sand. Would they bring in fresh sand if I died? Seriously, as sick as I was, I felt I could croak at any minute. When they helped me onto the cot, I was just glad to be horizontal, and suddenly I felt very sleepy. Juana opened my shirt and bathed my forehead, neck, and shoulders with hand towels soaked in cold water. "I worry about this high fever," she said.

I must have slept, and when I was awake again, Juana was beside me asking if I could hold a thermometer in my mouth. The reading must have been shocking because I heard the family shouting at each other in three languages, apparently not in agreement about what to do about me. I was burning up and I remembered those sports clips on TV where the winning coach is doused with a huge bucket of Gator-aide, and I thought that would feel pretty good right now. It might at least save Juana and Brenda the work of providing a constant supply of cold wet towels. I drifted in and out of sleep, trying to piece together a discussion that was being held about me as if I wasn't there.

"I'm worried about his fever." I thought it was Magdalena's voice, but in Spanish.

Abuela Paulina said something that ended in the word curandera.

"He won't like that," Juana said. "He will think it is a witch doctor."

"Better than the priest for last rites." That sounded like something Brenda would say, thinking I was asleep.

"Maybe it was the sudden change of temperature today. It was very hot this afternoon." Was that Magdalena?

"I saw him walking with Cecelia," Brenda said.

"Cecelia?" Juana asked, alarm in her voice. Then she screamed out, "Cecelia, get out here this minute.

"Shh!" someone said. You'll wake him up.

It did awaken me more, and I tried to sit up and couldn't, but I did rouse myself enough to say, "She bought me a horchata."

"Oh, my God. Where?" Juana asked.

"At this little stand by the church," I managed to whisper.

At that moment, Cecelia arrived. "Did someone call me?" she asked with that high voice of an innocent child.

"Did you buy Carl a horchata at Señor Pepe's stand? You know we don't do that." Juana's voice grew louder. I'd never heard her speak sternly like that before. "Americans have very sensitive stomachs." She was screaming now. "Were you so jealous you tried to kill him?"

"And are you so in love with him that you dare to accuse me of that?" I knew that was the high-pitched voice of Cecelia.

Brenda said in a calm voice, "Now that we know what it is, maybe I should run up to the clinic and get a doctor to prescribe an antibiotic.

Somehow, I managed to sit up and say, "That sounds like a really good idea." Then I flopped down again and must have fallen asleep, apparently for a long time, because it was dark when I awakened next.

I opened my eyes. The moonlit courtyard was still, not a sound of anything, not even the peeping of birds. It took me a moment to realize where I was and why I was there. Was I alone? I glanced to my right and there was Juana in a chair beside me gazing down into my eyes with a tender expression. "I think the antibiotic is working," she said. "The fever is breaking."

I hadn't remembered taking any pills, but I nodded in agreement. She smiled. That smile would cure a leper. Maybe raise someone from the dead.

By Sunday afternoon, I was feeling better, but weak. Juana told me to stay home from tutoring on Monday and said she had already told Padre Paulo I would miss Tuesday and would begin my work in the pre-school on Thursday if I was fully recovered.

I needed to get my digestive system working again, and for that Abuela Paulina made me some delicious chicken soup. Then Juana fixed some toast with guava jelly. By Sunday evening, I was back upstairs in my room.

Brenda stopped in after class on Monday to tell me that everyone missed me and hoped I was feeling better.

"By the way," I asked, "How sick was I?"

"On a scale of one to ten, I would say you were about a nine."

"Could I have died?"

"If it got worse, perhaps without the antibiotic. Yeah, that's why they were so worried about controlling that high fever."

"I had good care," I said.

"Especially from that little dark-eyed nurse with the cute smile," Brenda teased. "She stayed up the whole night with you. I think she really loves you."

"Really? More than a friend?"

"Yes, more than a friend."

That's all that was said and Brenda went back to her room.

After watching the services for Osvaldo and then having a near-death experience myself, I began to do some serious thinking about living and dying. I remembered talking to Marv about "suicidal thoughts" in my first year and then studying later on about how suicide is the only logical answer to an absurd world. Well, I have to tell you, that after being that sick, drifting in and out of conscious awareness with that high fever, I had no interest in suicide. Not waking up in the morning? Non-being? No way! I felt damn lucky to be alive and I couldn't wait to get on with my life, whatever it was going to be.

On Thursday, I walked up to the church and found the room where the pre-school meets. The class is in the refectory—we would say dining hall—of the old convent, a cavernous room filled with straight rows of unmatched, low oblong tables and a conglomeration of child-sized chairs. It looked like a gathering of elves in a medieval castle and was certainly unlike any idea of pre-school or kindergarten that I could recall. The children's voices echoed off of stone walls, tile floors, and the vaulted wood ceiling, but there was no shouting or screaming. My first impression was of a really strict classroom, like a military school, more conducive to order than creativity.

I loved the children immediately although it took some time for them to like me. The boys were dressed in denim pants and white t-shirts and the girls wore cotton dresses in pastel shades. The children looked similar enough to call their outfits uniforms, and of course they all had uniformly dark eyes, shiny black hair, and copper-colored skin. How was I going to tell them apart? For sure, there were no blue-eyed, Barbie doll blonds in this school. I watched them for a few minutes, wondering what to do.

I knew I had to get down to their level to interact with them, but I was afraid that if I sat on one of their chairs, I would smash it. What were they speaking? Zapotec, of course, but also some Spanish. Bi-lingual pre-school kids? Maybe I could practice my Spanish on them. The children looked up at me half-curious, half-scared from their tables like I was some gigantic outer-space alien. It was the first time that I had thought my height was a handicap. I decided to kneel down on one knee next to a sweet little girl seated at her table, but when I put my arm around the back of her chair, she looked up, screamed, jumped to her feet, toppled over her chair, and ran straight for the arms of one of the volunteer teachers for a comforting hug. Then she just stared at me, terrified, trying not to cry.

"Está bien," the little boy next to her said to her, setting up her chair and pointing to it. "Usted siéntese aquí."

"¿Hablas español?" I asked.

"Sí."

"Zapotec?"

"Zapotec," he said in a Zapotec accent.

"English?" I asked.

"A little," he answered in English.

I had made my first friend, Miguel, who I found out later was the mayor's son. With the help of the volunteer teachers, I made it through the morning.

That afternoon, I went to my computer and undertook an online search to try to learn something about pre-school education. I discovered a huge professional field called Early Childhood Education and noticed that many experts had studied it and written about it, and that there were a lot of different philosophies and theories about how young children learn and what type of teaching they need to be able to succeed. I stumbled onto a Wikipedia article on Montessori schools and a theory of early childhood development by Maria Montessori, an Italian physician and educator of children with special needs. Her philosophy seemed a bit abstract, but what I took from it was the idea of free activity within a prepared environment. Give the kids a lot of stuff to manipulate and experiment with so they can explore the world and use their imagination.

So, I started collecting stuff and just threw it in my backpack. On the following Tuesday, I showed up with some raw wool, paints, paper, ears of dried corn, chicken bones, nuts in the shell, pieces of cloth, and flowers. And, of course, I had those things I had purchased at the Oxxo. I would put out one thing at a time on their little tables, and when they got tired of that I would collect it and put out something else in its place. The other teachers looked a little bewildered, but they got into it, too, asking the kids a lot of what-if questions, and the little kids seemed to enjoy it. Gradually, over the next few days, we were able to focus some of that exploration on learning shapes and sizes and colors, and even numbers. I was having a lot of fun with these kids, and Miguel, the mayor's son, became a kind of self-appointed assistant to me as he helped pass things out and collect them back up again.

I felt fully recovered from my serious illness, and I had joined the others again to drive into Oaxaca in the green bean machine to tutor the English language students. On the following Wednesday morning, while Brenda and I were finishing up our breakfast at the little table in the kitchen, I glanced through the open door and noticed Francisco striding across the courtyard with a newspaper in his hand. It was not his habit to be reading a newspaper in the morning, so there must have been some special news in it today.

"Where did you get the newspaper, Francisco?" Juana asked.

"I bought it up at the Oxxo. I was just buying some stuff I needed, and the headline jumped out at me, so I picked up a copy. I thought our two guests might be interested." He nodded at me and Brenda and placed the front page of the paper before us. The headline read: FATHER AND SON MURDERED. Drug dealers from Jalisco were found…

Brenda grabbed the paper and started reading, as Francisco said, "See, it happens."

"Oh, no," she said, "this is horrible. It's Ismael. Ismael and his father"

"You knew them?" Francisco said, looking confused.

"Well, yes and no." She brushed away a tear and said to Francisco. "You met him. He's the one with the fine clothes and rings. Remember? I was trying to help him. He was trying to escape his horrible life."

"Oh, I'm sorry," Francisco said. "I didn't know he was the one who was killed. I was just bringing the newspaper headline to make a point about going into the city alone."

"Don't say I told you so," Brenda said.

"No, nothing like that. If I had known that's who it was, I wouldn't have broken the news like this. Honest. I'm really sorry."

"Believe me, Francisco," Brenda pleaded, "I was just trying to help the guy. To listen to him. To help him think about a way out. Nothing more. Now look what's happened to him. And his father, too."

Francisco put a hand on Brenda's shoulder and looked up at Juana as if to ask for help in finding the right words.

"We are both really sorry," she said, nodding her head up and down. "We lead a very sheltered life here in the village, but Francisco is right when he tells you that Mexico can be violent and dangerous."

10

Falling In Love and Struggling With a Divided Heart

Mom's new half-sister. An offer to stay through the summer. The family discussion. Juana's deal. A job posting. My dilemma. Moonlight at Mitla. Mural painting and a science lesson at pre-school. A night out at the tavern, discussing virginity. The legend of the Zapotec princess. Emails from Marv and Mom. Brenda's decision. So easy to talk with Juana.

I had been corresponding by email with my parents, usually on a Sunday night, once every two weeks, mainly to assure them that everything was going okay with my stay in Mexico. As usual, I wasn't very communicative, keeping the correspondence on a fairly brief and shallow level, leaving out a lot of things that might be upsetting or require a lot of explanation, such as Osvaldo's fiesta, the murder of the drug dealer Ismael and his father, my near-death high-fever illness, teaching pre-school in a Catholic church, and my unexpected but growing friendship with Juana. Over the years, as I have explained, my parents made many selective omissions in what they chose to tell me—like my father wasn't really my father—so I didn't feel particularly guilty leaving out certain things when I emailed them. I have chosen to omit these superficial exchanges here, though I still have the emails. One email from Mom, however, deserves inclusion in my story. It was about the family heritage on my mother's side.

Brenda had heard weeks ago from her mom about their DNA testing, and she told me immediately that the results showed that the common DNA with her mother established that she was not adopted. That was a relief to her, but she was still haunted by thoughts of her stillborn sister.

When I hadn't heard from my mom, I began to wonder if Mom was not my actual biological mother. That would mean that I had neither a mother nor a father. How could that be? Why hadn't she shared the results with me?

When I finally received a rather astounding email from her, I printed it out, and after the others had gone to bed, I went into Brenda's room and read it to her.

Dear Carl,

I should have told you earlier that our DNA tests, yours and mine, came out fine. Yes, the little egg that grew into my baby boy was really mine and we are related by blood as mother and son. Please excuse my delay in reporting this, but the explorations of my own ancestry produced some surprising results which the scientist in me had to pursue.

I won't go into the details of how I discovered what I did, but it turned out that besides me, there was another child who shared DNA with me. I had not known of this older sibling, so the search began. I flew to Minnesota during spring break to see what my father knew about this and to try to locate birth records.

"Here we go," Brenda said. "Now she has to deal with family secrets. Read on."

When I discovered a certificate of birth for a girl three years older than I, registered with my mother's maiden name at the county courthouse, I asked my father, your grandpa Anders, what he knew. At first, he was reluctant to speak, saying he couldn't remember, but when I showed him the evidence, he changed his story, saying that it was probably okay to tell me, now that his wife (my mother) had passed away. He said that she had told him the truth on condition that he would never ever tell anyone else.

"At least not until they were mature enough to handle it, right? Maybe there is a genetic predisposition to keeping secrets in your family. Sorry. What did she find out?"

What my father told me was that before he met my mother, she had been raped by a hired hand who worked on the farm where she lived. She had the baby and put it up for adoption. My mother told this to my father right before they were to be married. It was a huge shock, of course, for him to learn this, but they were so in love that they went ahead with the marriage anyway, which was happy and fruitful, producing another child, which is me. While I was visiting in Minnesota, I began the process of trying to discover the whereabouts of my older half-sister, born before my parents were married. Naturally, I was very annoyed that no one had told me about this.

"Annoyed?" Brenda said. "Now she's finding out just how annoying it is to be the victim of family secrets. I'm sorry, Carl, I know she's your mother, and I shouldn't be saying these things, but you shouldn't have had to go through what you did."

"Or you either," I said, "I have to tell you, Brenda, it's really been pleasant living here in Mexico with this lovely family, not having to think about my own. But let me finish."

It will take some time to do that tracing to find my half-sister, and we may never be successful. Nonetheless, I must try. I feel compelled to know, and I understand better now your desire to discover your actual ancestry. I can assure you of one thing; there will never be any more family secrets between us. You have my word.

With love and understanding,

Mom

P.S. I asked my father what happened to the rapist and he said that as far as he knew, nothing. He skipped town.

Brenda shook her head back and forth over and over. "And so it goes," she said. "Men seeking their own pleasure in women and getting away with it."

"It's terrible, isn't it?"

"Actually, it's terrifying. Let's hope this is the end of the story for you and your family now, Carl. I mean, really, what more can be discovered about a sperm donor?"

On the first Friday of May, after the Cinco de Mayo holiday, Señor Valdez called Juana, Brenda, and me into his office for a private conversation. He was very direct, and he just said, "At my request, the University has approved the extension of the internship positions through the summer term. You, Brenda and Carl, are invited to stay on through the end of August, and you, Juana, may ask your parents if they are willing to continue to provide housing and transportation as hosts under the same financial arrangements. I hope you will give it serious consideration," he said, turning to Brenda and me. "The summer term is very busy for us, and we need your help." Brenda and I just stared at each other, not knowing what to say. I could see that she was struggling to conceal a smile of inward happiness.

Then I said to Professor Valdez, "I want to make sure you know how much we have enjoyed our tutoring with you and our living arrangements in Teotitlán del Valle. It has been a wonderful experience for us."

He smiled and said, "If you stay, it will surely help me out, but also give you and Juana and Brenda and Francisco a chance to get better acquainted."

Oh, my gosh. Why did he link us together like that? Did he know? How would he know? Was he trying to be a matchmaker? If he knew, then he must also have known that his offer would be very disturbing to the family. The last thing in the world they needed was more time for their son and daughter to get better acquainted with the American interns.

When something you had vaguely dreamed about suddenly becomes possible, there is a tendency, you know, after initial rejoicing, to wonder if what you had hoped for is really a good idea or not. Now I had a huge conflict between wanting to remain in Mexico to build my friendship with Juana, and needing to return home to Texas to finish my college degree, which was surely what my parents would expect.

On the following Monday, after we arrived home from classes, Juana suggested that we go for a little walk, down past the public schools toward the cemetery.

"Have you told your parents about the offer from the university?" I asked.

"That's why we are out here walking, so I can tell you about that."

"And..."

"In the early evening after dinner on Saturday, when you guys had gone to your rooms, the family was sitting at the round table under the mango tree, and Francisco was with us. That's when I explained to Mom and Dad about the offer for the interns to stay through the summer. They were taken by surprise, unable to hide their concern, and everything became quiet until our father spoke first. He said he was worried about the friendships that had developed. I admitted that the interns had become our good friends, and Francisco agreed, saying it was a natural result of being together, taking good care of them, and seeing that they were happy.

Then my mother spoke up, calm but firm. You know how she is. She wanted to know if our friendships had become romantic, you know, like Cecelia had told her. So I said, 'You mean with Brenda and Francisco?' And Francisco said, 'Or did you mean Juana and Carl?' It was pretty stupid of us, because my father picked right up on it and pointed out that we seemed to be admitting that there was at least some element of romance for both of us. Then Francisco said, 'But we aren't doing anything wrong.' Then my father said, 'But are you admitting that romance could be a possibility?' So I answered with the most respectful voice I could find, 'We are not experienced in matters of romance. Perhaps you could advise us.' 'Well,' my father said, 'our parents decided things like that for us. Your grandparents brought us together, and we are grateful that we were able to develop a love for each other.' Then my mother said, 'Today, young people want to fall in love first and then get married. It seems backwards to us and that they make a lot of bad choices.'"

"I was afraid this conversation wasn't going the right way, so I said, 'If Brenda and Carl could stay a little longer, maybe we could discover whether we are anything more than just good friends.' That sparked a long wandering discussion."

Juana and I had walked as far as the cemetery while she had been telling me this, and we had stopped to decide whether we should go further or turn around and go back. "But what happened?" I asked Juana. "Did they accept the university's offer to the host family, or not?"

"I'm getting to that," Juana said, "but there is more to the story. Let's go into the cemetery here and follow this path past grandpa's grave and the markers of my ancestors to a private little stone bench that I know about back in there. I can tell you the rest there."

So that's what we did, stepping respectfully around the graves, and when we were seated side by side on the bench, with a beautiful view overlooking the valley, Juana continued. "We were getting nowhere when

Abuela Paulina came hobbling across the courtyard with her cane. She told us she felt like she was being left out of an important family meeting. My father invited her to join in, helped her get seated, and told her about the offer from the university. He expressed concern about the friendships developing between Juanita and Carl and Francisco and Brenda. 'Yes,' Paulina said, 'they have all become quite wonderful friends, haven't they?' And my mother said, 'Maybe more than friends. What if they are falling in love?' Paulina smiled and continued, 'Oh, you know young people, they fall in love one day and fall out of love the next. Have you forgotten that you both thought you were in love with someone else when Osvaldo and I brought you together?'

There was a hushed silence. Francisco and I glanced at each other and tried not to smile. I think my parents were a little embarrassed. Then Paulina added, 'The times are very different today.' My father said, 'But mother, don't you understand what this could mean for our community if these friendships are allowed to continue? Brenda could take Francisco back to the United States with her, and look what that would do to our weaving business, the farm, the family.' But Paulina had an answer for him. She said, 'Oh, I don't think Brenda would do that. She likes it here. I'm even teaching her about Zapotec cooking.' Then my mother said, 'Well, it looks like you have become good friends, too.' And Paulina said, 'Of course, who could not become friends with Brenda?' And Francisco said, 'Apparently me.'"

Poor Francisco. Juana and I had to laugh quietly about that back there in the silence of the cemetery, knowing that Osvaldo's remains were not far from us.

"But then my father said, 'What about Juanita? Do you think she is in love with Carl?' And Abuela Paulina said, 'In love? My gracious, you will need to ask her about that. I know she is very devoted to him after he got so sick with that high fever.' But then my mother said, 'Do you think Juanita will go off with Carl to live in the United States?' And Paulina replied, 'Well, yes, Carl or someone else. You know our little Juanita. She wants to see the world and that's what she will do anyway, so wouldn't we all prefer that it be with a handsome and responsible young man like Carl rather than someone she finds on the street in California?' It got quiet again until Paulina said, 'You will accept the offer to let Brenda and Carl stay, won't you?' We sat through a long silence and I started to get really nervous. Finally, my father said that he would accept the offer from

Professor Valdez, but with a condition. I was pleased with the decision, but I didn't want to hear that condition. 'What is it?' I asked. Then he said, 'We want you to meet some men from our community. We have accepted a formal offer for you to have dinner with one of them.' I knew I didn't want to know, but I asked, 'Who?' They said it was Guillermo Ortiz. Can you believe this? 'Where?' I asked. 'In downtown Oaxaca at the restaurant in the Hotel Quinta Real,' my mother said. Oh, man, I was in a mess. I had to think fast. Suddenly I got a terrific idea. 'I accept, if both interns get to stay, but I have a condition, too, well, not a condition but a request. I don't know this guy very well, so I will need a chaperone. I want Francisco to come with me.' As you might guess, Francisco was not happy about that at all, spending an evening chaperoning me with his amigo."

I was taking it all in as Juana was telling me what happened, and I said, "I can't believe you did that. To Francisco? Your brother? You can really be a little devil."

"Only when I'm trapped," she said. "But don't worry about the dinner with Guillermo. I have no interest in him at all. Pardon the expression, but he has the mind of a lizard. I thought it was the least I could do to help you guys stay through the summer if you want to do that. I'll bring you some churros. Then she hit me with that smile, and I knew everything would be okay.

That night I told Brenda about the deal to extend our stay with the host family, and we laughed a lot as I recounted, as best I could, Juana's report. Brenda was really pleased, and said, "Thank God for Abuela Paulina. She's such a dear old lady."

Juana told me you are learning how to cook Zapotec food from her.

"Oh, yeah, on Tuesdays, Francisco drops us off at the market and we shop. Then we come home and I watch while she shows me what to do and chatters away at me in Zapotec."

"What do you cook?'

"The things you eat on Tuesday nights. We made amarillo con pollo, that tasty chicken dish with cumin and chili sauce; picadillo, a spiced shredded pork stuffing for chili rellenos; and coloradito, chicken in red chili and tomato sauce. Remember them? Paulina is a wonderful teacher. This Tuesday we will make Oxaqueño, a dark mole sauce, Oaxaca's most famous food."

"So you are turning into a little Zapotec housewife." I knew I shouldn't have said that, but Brenda just shrugged. "Let's say I'll be ready if anything develops. If not, I've got more material for my Independent Study in anthropology on Zapotec culinary culture."

On Friday afternoon, after we finished our tutoring in downtown Oaxaca, Brenda and Juana and I sat down in the sun on the steps of the old church near the Zócolo. Brenda seemed very anxious to tell us some news. "Listen, you two, I need to tell you what just happened. Señor Valdez invited me into his office and showed me this." She held up a piece of paper so we could see.

"What is it? Tell us," Juana said.

"A job posting."

"Where?" I asked.

"At the Monte Albán Museum for an assistant curator. Two days a week."

"Starting when?" I asked, thinking it would be in the fall.

"Now," she said, "starting now, Tuesdays and Thursdays. Señor Valdez says he thinks I would have a good chance to get it. He says he's already told them about me."

"That's great," Juana said.

"Congratulations," I said. Then I began to deal with all of the implications bouncing around in my head. She would definitely want to extend her internship through the summer now. In fact, if she didn't have the teaching internship, she could probably just stay for the job, I mean, a paying job at a museum. But would she want to stay through the fall? Live here permanently? Become a Zapotec housewife and museum curator? Finish her degree online? Could she even do that? Was she testing herself?

I knew that Juana was having similar thoughts, and we exchanged knowing glances. Then I said, "That's really a nice opportunity, Brenda." But I thought about her parents back at Little Texas College and her dad urging me to watch out for her. What would he think about this now? Then I said, as gently as possible, "At some point we need to share some of this with our parents and ask their permission—"

"I don't plan to ask their permission," Brenda said firmly, shaking her head from side to side. "I plan to tell them what I have done after I get the job and accept it."

That evening, after we arrived home, Brenda went straight to her room, no doubt to work on her resumé and letter of application, but Juana and I lingered in the courtyard for a while to drink fresh fruit drinks from a can and share our feelings about the future.

"Were you surprised," I asked her, "about what Brenda said about telling her parents?"

"Yes, a little. I disagree with my parents on some things, but I always try to respect them and keep them informed. On certain matters, I still feel that I need their permission."

"It is really nice that you are making it possible for us to stay through the summer, but I have to tell you that I am really confused about whether I should stay or go home. I've never met anyone like you, Juana, and I want to stay here to get to know you better and have more fun with you. But I am very close to finishing my college degree, so that if I go home, work hard, and take some extra courses this summer and fall, I think I might be able to graduate by December. Then I will be free to do what I want and be who I choose to be. But I hate to leave you."

"How do you call that?' she asked. "A divided heart?"

"Actually, a broken heart that is tearing itself apart over you."

"Oh, don't let that happen. There's no need to suffer. The future is in God's hands, and if we are meant to be together, we will be. So don't worry."

"I really admire your faith and the trust you have in the future. It helps me relax, but I'm still very nervous and confused about what to do."

"It's okay," she said. Then taking my hand in her two hands she said, "Let's just enjoy the days we have together now."

On Tuesday night, after a chicken dinner with the famous Oaxaqueño mole sauce prepared by Paulina and Brenda, Francisco suggested that the four of us sneak away on a little excursion to Mitla. "There's nothing like Mitla in the moonlight and tonight there's a full moon."

I had heard of Mitla, but I wasn't sure what it was or where it was.

"The ruins?" Brenda said. "You know me, I'll visit ruins any time of day or night, but what's so special about Mitla in the moonlight?'

"You'll see," Francisco told her.

So we all piled into the green bean machine and drove off to Mitla, which turned out to be not very far away at all. Why hadn't we been here before? "What's Mitla?" I asked as we arrived.

"I'll give the explanation," Juana told Francisco, "but it's going to be in English.

"Go ahead, sis."

"Mitla is another set of ruins, not nearly as big as Monte Albán, and not nearly as old, thriving somewhere between one thousand and fifteen hundred A.D. The word Mitla comes from the ancient Mictlan, meaning the place of death."

"Sounds scary," I said. "Will we see any ghosts?"

"The spirits of our ancestors are always around," Juana explained. "We just don't see them. What you will see is some old stone buildings with small courtyards, a church, and the remains of a long wall that enclosed some small sleeping rooms."

"They had walls, like yours?" Brenda asked.

"Same idea. At its peak it had ten thousand inhabitants. But the interesting thing about Mitla is the designs cut into stone. You'll see them even at night with this moon."

When we had arrived, Francisco parked the van on the street. No entrance fee, no guides, no tourists. We just walked in. It was empty and quiet, isolated and insulated from the street noise. The full moon brought a strong, clear light, illuminating the buildings in shades of tan and gray, creating a special atmosphere both eerie and peaceful. As we moved into one of the open courtyards, Juana pointed up at the decorative friezes at the tops of the still-standing walls.

"Do you see anything familiar?" Juana asked.

I looked up and it hit me immediately: these were the designs used in the weaving of many of the rugs and blankets.

"Oh, my God," Brenda said, "you use these designs. Look how they stand out in this moonlight."

Right there in front of us were the repeating patterns borrowed for the rugs: stair steps, boxes like a maze, and triangles, lots of triangles in different positions, stacked or adjacent, sometimes forming or surrounding diamond shapes.

"All in stone," Brenda continued. "That would be so hard to do without modern power tools. I can see the workers up there on their wooden scaffolds, tapping away with a rock hammer on some kind of iron chisel, chipping at the stone." Francisco was helping her learn some new words in Spanish as she gestured and pointed at the designs. "I can picture the people working here and walking around in these courtyards."

"Maybe not so different from our little town today," he said.

"It's so romantic," Brenda clasped her own shoulders with both hands.

Suddenly, Francisco grabbed her hand and they started off in a different direction.

"Let them be," Juana said. "We'll go this way."

She led me off into another courtyard of more stone walls with designs at the top. "Your family is very clever at adapting these designs" I said.

"That's my father. Other members of the community turn to him for ideas. But borrowing ideas from Mitla has been going on for years, maybe centuries."

We came upon a long wall with three doors, actually just archways now, leading into three small rooms. "And what will we find if we go through these doors?" I asked.

"We never know until we try," she said. As we walked through the arch and into the first room, she positioned herself at the opposite wall, leaned back against it, and looked up at me with coy innocence and said, "If you want to kiss me tonight, this would be a good time and place." Then she smiled that smile, and who could resist that? We stood there kissing for quite a while actually, our bodies pressing against each other, our lips shifting to new positions, and we both got really excited. Then Juana said, "We better stop. I just wanted to find out what it would be like to have you kiss me. Did you like it?"

I just nodded. She knew my answer. I took her hand and we walked to the next archway and entered that room, and then the next, stopping for a few kisses in each room. By then I was completely out of my mind with love for her. So this was moonlight at Mitla. As for Brenda and Francisco, we had to wait for them for quite a while to come back to the van. Was Brenda getting over her dislike of physical contact with men? Or was she resisting the advances of Francisco? And would I ever know?

My days were divided between tutoring, my primary assignment, and working with the little children at the pre-school, but I had trouble keeping my mind on what I was doing at both jobs after moonlight at Mitla. How could I forget that? The children had learned to trust my blue eyes and not be afraid of my size, and I grew to love them because they were so darn cute. As an alternative to coloring-book activities, I established "free drawing" time, so that they could use their imagination to alter the shape or size of an object and give it a color other than its natural color, like a purple dog the size of a horse. Maybe like a Chagall or Picasso? They loved to break the rules when they were encouraged to do so.

One day, on the outskirts of town, I found a large piece of left-over drywall board near a construction site. Francisco helped me put it in the van and bring it to the school. We propped it up so that it wouldn't fall and gave each table of children the task of painting a designated part of it, turning it into a cooperative mural. The volunteer teachers were amazed at how well it progressed and praised the students for their good work. When it was finished, one of the teachers found Padre Paulo and invited him to come and see the mural the children had painted. He was impressed and pleased. Was mural painting in the genes of Mexican children? My parents, of course, would say no, but there did appear to be a culture of Mexican mural painting that even little children could pick up from their surroundings. After all, there were murals in the nave of the church, in the entry to the refectory, and occasional murals here and there on the walls around town that they couldn't help noticing as they walked to and from school. With so many walls, who could resist painting them?

Miguel, the mayor's son, who helped me distribute and collect the materials I brought to class, came up to me one day with a large jar, and when I asked him what was in it, he said, "Bugs."

"Where did you get them?" I asked in English.

"Collected them." Then he looked up at me with his big brown eyes and said, "Can we use them today? They're all dead."

That turned into a science lesson. He distributed a few insects to each table, and I gave instructions in Spanish to examine them carefully, describe and count the parts, and figure out how they could eat, walk, fly, and protect themselves. That was an interesting lesson: observing, counting, making hypotheses, and interpreting—the basic elements of science, or any other discipline for that matter. I was surprised to see how young children could do, almost instinctively, what I had struggled to learn in college. During "free drawing" on that day, the children were asked to imagine and draw an unusual insect with their crayons, and they came up with a lot of big scary creatures. When we were finished, Miguel collected his bugs and put them back in their jar. Oh, man, how was I going to leave this town, this school, these kids?

On Friday night, Francisco invited the four of us to go together to

Pepe's Taberna for drinks and something to eat. Juana and I were reluctant, but then Francisco said, "Come on, you guys, you can't go back to Texas without having a little tequila." I wanted to tell him that Texas had plenty of tequila of its own, imported directly from Mexico, but he insisted that Juana and I join them. By now the town had grown accustomed to seeing the brother and sister out with the Americans, and Francisco made it clear that he really didn't care what anyone thought about that. I could tell that Juana was not very enthusiastic about going to Pepe's, but she gave in. "Okay, sometimes they have good music," she agreed.

Pepe's Taberna is four blocks from the center of town on a cobblestone street that soon turns into a dirt road with a few small houses, but seeming to be leading to nowhere. Everyone in town appears to know where Pepe's is located, and that night the place was jammed. Most of the seating is outdoors under flowering, sweet-smelling shade trees, and the tables are separated from the street by a black wrought iron fence. Soft light comes from colored bulbs strung along the top of that fence and in the low-hanging branches of the trees. A small mariachi band provides peppy songs that everyone seems to know, interspersed with an occasional tragic love song with a woman belting out high notes that I swear could break a water glass.

Francisco ordered four tequilas, and when they arrived, Juana pushed hers in front of her brother, who insisted that I at least taste a little. I took a few sips and pushed mine over to Brenda. They would take care of the tequila while Francisco tried to respond to Brenda's request, "Tell me about Zapotec marriage traditions." He looked a little surprised until she said, "Nothing personal. I might be asked about that if I'm interviewed by the museum director."

"Oh, okay. Are you talking about ancient or modern? I don't know about ancient, and modern gets all mixed up with Spanish traditions, so all I can do is tell you about one of the customs I know about. It's a little unpleasant, though. Are you sure you want to hear this?" He made a face to match the question.

I didn't know what to expect, so how could I object, but Juana seemed to know what was coming and said, "Maybe not out here, Francisco. Let's just enjoy the music." Just then our order of shrimp ceviche arrived with a stack of tortillas and four plates.

Then Brenda said, "Well, if we are talking about marriage customs, it can't be so hugely unpleasant, but if it is, you can blame me for asking."

"Well, I'll tell you about the local tradition, but not everyone—in fact, hardly anyone— practices it anymore. Let's say only some do."

"What?" Brenda asked. "Just tell us."

Now, Francisco was looking a little nervous as he began, with his sister sitting right there across from him. "Well, first of all, a man is supposed to marry a virgin."

"Even if he isn't one himself?" Brenda asked, but it was more of a statement than a question.

"Well, yes," Francisco replied, "there's been a double standard but things have changed recently."

"How?"

"Well, in the idea about having to marry a virgin."

"Why? Because they are in such short supply?" Then Brenda slammed a hand over her mouth. "I'm sorry. I won't interrupt anymore. Just tell us about the old tradition."

"The couple would be married at the church," Francisco continued, "but they didn't go off on a honeymoon, you know, like the Americans go on a cruise to Acapulco or something like that. No, the couple stays somewhere right here in the village."

I noticed beads of sweat forming on Francisco's forehead, and he took out a clean white handkerchief, but didn't use it, as I thought he would, to blot his forehead. He just held it in his hand as he continued the explanation.

"On the wedding night, the bride and groom go off by themselves to a little nearby hotel. After a short time, the groom emerges with a blood-stained handkerchief and walks through the streets waving the handkerchief over his head."

"Gross," Brenda shouted out in English. "How completely disgusting!"

People at other tables were staring at us now. Juana looked very uncomfortable. Francisco had covered his face with the handkerchief so that just his eyes were peering out over the top of it. Then he shrugged and said to Brenda, "You wanted to know. Now you know."

Brenda and Francisco appeared to be enjoying their tequila, which seemed to be having its usual effect. She had been nodding her head back and forth for a while, as if she wanted to say something more. Finally, she said, "What is this obsession with virginity?"

"I don't know," Francisco said, returning the white handkerchief to the rear pocket of his jeans. "You're the anthropologist. Maybe you can explain it. Something about purity? The blessed Virgin? It goes way back, I know that."

"Well, yes," Brenda said, "I didn't mean to put the blame on Mexico. We have this virginity obsession in the United States, too. But for us, it's not how long you can keep it, but how quickly you can lose it."

"What do you mean?" Francisco asked, frowning.

"My high school friends were obsessed with losing their virginity, to the point that they would go out with the worst jerk in the world, just to get it over with, to be free of it."

"You're kidding," Francisco said.

"Not kidding at all. In fact, they would brag about it, compare experiences, and tease the other women who still claimed to be virgins."

What was Brenda meaning to communicate to Francisco by talking like this, that she was claiming to be a virgin, or wasn't? Was she a little loose in the mouth from the tequila?

As Juana and I nibbled on the shrimp, I had been watching her through this discussion, and I could see her growing more and more uncomfortable. Now she was looking around like she was searching for a way to escape.

"Young women here try to hide it if they aren't virgins." Francisco observed. He put his hand on Brenda's forearm and said, "That's pretty disgusting what you just described."

Then Brenda delivered the clincher, this time partly in English, maybe not realizing how offensive her offhand comment would be. "I had a friend in high school who called virginity the immaculate misconception."

Silence. Okay, it's hard to get puns in another language, so I didn't know if Francisco got it or not. Was Brenda trying to show she was comfortable with sex by talking about it like this? Then Juana whispered to me, "Could we leave? I'd like to walk a little." She stood up. "Thanks for the shrimp, Francisco. We're finished."

We left our table at Pepe's Taberna and headed back down the cobblestone street toward the plaza and the church. I knew Juana was upset, but she didn't say anything. We just kept walking on past our gate, over to the cemetery, where we found that same stone bench overlooking the valley, lighted now by the still strong half-moon. A soft breeze had blown away the heat of the day, and the evening was pleasant—at least the weather. The lights of the houses in the valley flickered in the dry atmosphere.

When we were seated on our bench, Juana said, "I'm sorry, Carl. I'm just not accustomed to speaking about such private matters in public places like a bar. We never know who's listening, and my brother wasn't exactly whispering. And waving that handkerchief. It was really embarrassing for me. To tell the truth, I don't like talking about things like that at all."

"Maybe it would be best to change the subject," I said. "Forget what happened at Pepe's, if we can."

"Yes, please do. I would like that," Juana replied, smiling for the first time that evening.

Having suggested that we find a new topic, I guess it was up to me to come up with one, so I asked her, "How did you get the name Juana? I notice that they call you Juanita sometimes."

"Little Juana? Oh, Juana is a fairly common name around Oaxaca because of an old Zapotec legend, but I don't know if my parents named me for that Juana or not."

"Do you know the legend?"

"Yes, but it is a little disturbing. Do you think you really want to hear it?"

"Well, yes, if that's how I can learn about your name."

"Okay. This is it. When the Zapotecs left Monte Albán, the Mixtecs took over. This is long after the classic period represented by the artifacts displayed in the museum today. The Mixtecs had a final battle with the Zapotecs and defeated them badly. To seal the treaty and assure peace in the future, the Mixtecs kept the Zapotec princess Donjai with them."

"There was a Zapotec princess?

"Yes, but then the Zapotecs tried to launch one more surprise attack, and the Mixtecs ran off with the princess and decapitated her. Is that how you say cut off her head?"

"Yes, but how dreadful. They did that to a princess? Then what?"

"The Mixtecs confessed where her body was, but never revealed the location of the head. And this is where the legend begins. Apparently, a young shepherd boy tending his sheep at a site called San Agustin de las Juntas, near where the airport is today, noticed a continuously blooming lily and began to dig it up by its roots to take it home. As he dug, he noticed that the lily was growing out of a human ear."

"Oh, no."

"Which was part of a human head."

"The princess."

"Yes, preserved in perfect condition with the ornamental jewelry of the Zapotec princess. So they dug up this head, reburied it with the rest of the body in the Temple of Cullipan, and rebaptized the princess as Juana Cortez."

"Juana? With your name Juana?"

"Well, it's the same name I have anyway."

"So you are named for a princess and I am named for an astronomer."

"Really?"

"Yes, Carl Sagan. I like Princess Juana better, but it's really a ghastly story.

"Ghostly?"

"No, ghastly. It means shocking or horrifying," I explained.

"Ghastly, but also very beautiful. That's Mexico."

"But tell me, what does the legend mean?"

"Many things. Some say it demonstrates how the beauty, goodness, and power of the Zapotec people are preserved, no matter what, through many generations and all ages. That severed head appears on the coat of arms of the City of Oaxaca."

"Really?" But then I smiled as I said, "It could also mean, be especially careful with anyone named Juana," I said.

"Like don't lose your head?"

"I already have, Juana. Could I be falling in love with a Zapotec princess?

As she turned her head upward toward me and smiled, I gave her a kiss, and then some more. "I like this," she said, "kissing you under the stars in the cemetery here where my ancestors are watching. You've made me happy again after a terrible evening."

I didn't know what to say, but she wasn't objecting, so I kissed her some more.

On Wednesday night, the Ford Focus driven by Guillermo Ortiz was parked outside the wall, and when he came through the door, Magdalena, Sebastian, and Francisco greeted him warmly. Juana came across the courtyard to join them, dressed in a beautiful dress that I had never seen her wear before, looking like a true Zapotec princess. Had it been purchased new for this occasion? I glimpsed all of this for a brief moment sitting on the top step of the staircase, hidden, I hoped, by the wood banister, before I retreated to my room.

I knew there was no reason to worry about their evening out, with Francisco going along as chaperone, except I could empathize with Juana's unhappiness at having to go to dinner with that boring Guillermo at the Quinta Real, just to get her parents to extend the stay of the interns. But I knew I needed something to occupy my mind that night, so I decided to send an email to Marv.

I really hadn't written to Marv very often during my stay in Oaxaca because I was so relaxed and happy, so at peace with myself and at home there, that I hadn't felt the need for a counselor. I wasn't having those emotional problems about my ancestry and identity like I was when I was at Little Texas College. I told him that a couple of times, once in February and again in April, and he sent back brief notes saying he was happy to hear such good news about me. I still had (and still have) those emails. I also thanked him again for all he had done for me. But tonight, I felt that old restless anxiety coming back, and I knew what it was about: my decision to stay here or go back to LTC.

I told Marv that our internships were extended through the summer months of July and August, and that we had the opportunity to stay if we wished, but that I was badly confused about whether to stay or come back to Texas. I had already told him about the gentle and welcoming family, the strong Zapotec culture, and my volunteer work at the pre-school, but I hadn't said much about Juana, not wanting to tell him about my friendship with her until I knew more about where it was going. Now, I told him, my decision about coming home was getting really complicated by my unexpected attraction to Juana. I knew I should probably return home and finish college, but I really hated to leave her. Never having been in love, I didn't know if I was. I just couldn't picture telling her good-bye.

As I wrote all of that, I got pretty nervous trying to picture what it would be like to leave Juana in Mexico and live without her back in Texas. I told Marv that everything felt totally comfortable here now, and I was afraid that things back home would seem foreign to me and I would go back to being lost and anxious again. So I described my dilemma to Marv and sent off my email.

He was either working late or just had the habit of answering his emails when they came in, but he wrote right back.

Hi, Carl,

It's always good to hear from you. It often happens: the foreign becomes familiar and the familiar becomes foreign. The decision is yours, of course, and I am sure you are weighing your new friendship against what I am sure your parents' wishes would be as well as the delay in completing your studies. You must be close to graduating. The exciting thing is that you seem to have found yourself, the real you, through this wonderful experience in Mexico, and it is natural to want to hang on to what is making you happy.

As for love, almost no one picks out their partner: it is a non-choice shaped by proximity, availability, and puzzling coincidences, an exception to Thoreau's idea of the life of deliberate choice. There's no way to be prepared for the unexpected, especially in romance. That's why we have the myth of cupid, a capricious figure who sneaks around behind the scenes shooting us in the heart with arrows when we least expect it. Don't let it make you miserable. Enjoy it.

Marv

Oh, God, vintage Marv, full of insight about the problem but without any clear direction, leaving the agonizing choice up to me as always. I sort of believed what Juana had said about everything working out somehow, but how could I tell her that I had to go home? How could I tell myself that I must return home to a home that wouldn't be home anymore? Leave my life at Teotitlán del Valle for a residence hall room at Little Texas College? Give me a break.

After reading the email from Marv, I noticed one from my mom that had just arrived. Here is what I found:

Hi, Carl,

I want to let you know about your father. On Saturday, we rushed him to the hospital in the city with heart attack symptoms. They diagnosed it quickly and put in two stents, as they do now, to widen the arteries in the heart, and he responded quickly. In fact, he is home now and is beginning to grade some papers. So don't worry about him. He's fine.

I didn't contact you immediately because I was caught up in getting him the proper treatment and monitoring his recovery, and I wanted to see what the outcome would be. As it turned out, there is no need to change your departure plans. You can just use the round-trip ticket that we purchased for you back in January, which coincides with the ending dates you gave us for your service-learning term. In other words, there is no need to come home early to see your father.

We are both glad you have had such a good experience in Mexico and can't wait to hear all about it from you in person. Your father is alive and well, saved by sound science applied through modern medical practices.

All my love,

Mom

Oh, geez, a heart attack. And Mom expects me to come home right on schedule, of course, because I never mentioned I might stay through the summer. That was dumb. I knocked on Brenda's door to tell her the news. Of course she was there, because Francisco was busy being the chaperone for Juana at the dinner with Guillermo. I told Brenda about the email, my dad's heart attack, the round-trip ticket home, and the expectations.

"So you're thinking of returning because of your dad's health. Have you forgotten that he isn't even your dad?"

"Oh, but he is. He's not my biological father, but he's the only dad I've got. He raised me." Why did I sound so defensive?

"Well, do you want to go back to Texas?" she asked with a horrible frown.

"To Texas, no. But to finish my degree. I just think it would be awfully hard to convince them to let me stay."

"To let you? There you go again, asking for permission."

"Haven't you asked your parents if you can stay?"

"No. Like I told you, when I know for sure, I'll just tell them."

It looked like Brenda was planning to stay. As for me, Mom's email was kind of a tipping point pushing me toward return. But if I was going home, I needed to tell Juana.

On Friday afternoon, as soon as we arrived from downtown, Brenda and I sat down at the round table in the courtyard before going to our rooms. "Here. Sit down," she said. "I want you to be the first to know the news. I haven't even told Francisco."

"What?" I asked, being fairly sure what this news would be.

"I got the job at the museum. I interviewed yesterday while Señor Valdez was there to coach me, and I received word just this afternoon.

"Will you take it?" I asked, wondering if she was thinking more about whether to stay or go home.

"I already told them yes."

"So you are staying."

"Sure, aren't you?"

"No, I'm going back." I hated to say back home.

"But what about Juana? I thought you two were…pretty close."

"We are. Don't say anything. I haven't told her yet.

"Are you doing this for your parents?"

"Not just for them. I respect them, like a good Zapotec man would, but I need to finish my degree."

"It's possible, you know, to get a job without a degree. I'm living proof of that."

"I almost forgot to tell you congratulations. But my education isn't about getting a job. I just need to finish figuring out who I am. Complete my degree. But what about you, when will you tell Francisco?"

"Tonight. We'll celebrate at Pepe's Taberna."

"You'll stay here. You're in love. Do you think you might stay forever?" I asked her boldly, but back in my mind I was wondering if she knew what might be required of a Zapotec bride.

"If I'm asked, I would consider it."

"Wow!" I wasn't quite sure how that would work out. Abuela Paulina would have to spend more time teaching her how to cook Zapotec food and then plead her case convincingly with the rest of the family. And Brenda would have to get over some of her hang-ups. Could she do that? Maybe she wants to stay and experiment a little with Francisco so she can find out. Then I said, "Well, Brenda, so much for our codependence. It looks like we are taking different paths." I was okay with that, but it still felt a little strange after so many years together.

"Yes, at last," she said smiling, but looking nervous, too. "So let's hope for the best."

Brenda left then, like she was eager to end this conversation and get out of there. But what she said was that she had to go get dressed to meet Francisco, who was already at the bar with his amigos, and tell him her good news. Meanwhile I would need to figure out how to break my bad news to Juana.

I rehearsed what I would say to her over and over again in my head, changing my message each time. I didn't want to use my father's heart attack as an excuse. I needed to explain to her the importance of finishing my education and getting clear in my own mind about the purpose of life and my life in particular. Should I tell her I love her? Did I love her? I was sure I did, but if I started into that, I might have to fight off the tears. Oh, man, how was I going to tell her I was leaving?

I didn't set a time or place. We just happened to meet late on Saturday morning at the round table under the mango tree where all of the important family decisions were made. She had been weaving all morning and needed a break. She brought us some fresh mango juice from the kitchen. The birds were singing. Maybe this was the time to tell her.

"Francisco told me this morning that Brenda got the job in the museum," she said. "And she's staying," Juana told me as she sat down beside me.

"What do you think about that?" I asked.

"The job? A pleasant place to work, but part-time and low pay."

"No, I mean, what do you feel about her staying?" I sounded like Marv.

"Well, Francisco is all excited about it, but if you won't tell him I said so, I feel it's a mistake."

"A mistake? Why?" I was really surprised to hear Juana say that.

"Francisco will never leave. He can't. He's the oldest child, the son. Bringing Brenda into the family and into the community, while not impossible, will be very difficult for him. She might be better off going home, finishing her studies, and forgetting about Francisco."

I was really jolted, completely shocked, to hear those words from Juana. And I was sure that I needed to forget all of those speeches I had prepared for breaking the news to her. "That would be a shame, her going home, after you put so much work into making it possible for both of us to stay through the summer."

"Effort? Eating that elegant dinner? Oh, by the way, I have the churros. I've been saving them for you in the kitchen."

"And what about me, Juana? Should I go home, too, back to Texas?"

"That's your choice, but if you are asking me, I would say finish your studies. How many people get that chance to earn a college degree? Not many in Mexico, that's for sure."

For a brief moment, I was starting to worry that I was in love with her but she wasn't in love with me. "What about us, Juana? Should I just go home and forget about you?"

"Oh, I hope you will never forget me," she said with a contained smile.

"I will never forget you, Juana. Never. And I think I'm in love with you. I mean, really in love."

"Me, too," she said.

"Then it will be very difficult for both of us if I go home. I mean, it won't feel like home at all to me after living here with you. I'll miss you really bad."

"Me, too, she said again. "But I'm hoping it won't be forever. I'm thinking you might come back."

"But is there any hope for us? Won't it be just like you described for Brenda and Francisco?'

"Oh, no. Completely different."

"Why?"

"Francisco is the son. I'm the daughter. It's not easy being the daughter, missing out on so many opportunities the son gets to have. But in this case, I have the advantage. Of course my parents are concerned about me, but not in the same way as with Francisco."

"What will happen to us?"

"I told you, only God knows the answer to that. We don't know. Many things could happen."

"It's true, isn't it?"

"Abuela Paulina told me bedtime stories every night when I was a child to put me to sleep. They were in Zapotec, and she just made them up. But here's what she did. Every story started out almost the same way. The setting in the beginning was the same, the characters, the situation, always the same. But the ending was always different. I don't know how she did it, but every night there was a new ending."

"I think I know what you are saying. Life is like that."

"Most people can picture only one or two things that might happen to their life, when, in fact, there are a lot of possibilities. Stuff we can't even imagine." She took my hand in her two hands. "There is a long list of things that could happen to us, Carl, we just don't know what's on it. That's why I'm not worried. Abuela Paulina taught me that there can be many happy endings to the same story."

"You won't be sad if I go home?"

"Of course I will be sad, and you will be sad, too, but we won't cry our hearts out because it's not the end of the story."

As I look back now while I am writing this, I'm remembering how calm and at peace Juana was compared to me, always worrying about what to do and say, until my brain is in an uproar. Oh, my gosh, what a beautiful person, not just her looks, but in her heart, too. I didn't need any rehearsed speeches to have a conversation with Juana because it was so amazingly easy to talk with her. I just wanted to be able be with her for the rest of my life to hear her calming words, to share her sense of trust in the future, to see that smile. Now I knew that I loved her for sure. Juana, my Zapotec princess.

11

Feeling Like a Stranger Back Home in Texas

Everything foreign. Summer session studies. Selling houses. Jolene's story. Housing plans for fall term. Dad as department chair. Origins of Life without evolution. Brenda's engagement. Searching for the right word with Marv. Ken will return. So will Brenda.

Juana didn't want to go to the airport. She said she would prefer to say good-bye to me in the courtyard, where we could be together but alone in our final moments. Besides, Francisco had arranged with Guillermo Ortiz to drive us, and that would mean Juana would be riding back home with just Guillermo, and for sure she didn't want to get caught with the lizard in that trap. He seemed eager to put me on a plane bound for the US, loading my luggage quickly into the back of the Ford like a hotel bellhop. So, I rode out to the airport with Guillermo in silence, and he rode home alone.

As I changed planes in Mexico City, I had this strange feeling about leaving Brenda behind. We were definitely going our separate ways, and that seemed odd after being such close friends all the way back to elementary school. But why was I going home while she was staying? Was she really in love with Francisco, and if so, how was that going to work out? What were her parents going to think about that, and how would I ever explain to her dad about Francisco? But hold on, was that really my job?

As I approached the gate in Mexico City for my flight to Texas, I wanted to turn around and catch the next flight back to Oaxaca—probably just the same plane going back and forth every couple of hours anyway—because I was already missing Juana really bad. I knew that the weeks and months ahead would be difficult without her. I just didn't know how difficult.

My parents met me at the airport, and it was good to see both of them, although my dad's gray hair was now thinner and completely white. My mother was still full of energy and enthusiasm, but she had a worried look in her eyes, as if something was wrong that she might tell me about later. She drove the new Honda with my dad up front on the passenger side, as I leaned forward from the back seat, chattering on about Mexico most of the way home. I told them in more detail about the food, the weaving community, the family funeral, teaching pre-school, and my internship as a tutor—everything but my romance with Juana. I think they were pleased and amazed at how happy I seemed to be.

On the plane, I had been able to see from the air the terrain of Mexico slowly fading away behind me as we approached Texas, and I had wondered then what it would feel like to be back on US soil in the Lone Star State. Well, as I remember it now, everything looked really different to me, huge and spread out, as opposed to compact and cozy like Teotitlán del Valle. The massive thruway from the airport with its curving on and off ramps contrasted with the simple road coming to and from the airport in Oaxaca. As we drove through our town, I noticed that Main Street was wide enough for two or three Avenidas. Even the two-lane highway out to our house, where I had had the accident with Ken, felt excessively wide with its center stripe and finished shoulders compared to the narrow cobblestone streets to which I had grown accustomed in Mexico. Here in Texas, there were no walls or doors, no enclosed courtyards, no plaza or church, nothing to provide a sense of community, just our one small house on the prairie built at a safe distance from the others to preserve everyone's privacy.

When I entered that house, I felt like a complete stranger although nothing had changed as far as I could tell. The shared office of my parents was cluttered with papers as always, the dining table had three placemats, and my dad's recliner was positioned at its usual angle in the living room in front of the TV. My lonely bedroom downstairs in the guest room was exactly the same, but I knew immediately that there was no way I could stay there for more than a few nights. I couldn't understand why everything looked so foreign to me, as if I were visiting for the first time, like a tourist popping in off of a cruise ship. Both parents were especially welcoming, obviously happy to have me back, and more demonstrative, it seemed, in their affection for me than before I traveled to Mexico. Did they miss me?

But this was not home to me anymore. As soon as I could, I needed to get back to the campus, where I probably wouldn't feel at home either.

After two weekend nights at the house, I rode in with Mom and Dad on Monday morning as they went to their respective offices in the Science Building. I visited Campus Housing to persuade the assistant there to assign me a single room for the summer. I would worry about housing for the fall term later. Yes, the room seemed small, plain, and lonely, but I had plenty to do and only planned to sleep there. The next day, I brought in my stuff and set up my laptop. I described in a long note to Juana my feelings about being back, the first of many emails, through which we were to become even better acquainted. On Sunday nights, as became our custom, we also talked by phone, and she always volunteered without my asking, some bit of information about Brenda and Francisco, so that together we could trace the progress of that odd romance and maybe learn from it.

Next, I needed to check with the professors for whom I was doing Independent Study projects to register for them and add the appropriate title for each. Professor Adams and I agreed on "Zapotec Religious Beliefs." For Professor Martinez in anthropology, it was "Zapotec Marriage and Funeral Customs." I had plenty of information and photos enough for a study of "Zapotec Design" for Professor Winter in art history. I hadn't had time to write up these projects in Mexico, but I had a good start on each one. I just needed to use my notes and finish them up.

I also checked out the summer workshop schedule and found a course on Early Childhood Education, and when I looked at the course description, I was surprised to see how interesting it sounded. There was that name again: Maria Montessori. I was pretty sure I would be the only guy in the class, but I didn't mind that. Maybe I could learn something useful in case I ended up back in that pre-school at the church again. The other summer workshop that caught my attention was a course in accounting. If I ever got involved in some small business, it might be good to understand how they keep the books. With the two workshops and all of those independent studies to complete, I had plenty to do to keep my mind off of Mexico.

I received an unexpected call from the Homestead Real Estate Agency in town, the one that sponsored me for that summer workshop where I learned to take and pass the licensing exam. Two agents had left the firm and they had more clients than they could serve in a hot market, so they wanted to know if I was interested in filling in. For money on a regular commission? Straight up, man. What a surprise that was. One listing was a house some distance north of town with the same design as my parents' house. I had to persuade potential buyers of the advantages of living in the country in a single level ranch with a finished guest room in the basement although I hoped I wouldn't ever have to live in a place like that again. I made five thousand dollars commission on that. My parents were smiling from ear to ear. Maybe I wouldn't turn out to be a loser after all.

I had done so well on the first deal that the agency threw me the challenge of selling a little bungalow in the black neighborhood south of town. I established good rapport quickly with prospective buyers when they discovered that I had read Uncle Tom's Cabin and knew about James Baldwin and jazz. I didn't make as much commission, but I impressed the agency, which I discovered was the same agency that sold my parents their first and only house when they arrived here in Texas. By the end of the summer, I had earned fifteen thousand bucks, more than enough for a ticket to Oaxaca and a backpack full of supplies for my pre-school kids at the church.

I stopped for dinner one night in the residence halls cafeteria, the only one open in the summer, and I ran into Jolene. "Oh, my gosh," I said, "you're still here.

"At the college, yes, and still unbelievably alive on planet earth as well," she replied. "Literally amazed to be here!"

Oh, oh. Had she tried to suicide? Overdosed? "I was looking for you fall term. You must have been gone."

"Oh, yeah. I missed a whole frickin' year," she said.

"Where were you, if I may ask?"

"You already did," she said. "But if you really want to know what happened, you need to sit down with me here tonight. Okay?"

"Yeah, sure. Over here," I said, pointing with the corner of my tray.

"And where have you been?" Jolene asked.

"Mexico. Service-Learning Term. Just got back." I took a bite of whatever it was that was on my plate and nearly choked as I asked, "Where were you? Can you tell me?"

"I'm literally ashamed. Embarrassed AF."

I couldn't imagine Jolene ever being embarrassed about anything, so I asked with a quick little frown of concern, "Something serious? I promise I won't tell."

We just sat there all quiet for a while, shoveling in that college food. She took a few more mouthfuls and pushed her plate away, half finished, signaling she was ready to tell her story. "Remember that night in the Arb when we were vaping? Well, things got a lot worse for me. Not just THC. Everything. Meth. Opioids. A lot. I really got hooked. So my parents sent me away for a year to a fancy rehab facility. Dad literally spent his entire architectural commission from a new building he had just designed, but, hey, it worked. I'm over it. Seriously clean. And I never touch anything anymore. I had a lot of counseling with it, and now I know that I'm definitely not nobody."

"Oh, oh, sounds like you caught the nothingness bug sitting next to me in Origins of Life."

"I won't deny that the class might have had something to do with it, but it was very much more complicated than that, Carl. I had a literal physical addiction, you know."

"I was afraid you were off at some cloister having a baby."

"Well, that, too," she said, watching my reaction.

"What? What do you mean?" I was shocked and couldn't hide it. Why did I say that?

"Yeah, I was pregnant. Briefly. I took care of it."

"Here, in Texas?"

"New Mexico. Then they sent me to California. So now you know my story. But getting well was everything." She gave me one of her coy smiles. " Do you think you will like me better now? I'm changed, Carl. I'm telling you I'm totally different."

"I notice that," I said, nodding my head yes, and smiling. But it felt like she was the same old Jolene when it came to flirting with me, and it felt weird being flirted with when I was pretty sure I was already in love with a Zapotec princess. "So, you 'll be here another year?" I asked.

"At least. But let me tell you what I'm cooking for fall term. A lot of faculty brats are still here, and most of them have friends now, so I'm working to fill a couple of floors of one of those Senior Suites with all of us extremely serious types, of which I am one now."

"That sounds cool."

"So, talk to your friends. Have them contact me. She pulled out what looked like a business card with all of her contact info and gave me one. "What about the Chinese guy that you damn near killed?"

"Ken? Hey, give me a break, Jolene. We convicted the driver last fall. It was never my fault."

"Oh, I remember now. Yeah, I called you. Well, get Ken to come back and join our group for his senior year."

"Do you think?"

"Won't know 'til you ask him. And what about Brenda?"

"Oh, we've gone our separate ways now."

"Really? That's a pleasant shock. But aren't you still friends?"

"She stayed behind in Mexico. I don't know when she will be back."

"Well, invite her anyway. She's welcome. Come on, Carl. Invite your old amigos to the Suites. It's going to be a residence hall full of our kind of upper-level students. It'll be everything."

"Birds of a feather…"

"Fuck together. Just kidding. Oh, I'm so sorry, Carl." She put a hand over her mouth. "The new me just shouldn't have said that." I shrugged to let her know I didn't care. "I just want to gather up a group of really fine people to live together during our last year at LTC. The college is kind of crazy falling apart now. Have you heard? Oh, that's right, you just got back. Well, keep your eyes open." She piled her dishes on my tray and slipped her tray underneath mine. "Can you take these back? So much to do. I can't even. I'm the editor of the student newspaper now." I nodded my head and tried to look impressed. "That's my business card," she said, pointing to the one she had handed me. "Don't lose it. And phone me."

Dad called and invited me to lunch. I wondered what else he could possibly tell me about my ancestry, but he said he just wanted to fill me in on a problem he was having in the department to get my take on it. Was he asking my advice on something? That would be new.

I met him at his office, and as we walked into town, I noticed that he was a little slow, even though he had lost weight and looked trim. After his heart attack he was on a restrictive diet, so he told me that Biscuits and Brisket was off limits, and that we would need to go to Danny's Diner instead where we could get a salad. It was closer, just a block down to the left on Main Street. It had an aluminum exterior and with the look of an old railway car, a place mostly for burgers and shakes, but with a popular salad bar full of interesting options. We designed our own salads and took them over to a small table.

It's hard to talk and chew salad, so we just chomped away like two grazing horses for a while until Dad was ready to speak. "Okay, I'm finished," he said, blotting his mouth with a paper napkin. "You remember how I told you about not being very happy about having to take my turn as department chair? Well, wait until you hear this. I'll not name names to protect the not-so-innocent. One of our faculty, a family man, is having an affair with our administrative assistant, a married woman."

"In secret?"

"No, right out in the open, with hugs and kisses for everyone to witness. Slobbering all over each other. But here's the problem: they are consenting adults. Everybody's all righteous and wants me to do something about it. Students, faculty, other staff members in the building."

"The building? Other departments know about this? Chemistry? Biology?"

"Oh, it's the talk of the entire campus, but that doesn't bother the unprincipled principal players. I went to Human Resources, and they said that if the two parties were consenting adults, there was nothing I could do about it."

"Does the professor make decisions about her salary?"

"No, I do. But that's a good point. But if I used that to apply pressure, it would be discrimination." He rolled his eyes and held a fake smile. "Everybody has an opinion. It's immoral, some say. No, it's not, it's cool, others say. Someone should tell their spouses. Block his efforts to get tenure. Assign her a job on the other end of the campus. Shame them somehow, even though they have already proven to be shameless. I spend my whole day listening to that crap. Then I tell my critics that there is nothing I can do. A group of students came in last week and asked why I wasn't doing something about that immoral affair in my department. The prof is a very unpopular teacher, content to flunk out the poorer students instead of teaching them. The students want me to use this opportunity to get rid of him. So, what's your opinion?"

"Well, the teaching issue is separate from the affair, but if you want to know what I think, I'd say you should resign."

"Resign? As chair?"

"Sure. For health reasons. You don't need this stress."

"But that just leaves the problem unsolved for someone else to deal with it and spoils my reputation as a problem solver."

"It's not your reputation that's at stake, it's his. I just think you shouldn't have to face all those unreasonable people."

"But that's my job: teaching unreasonable people to be reasonable."

"In class, yes, but this job of department chair may be wasting your time and talents as a professor."

"Hmm. That's an interesting point."

I just wished I had a better solution for him. I realized that I cared for him as my dad, and I didn't like seeing him suffer. What was all this stress doing to him?

He looked at his watch and noticed that we needed to start back. After he took care of the check, we strolled along Alamo Avenue chatting about Mexico, Texas, and Trump's wall. Then he said, "Things have always been difficult in this country, especially in this state where politics can be terribly irrational. But recently, with the president we have now—I mean of the United States, not the college—it seems that lying, cheating, and stealing have been so glorified, that everyone thinks they can do it, and right out in public. Hey, who needs morals? Leadership is important, and that kind of leadership spreads right across the whole culture, even to a gem of a little college like this."

We walked a little further, and then I said, "It seems like people in the United States love to hold strong opinions and argue about them, without much regard for the evidence."

"You sound like you are my son, son." He grinned at me. "Ah, yes, we are a very badly polarized country now. In earlier times, people would just look the other way at the infidelity problem I've described to you in our department. Now, it's everybody's business, and, yes, they all have an opinion, like a revelation from God Himself, about what I should do."

"You're in the eye of the hurricane," I said.

"Well, I didn't expect you to have a solution. I just needed you to listen and understand me."

"I think I do, but I still think you should resign. You need to protect your health."

"Ah, yes, stay well so you can have a long life. For what? To devote myself to the lost cause of teaching unreasonable people to be reasonable?"

I didn't know how to take that last remark and didn't reply, but it was disturbing. Was he just unloading his frustration, or was it a clue that he might be giving up on life?

I decided to initiate a conversation with my mom to see how she was feeling about her work. The next day, I phoned her and told her I would bring over two smoothies if she had some free time. An appointment had just canceled, and I could take it if I could appear in ten minutes with the smoothies. When I got there, I noticed that even her office felt strange to me. A plant she kept in one corner looked withered. The botanist's plant is dying?

We chatted for a few minutes, and then I asked her, "What's happened with the search for your half-sister?"

"We found her. Her name is Lena. She was living in a small town two towns down the road from the old Swenson family farm."

"Living that nearby, but unidentified for all of those years? Interesting."

"Yes, I went back to Minnesota to visit one more time while you were in Mexico."

"Did she know what happened?"

"She didn't, but she does now."

"So, she never met her mom, which of course is your mom, too."

"Correct. And I had a lot of fun sharing pictures of our mom and of you. She's actually your Aunt Lena, you know."

"I wanted to say 'half-aunt,' like they do with half-brothers and half-sisters, but it sounded funny in my head, saying half-aunt, picturing an ant cut in half. I wondered if I was her half-nephew. "Does Lena have kids?" I asked.

"Two."

Were these my half-cousins? This was getting ridiculous and I had to get control of my brain, so I asked, "Did she like being discovered?"

"I think so, but she said it wouldn't really change how she thought about herself. Her life, she said, was already too much in motion for her to change anything. She teaches school. Kindergarten and first grade."

Was there a teaching gene in this family that I had caught along with my blue eyes? I was reminded of Mendel's peas. Inherited characteristics are not linked "It was nice that you found her and told her the truth, at least nice for her to be able to know."

Mom smiled at me, perhaps reminding herself of what I know now that I didn't know before. Was there more to tell me? I hoped not. I changed the subject and asked her if she knew about dad's stressful situation as department chair. Had he told her about the affair?

"Oh, yes, I hear something about that blasted scandal every night."

"I told him to resign, but he seems to think his reputation is at stake."

"Well, with three books and nine journal articles to his credit, I don't think he needs to worry much about his reputation. But I know he worries. Did he tell you that he was promoted to full professor this spring?"

"No. He never mentioned any of that, only his problems as department chair. I'll congratulate him when I see him next time." I took a few sips of my smoothie, and then I said, "Tell me what's going on in your life. You look worried sometimes. Is everything okay?"

Well, for now, yes, but there are two new trustees on the board and they are making waves."

"About what?"

"Teaching evolution."

"You're kidding. Come on, this is a private liberal arts college. Hands off."

"Well, that's what I say."

"So the trustees are starting to interfere with the academic freedom of professors? But what could happen?"

"Our course Origins of Life could get cancelled, or seriously modified. They have already asked us to give trigger warnings to students when the material we are presenting could be disturbing."

"Disturbing? I can't believe what I am hearing, Mom. Of course it's disturbing. But what do the students think about the course?"

"About half of them say they really like the course the way it is and don't want any changes, but then the other half want the evolution part taken out."

"Taken out? How the hell—excuse me—how can you teach about the origins of life without evolution?"

"Some want the Biblical version side by side with the science."

"Oh, if they only knew what they are asking for. Herr Schmidt could teach that and really get them upset when he describes the creation myth."

"Does he call it that?"

"Of course, Mom. He's a Biblical studies scholar from a German university and very sophisticated. I'd say the trustees better back off and not get involved in this, especially when the students are divided. Dad would say polarized."

Then Mom told me about how they had already cancelled Professor Richardson's summer workshop on Texas history. "Yeah, I noticed it wasn't on the course schedule," I said.

"They put pressure on the academic dean to suspend it for a year while they investigate whether he is teaching critical race theory."

"What's that?

"That racial bias is deeply embedded in the US social and political structure."

"Of course it is. You mean the dean canceled Richardson's course for that?"

"The dean felt he had to."

"That's not a good sign at all, Mom." Then I changed the subject and told her about Jolene's plan to bring a so-called upper-level group of us together to live in one of the Senior Suites this fall, and Mom thought that was a terrific idea.

Then she asked, "What's going on with Brenda? Why didn't she come back with you?"

I hesitated. What was I supposed to say and not say? "Brenda got a nice job opportunity to work in a museum at one of the ancient ruins."

"Something good for her resume? But tell me, does she have a boyfriend there?

"You need to promise me that you won't tell her parents."

"I'd never tell them something like that. I hardly ever see them anymore."

"Let's say that she does have a friend, but I'm not sure how it's going to work out. My guess is that it won't. I've been avoiding her dad, because I don't want him asking me."

"Well, he needs to ask her not you. Oh, the poor dean of students, this is all he needs for a complete nervous breakdown. He is already up to his ears in problems with the fraternities and sororities, all kinds of allegations about sexual misconduct, drinking, and drugging women for sex. And he has the job of trying to find out who's telling the truth."

"Maybe no one."

"You hit that on the head."

It was a wonderful conversation I had with Mom, but also upsetting. What was happening to my parents and to Little Texas College? And in such a short time. For sure, I didn't want to get involved in any of those controversies, so I decided to focus on my Independent Studies, my workshops, and selling real estate properties. As for my friendship with Juana, I would save that conversation for another day when I could find the courage to bring it up. Oh, geez, was I the one now, keeping family secrets?

On Sunday night, I called Juana at the usual time, and she had some rather startling news.

"Francisco usually picks up Brenda after work on the days she goes to the museum," she began. "On Thursday night, he invited her to climb one of the big pyramids with him, you know, right there in the Mount Albán ruins, and when they got to the top, he pulled out of his pocket a small box containing a silver ring with an emerald setting, the green to match her eyes, he said. He asked her to marry him."

"Oh, my God, Juana. I can't believe this. Are you kidding me? What did she say?"

"He told me she said yes. But before you pull the panic lever…Is that right?"

"It's press the panic button."

"Oh, yes, I remember now. Anyway, don't worry because Francisco didn't check with the family first."

"So he may be in deep trouble."

"Don't you say deep shit?" she asked.

"Your English is getting very sophisticated, Juana. But tell me, what will the family say."

"Much."

"Can they object?"

"They can, and they already have. We will just need to wait and see if he backs down."

"I'm shocked. Please let me know what happens."

Then we talked some more and I told her about how my parents were being so nice to me, but that I was worried about them. I told her I was working really hard, and that I was missing her, Teotitlán del Valle, and the children in the pre-school.

"The courtyard is not the same without you here, Carl. I just weave all day long. I don't even go into Oaxaca to the English classes."

"You don't need any more classes. Just keep practicing."

"That's the problem. With who?"

"Whom."

"See."

"Me."

I certainly didn't need to run into Brenda's father as I was sneaking past the Dean of Students Office on my way to see Marv, head down, eyes straight ahead. I hadn't seen Marv since I had returned, and I needed some counseling on my romance with Juana.

I went in and sat down, and in a few minutes, he wheeled in through the door to greet me with a smile and strong handshake. Oh, my gosh, it was so good to see him. But it was also a sad reminder that as time passes, Marv will still be sitting in in that same wheelchair.

"It's so good to see you, Carl. Tell me all about your travels."

I tried to do that, but there was so much to tell in that short hour, and I felt the clock ticking because I wanted to talk to him about Juana. I stressed the attraction of a stable culture and unique way of life with the Zapotecs where they took time to enjoy each day, each meal, each sunset. I told him about my teaching at the pre-school and about almost dying and how it made me want to live.

"No more suicidal thoughts," Marv and I repeated in unison, then laughed about it. Then I told him about Juana, how cute she is and how much I miss her. How I called her my Zapotec princess.

"Nothing wrong with missing someone you love," he said. "And you came home to test the strength of that love? What are you finding?"

I told him that I was sure I loved her now, but that it was hard to project how things could ever work out for us because of the way the family controlled the marriage of their offspring. Then I explained to him that when Juana was a kid, her grandmother told her the same story every night with a different ending each time, and that Juana thought we couldn't anticipate how things would come out for us, and that we didn't need to."

"Wow! Two wise women, I'd say. She's right, you know. Happiness comes in unexpected ways. So it will be interesting to see how your love story ends."

"One more thing," I said. Now that I'm back, everything looks really strange to me here."

"Reverse culture shock? You know about this?"

"I do, but it seems worse than that, like it might be permanent. Everything here seems foreign to me. My parents have been telling me what's been going on here at the college, and I can't quite comprehend how that shit could be happening here.

"I know what you are talking about. And they are both right in the middle of it, being shoved around a lot by unreasonable people. It's scary, what's happening here, even for an ex-marine."

"I just feel so—what's the word—estranged."

"Estranged is a good word for it. It refers to couples who no longer get along, but the broader meaning is that you become disaffected with almost everything you encounter, alienated, just not feeling at home with anything. Something like that?"

"Yes, like I watch what's happening here at the college, in the State of Texas, in my country, and I don't feel a part of it and don't want to be. People telling other people what to think, right and left constantly battling each other over politics so that nothing gets done. I just want out. I want to lead a completely different kind of life. A simple life. Somewhere else."

"As a Zapotec prince? Well, it wouldn't surprise me, Carl, if your story had a rather unusual ending. Grandma's right. We don't know what the end of the story will be, but you can feel free to be as unconventional as you wish. Invent a unique life that will make you happy. What's wrong with that? I really believe you could do it now."

"Oh, Marv, you are amazing. I've missed you." How could he grasp so quickly what was going on with me? How does he find just the right words to express his understanding and support? I shook his hand, and then I had to get the heck out of there because the tears had started pouring down my face as I glanced down at his legs. Had he had a girlfriend, I wondered, before he went off to war? Had cupid ever struck his heart, or was it just that exploding landmine?

I had emailed Ken to see if he had recovered from his injuries and told him it would be really cool if he could come back to Little Texas College to finish up his degree. I didn't hear anything back for a couple of weeks, and that bothered me. Then I received this email:

> Hello, Carl,
>
> Sorry not reply sooner. I talked to parents and persuade them. It took long time. Also had to find out about transfer credits. It all works. I can finish last year at LTC. I'm returning. Happy to be your roommate again. Is Amy Chang still there?
>
> Your friend,
>
> Ken

That made me really happy. So I sent Jolene a text and asked her to meet me for dinner to go over the list of students she had invited for the Senior Suites residence hall. I told her I had some news about Ken.

We unloaded our trays and she pulled a folder out of her backpack. We read through the names together, and I was really impressed. First, she had rounded up the faculty brats. Suzette had lost credits during her study at the university in France and needed to stay another term, possibly the whole year. Olivia Richardson was pretty agitated about what was going on with her father's course on Texas history, and she wanted to make sure she finished her degree before they fired him. Hans Junior, son of Herr Schmidt, played cello and was a music major, and he wanted to bring along two guys who played in a string trio he was in.

"What about my former roommate, Alexisius Jefferson?" I asked.

"Do you think he would leave the Black Student Alliance?" she asked.

"Try him. He might. Ask him to bring some of his friends. And while we are multiculturalizing, what about Rachel Katzenbaum?

"Is that even a word? Why? Is she Jewish?"

"From Brooklyn? For sure. Smart and talkative. Ask her to join us. And I'm sure she has a good friend or two."

Jolene was counting the list. "I'd really like to have twenty-four, enough for two floors. Obviously, Olivia and Suzette have friends, too, and I know a couple more that I could ask."

"Looks like we're almost there." Then I told her to add Ken's name as my roommate, and to locate Amy Chang and invite her to join us.

"Matchmaking?" she asked.

"Hey, Ken and Amy were already good friends, and she was heartbroken about his going back to Taiwan. She thought she would never see him again, and now look what's happening."

"Is that a long yes to my question about matchmaking?" She smiled and raised her bushy eyebrows. "And what about Brenda? What do you hear from her?"

"Nothing."

"Well, email her. See if she's coming back."

When I got back to my room that night, I sent Brenda a message telling her I hadn't heard from her and was worried. Then I told her about the group of students that Jolene had assembled to live together and invited her to join us autumn term. I didn't mention anything about Francisco's marriage proposal. She wrote back, but only a short note.

Hi, Carl,

Sorry to have lost touch. The job turned out to be enjoyable and I learned a lot, but the pay is low. I barely saved enough for my ticket home, which I've already bought. Wow! That's only two weeks away.

Count me in for the Senior Suites. That sounds like fun. It will be good to see you and tell you what happened with Francisco.

Brenda

Did she think I didn't know what happened, that Juana had not told me about the marriage proposal? There's more? I'm sure there is. Well, hey, anyway, Brenda would be coming back, no doubt with a bruised ego and some regrets. But she would join our group. That would be interesting. I would ask Jolene to put us on separate floors because I didn't want to start up that codependent crap again.

I finished up my workshops, completed all of my Independent Study papers, and counted up all of my credits one more time. With the advance placement credits from Honors courses in high school, my numerous Independent Studies, my completed write-up of my experience in Mexico for my service-learning credit, plus the classes I was taking that summer, I would be able to graduate at the end of the autumn term if I took a heavy course load. No problem. Between summer and autumn terms, I sold two more houses.

12

Living in the Senior Suites and Finishing My Degree

The Senior Suites. Music Appreciation. Brenda tells what happened with Francisco. Breaking news! Maybe a minstrel show? Sorority wars. Giving Dad suggestions. Campus uproar. Demonstration. A walk with Mom in the Arb. Chamber music salon. Openly black? Pro-Choice choices. Rescued by the athletes. No one wants kids. Grandpa Swenson's wisdom. Universal love.

The Senior Suites, reserved for students in their fourth year of study at Little Texas College, had a reputation across campus for being stylish, spacious, and the best place to live among all of the residence halls. From the outside, the suites looked like well-appointed condominiums in a modern glass and concrete style. Inside, the attractive main lobby had a stairway and elevator serving four floors. Each suite consisted of six double rooms, men's and women's bathrooms, and a central lounge with study tables, a widescreen TV, and a couch. We quickly turned the lounge on the fourth floor into the social lounge and the one on the third floor into the study area, swapping out some of the furniture. The group of us that Jolene put together occupied those top two floors, and the first two levels of the building were filled mostly with male and female athletes who competed in the Division III sports at LTC.

I lived in a fourth-floor corner room with Ken Lee, and we had a nice view from our window looking north across the athletic fields. My former roommate, Alexisius, was next door with Jacob Zimmerman, an econ major and old friend of Rachel Katzenbaum's from Brooklyn. Jacob—he called himself Jake—told Jolene he would enjoy having a black roommate, and Alex was available because he was sick of living with the brothers and sisters from the Black Student Alliance. Jolene lived down the hall with an old friend from Sacred Heart named Roberta Rivera, a studio art major whom I had met in my painting class. Jolene was a communications major now and spent most of her out-of-class hours working on the newspaper which was called The Student Voice. Her associate editor, Tommy Tuttle, lived next to Alex and Jake with his roommate Jimmy Lindell, a psych major who knew Brenda, which made her happy that there was someone from psychology living in the Senior Suites. My friend, Suzette Bouchardet, was still around after her year in France, and her roommate was Bridget Lyon, a French friend she had persuaded to study in the US for a year, without actually telling her much about the size and location of Little Texas College. Rachel Katzenbaum, was rooming with a friend from art history named Eleanor Lippmann. And that's only the fourth floor.

It took me a while to get everyone straight down on the third floor, but Ken's old non-girlfriend, Amy Chang, was there with her roommate, Linda Ho, a biology major who had taken courses from my mom. Hans Schmidt, called Junior, you might remember as the son of my Biblical Studies professor, Herr Schmidt. Hans Junior was an accomplished cellist and he brought with him a violinist name Eric Lawson, and next door to them lived Emil Brandt, who played viola, and his roommate Desi Aguilera, a classical guitarist of Cuban descent. Hans Junior, Eric, and Emil made up the string trio that provided us with Friday night concerts in the fourth-floor lounge. I'll describe those later. I can't remember exactly how Sammy Sitwell and Dwight Dundee became part of the group, but I suspected they may have been a couple of Jolene's former boyfriends. Of course, Brenda was on that floor, too, with Chanda Clay, an assertive but thoughtful black student majoring in sociology, a close friend to Alex, and like him, a little tired of the Black Student Alliance. Olivia Richardson, the daughter of the Texas history professor I liked so much, had brought her friend Maria Archuleta, and they were both doing their student teaching in secondary social studies, so they weren't around much.

This was an amazingly diverse but compatible group of students, but as you can see, woven together like a spider web with our pre-existing ties and coincidental connections. We tended to agree with each other on most things, and when we didn't, we were civil and respectful to each other. We were somewhat set apart from the rest of the campus because of our strong interests in our studies, and as the weeks passed, we came to feel alienated from much that was taking place that term at Little Texas College, or to use the word that Marv and I had identified: estranged. Other students found us difficult to understand, with our strong intellectual and cultural interests, and they were sure that we were elite snobs. Our way of supporting each other contrasted sharply with the polarizing nonsense that permeated the rest of the campus, and during the autumn term that year, as you will see, there was plenty of nonsense. The names that the other students had given to our group gradually drifted up to the third and fourth floors of the Senior Suites. Are you ready for this? They called us "The Multicultural Nut House," "Woke Joke Paradise," and a name using the N-word that I refuse to include in this account.

As soon as Ken arrived from Taiwan and found the way to the Senior Suites, I shook his hand as he bowed slightly, and we took a moment to talk about how he was doing physically after his injuries.

"No problem. One arm here doesn't go straight up." He lifted one slightly bent arm to demonstrate.

"Making it difficult to hold up the sky." I observed. We laughed together like old times.

"But no problems walking. Just little stiff sometimes."

"What about emotionally?" I asked, realizing as soon as I said it, that I wasn't being clear.

"Still have feelings. Injury to head not bad."

"But do you have fears and worries about riding in cars?"

"Don't like ride in cars. Prefer walk."

"I'm really glad you could come back to Little Texas College to finish up. Where did you study at home?"

"In Taipei. At National Taiwan University. Thirty thousand students. Some classes in English, but mostly Chinese. Very competitive. No friends. Not like here. I wanted to come back to the US where I could speak English to friends. You. Amy." It made me feel good that Ken still thought of me as his friend. "And friendly professors, too," he said. "Very personal here."

I had taken courses that term with more of those friendly professors, new ones that I wanted to get acquainted with and learn what they had to teach, their methods and subjects. I took a course in economics and one in political science, hoping to perceive better what was going on around me in the US, but I only became more alienated, as I came to understand the gap between how things should and could be done, based on solid scholarly findings in those fields, and what was actually happening at the time in politics. I liked learning about macroeconomics and also the way the federal system, just by its structure, worked against equal representation, especially in the Senate, like Alaska and Wyoming both with two senators, but hardly enough population for one representative each.

A course in Music Appreciation fit nicely into my schedule. Because I had taken piano lessons, I had learned to read music and appreciate classical composers, so I had a head start on being able to identify which styles belonged with which historical periods, like Baroque, Classical, Romantic, and Modern. Some of the examples that Professor Woodley played for us really grabbed my emotions, both for joy and for sadness, and I began to see how music could dig its way into the soul in such a way as to give new meaning to the word soul, like I actually had one and music knew where to find it.

One day, Professor Woodley said that music was the universal language and that people of all different spoken languages and cultures could understand each other's feelings through the common language of music. Naturally, that made me long for Juana, as everything did lately, and I realized how much I wanted to be able to share some of the music from the course with her to see how it made her feel, using that common language of music without having to skip back and forth from Zapotec, to Spanish, to English. For example, I wondered what feelings Beethoven's Fifth Symphony would awaken in her and dreamed about being able to sit side by side with her and listen to it with a live orchestra? Wow! How cool would that be?

I also signed up for Senior Honors Thesis in religion so that I could graduate with honors in my major, whatever that meant. I wasn't sure. I decided to make a comparison of the religions I had studied to note their similarities and differences. People who haven't studied the world religions like to say that all religions are the same, which, of course, they are not. But sometimes there are some similar beliefs and teachings. I wanted to find and describe those similarities. I'll tell you later how that came out.

One night early in the term, while I was studying in the third-floor lounge, Brenda came in and sat down beside me without any books or her laptop, signaling she wanted to share something with me, and because no one else was there, it looked like we would be able to talk privately and seriously. We had been passing each other in the residence hall, sometimes using our Mexican greetings and a smile, but we hadn't really talked seriously since she got back. Maybe she was ready to tell me what happened with Francisco.

She said she really liked him and she was pretty sure he liked her, too, but she never learned how to be comfortable when he started to express his affection physically, like touching or kissing her. "At first, I just thought I had some hang-ups I needed to get over, and I wanted to explore that with Francisco—kind of experiment a little and test myself out—because we seemed to have a really strong emotional connection. I knew I liked men, not women, so I figured I just needed to learn how, if you know what I mean."

"So, you were exploring a little?"

"Oh, yeah, even before you left, you know, like moonlight at Mitla. But after he asked me to marry him, I think he took my resistance to mean that I wanted to wait until after we were married, like I was a virgin or something."

"That's reasonable," I said, remembering the story of the blood-stained handkerchief.

"Only what I discovered through my exploring was that I wouldn't feel any different when we were married, and then I would be in big trouble."

"Because then, there would be an expectation—"

"Which to a Mexican man like Francisco becomes his right. So, I was pretty relieved when his parents made him withdraw his proposal."

"They didn't know it, but they were doing you a favor."

"Exactly."

"And now that you've had a little time to think about it, what do you conclude?" Oh, geez, I was sounding like I was the psychologist and she was my client.

"Well, I liked the close friendship and loving relationship with Francisco, and that was enjoyable and good for me, but what I've learned is that I don't like sex and, face it, I probably never will."

I found this a little hard to understand because it seemed so contrary to me and Juana, but, hey, I had to remember, this was Brenda. "So at least you have discovered who you are and what you want and don't want."

"Yeah, I've been doing a lot of Google searches recently, and what I know is that I'm not a lesbian or trans or anything like that. They call people like me hetero-romantic, where I'm attracted to people of the opposite sex and I like the romance, but I don't want to have anything to do with them sexually."

"So, is it correct when they call that asexual?"

"ACE? Yes, that's correct, too, but you know how I hate labels, so if people have to call me something, I would prefer hetero-romantic."

I just sat there nodding a lot, wondering if there was a shorter version, like hetero-ro or just ro-ro. Then I couldn't think of anything else to say, and eventually Brenda told me, "I just wanted you to know." I nodded some more and she asked, "And we're still friends, right?"

"Yes, of course. Of course." As I sat there thinking about what she had said, it seemed to me that things hadn't changed much for her from when we were in high school and people used to call me Brenda's boyfriend. But for me? Well, Juana had awakened something that would never go back to sleep. I was glad for Brenda, that she got it figured out, but I felt kind of bad for Francisco having had to go through all of that with Brenda.

Then she started talking about her father's frustrations as Dean of Student Life. "I'm really worried about him," she said, shaking her head slowly, over and over from side to side.

"Because?"

"The students are getting really crazy, doing things to test the rules, picking fights over the most trivial issues, and annoying each other, like they've lost their minds and are taking instructions directly from TikToc. And they seem to be setting up intentional confrontations with the administration. I had lunch with Dad yesterday," she said, "and I've never seen him so down. He had his glasses pushed up onto the top of his head and started searching around in his pockets like he'd lost them."

"Well, people do that as they get older," I said, trying to hide a smile.

"No, it's more than that; it's serious. I think he's having anxiety attacks. At the end he told me he was starting to look for a job at a different college, but when he got in touch with some of his colleagues in NASPA and ACPA, you know, the national associations, they all reported the same thing, like they wanted to leave their jobs, too, but there was no place to go that was any different."

"Sounds serious." I nodded my agreement and then asked, "What's going on? My parents are worried about what's happening here, too."

"Maybe the times," Brenda said with a shrug, but the conversation ended there because neither of us ventured any interpretation of what that meant—the times?

Some of us would gather each night in the fourth-floor lounge to chat or flip on the TV news, usually those channels that were constantly exposing the president's lies, or his pseudo friendships with Putin or that Kim guy from North Korea. Or if my friends really wanted some laughs, they would tune in Fox news and mock it. Time to mock the Fox, they would say. The president was in his third year and people either loved him or hated him. As for me, I was pretty much indifferent to all of that TV news although I thought it helped me sometimes to understand what Brenda was calling "the times."

One night, still in early October. Jolene came in shouting "Breaking News! Literally. Breaking News!" She and her associate editor, Tommy Tuttle, were just coming in from a long evening of investigative journalism for the Student Voice. Alexisius and his roommate Jake were there, Linda Ho was there, and so was Brenda and her black roommate Chanda Clay. Roberta Rivera drifted in when she heard her roommate Jolene proclaiming 'Breaking News!"

"What's up?" Alex asked. "Tell us."

Jolene plopped down on the couch as Tommy put the TV on mute. "We've been researching the backstory on this all night. It looks like the guys over at the Theta Chi house are planning a little minstrel show."

"Unbelievable. You're kidding," Alex and Chandra said almost in unison. "Why would they want to do something so stupid?" Alex asked, looking very upset.

"Well, apparently there is a big controversy going on down at UT..."

"University of Texas at Austin," Tommy explained.

"Yeah," Jolene continued, "over the singing of that famous fight song with the words 'the eyes of Texas are upon you.' It has just surfaced that the song was first performed in 1903 at a minstrel show. So now, the UT campus is totally divided, some defending the song and others wanting to cancel it immediately. The poor UT president is caught in the middle between students with progressive ideas, saying it has racist origins, and wealthy conservative alumni threatening to stop their donations if that song is banned.

"What's that got to do with Little Texas College?" Linda Ho asked innocently.

"Nothing." Tommy said. "At least it shouldn't. But the fraternity brothers at Theta Chi apparently want to take a stand in support of keeping that song, which is so famous now that everyone in the State of Texas knows it and sings it."

"To some Texans that song is everything," Roberta added. "It's to the tune of 'I've Been Working on the Railroad.'"

"That's the one," Jolene said, "and the attitude of the Thetas is like, we'll just show everybody what we think of this stupid woke controversy by putting on our own Theta Chi black-face minstrel show right here at Little Texas College. We'll show 'em."

"Sweet," Alex said. "Don't they know what that means today, white people in blackface portraying us as these jovial dimwits? The Black Student Alliance will go crazy."

"Along with a lot of other students who know that a minstrel show is completely unacceptable today and always has been." Chanda said.

I hadn't said anything, having fun just watching and listening. Brenda took off her glasses, raised her eyebrows, and shot me a stare with an outstretched palm, which I interpreted as her way of saying, "See, here's another mess for my father."

"So when is this minstrel show supposed to come off?" I asked.

"Well, we will be on it," Jolene said. "That will literally be the story for our next issue, right, Tommy?"

Two nights later, Jolene came into the lounge again shouting "Breaking News!" It was a different group that night, mostly women: Rachel Katzenbaum, her roommate Elinor, Suzette and Bridget, and Hans Schmidt and his roommate Eric. Luckily, Brenda wasn't there to hear about another problem for her father. "What's the breaking news tonight?" Rachel asked.

"Well, it seems that two of the sororities are about to go to war with each other," Jolene explained.

"Each other?" Rachel asked. "Over what?"

"Clothes," Tommy Tuttle said. "The Delta Gammas are saying that the time has come to stop dressing like a sex object if you don't want to be treated like one. You can't have it both ways. Tone down the sexy tank tops and tight exercise stretch pants."

"Makes sense," Elinor observed.

"Not to the Sigma Kappas," Tommy continued. "They say that a truly liberated woman can wear any damn thing she pleases. Even display her bare boobs if that's what she wants. The whole point of liberation is to dress for yourself, not to attract some hypermasculine cowboy."

"The Delta Gammas," Jolene explained, "are going to demand that the Dean of Student Life put the Sigma Kappas on probation for the way they dress and for advocating lewd behavior."

Suzette and Bridget both jerked back and exchanged frowns. "I can't even," Suzette said.

Then Bridget said in her lovely little French accent. "Do they want the dean to create a dress police like in Iran? Is this really anyone's business what a woman will choose to wear? I don't mean to be critical, but some things in this country are quite comical to me, like a Moliere farce perhaps?"

My dad phoned and invited me to walk over to Danny's Diner for lunch. He said he would like my opinion on something. I was flattered and hungry, so I met him at the Science Building and we walked into town. After finishing our salads, I asked Dad about the status of the love affair in his department.

"It's over," he said without smiling. "Their spouses found out. Our physics professor's wife wants a divorce. The husband of my assistant said he still loves his wife and would help her find another job off-campus in the real world where people still have morals. When she leaves, I'm worried that the budget people in the dean's office will eliminate that position—that's what they do now with vacancies—and I won't have an assistant, so I'll have to do my own clerical work even as chair of the department. It's happening all over, Carl. Faculty are becoming high-priced secretaries. People are already saying that it would serve me right to lose my assistant for letting that ugly drama go on without stopping it. But you know, my hands were tied."

"At least this episode is over. I still think you should resign as department chair before some new problem arises."

"Well, that would be nice, but probably not," he said. But he paused for a moment like he was giving it some thought. "But I want to tell you about a Faculty Senate sub-committee I'm on. Some of us have become concerned about the assault on our academic freedom, not only from those two crazy new trustees, but by some of the students, alumni, and administrators as well. Everyone wants to tell us how to do our job. Being a professor isn't easy in a society where the truth is called fake and the false is called true."

"But it's the responsibility of the scholarly disciplines to conduct research and teach the truth without interference." I sounded as if I were on the committee myself.

"See. You understand the academic enterprise now. You know how it works, or is supposed to work. The problem is that the discussions of the sub-committee are getting bogged down in our own disagreements so that we are starting to lose focus and deviate from our original purpose, which was to draft a statement the Senate could bring before the entire faculty and let them vote on it. But a new assistant professor from the philosophy department wants to describe what's happening here at Little Texas College as an example of a broader cultural malaise, and he wants to call our report 'The Epistemological Crisis.'"

"I'm not sure how many people outside of the philosophy department will know what that means," I said.

"Exactly. It is a crisis certainly, and it threatens the scientific traditions of empirical observation, verification, and peer review. You know about this?"

"Of course, Dad. I learned it from you and Mom by listening in to your conversations at the dinner table, and now I know how it works in the other disciplines as well. But to call your report 'Epistemological Crisis' could turn a lot of people off, even those who know what it means. May I make a suggestion?"

"That's why I am telling you about this. Please do."

"What if you called it 'Teaching for Truth' and after one short paragraph on the societal crisis, spell out what is needed here at Little Texas College to be able to teach without interference. Maybe a bulleted list. Something like this. To be able to teach the truth, we need to develop the course syllabus as we understand it without interference. We need to choose the texts and develop the reading list. Our classes must be an open forum for discussion of the truth based on facts. Above all, we don't need to give students trigger warnings about disturbing material. Our job is to disturb people."

"Oh, that's marvelous," he said, taking out his phone to make notes on what I said.

Three to five pages at most," I continued. "Plain language. Take a stand. This is what we need at LTC to teach the truth."

"Brilliant. I'll mention it to the others, and we will let the philosopher write his own statement for an article he can go publish in a scholarly journal. That's where it belongs. Epistemological crisis, indeed. Yes, yes, thank you."

As we walked back to the campus, I felt like I was nine feet tall. How had this man and I—not my biological father, nor I his son—become such good friends? How had I earned his respect? Why was I now able to feel what he was going through at this point in his career as the old ways were crumbling. I liked these serious conversations I was having with him, and I recognized that in trying to understand him, I had grown to like him even more. Should I dare call it love? Yes, I had learned to love him as a father.

Theta Chi tried to put on its black-face minstrel show, but it was pretty much of a bust. The other fraternities didn't attend because they were sure the Thetas would be seriously disciplined for breaking college policies about inclusion, so they just stayed out of it. The DGs and Sig Kaps didn't attend either. Some students joked that it was because the sorority sisters couldn't decide what to wear. A sizable crowd led by the Black Student Alliance assembled out front on the Theta Chi lawn where a small stage had been constructed, and they booed and yelled so loud that the "show" couldn't go on. Surprisingly, no one that day tried to sing a note of "The Eyes of Texas." No violence, no overt conflict, but the racial tension was smoldering there beneath the surface. I'm sure the folks on the "town" side of Alamo Avenue were taking it all in as they stopped to watch and comment to each other, not sure what was going on at that frat house over at LTC.

A week later an incident occurred that also divided the campus, but this time the racial lines broke down as other issues surfaced, like: Who the hell is actually telling the truth here? A black student named Angel Johnson, who Alexisius and Chanda hardly knew, had gone off with her boyfriend for a late-night rendezvous in an equipment shed at the north end of the athletic fields used for storing soccer balls, tennis nets, and lacrosse sticks. The shed was unlocked, so they entered, outfitted with blankets they had brought with them for the occasion, and closed the door. Actually, that door should have been locked, which was later identified as an error of the athletic department. Officer O'Reilly, the guy from campus police who helped me track down Billy Bob Wilson, the hit-and-run driver, was making his nightly rounds of the campus and noticed that the door to the shed was unlocked, so he locked it. He was only a few steps away when he heard terrified pounding and screaming, so he returned to the shed, unlocked the door, and found the couple naked but wrapped in blankets. He said to them, "You will need to leave." That's all he said. They grabbed their clothes and disappeared, and he locked the door again.

I know all of this—O'Reilly's side of the story—because I ran into him the following night as I was walking back to the Senior Suites from the library. Because we knew each other pretty well by then, he told me what had happened. We laughed about it a little because he said he had no idea that there was anyone in there when he locked up the shed and was surprised to hear people screaming. And then to find naked lovers. He said he was worried because they were black, and I told him that probably nothing would come of it, but I was wrong.

Three days later, Angel filed a complaint with the Office of Campus Police and sent copies to the Dean of Student Life and the President. In the complaint, Angel said she was harassed and humiliated by a campus police officer, her privacy had been violated, and she and a friend, for no reason at all, had been thrown out of an unlocked storage shed near the athletic fields at midnight. She complained of racial bias in the officer's ordering her to leave. She said she was afraid of being shot, which might have been the first clue that she was embellishing her story, because we knew that our campus police were unarmed.

After that, Officer O'Reilly was suspended without pay while an investigation was initiated, but it was difficult to conduct because there were no witnesses to substantiate or deny the charges Angel had made. Based on what I had learned from Officer O'Reilly directly, I told my former roommate Alexisius what had actually happened, and he and Chanda began their own investigation. He tracked down the boyfriend as a check-out clerk from the local supermarket, not a student at LTC at all. As for Angel, well, she really wasn't one, as her name implied, but was a first-year student, admitted provisionally for low grades from the local, mostly segregated, South High that she had attended with her boyfriend, and she was known there, sorry to say, as a troublemaker.

Well, of course there would be protests, and when the day came, people marched in front of the offices of the campus police in the Student Union. Alex, Chandra, Brenda, and I, along with several others from the third and fourth floors, carried signs we had made reading "O'Reilly is Blameless," and "Angel is no Angel," and "Reinstate O'Reilly." Our signs were actually pretty classy because our studio art major, Roberta, designed them. When we showed up at the protests, students from the Black Student Alliance were shocked to see Alex and Chandra carrying those signs and marching with us in a crowd that had grown quite sizable, composed of students, as ourselves, who just wanted the charges dropped against O'Reilly, a strong representation from the Greek-letter frat houses with their veiled racial sentiments, and on the other side a surprise invasion of students from the mostly-black high school supporting their brother and his honey. It was an odd mix, but a lot of students believed that Angel had fabricated the charges to keep from jeopardizing her provisional admission status, although there was no specific provision about not being caught naked in an athletic shed.

What surprised everyone was the line of armed police from the town force standing in front of the Student Union like they were guarding it. Why were they there? Were they expecting a race riot led by the black high school students? Were they hoping for one? Later I asked Brenda's father about those police, because by then I was pretty suspicious about the town police under the mayor's direction. He said that the police were on call if the campus police couldn't handle some bad situation. When I asked him if he had called for help, he said no. He wasn't happy about the uninvited intrusion, as he called it, of the town police. Of course, Jolene and Tommy published a big story about "the intrusion" in the next issue of The Student Voice, and I'm sure the police weren't happy when they saw copies of that.

Even though Angel's charges were denied and Officer O'Reilly was reinstated, the President of the College sent a memo to all of the divisions and departments—against the recommendation of the Dean of Student Life—mandating racial sensitivity training for all employees, new and continuing. It was as if Angel had prevailed anyway, and now the campus was in an uproar over the President's order. Did everyone need the training? Like Mom and Dad? Hardly. No one was happy.

I hadn't participated in any demonstrations like that before, and to tell the truth, I felt kind of foolish walking around grasping the edges of a posterboard sign that said "Reinstate O'Reilly," wondering how its message could possibly have any effect on the made-up minds of those who might read it. Was that really me out there? And why was I doing it? I felt very out-of-place and all I could think about was being back in Mexico with my pre-school students, painting murals and studying bugs. It was time to go talk to Mom about this protest experience and see how she was getting on with her issues. I texted her and we agreed to meet for a walk in the Arb at three o'clock the next afternoon.

Because she had time to plan for a walk, she appeared in comfortable hiking boots, a wide-brimmed straw hat, and khaki pants, as if ready for a safari, a botanist in the wild. Sometimes she could be so darn cute. The sun was still warm in late October and broke through light clouds frequently, giving us pleasant conditions for our walk and talk. As we strolled along the path, she pointed out some of the trees that had been brought in to increase the biodiversity, or at least the diversity of trees, now thriving in the arboretum. The leaves had turned into those attractive "fall colors," and we found some acorns under a tall old oak. She showed me the pointed, almost needle-like formations at the tips of the pin-oak leaves, like a teacher who seemed unable to stop teaching.

As I mentioned, I'd been to the Arb at night with Jolene long ago, and then later to do yoga and meditate, but this was the first time I could remember covering such a distance in the daytime on an actual hike, and I was surprised to see such a well-cared-for expanse of greenspace with so many trees and birds, and even a small spring-fed stream. The birds were really chirping that day, like they had strong opinions, too, and, of course, Mom knew them all by name.

I told her about Officer O'Reilly and the disputed charges of Angel, and I could tell that Mom had definitely been following it. She told me, "I got to know him when he was helping us make the case against the mayor's son, and Officer O'Reilly seemed very professional to me, not the sort of person to do what he was being accused of at all."

"That was my view, too. It was my old roommate Alex who dug out the background on Angel. I was actually in the protest, but it felt really strange to be there."

"I think I saw you in a photo that someone sent to me."

"Really? How did I look?"

"Not very enthusiastic."

"I'm not cut out for causes."

"I understand. But it doesn't mean you won't have them someday. I hope you will." We came to the end of the path although the vegetation of the Arboretum continued on for a few yards until the campus boundary met the prairie. As we turned around and started back, I asked Mom how it was going for her and my dad with the course, Origins of Life.

"The trustees still want to know more about what we are teaching, and the dean has requested our syllabus. I sent a copy, but with a note that warned him that this belonged in his file as chief academic officer, but that it should not be made public. It is, after all, what students pay tuition for: our courses."

"And what about Professor Richardson?"

"If there is a course review for Texas History, it is being done privately. There is not a faculty committee, nor any discussion of it."

"What else is going on?"

"Well, we were to have brought in a speaker on global warming from NYU, where, as you know, your father and I did our doctoral studies. But a member of our department discovered that our speaker had been accused of unwanted sexual advances."

"Accused. But is it established that they were unwanted?"

She smiled at my remark. "Not yet. But they voted five to four to cancel him."

"Cancel him? How much can this little college take before it tears itself apart?"

"Do you watch the news these days?" she asked.

"Sometimes it's on in the lounge, and I catch a little while the other students are watching. But I know what you are getting at. The tensions aren't just here; they're everywhere. People are at each other's throats about everything."

"And they are armed. Your father is very disturbed about it."

We walked on in silence for a short distance while I rehearsed the best way to tell her about Juana. I was determined to make myself tell her this time. "I've told you about my good times in Mexico," I began, "but I've left out an important part. I think I'm in love with the young woman in our host family who made our housing arrangements on behalf of the university. Her name is Juana, like Juanita. She's really cute, and I've never felt like this about anyone before."

"I've suspected as much, but I wanted to give you time to tell me when you were ready. Now that you have, I'm happy for you."

"I call her every Sunday night, and I'm sure now that I need to go back and visit her again."

"Will you move to Mexico? That would be my first thought, wouldn't it? Sorry."

"I don't know how our story will end, Mom. I really don't. I like the stability of the Zapotec culture, the caring support within the weaving community, the way of life, but I don't know if they will accept me."

"And Juana loves you, too? That must also pose a dilemma for her and her parents."

"I'm sure she does, and I know she struggles with it. Francisco, her brother, proposed to Brenda, but the family made him withdraw it."

"Really? I didn't know this."

"To tell the truth, Mom, I think you would love it in Oaxaca. The climate, the vegetation, the plants used for dyes…"

"The medicinal herbs. I can picture it." She gestured with both hands as if to draw a horizon line. "If you go there, I would love to visit you. With your father, of course."

Wow! What had happened to my parents? They were both so understanding. So respectful. Or was it something that had happened to me? Did they see me differently or was I actually different? At last, I felt at ease with them. Like they were finally telling me the truth about everything and accepting me as their adult son.

I know it may be hard to picture this in a college residence hall, but on Friday nights at ten o'clock, the fourth-floor lounge turned into a chamber music salon as our resident trio performed something they had been working on that week. As I mentioned, Hans played the cello, his roommate Eric took the first violin part, and their friend Emil the viola. That night it was a Haydn string trio, a rather lively piece in places with lots of contrasts in loud and soft. Not all of the students came to these concerts, of course, having other things they preferred to do, but there was always a small crowd that soon became larger as the sound of the music drifted down to the third floor.

As for myself, I wouldn't miss it. I had grown more and more interested in classical music that term and began to download some of my favorites, but really, there was nothing quite like a live performance with its authentic sound and the feelings conveyed by the players through their movements and expressions. They were astonishingly good, by the way. So, we had our own live concerts provided for free by our friends.

That night, after our musician friends had left and most of their audience had wandered off, Ken and Amy, Alex and Chandra, and Brenda and I were commenting on how accomplished they were, when Brenda said, "I'm wondering if they're gay."

Nobody said a word until finally Alex said, "Why would you wonder that?"

"It's not a prejudice or anything negative, Alex. I've just become interested in sexual orientation. They've never said."

Then Chandra pointed out, "If they haven't said they are openly gay, then who are we to say?"

Alex nodded his head a few times and then he said, "I'm fastening on this phrase 'openly gay' like there is a choice to reveal one's sexual preferences or not. Can I say that I'm openly black? I mean, I am, of course. Openly, only because everyone can see my skin."

"Oh, Alex," Chandra said, "give it a rest. Maybe we just need to leave them alone."

Then Brenda said, "Forget it. I'm sorry I brought it up."

"Yes. Not spoil nice mood of concert," Ken suggested.

On Sunday night, after I called Juana, I came back to the lounge to find a lively discussion of abortion taking place. The room was filled with women, and the few men there were mostly quiet. Many of the women expressed concern about the fate of legal abortion now that the President and Senate were filling the vacancies on the Supreme Court with people who would for sure overturn Roe v. Wade. Others pointed out that if that happened, the states could go a little crazy with their own strict, or even more strict, anti-abortion laws. Because most of the women in the room favored legalization, the "Pro-Choice" position, the discussion quickly moved to what choice a woman might make if actually faced with it. There was some thoughtful discussion of the questions: At what point can we say that a viable human fetus exists, and on what do we base that view? What about the adoption option? I was struck by how knowledgeable the women students were on the fine points and how seriously they took the discussion. I also noticed how quiet Jolene had become, just listening, while her eyes were darting back and forth at the others. She appeared to be taking in all of the details and I thought I saw her taking notes on her phone.

On Wednesday, an editorial appeared in The Student Voice with the headline "Pro-Choice Choices," and it summarized the thoughtful discussion held in our lounge, identifying the source of the ideas as students, but without their names. It was signed off as "Editorial Staff" with the names of Jolene Winter and Tommy Tuttle, along with two others who worked on the paper with them. That was all it took to create the storm that blew across campus like the high velocity winds of a Texas tornado.

Apparently, many students had only read the headline and formed their opinion immediately that the school newspaper had taken a pro-life stand, which it hadn't. It should not have been surprising, but it was, to see how many students had quickly assembled to protest the next day. A sizable number of older "grown-ups" from town joined them, gathering on the sidewalks and lawn in front of our Senior Suite. The protestors carried signs of "Pro-Life" and "Stop Killing Babies," and they chanted those same slogans loudly, over and over. Apparently, word had spread that the authors of the editorial, lived in Senior Suites along with a bunch of other liberal snowflakes.

The protest was scheduled for Thursday at noon, just as students were returning from classes and heading out to others. It turned ugly when the protesters started to block the residence hall entryway so that students couldn't come in or out, or if they pushed through somehow, the protesters would harass them, so that they had to run a gauntlet of verbal abuse. It got pretty scary with all of that pushing and shoving and yelling and chanting.

What the demonstrators had not considered was that the other floors of students living in this Senior Suite also needed to pass in and out of their residence hall, and they had no intention of enduring such harassment. Some of us—Brenda, Jolene, Tommy, Rachel, Chanda, and I—were watching from the windows of the fourth-floor lounge when students from the first and second floors began to pour out single file onto the sidewalk in front of the entrance. They made a long line, like a Civil War battle line, but instead of holding guns, they were holding hands with each other and advancing slowly toward the protesters.

Some among the student protesters must have recognized certain individuals as stars of the men's and women's basketball, soccer, and volleyball teams. Others, perhaps the people from town, only recognized the size and muscular bodies of those in the line coming toward them, and it didn't take them long to decide that they didn't want a physical confrontation with such formidable-looking young adversaries, slowly and persistently marching at them. The crowd of protesters dispersed quickly, and some actually began running away towards the main entrance to the campus on Alamo Avenue, where they had entered. It was fun to watch from a distance. But why had the athletes cleared them out?

Those of us who had been watching from the lounge window charged down the stairway and arrived in the lobby in time to meet the returning athletes. "Looks like we won for once," a tall young woman said. I thought I recognized her as a basketball star. "For sure one of our easier victories," another said.

When Brenda arrived on the scene, she said to them, "Hey, you all, thanks for breaking up the mob."

"Well, we had to get to class and to our practices. Hey, we live here, too. I mean, they can think what they want about abortion, but they had no right to try to shut this place down like some clinic."

"Well, we appreciate it," Chanda said. "It was getting incredibly scary, and I sure didn't want to go out there by myself."

"For sure," the student said. "What you hope is that no one has a gun, you know, people coming in from town like that could be armed. It only takes one crazy dude."

"That took some guts," Brenda said.

"No worries. It worked."

I'm not sure whose idea it was, maybe Rachael's, but that night we ordered a bunch of different kinds of pizzas from a place in town and threw a little celebration for the athletes on the first and second floors. Desi played his guitar and sang some hot Cuban numbers, and everybody had a blast. After that we began to mingle more with the athletes on the lower two floors.

We continued through the term, watching the late evening TV news, listening to Jolene's "breaking news," enjoying the Friday night salons offered by our string trio, and continuing with our interesting discussions. I had grown to enjoy my classmates in the Senior Suites a lot, including now some from the first two floors. The stereotype of "dumb jocks" did not hold at Little Texas College because there weren't any athletic scholarships. The focus of the athletic department was on "student athletes" with a strong emphasis on the student part as demonstrated by good grades. What I'm trying to say is that the students on the floors below were no dummies, and as we got better acquainted, we invited them to join us in our music salons and discussions, and they seemed to like that.

I remember one night in particular when some of them were there, a discussion began to take shape after one of the students asked what people thought about bringing children into this crazy world we have here today. Immediately, someone said that they had read that there were environmental groups now advocating no more babies. I was surprised—no shocked— at how many said they didn't want to have any children, and it wasn't just the women students either. They gave some interesting reasons, and as I listened, I took it to mean that many of them felt estranged from the society in which they found themselves living, just as I did. Not having children was just one aspect of their estrangement. They wanted no part of the world of corporate greed and the pressure to do two jobs at once while being paid for one. They complained about the income disparity of the social classes and the inability of a paralyzed government to do anything about it. They were alarmed about what was going to happen to the environment in the next thirty years, terrified about their own personal safety in public places and that of their hypothetical children at school, and completely distraught by the widespread availability of military-style weapons.

Some were going on to graduate school but weren't sure how they would use their professional training once they graduated. Others, like our musicians and artists, were hoping to live isolated lives within little cultural islands where they could pursue their interests but ignore society. Others spoke openly about leaving, going to some other country to live, to France or Austria, Canada or Mexico, or to a completely different culture like Japan or New Zealand. I heard the word expatriate a lot, and when I mentioned the word estrangement, a lot of heads nodded. We got off on all of the weird things that people do to avoid the seriousness of life. Then I gave them the word absurd, and they devoured it, using it over and over. I was surprised at the direction of this discussion, and it made me feel that maybe I wasn't so out-of-step with my peers after all. My god, what was going to happen to all of us when we left Little Texas College?

Grandpa Swenson, my mom's dad, had planned to visit us in late August, but his health had deteriorated badly, and he thought it best to cancel his trip to Texas. He had had two heart attacks the previous year, and knew the symptoms well, so that when he noticed them, he would go to a doctor. Naturally, the doctor would prescribe some pills—that's what doctors are expected to do—but grandpa never seemed satisfied with the doctor he had just visited, so he would go to a different one in town, and then try one in a neighboring town, and then another, each time receiving a prescription for a new batch of pills, which he took conscientiously along with the others. Mom found out that this had been going on for almost a year, and by then he was taking more than twenty pills each day.

As his condition worsened, he sometimes called 911, and an

ambulance would take him to the ER. Because it was a small town, the ambulance drivers and ER medics all became well-acquainted with Anders Swenson, but then one night the ER folks kept him at the hospital and things went downhill fast, both physically and with his morale. The town where he lives in rural Minnesota has a sweet little Hospice called Teresa House, so when the hospital staff said they could no longer help him, they sent him there to die. In the hospice, as is the custom, they took away all of his medicines, and guess what, in a few days he got better. So much better, that they had to dismiss him.

When the nurse called Mom in early November to report what was going on with her father, Mom decided to take a long weekend, Thursday through Tuesday—my dad would cover the classes—and she invited me to go with her to Minnesota. I surprised myself by agreeing to go, because I was really busy with my studies, but I had always liked Grandpa Swenson, and besides he was the only real "grandperson" I had in my life. It might be my last chance to learn something about my Scandinavian ancestry.

What we found when we arrived was encouraging. Grandpa had already gone home from the hospice, and he hardly needed the homecare he had arranged because he was able to navigate the house with a cane, and the neighbors were forever bringing in meals, not "on wheels," but in their own loving hands.

One night, I pulled up a straight chair from the dining room and sat beside Grandpa Swenson in his antique rocking chair for some conversation. Like Abuela Paulina, he seemed to be loaded with wisdom. I asked him to tell me about life in the hospice. He said it was a remodeled old Victorian house staffed by dedicated volunteers who all seemed to know each other. The ladies from town dropped off food, and now and then an actual hospice nurse would stop by. "Other volunteers, high school students, came in to talk, play games, feed us ice cream, or read to us," grandpa said.

"Why did you go to the hospice?" I asked. "Did you want to die?"

"Heavens no! Who wants to die? Not when there are Minnesota sunsets and maple walnut ice cream."

"You liked living?"

"Still do."

"You got better and they sent you home?"

"Let me tell you about that. The principal of the high school stopped by to look in on the student volunteers, so when he came in to talk to me and we got acquainted a little, I told him he should be proud of me because

I was graduating—from the hospice, that is. And he said that's what he had heard. Then he grinned for a second and told me that I wasn't really graduating because actually I had flunked out."

"Flunked out of hospice," I said, "that's a good one." We enjoyed a good laugh. Then I asked him what wisdom he had to share with me about life.

"Wisdom? That's asking a lot," he said. "Let me think a minute." He scratched his forehead. "I'd say respect nature, be kind to animals and people in that order. Work hard at whatever you choose to do. But I'd say the most important thing is to find someone you can love, and do your best to show them that you love them. I guess your mom told you what happened to my wife before I met her. That was horrible news for me, and then to hear that she already had a child. But it weren't her fault and I loved her so much, I still wanted to marry her anyway."

"Would you say that's the most important thing, having someone to love?"

"Oh, yes, by far. Most everything else is kind of pointless. It's amazing to see the asinine things people do to try to make themselves happy. Me, I spent seven days a week milking cows. You can't get much more pointless than that although the cows seemed to appreciate it. But then I had my love—we used to call each other Love—and that one person made life worth living. Oh, my how I miss her." He started to sob, trying to hold it back, but couldn't.

When I got back to Little Texas College, I had a lot to think about from the visit to Grandpa Swenson. He used the word pointless instead of absurd, but I'm sure that's what he meant. So an ordinary person without so much "book learning," as he called it, could also find life to be pointless. And the meaning he made for himself was with my grandma, the violated woman he called Love. She was the love of his life that made life itself worthwhile. So instead of suicide, which was probably never a conscious choice for him, he chose life and is still choosing life. Even with the loss of his wife, he is still enjoying the small pleasures in life that bring him enjoyment. I would definitely call that wisdom.

Had I already found the love of my life? Did I need to wake up to the fact that Juana was actually that person? Alright, so she was from another country and culture, and her parents probably wouldn't approve of marriage, and the probability of my being accepted into that Zapotec family was very low, but I could still love her. All I knew was that I missed her desperately and wanted to see her again as soon as I could. I needed to stop fretting about how the story would end and go down there to tell her what I felt about her and do my best at creating a happy ending.

During reading week, I finished up my Senior Honors Thesis for my religious studies major, the comparison of themes in the world religions that I mentioned earlier. I worked my way through the differences, giving examples of ideas about God, creation, and human nature in a scholarly and systematic way— I certainly knew how to do that by now— and ended with what I called "the universal principle of love." What I discovered was that several of the religions have some version of what Christians call the Golden Rule: "Do unto others as you would have them do unto you." Naturally the concept in Matthew comes across in a slightly different way from Mark's "Love your neighbor as yourself." But the interesting discovery was to find similar "rules" in other religions, though not always expressed in the same words. In Buddhism, it is "Treat no others in ways that you yourself would find harmful," and in Confucianism it is "Do not do to others what you do not want done to yourself." In Islam it is "Wish for others what you wish for yourself," and in Hinduism I found, "Do not do to others what would cause pain if done to you."

I made the point in my thesis that all of these "golden rules" assumed the human capacity for empathy, the ability to understand another person's feelings as well as one's own in such a way as to project what that person might want or need. In my arduous quest for the meaning of life, perhaps this was the simple principle that could guide me. It appeared to me, that human beings across many ancient cultures had been able to grasp the concept of empathy as the foundation of love, providing a profound guide for how to live one's life. Was it really as simple as "love one another"?

As I finished up my thesis, studied for my exams, and turned in the rest of my work, it dawned on me that not only was the term ending, but my time at Little Texas College was finishing. I had nostalgic remembrances of my favorite professors and their courses: Professor Adams, Herr Schmidt, Professor Richardson, and Jolene's mother, Vanessa Winter. And what about Marv? Could I squeeze in one more visit with him because I might never see him again? I told myself to let go of every square foot of that campus I had come to know so well, the classroom buildings, the Student Union, and the Arb. Prepare to exit. Break the attachment. I tried to imagine how

I was going to say good-bye to all of my close friends: Ken, Alex, Suzette, Rachel, and of course Brenda. I had counted my credits carefully and had just the right number to graduate, so there was no reason for me to stay at LTC, even though I had no career plan, no life plan, just a persistent call to catch the next plane for Oaxaca and visit Juana.

I had told Ken that autumn term about how I would probably be his roommate for only one term, and he said no problem. When I asked him if he was going to replace me, he said he would "leave vacant." I suggested that maybe Amy could sneak upstairs and spend a little time with him, and he just smiled. Had Amy become the love of his life? Suzette was planning to live in France next year, and Hans Junior, Eric, and Emil were hoping to get into a music conservatory in Salzburg, Austria, called the Mozarteum, so that their trio could stay together. Jolene was headed toward Northwestern's journalism school, and my old friend Brenda was trying to decide among graduate programs in clinical psychology. Because all of my friendships had become so close, it was very difficult to leave campus a term early, but I kept reminding myself that all of those relationships would need to be broken off anyway if I stayed until graduation in June, and by then it would be even harder.

I remember feeling good about my last term at LTC because I actually had a lot of close friends and finally a deep immersion in college life, being glad that I hadn't missed out on that. I was less estranged and alienated and even had a vague sense of where I was going. Vague being Mexico. I discussed with Mom and Dad my plans to return to Oaxaca, and they both encouraged me strongly to go. "It's the only way you will know for sure," Mom said. The sadness of all of those good-byes was offset by the excitement of seeing Juana again. Maybe I would surprise her and just show up at the door in the wall unannounced.

13

Accepting Tor's Offer to Sell Rugs and Blankets in Aspen

Surprise! A friendly welcome. Eating burritos on the bench. Pre-school reunion. Meeting Tor. An offer for selling weaving in the Ashcroft Valley. Two plane tickets to Aspen. Designing a fund-raiser for Gabriella. Preparing for summer. Landing in the mountains. Alone in an isolated cabin. Ghost-town tour. Hiking in the valley. Back to Teotitlán to get organized.

I wanted to surprise Juana. We had continued our Sunday night phone conversations, and I had told her that I was thinking about coming down to visit her, but I never said when it would be. So I continued to call and send her emails right up to the time I left for Mexico. The situation was a perfect set-up for a surprise, but I never considered that I could be the one who would be surprised.

I took the same flight through Mexico City to Oaxaca, and when I arrived at the airport, I hired a taxi to drive me out to Teotitlán del Valle. It was a little expensive, but I had a pocket full of pesos converted from my dollars earned on real estate commissions. It was still daylight and the route was familiar. I felt at home again in Mexico right away and realized how much I missed the warm weather, clear skies, and dry landscape as we drove through it on the way up the hill. We eventually turned onto the cobblestone streets of the little town that I knew so well. I remembered exactly how to get to Avenida Juárez and to the place where the dark wood door in the wall was located, so that I was able to point it out clearly to the driver. I paid him, adding a generous tip, and gathered up my luggage and backpack, to go stand in front of the familiar door. Now what? Should

I knock? I couldn't just barge in, so I tapped on the door twice. No one responded. I turned the handle and entered slowly peeking around the corner. When I looked up, I saw Juana sitting at the table under the mango tree talking with someone. Who was it? I took a step closer and recognized Guillermo Ortiz. Oh, my god, was she with him?

As I walked over to them, she saw me, and I could see a little glimmer of excitement in her eyes as she smiled that smile at me, but she didn't come to me with hugs and kisses as I had expected. She just sat there, providing what seemed to me a very restrained welcome in front of Guillermo. Why was he there? Was he still trying to court her? How many times had they gone out to dinner? Why hadn't she told me? Was I interrupting his visit with her? I remember now how those questions flashed through my mind as I tamed a strong urge to pick him up and throw him over the wall. Had I come all of this way back to Mexico to see Guillermo with Juana?

Just then, Cecelia, Juana's younger sister, came across the courtyard, all dressed up and smiling as Guillermo rose to give her a hug. "Well, look who's here," she said, glancing at me. She threw her sister a half smile and popped her eyes open wide as she bobbed her head back and forth.

As I hugged Cecelia, I remembered how she had nearly killed me with that Horchata drink, but something about her looked more grown up now, more settled, and happy. She took Guillermo's arm as they went out through the door. I shrugged, and as I turned back to look at Juana, I saw her running at me full speed, ready to throw herself into my arms. Somehow, I caught her and we enjoyed a barrage of kisses, grasping each other amid sighs of "Oh, I missed you so much. So much." Finally, I set her down gently and asked about Guillermo. "What's going on?"

"Oh, he's courting Cecelia now. I was just being polite to him as we waited for her."

I resisted the temptation to say that Guillermo and Cecelia seemed to be made for each other. Instead, I admitted, "You had me worried for a minute."

"I could see it on your face," she said, "I'm sorry and I apologize, but I had to control myself. It wasn't easy."

"How are you?" I asked.

"I'm fine, now that you are here." She said, nodding her head and smiling.

"And the family?"

"Everyone's okay."

"Abuela Paulina?"

"She's still good. Older. A little wiser. She keeps telling me to be patient."

Just then Magdalena and Sebastian came across the courtyard. "We heard your voice," Sebastian said, coming forward to give me a hug and a pat on the shoulder.

"Yes, welcome," Magdalena said, and it sounded like she meant it. They were speaking a few words in English. Had Juana been teaching them?

We sat at the round table as Magdalena went to the kitchen to bring us something to drink. I didn't know what to say, how to explain my surprise visit, but Juana told her father in Zapotec how I had arrived while she was with Guillermo and it had made me jealous. I couldn't understand the words, but I knew what she was telling him because of her gestures and the way it made her father laugh. Then she told me she was explaining to him my surprise visit and how happy it had made her. Her father was smiling, openly sharing in the happiness of his daughter.

I looked up and saw Abuela Paulina coming across the courtyard using a cane, and she was coming so fast I was afraid she would fall. Juana jumped up and ran over to steady her by taking the arm not using the cane. Grandma exclaimed something in Zapotec as she picked up speed to reach me. I bent forward to give her a gentle hug. Then Naxeli and Naconda materialized, like ghosts become flesh, and bounced over to give me hugs, both looking a little taller and stronger on their way to becoming young men. But where was Francisco? They said he was out working on the farm.

What a friendly welcome I had received. I hadn't really expected that. We sat at the table drinking our drinks, something with mango, lime, and sugar, as I listened to what seemed to me to be a very positive family conversation in Zapotec. Juana must have shared with them all along these many weeks how much she had been missing me. They seemed happy, for her sake, that I had returned. Everyone shared in the enjoyment of the moment, apparently with no thought about how long I might stay or how the story would end. At least the book was open and the page was blank. I had a chance to start writing our future. Maybe Abuela Paulina could invent a happy ending for us.

We took my luggage up that magnificent tile stairway to the same room where I had stayed previously, and I noticed that the bed was made up and everything was clean and in order, as if Juana had been perpetually expecting me to arrive, sometime at least, if not today. When I finished unpacking, I asked, "May we walk into town? I need to see the church, the square, the market. I've been missing them, too. You know, the wonderful way of life you have here."

"Of course, let's go." And we bounded down the stairs together and made our way through the courtyard. As we strolled along Avenida Juárez, the bell in the church tower tolled five o'clock, and although the sun was beginning to set, the temperature was warm, actually ideal, and the sky was clear. We went into the market, and I suggested that we buy two burritos and take them back to our special bench in the cemetery, where we could look out over the valley. I never knew that eating a burrito could be so romantic.

Over the fall term, when Juana and I had talked by phone each Sunday, I told her a lot about life in the Senior Suites, and although the events I described had to be difficult for her to comprehend, she appeared to remember them now and even the names of some of the students who lived there with me. She wanted me to tell her more about Ken and Alex, Jolene and Rachel, and the musicians in the trio. It was as if her imagination had made my friends into her friends. We never mentioned Brenda.

As I responded to her questions, I was surprised at how distanced I felt from my classmates already, without much enthusiasm for talking about them. How could that have happened to me so fast, leaving one life behind in Texas and picking up another so quickly here in Mexico? It made me feel confused, all over again, about who I really was: the conscientious student from Little Texas College or the time-traveler rediscovering his love for the Zapotec princess. Although I cherished what I had studied and learned as a student and knew that it had definitely shaped me into who I was, I also sensed that side by side with that student, there was another person emerging now right here, who might well be the authentic self I was hoping to become. But at that moment, sitting there on the bench trying to respond to Juana's curiosity about my friends, I was flat out confused.

Before I went to sleep that night, Juana asked me what I wanted to do the next day and I said, "Go to the preschool and see the students."

"We can do that. Around nine o'clock?"

So, after a breakfast of rolls, honey, and that wonderful cocoa made with Oaxacan chocolate, we went up to the school at the church. As we entered the old refectory, the teachers saw us, and one of them said, "It's

Carl." All of the little heads turned toward the doorway, and when the mayor's son came running at me, the others followed, and soon they were pulling on my arms and legs and guiding me toward their little tables and chairs.

"It looks like they aren't afraid of me anymore," I whispered to Juana.

"Afraid? Padre Paulo has told me that they are always asking for you and wanting to know when you will come back."

I had a backpack full of supplies that I had brought with me, including some fascinating Montessori puzzles I had learned about in my Early Childhood Education class, but I was dying to try out a building activity with three by five cards that my business professor had done with our class to teach teamwork. I opened some packs of blue, pink, and white cards, and distributed a little stack of each color to their tables. I showed them how to fold the cards two different ways, the long and narrow way vertically, and the short horizontal way, both being sturdy for building by placing some unfolded flat cards on top of them. I showed them how to stack the cards on top of each other and told them that the goal was to make buildings as tall as possible but also very beautiful.

They experimented with the cards for a while, quickly discovering who was good at folding, who was better at carefully stacking the cards, and who had the best design ideas. My prof would say that they had already figured out how to work in teams taking on different roles. Their teachers gave them hints and suggestions, but also the freedom to work independently. The interesting thing is that the students also became curious about what the teams at the other tables were doing, sending runners out to gather up good ideas. It was not a competition, as it might have become in the US, seeing who could build the tallest tower, but an exercise in cooperation. I was stunned at what those little kids actually built, the way they engineered stability, and how they managed the creative options of shapes and colors. Well, they were, after all, the sons and daughters of generations of Zapotec artisans, so it should not have been surprising that they were good at it. They kept coming up to me and pulling me by the hand, saying to me in Spanish, "Look at ours. Do you like it? Isn't it beautiful?"

After class, Juana and I talked about how just one activity like that could teach so many things. "You need to get involved again with those kids," she said. "They like you and you add a lot with your clever activities."

"I like them, too," I told her, "and I like working with them. Maybe I can go for two days a week as before." But then I realized that this implied that I was going to stay. Was I? How long? I didn't know. We weren't ready to talk about that yet.

Juana also told Señor Valdez that I was back, and he offered me a job teaching an intermediate English class of my own. I told him I was just visiting and wasn't sure how long I would be around, but he insisted that it didn't matter. I could start the next day. He would split one large class into two sections. So I began teaching English three days a week.

After two weeks, as I was settling into my old routines in Teotitlán del Valle, Juana received a phone call, followed up by an email, from someone visiting from the US who wanted to sell handwoven Mexican rugs and blankets in Colorado. As it turned out, that call was a life changer.

"I know Colorado a little," I said. "Our family vacationed there once. It's beautiful. Where in Colorado?"

"He says he's from a town called Aspen."

"Oh, the famous ski resort? Really?"

"He's in Oaxaca and wants to come up here and meet my family and our neighbors. Stay for the day."

"Do I need to sleep in the courtyard?"

"We still have one more room, amigo."

"Invite him. Who knows what could develop?"

Juana called him back and the next morning Francisco picked him up in the green bean machine at the Zócolo in Oaxaca and brought him out to us.

Tor Gustafson was an American, but only because he was born in the US; otherwise, he was thoroughly Norwegian. Tall, strongly built, aging well, with blond and gray hair and blue eyes. Both of his parents immigrated from Norway, originally having settled in Minnesota in a town with a name that I thought I recognized as being not far from where Grandpa Swenson lived.

Tor's family eventually migrated to Colorado to open a cross country ski course in the Ashcroft Valley, home to an old mining village called a ghost town. "Just a name, Juana. No ghosts there," I said. Tor's family had maintained the Norwegian customs and diet, and when his parents passed away, he continued their way of life in the ski business, adding a small inn, more like a bed and breakfast place, he said, and a popular new feature: dog-sled rides with authentic Alaskan huskies. While downhill skiing thrived in Aspen, cross-country Nordic skiing survived in the Ashcroft

Valley. Word spread about moonlight rides in sleds drawn by actual huskies, and customers soon learned that they needed to make reservations well in advance. Tor was quite a talker, and it was fun listening to his descriptions of yet another way of life at Ashcroft, but so far, we couldn't figure out what this talk had to do with Mexican rugs. So I asked him.

"I've seen examples of these rugs in my travels," he said, "and people always told me they came from a weaving village outside of Oaxaca, Mexico. When I heard about the spinning of the wool, the natural dyes, and the traditional but modern patterns, it reminded me of the old, hand-crafted Norwegian goods, very authentic, you know, not manufactured. As you can see, I have a personal appreciation for the workmanship."

"And what is your business interest?" I asked, hoping to get to the point.

"My wife died two years ago, and last year I moved back to town."

"To Aspen?"

"Yes. Well, in the river valley coming into Aspen. The winters were getting lonely and difficult for me up there in the valley at Ashcroft, even for a hearty soul like me. The business had dropped off, and feeding and maintaining the dogs had become challenging, so I closed off the business and sold a piece of my land to some people who wanted to open a small restaurant. Now my inn, more of a cabin than an inn really, sits vacant on a little plot of private property completely surrounded by National Forest Land full of spruce trees and aspen groves. In the summers it would be a perfect place to sell these rugs because a lot of tourists come by to visit Ashcroft, which sits just across the road, and to have lunch at the thriving little restaurant.

"Ashcroft? People come to visit a ghost town?" Juana asked. "Sounds creepy."

"Well," Tor continued, "there's the remains of an old mining village there with weathered, barn-wood buildings: a post office, saloons, and even an old hotel. But people also come to see the valley, which is one of the most beautiful spots in Colorado—maybe even in the whole world—and to imagine what it must have been like to live there in a silver-mining town in the late eighteen hundreds, when Ashcroft was larger than Aspen."

"You think it would be a good place to sell rugs and blankets made in Mexico?" Juana asked, a skeptical frown on her face.

"Yes, of course. The tourists have good taste and plenty of money. They come from all over the world."

I was reminded to ask again, more specifically, "And what is your financial interest in the rug business?"

"I don't have any financial interest. I've made my money. I'm kind of an odd duck, and an old one at that, and I'd just like to see some honest, hard-working folks from Mexico be given a chance to sell their marvelous weaving at a good price in a nice setting. It would put the cabin to good use in the summer months. There is plenty of space to live there and set up a nice display in the rooms up front." Then he paused for a moment and started shaking his head back and forth before he resumed "It's terrible what's being said in the US these days about Mexican people. It's wrong and it's downright embarrassing. Maybe this is my own small way to say sorry."

"You don't want a share of the profits?" I asked directly.

"Not a penny."

"No rent for the cabin?"

"None."

"No requirements?"

"My only stipulation is that after modest living expenses are taken out, along with the costs of transport, the rest of the money will come back to this weaving community right here as a fair return on the product."

"You're serious," I said, looking him straight in the eyes, but not doubting him.

"I am. And to show you just how serious, I will send you two plane tickets to Aspen for late May so that you can see the cabin and the valley. We might say this is my charitable contribution from one valley to another, and I want to get it started this summer before I get any older. It's my dream to do a little good in this world before I pass on. Do you think you and your neighbors can produce a hundred rugs and blankets by June?"

"Wow! That many? I'll check with my father," Juana said, "but, yes, we will try to make as many as you think we can sell."

"Well, good." Tor ran a hand through his graying blond hair as his head nodded gently. "That sounds good. So, who's coming to Aspen? The two of you?" His dancing eyes glanced back and forth at us.

I looked over at Juana and her gaze was fixed on me with a big smile on her face. Then she turned to Tor. "Yes, the two of us," she said with assurance, pointing at me and herself. "That's who it will be."

Then we found Sebastian and Magdalena to help us show Tor around the weaving operation in the household and introduce him to some of the neighbors. He grew even more excited about fulfilling his dream as he saw more examples of the weaving, more patterns and bright colors.

Juana drew me aside at one point when Tor was occupied and asked, "Is this guy serious?"

"I believe he is for real, Juana. The test will be if he sends us the tickets, but I'm sure he will. Sometimes you need to trust people."

A hand flew up in front of her mouth, but she couldn't keep the words from popping out anyway. "Even Americans?" she said.

"Some Americans," I replied. "Some."

That evening Abuela Paulina made her tasty Oaxaqueño dark mole sauce with a hint of that chocolate taste to spread over the chicken as we served Tor a traditional Zapotec dinner. When we showed him to his room, he apologized for being exhausted and asked if he could retire.

Then we quickly assembled the whole family at the table under the mango tree, and I laid out the proposal from Tor as Juana translated the English into Zapotec. Naturally, the family had a lot of questions, and needed considerable reassurance about Tor's background and motives in this deal, but eventually Abuela Paulina said, "Try this as an experiment. If it fails, nothing is lost. We still own the rugs and can sell them somewhere else. If it succeeds, it could be very good financially for everyone who participates. I'm sure that Carl will see that no one takes advantage of our family."

Then Juana told them about the two tickets to Aspen, explaining that I had taken courses in business so that I would know how to set things up. And she was the only one in the family with good enough English to understand Señor Tor and be the salesperson in Aspen for the weaving. Everyone agreed, or at least no one objected, even though this involved Juana's going off to the United States with me.

"At least she won't be alone," Sebastian said, glancing at me as if to underscore my responsibility for her safety.

"I'm sure Carl will take good care of my sister," Francisco said, after keeping mostly silent through the discussion. "I think this is a good opportunity for the Hernandez family. I will try to buy a few more sheep this week. We may need to find some more looms. But don't worry, we can produce the goods. The neighbors will be excited when we tell them tomorrow."

And so, with the blessing of the head of the household, Sebastian, and the eldest son, Francisco, we were on our way to Aspen, that is, if the plane tickets arrived as promised.

One day, after the pre-school class at the church, Padre Paulo came up to me with Juana. He had been talking to her about one of the former pre-school students, now in second grade, Gabriella Gutiérrez. The priest was pointing to a picture she had drawn of a child in a hospital bed and an ambulance with a big red cross. Coins were coming down from the clouds like rain. As he spoke in Spanish, Juana translated for me although I found myself understanding quite a lot of Spanish these days.

Apparently, Gabriella had been operated on successfully for a brain tumor, but the drug for chemotherapy, coming from a company in the US that had raised its prices, was now even more expensive, and although the government paid a portion, the balance was too much for the family to cover alone. Without the drug, the tumor would return. No one knew what to do.

"I know this family," Juana said. "Of course, they can't afford it. They are weavers like the rest of us. Oh, and that little Gabriella is so cute."

Their eyes had shifted to me to suggest a solution, and I needed to think fast. We needed to raise some money. I recalled how that had been done in our town when I was in high school. A family had lost their home in a fire. I was never very positive about that town, but good-hearted people exist everywhere, and people in the US are good at organizing charity events. I remembered what they did and began to think about something similar for Juana and Padre Paulo.

"Well, here's an idea for a fund raiser," I began. "Let me see what you think. We will hold a breakfast on the plaza and get a restaurant to sponsor it."

"The Golden Rooster," Padre Paulo suggested.

"Okay. They provide the breakfast for free. That's their contribution. But we sell tickets, and people pay for these tickets, which are a little more expensive than usual."

"The ticket sales are all profit?" Juana asked.

"Exactly," I continued, "but the tickets also have numbers on them. There's a drawing for prizes we announce in advance, so that many people will be motivated to buy several tickets, hoping to win something."

"Where do the prizes come from?" Juana asked.

"All over Oaxaca." I told her. "We go to the city and surrounding communities to get stores to donate prizes free."

"So the prizes don't cost anything either," Padre Paulo said. "I'm starting to like this idea."

"And we get sponsors, too," I continued. "They will be businesses and non-profits who give cash to have their names projected on a screen over and over that morning at the breakfast."

"How many?" Juana asked.

"Maybe ten, but as many as we can get. All of the money goes to Gabriella's family to buy what is needed for the treatment."

"I think it will be a huge success," Juana said. "But who will organize it?"

"I'll help," I said, but Padre Paulo, here, knows everyone in town. Once we get the idea out there, people will volunteer and ask how they can help out. We just need to set a date and make it happen."

In the next few weeks, Juana and I had a lot to do. I taught pre-school at the church and English at the university. Juana had her usual weaving to do as well as household chores, which she never thought of as chores. Together, we had to set up the business in Aspen and learn about exporting from Mexico and importing to the US. We had to choose a company to ship the rugs—probably FedEx or DHL—and see what it would cost. We needed to get several families to contract for producing an agreed upon number of rugs and blankets. In every spare minute we could find, we worked on getting businesses to give gifts for the breakfast and on signing up sponsors. And this became our life. But we always found time to prepare and enjoy meals, to spend time with the family, and to enjoy the rising and setting of the sun.

Juana had learned to drive the green bean machine, and although she didn't drive much, occasionally she would shuttle the two of us over to the nearby ruins so that we could enjoy kissing in the moonlight at Mitla. Our romance grew stronger and no one in the family appeared to object. At times it seemed like they were encouraging it. Obviously, I had decided to stay on until our trip to Aspen. And after that, of course, I would need to help Juana set up the business that summer at Tor's cabin in the Ashcroft Valley.

I asked myself if all of this activity was something I was just making up to give a pointless life a little meaning. Well, so what if it was? None of it seemed foolish or ridiculous to me, in fact just the opposite, because everything we did was helping someone. Was I trying to build an authentic life by living according to the universal principle of love? That seemed a little grandiose to me. Maybe just fighting the plague. At least I had no thoughts of suicide—Marv would like that— because I wanted to enjoy to the fullest each moment of my precious life with Juana. That day the plane tickets to Aspen arrived.

In Mexico City we caught the plane to Denver and then boarded a small jet for Aspen so that we could check out the set-up there. As the plane descended to land, I noticed a mountain outside the window that seemed really close to the wingtip, and I glanced across the aisle to look through the opposite window and saw the same thing, a looming mountain. Holy cow! Were we going to crash into one of those mountains? I pointed them out to Juana, but she was already holding on tight to both armrests and looking straight ahead at the back of the seat in front of her as we bounced through the rough air. Apparently, the pilot was guiding us in on the usual approach to the only runway, because we soon landed safely, and when we disembarked, carrying our backpacks down the outside stairs of the plane, we could see tall mountains towering over both sides of a landing strip that stretched up through a narrow valley.

The airport building itself was small and compact compared to the terminals of the international airports in the big cities, so it was not difficult to find Tor standing alone, his hands clasped behind his back, waiting for us. We hugged and he asked about our flights as we waited for our luggage, one small suitcase each. Then he drove us out of the airport parking lot onto the highway and toward a roundabout, where he picked up the road with the sign for Ashcroft. Although it was definitely springtime and most of the snow was already melted beside the road, the tops of the mountains and some of the steep valleys were still covered in white. I had never seen anything like it, and Juana kept commenting on the beautiful scenery and how this was the first time she had ever seen snow. We made our way to our destination on an uphill ride of about twenty minutes over a winding road that seemed to be following along beside a rushing river. Eventually Tor pulled off the road into a gravel parking area bordered by a wooden rail fence in front of the cabin. When we stepped out of his SUV, we realized that we were standing in the valley of a pristine mountain paradise.

"Let's use what's left of this evening to get you settled, and I'll show you the ghost town tomorrow. Maybe we can even hike part way out to the restaurant then." The air was clear and moist and I took some deep breaths. "There's less oxygen here," Tor said, "but you'll grow accustomed, young as you two are."

We followed Tor along a board walkway that turned into a bridge crossing over a narrow fast-flowing stream as he led us up a slight grade to a cabin perched on a knoll overlooking the valley. As he unlocked the front door and entered, he said, "This is the room where you will display your rugs as hangings on the walls, with stacks and stacks of them to be examined by the tourists who will stop here to buy them."

I couldn't even imagine a tourist finding this place, and Tor must have read my mind or the expression on Juana's face, and reassured us, "It's not summer yet, and we're actually in low season at the resorts between summer and winter, but when summer arrives, so do the tourists. They'll stop off here when they come to explore Ashcroft. Just place some of the rugs on that rail fence down there by my SUV and hang a few across the porch railings here, and you'll see what happens. Maybe put up a sign down by the road." He pointed and moved about from place to place with enthusiasm as he made suggestions about what we could do to display the rugs.

Then Tor showed us the rest of the cabin, which I remembered that he had called an inn, and I could easily picture it as a bed-and-breakfast with what remained of a small kitchen, a dining room, and several guest rooms with beds all made up. "You lived here?" Juana asked him.

"My wife and I, yes for many years. I rented the rooms and she cooked the breakfasts. I still miss her a lot. Tomorrow, I'll show you the kennels where we kept the dogs. It's getting dark now. You need to get settled. There's a fireplace here and plenty of aspen logs and pine kindling out back. This place is yours to enjoy. I'll stop back again at ten in the morning, if that's okay. Oh, by the way, you'll find things to eat in the cupboards and frig." Then he left us.

We could have easily felt frightened being left alone way back there in such an isolated spot, but we realized that we would definitely be much safer in that cabin than being left in the downtown of some strange US city. We were going to be living by ourselves close to nature. What can hurt us" Juana shrugged, "alone out here in such a cozy place?" I almost said bears, wolves, and mountain lions, but I thought I'd better not.

We wandered around inside the cabin together, checking out all of the rooms, and I brought in some wood to make a fire in the moss rock fireplace because it was chilly. We fixed a snack and some tea and chatted for a while until the fire burned down and we both started yawning.

"Which room do you want to sleep in?" I asked Juana.

Without hesitation, she replied, "The one you're in."

That's when we began sleeping together.

The next morning, Tor stopped for us as planned to see the old village of Ashcroft, only about fifty yards—sorry Juana, think meters—up the highway and on the other side of the road, its parking lot clearly separated from ours and much larger. The small cabin at the entrance, that housed the guides in the summer, was closed, so Tor became our guide. The paths were boardwalks that led from one building to the next, providing a way through the grassy meadow that spread over to the edge of that same fast-flowing river. "It's the same stream that the road follows," Tor pointed out, "and it is dangerously close to overflowing its banks with the spring run-off."

"Run off?" Juana asked, looking up at me, puzzled. "Like rabbits that always..?"

"The snow melts at the higher elevations up there in the mountain tops." Tor pointed at them. "As it turns to water it runs off down the valley, collecting into the river here. That's why it's called run-off. Right there just below where the snow is still appearing, you can see what's left of the old silver mine that made this town prosperous. There were three mining towns: Ashcroft, Independence, and Aspen. They came into being after a prospector struck gold in 1879. Let's walk along here and take a look at some of the Ashcroft buildings." He led the way and pointed out the saloons, a store, and post office.

"Well, it's not Monte Alban," I said, taking Juana's hand, "but I guess we can still call them ruins. Just a little over two centuries back. Can you picture the miners walking the streets here?"

"Well, yes, I suppose, but I really can't picture a silver mine right here ruining this peaceful valley."

We passed several old buildings, some in better condition than others, none of them with any glass left in the windows. "This was a hotel," Tor said, when we came to the last building where the boardwalk stopped.

"Steps, a porch, two stories," I pointed out to Juana. "Quite a nice place for its time, I would guess."

"Yes," Tor said. Now turn around and look back down that walkway and try to imagine a lively little town here."

"I can do that," I said. "People walking around trying to make a life here."

~

"Now it's a favorite spot for weddings," Tor mentioned.

"Good," Juana said. "More customers."

"Would you like to take a little hike out toward the restaurant?" Tor asked. "It's not open yet, but it's a nice walk."

"Vamanos," Juana said, then switching back to English, "I mean, let's go." Where the boardwalk ended by the hotel, a narrow path continued on, uneven and rocky with an occasional fallen log across it. We plodded on through the forest with the river rushing along beside us. "What's that delicious smell?"

"The trees," I said.

"Yes, the evergreens and the aspen groves give off a fine scent that floats in on the moist air. You like it?" Tor asked, turning to Juana.

"I love it," she exclaimed, stopping to take in a few deep breaths.

We walked on and eventually Tor led us up a slope that brought us back to the highway. "We can continue on walking along the road here. In the summer, it will be full of cars and cyclists, over fifty people for lunch each day by reservation only."

"More customers." Juana said.

"Some of them will stop just to learn about your weaving, but many will buy."

We walked for about another quarter mile or so and as we came to a crest in the road, Tor asked us to stop for a moment and look both ways. Looking back, we could see the old board buildings of Ashcroft in the distance and across from them our little cabin. Looking ahead, in the other direction, we saw a long valley with three jagged peaks in the background, snow-capped against the bright blue sky. But the main impact was of an immense space filled with thousands upon thousands of evergreen trees covering the lower slopes of the mountainsides, the vastness of nature and the nothingness of the little humans trudging along the road. But instead of feeling like I was nothing, I actually felt I was part of it, like I belonged there with all of those trees and mountains, and I had this sense that everything was in its proper place and mysteriously unified.

"Maybe we should go back now," Tor said. "We can go to the restaurant another day when it's open."

How had this person Tor come into our lives and why were we living in his cabin in this magnificent valley? I was sure that I didn't know why such an unwarranted accident had happened to us. Later, when I mentioned that to Juana, she said she believed it was the hand of God guiding us.

The next day, Tor took us into the city of Aspen, and Juana and I were overwhelmed again, but in a different way. No ghost town here, but a pleasant mix of historic and modern buildings with several streets for pedestrians only, and a lot of upscale shops with famous brand names. Uneven brick sidewalks were woven through clumps of aspen trees. We passed a Planned Parenthood clinic, and I took note of where it was. Did we need to visit?

I turned to Tor and asked, "What brings people here in the summer? I know it's the skiing in the winter. But summer?"

"Hiking, mountain biking, and riding the gondola up Aspen Mountain for the thrill of it and the photo-ops of the views. Shopping and eating in the world's best restaurants, of course, but just being in the cool mountain air of Aspen and away from it all. But there's also a classical music festival and school here all summer long that attracts the best students and teachers, outstanding soloists, and famous conductors. You'll need to check it out. Naturally it draws sizable audiences, some of whom will visit Ashcroft."

"Oh, wow! That sounds fantastic," I said, sharing with him my new appreciation of classical music.

"You can sit outside on the lawn under the aspen trees and listen to the concerts for free," Tor told us. "We can drive over there now, and I'll show you what I am talking about."

So we did that, cutting through a neighborhood of some of the most fantastic homes I had ever seen. Some old, some new, all with beautiful landscaping.

"Many of these are worth millions," Tor pointed out. And most of them are second homes used mostly in the summer and for a few winter visits during the ski season." Passing a property with a realtor's For Sale sign, I wondered what the heck the commission would be on a house like that.

We parked in the lot for the music festival and Tor walked us along a little path through a grove of aspen trees. "Everyone refers to this as 'the tent' and that's because it has a pointy fiberglass tent-like structure. During the concert you feel an openness, the breezes blowing through, or an occasional thunderstorm passing over."

"Part of nature," Juana observed.

"Like everything else in Aspen," Tor said. "It's a town that attracts people who want to be outdoors and active, close to nature. I think you will like it."

"We already do," I said. "How can we ever thank you?"

"By selling a lot of blankets and rugs from your community. Make my dream come true."

When we arrived back in Teotitlán del Valle, we were running around like a couple of Zapotec warriors, gathering up the weavings to be sold, identifying the family that produced a particular piece by tagging it, and making arrangements for the shipping. Everything was to go to Tor's address in Aspen, and the plan was for him to take the rugs and blankets to the cabin in his SUV. We had a good supply, and it was not going to be cheap to send them, but we only needed to sell a few of them to cover the costs of shipment. Magdalena and Sebastian were very excited when they heard about what we told them about Aspen, and Francisco, bless his heart, worked long hours to help us get everything done, running here and there in the green bean machine. The pre-school children at the church were ready for their summer break, and my English classes downtown were finished, so we could devote all of our time to preparations, including the weaving produced by Juana and her family. I had become fairly skilled at spinning wool into yarn, but I still didn't know the first thing about weaving. In the midst of all of that activity, I somehow found time to explore what I needed to do to study for the Colorado real estate licensing exam online.

Back at Little Texas College, my classmates from the Senior Suite were graduating, and they were sending me a bunch of emails and text messages to say good-bye. They didn't forget me. Ken was going home to Taiwan and he had invited Amy Chang for a visit, although she was nervous about how she would be received by his parents. Alexisius, Olivia Richardson, and her friend Maria Archuleta all had jobs teaching social studies in a high school, but not in Texas. Alex was headed to Topeka, Kansas, and Olivia and Maria had positions in Albuquerque, New Mexico. Rachel was moving back to Brooklyn and had a lead on a job in an art gallery in Manhattan. The string trio was on its way to Salzburg, Austria, and Jolene and Tommy Tuttle both had fellowships to the Journalism School at Northwestern university. She said that they were a couple now, but she still missed me. Brenda, on her way to studying clinical psychology at the University of Minnesota, said she missed me, too. A lot! Suzette was returning to France for graduate study with her friend Bridget, and Desi was headed for Toronto, Canada, where he had a gig singing and playing guitar in a Cuban night club.

As for me, I was going to Aspen for the summer to help my princess sell hand-woven rugs made in a Zapotec weaving community in Mexico. It sounded weird, and I didn't have much to report compared to the impressive achievements of my classmates, but I was okay to be dividing my time between Aspen and Oaxaca and living a simple life with Juana. I didn't really think of myself as an expatriate because I hadn't left the US completely. It seemed more like I was some kind of citizen of the world, or maybe a galaxy, or one of the universes, trying to make a home close to nature in Tor's cabin and in the enclosed courtyard with Juana's Zapotec family without waving anybody's flag. But actually, it seemed to me that many of my classmates, in their own way, were trying to do that, too, hoping to figure out how to live their lives in some small corner of the global village, being already sick of the endless arguments about politics, politically-correct language, and the toxic bickering about the truth. Was our estranged generation the wave of the future? What would they call us? I knew what they could call me. Happy!

14

Meeting One Father and Losing Another

Marketing rugs and blankets in paradise. Mom's urgent call and a quick trip to Texas. Introducing the sperm donor. Dad's note. Our angel with wings in Aspen. Selling a house, attending concerts, and meeting people from around the world.

Juana and I flew back to Aspen for the summer at Tor's expense, hopefully for the last time free, until we generated enough capital to include travel as a business expense. I went through the formalities of setting up a small business in Colorado and giving it a name: ZapoRugs. I installed the formats for an accounting system on the computer using software I had worked with in my accounting class to keep track of every sale and any expense related to the business. Then I set up a separate account at the bank. Tor helped us with the pricing of individual products, suggesting that we were much too low and showing us how to base the price, not just on the size and the hours it took to produce it, but on the artistic appeal to potential buyers and what they could reasonably afford to pay in the US tourist market here in Aspen. He wanted us to sell as many rugs and blankets as possible at the best price per item in order to help the whole weaving community. It turned out that our angel had a good head for business.

Juana and I soon realized that we would need a vehicle for transportation into Aspen, so Tor took us to a neighboring town where we found a used Honda CR-V at a fair price. He told us it was a business expense and put enough money down on it to make the payments low.

Now we could shop for food and other supplies in local stores scattered out across the Roaring Fork Valley, named for the river that runs through it. We learned that this was also the location of Tor's modest ranch, if there is such a thing as modest in Aspen.

The day we opened for business, we selected a few rugs to hang on the walls of our "show room," including a lovely "tree of life" design, another with rows of birds, and a beautiful big abstract blanket with geometric patterns drawn from ancient Mitla. Then we picked out a few with bright colors to lay over the railings of the entryway porch, and we carried a couple down to place over the railings by the parking spot. We propped up our sign, securing it with a few rocks so that it wouldn't blow away.

Not knowing what hours to be open, we got up early and stayed open late, but we soon learned that no customers would come before nine and most were on their way back into town by four in the afternoon. Juana was excellent at explaining over and over again about the spinning of the wool, the natural dyes, and the weaving process, augmented by several pictures that she kept handy on her phone, which showed members of the weaving community at their looms. Customers were very interested in the process as well as the colors and patterns of these artisan products, and in a few days the number of people stopping by had increased significantly. Some couples bought two or three rugs as Juana suggested how they could be used in hallways, in front of a chest of drawers, or hanging on walls as art. It didn't take long for us to know that we had a thriving enterprise, and we enjoyed watching our stacks of rugs diminish as sales increased.

In our spare time, early mornings and at sundown, which was considerably later in the evening here, we walked the road up through the valley, bordered by grassy fields extending up to the edge of the forest at the base of the mountains. Gradually, wildflowers began to appear in those fields, giving them a delightful light pink color, to match the clouds at sunset. Walking to the end of the road one evening, we discovered where the restaurant was that Tor had mentioned, and beyond that we came to a place where the road ended in a parking lot for the trailheads to hiking paths that led into the National Forest at a point marked "Wilderness Area." We were truly living on the edge of an actual wilderness. We promised ourselves to drive out there early the next morning and go for a short hike, and we did that.

Everything was a paradise. The rugs were selling well, we were meeting interesting people, even a few celebrities, and our life together in that cozy cabin was delightful and romantic. We had discovered a small bookstore on Main Street, and we bought some paperbacks to read as we were waiting for customers. In spare moments, I studied for and took the Colorado real estate licensing exam, with the hope that I might one day be able to sell one of those big houses in Aspen. Yeah, dream on. Sometimes Tor would tend the store so that we could take trips to go sight-seeing around the Aspen area. We went to the Maroon Bells Scenic Area with its three peaks as backdrop to a gorgeous lake. We took the gondola up Aspen Mountain, visited The John Denver Sanctuary—a famous singer from Grandpa Swenson's time—to see the words of his songs carved in stone. We visited the ice caves, which they call grottos. Tor even took us fly-fishing in the Roaring Fork River and it was great fun until Juana caught a trout but didn't want to kill it, so Tor helped her to release it back into the river. We couldn't have been happier together living in the most beautiful valley on earth. What could possibly go wrong?

In late July, on a Tuesday, I received a call from my mother. We talked occasionally and I sent her text messages, but with this call there was an alarming urgency in her voice that I noticed immediately. "I'm sorry to bother you, Carl, but I need you to come home right away."

"What is it, Mom? Is Dad okay?"

"If I tell you now, you will only get part of the story on the phone like this, and I don't want you to worry, but I do want you to know."

"You want me to leave Aspen and come to Texas? Why?" I wanted some good reasons for that request.

"Remember how I pledged to be completely honest with you about your ancestry now that you have become an adult? Well, this is an adult matter, and I need you here so that we can do this together. I need to keep my promise."

I'm sure my face was all contorted into a big frown as Juana stared at me with concern. "Just answer me one thing: Is Dad okay?"

"For now, yes, but this can be upsetting to him, too. Here's what I would like you to do. I will send you a roundtrip ticket to get you here for a meeting we must attend this weekend."

A meeting? This weekend? I asked Mom to hold on for a moment while I asked Juana if she could manage the business without me for a few days. She shrugged because she didn't know what was going on, and then she quickly nodded yes. I told Mom okay.

~

After the phone call, I realized that I hadn't said much to Juana about my confused ancestry. If it didn't matter very much to me anymore, why should I bother her with it? So, I took some time to try to explain that my father wasn't really my father because my parents had used a sperm bank.

"A what?"

"It's where a couple can go to obtain sperm that have been given by an anonymous donor so that a woman can have a baby when her husband is sterile." I tried to keep the language simple so that she could understand, but I felt she was having trouble with the concept, not just the words.

"Are you one of those?" she asked pursing her lips.

"I am. It took my parents several years before they told me. But, yes, I am, and I suspect that my mom's urgent call for me to come home has something to do with this sperm bank thing."

"Then you better go. Don't worry about me. I'll miss you, but I'm strong. I'm not afraid being here. I never feel like I'm alone. I will keep selling rugs as long as we have them to sell." Then she became silent for a moment before she said, "It's hard for me to understand what you are saying because in my family we know we are all Zapotec. We know our father and our mother, and our grandmother and grandfather, and they know theirs, too. We respect and even worship our ancestors. This must be very difficult for you, not knowing who your actual father is."

I nodded to let her know that I understood and agreed before I said, "At one time, it bothered me a lot, and I was wanting to know, but I've stopped caring. Although, it might still be nice to know for sure."

"Then you should go to Texas," she said. "Yes, go."

As I came in from the airport concourse, I spotted Mom waiting for me in the terminal near a McDonald's, and after we hugged, I asked her if we could please get a snack so that she could tell me what was going on before driving home.

"You don't have luggage?"

"Just this carry-on and my backpack."

"Okay, I'll tell you now. It will be better than in the car."

I got some fries, she ordered a coffee, and we sat at a table in the back. "I know you want to hear about Aspen," I said, "and of course I want to know how you are both doing at the college, but I can't wait another second to find out why I am here. What's up?"

"Well," she said, blowing on her coffee to cool it before taking a sip. "This is very unpleasant, so bear with me. It has been discovered that the doctor who arranged for the sperm donors was himself the sperm donor."

"What? The doctor is my biological father?"

"Not just yours," Mom said. "He has apparently fathered many children through his practice."

"His practice of what? Fraud? Surely, it is against the law."

"Yes, he's actually under arrest now for fraud, breaking state laws that limit the sperm donation numbers, and using his practice for illicit financial gain."

"Oh, my god, this is horrible. How many of us are there? I guess I'm asking how many half-brothers and half-sisters I have."

"That's what the meeting is for, to identify the number. A notice has been posted for a class action suit, and as you might guess, it has been given extensive coverage in the newspapers and on TV. Not to mention the spreading of the scandal on social media."

"So we need to go to this meeting," I grumbled.

"You don't have to go," she said, looking apologetic and ashamed. "But I thought you should at least know about it and have the opportunity to attend if that is your wish."

"Well, I might as well go after coming all this way."

"Exactly. And it will be nice to have you with me."

"What does Dad think about all of this?" As I said that, I realized that the person I was calling Dad, who was not my dad, felt like my father in a way that this despicable doctor never would or could.

"He's a little nervous and doesn't want to go to the meeting with us. I'm not sure why. I think he's embarrassed."

"Will this sperm donor doctor guy be there?"

"I believe the attorneys for all of us have insisted on his being present."

"All of us? Are we part of the lawsuit?"

"Yes, at least for now. I have added my name to the list of women who were given misinformation."

"Fraud. A scam." My voice was growing louder and people were beginning to look at us.

"Yes, and there will be a list for offspring to sign as well, so that everybody knows who's who."

I suddenly began to wonder about this doctor, who he was and what he looked like. After all, he was my biological father. But did I care? "How disgusting," I said, standing up to throw my hardly-touched fries into the trash. "Let's go."

At home, Mom made a nice dinner that night, and we all stayed on at the table to talk after dessert. They loved my description of the Ashcroft Valley, and Dad applauded my success in helping Juana sell the work of the weaving community in Aspen. "As you know," he said, "I don't believe in angels or much else, but I must say that this Norwegian fellow you call Tor has been an unexpected blessing."

I remembered Professor Adams using those very words, unexpected blessing, to define grace. "We are both very grateful," I replied. "And we can't explain why it is happening to us. It has made me believe that there are good people in this world."

"Yes, even if they are the exception," my father said, "standing out in sharp contrast to the evil ones like this sonofabitch doctor. The contrast is striking, isn't it?"

"You don't plan to go with us to the meeting tomorrow?" I asked him in a gentle tone.

"No. I don't believe much good can come of it. Only the sharing of a lot of anger and embarrassment. I don't think you will see many of the non-biological fathers there. It's not for us. Once you attend, the cat is out of the bag, so to speak, and everyone will know you are not my son, that your mother and I used a sperm bank, and that we were duped by a fake. It will be very embarrassing for me, but sometimes the truth is embarrassing. So I suppose that you and your mother must go to stand up for the truth."

He spoke in soft, matter-of-fact tones without emotion, but I could see from the movement of his hands and the expressions on his face, that he was deeply disturbed. Mother seemed to realize the implications of what he was saying, but I don't think she comprehended how anxious he was about everyone knowing the intimate details of their personal relationship and my actual ancestry. "Your mother and I have talked about this," he continued, "and although we disagree, I respect her right as a woman to pursue justice under the law. It is her choice. As for you, it will be, perhaps, your only chance to see the man who is your biological father, and as you know, we have pledged that there will be no more secrets kept from you regarding your ancestry. Not letting you know about this and hiding it from you would have been like the obsolete secret-keeping of the past." His hands were very agitated now, beyond all reason, as if he were suddenly a victim of Parkinson's disease or cerebral palsy. "I understand that it will be good for you to go to the meeting, but it will just be too difficult for me.

Another of life's irritating dilemmas. How did we ever get into this mess? We just wanted to have a baby."

We dropped the subject, leaving it there at the dining room table, and I drifted into the living room where father sat down in his Lazy Boy chair as I filled in the gap in our conversation with more descriptions of the ghost town at Ashcroft and of Juana, which they welcomed with nods and smiles.

The physician was not from our small town. He had his gynecological office on the northern edge of the city in a medical complex near the hospital where Ken had been treated for his injuries. The meeting that day was held in the suburban Westminster Presbyterian Church, a large stone structure in the Gothic Revival style with pointed arches and stained-glass windows. The church had offered its facility without charge that day in keeping with its mission of social justice. Judging by the time it took us to find a parking spot, Mom and I concluded that the meeting would be well attended. The reporters had turned out like a flock of vultures, and the TV camera personnel were already at work outside, capturing shots and violating the privacy of the attendees as we walked into the church. For sure, there was no hiding place. A special section had been marked off for victims and their children, and it was so jammed that we had to squeeze into a space in a pew near the very front of the church to find two seats together. We took our places without comment as I glanced back and around at others to whom I must be related. What a weird sensation.

The meeting began on time and the lawyers representing the plaintiffs in the class action suit provided a summary of the facts. Here is what I recall. Instead of a varied group of certified sperm donors, as had been represented to the women patients, there was only one donor, and that was the doctor himself. How many offspring had come from this fraudulent procreation scheme? There were already sixty-four names on a growing list. Why was it important to gather these names? First, we were told, so that those on the list could know the truth about their ancestry. But even more important, those on the list needed to know that they were related, not as second cousins, but as half-brother and half-sister with important potential genetic consequences. Those implications were explained by two qualified physicians appointed by the attorneys. Their message was short and clear: Get on the list. Know who is on this list. Don't marry each other and don't have children together. Think of it as incest. Your children could have serious medical problems. Does this limit your freedom to fall in love? Yes, it does, but only with the people on the list.

I was shocked by the numbers and began to wonder about the sanity of the man who had perpetrated such a scheme. The offspring were of various ages, which meant that this devious activity had been taking place over several years. Some of the sperm bank offspring appeared to be my age or older, but others looked to be teenagers as young as thirteen or possibly still in elementary school. I wondered if we had a family resemblance, as children of the same parents often do. I tried to look around unobtrusively to check that out.

The lawyers for the plaintiffs asked the doctor's lawyers to present their client and give him an opportunity to make a statement. He appeared in his orange jail garb and when he was brought in bound in handcuffs under high security by three police guards, the assembled crowd became restless, whispering and groaning, with even some soft hissing and booing. I just listened and tried to get a good look at him.

He was introduced as Doctor Calvin MacGill, a person of Scottish descent, age fifty-six, and a lifetime resident of Texas. His name Calvin must have been an embarrassment to the Presbyterians who regularly worshiped there and were aware of their theological ancestor, John Calvin. I later looked up MacGill on my phone and discovered that like other Scottish names it had a meaning: Son of Stranger. That fit for me.

I don't remember what else they said about the doctor because I was fixed on his striking personal appearance, a handsome man of over six feet tall, well-built and muscular, light gray hair that suggested he was blond in his youth, and blue eyes that flitted across the crowd as if he were looking for his own features in those among us. I remembered reading later that blue eyes were the result of a single mutation and that blue-eyed people are all genetically related. I asked Mom if that was true, and she said it was possible to look at it that way. I preferred to think I was related to Mom.

I wondered how Calvin's genes had mixed with those of my mother, obeying Mendel's laws, even though he was an outlaw sperm donor. I looked down at my right hand and imagined how his genes were flowing through the blood in my veins at this very moment. I sneaked another look around at the crowd to see if there were offspring who resembled him, and I thought I saw a few, both male and female, but what I noticed most was the twisting of other heads and craning of other necks like a flock of geese, each goose trying to get a better look at the other, to see if they could detect any kinship resemblance to the doctor. But mostly I noticed a profoundly puzzled group of young people squirming in their seats, too baffled even to whisper to the mothers with whom they were sitting. Where were the fathers? Absent? Well, they were not really the fathers.

Calvin was asked to speak, so his attorney had him rise and face the crowd as a microphone was thrust in front of his face. He nodded and introduced himself as Doctor MacGill, although it was highly likely that his medical credentials, the doctor part, were soon to be stripped away through the criminal legal proceedings already underway. Then he smiled and said, "It's good to see so many of you out there." A chill descended on the stunned crowd. How dare he say such a thing! Was he so insensitive and unrepentant? Heads wagged back and forth as if to ask: Did I hear that correctly?

As you may have noticed, reading my story, I don't feel or express much anger, but at that moment I was struggling with myself to control a desire to stand up and shout out a nasty string of curse words at the guy, maybe to lead a physical attack on him, and to invite others to join me. As I looked over at Mom, I noticed the muscles in her face were twitching, as if she, too, were fighting a similar battle for internal control of her anger. But to me his remark was also a clue that this was a very sick man, who's megalomania had been expressed in his devious need to reproduce himself on a grand scale without regard for the consequences to those his "donation" had produced. Well, at least now I knew the truth. And Mom knew, too. She was brave enough to bring me, and I admired her for that.

But as I sat with her in the front of that beautiful church, the sacred space maliciously fouled by a sick man struggling now to find words for his insincere apology, I began to wonder if it might have been better for me not to know about my ancestry this time. What was the point of knowing that my actual biological father was a handsome but sick egomaniac who wanted to populate the world with his own precious sperm? Who needs to know about a father like this?

I was ready to leave, certain that this time I had learned more than I really needed to know about my ancestry. But we were kind of trapped sitting up front like that, and if we left, it would look like we were walking out instead of sticking together with the others. For sure, we would be stared at for it. Besides, we needed to stay long enough to get our names on those lists and sign up for copies. With nothing else on our schedule, no deadlines or plans for that evening, we could take our time.

Mom and I were quiet on the drive back home, but that was okay because we both enjoyed having our private thoughts without always having to express them. When Mom started to apologize, I was firm with her. "You don't need to apologize because you didn't do anything wrong. The doctor needed to apologize for misleading you, and he did a rather poor job of it. You and Dad did what other couples in your situation would do and have done ever since sperm banks were established by medical technology to solve a problem. Not create one. What little regulation there is in this state has not been well enforced. You are not responsible for any of that."

"I know, but I just feel bad for you."

"Why? I have a life, and I've decided now that even though life is pretty dang absurd, it is better to have a life than not have a life. I'm happy now living the life I have." Mom didn't respond, and I thought I saw a tear slipping down her cheek. "I won't even say that you need to forgive yourself because there's nothing to forgive. I have a father, and I would never think of that medical fraud guy as my father." Then I searched for some way to lighten things up, to insert a little humor. "If you want to worry about something, you can fret about what I might inherit from that asshole. Let's go back to Mendel's peas. What's the probability that I will feel the need to populate the world with children just like myself? Become a maniacal sperm spreader? Is that an inheritable characteristic?"

"Of course not," she laughed.

"What's the chance that I might inherit honesty, integrity, and a hard work ethic from the Swenson side of the family?"

She smiled fondly and glanced over at me. "I would say that possibility is a little higher, but it's not inherited."

"Okay, so if it's not inherited, but learned behavior, what then?"

"Let's just say that you've already learned it from the parents who raised you."

"That's a nice compliment," I said. "Thank you. I'm grateful to those two parents." We were silent then until we pulled into the driveway to our house.

Mom eased the car into the garage, opened the door into the kitchen, and yelled in sweetly, "We're home." There was no answer. As we went inside, I echoed her call, "We're home, Dad." Where was he? His car was beside Mom's in the garage. I went through the kitchen and dining room and found him sitting in his Lazy Boy chair in the living room, sleeping soundly, but his eyes weren't completely closed. I stood by him for a moment to see if I could detect any irregularity in his breathing, but to me it looked like he wasn't breathing at all. I touched his arm to rouse him as I called, "Dad. Dad," but he seemed cold. "Mom," I screamed. "Come fast. Something's wrong with Dad."

"What is it, Carl," she said, as she flew into the living room. She reached for his wrist to find a pulse. Then she started screaming and calling him by name, "Leon, Leon. Can you hear me?"

"Has he had another heart attack?" I asked.

"I don't know. I think he's dead, but call nine-one-one. Maybe there's a chance they can revive him. "Oh, Leon, wake up. Please, dear." I phoned for emergency.

Both of us were screaming and crying, nearly hysterical, and then I thought of what he had taught me: keep your wits. I glanced at the small table beside his chair. I saw a glass, nearly empty, a piece of paper folded in half, and a mechanical pencil with an eraser, his favorite. Although I knew I should leave things in place, I picked up the glass and sniffed the contents. Not water or alcohol, but a chemical smell. As I set the glass down, all I could think was sulfuric acid. Dad had access to chemicals through colleagues in the chemistry department. He knew all about them and what they could do. This was no accident. I grabbed up the piece of paper and read it silently as Mom stared out the front window, waiting for the arrival of a square red vehicle with a siren and flashing lights. I still have a copy of that note, although the words have also been burned into my memory.

> I am sorry to do this to you, my dear family, but I can't go on. My heart is still beating; that's not the problem. I just have no will to live, no courage to face the photos in the media, the gossip of the entire campus and community. Now they will know that I was unable to father a child, that you, Carl, are not my son, and that we the professional scientists were easily deceived by our own doctor. Students will have fun mocking us as that couple who taught The Origins of Life. My reputation in the department as a professor and scholar is ruined. I'm nothing. Now I will simply be remembered as the fool who was fooled. Best wishes, Elsa and Carl, for your future in this ridiculous world. I've had enough of it.
>
> With my remaining love,
>
> Leon

Mom was staring at me now. "Can you read it to me?" she asked.

"No, I'm sure I can't get through it. Here." I handed it to her and went into the dining room to sit at my place at the table and wait for the ambulance that would surely take him to the local funeral home to prepare him for cremation. Would there be an autopsy? I was too frightened to cry just then. The tears would pour out in the next few days as Mom and I tried to cope with Dad's despair and our own. How could he do this to us?

I called Juana and tried to explain what had happened to Dad in the best way I could between sobs. She was shocked, not being familiar with any instance of suicide in the Zapotec weaving community. But she was very understanding of what Mom and I were going through, the horror of finding him, the grief at his sudden absence, the sense of being left behind. She suggested that I should stay a few more days to be with Mom to help her with the mourning period, and I told Juana I would, even though I was missing her terribly and wanted to be with her in Aspen as soon as possible. "Help your mom," she said. "She needs you."

So in the next few days, Mom and I tried to help each other as the survivors of this horrible suicide. We both broke into sobbing fits at first, and we talked when we were able to as we were sorting through Dad's belongings here and at work. Mom was filled with guilt at having missed how strongly her husband Leon must have felt about our going to that meeting and revealing to the whole world the private matters of our family. I told her it would be revealed anyway, but that didn't seem to help.

"I knew he was opposed to our attending the meeting," she said, "but I had no idea of how intense his feelings were about our going."

"Looking back, it is easy to say we missed it, Mom, but remember, he didn't actually object. He didn't say we couldn't go."

"Oh, Leon would never do that. He hated conflict and arguments. He would just express his viewpoint and let it go at that. He would never tell me what to do or not do as a woman and wife."

"But in withdrawing to avoid conflict, he didn't let us know how strong he felt about certain things. It was easy to miss it because he didn't really express it. It's not just a matter of misreading the situation, Mom, he didn't put much out there for us to read. If he did, it was in fine print." I noticed that I sounded like Marv.

"Well, that gives me something to think about," Mom replied. "I just had no idea he would ever do this. He never talked about it or gave me any clue at all. I'm flabbergasted."

"Me, too. But let's not blame ourselves too much. My problem is that I have lost a father that I have just begun to know and love. We had some wonderful conversations last summer and fall." Then I really broke down sobbing. I knew how much I was going to miss him because I already was.

"Your father told me about your conversations. He had grown to respect you and was proud to have you as a son. He thought you loved him."

Well, that was too much for both of us, and we were both sobbing now. We stopped what we were doing and just stood there crying at each other, paralyzed. Then we hugged. Held on.

After dinner two nights later—she was still cooking dinners—I asked her what she was thinking about for her future.

"I think I will resign my faculty position. What Leon said about the gossip in his note was true. Now it will all be directed at me, including my being the cause of Leon's suicide. I can't imagine continuing to teach at Little Texas College."

"Really? But what will you do?" I asked.

"It is much too soon to know. I have insurance, a good retirement fund which I can draw on soon, the house is paid off and worth many times what we paid for it."

"You'd move out of here?" I know I sounded surprised, maybe because I wasn't sure what it would feel like to have no home although I no longer thought of this as my home anyway.

"I know I will need to try to build a new life," Mom said.

"I have an idea." The idea had just occurred to me at that very moment. "Why don't you come to Mexico with me and Juana? I love it there. If you like it, too, I'm sure you can find a way to stay, something to do."

"But what would I do at a weaving community in Mexico? I don't even know how to crochet," she said with a self-conscious smile.

"Well, visit me and Juana at least. Take a little vacation. If you like it, perhaps you can find a new way to be a botanist in Mexico."

"That sounds intriguing actually, but for now, let's just say I will visit. And, of course, I want to meet Juana."

"Which you could also do in Aspen before we return to Mexico."

"You're so thoughtful, caring about me like this."

"I can't help myself; it's how my mother raised me."

We spent the remaining days working hard together, retrieving Dad's belongings from the college, packing up his library and collecting the papers and books he had written, transferring precious information from computer files to flash drives, and completing paperwork in the office of the dean and in human resources. His colleagues in the Science Building were very kind to us, answering our questions and providing praise for his work in the thankless job of department chair, but when we ran out of things to say, they just shook their head and said things like "I can't believe it. We're so sorry."

We completed the information for the death certificate and made arrangements to pick up the ashes. Mom always paid the bills so she had a good grasp of the finances, but we still had to notify Social Security and visit the bank to take Dad's name off of the accounts. His Will left everything to her. I got a good taste of what's involved when a loved one disappears from the face of the earth, the multitude of markers of their presence and absence.

It was a difficult good-bye, my leaving Mom all alone in that house. Although she expressed a desire to resign, the dean persuaded her to complete her fall teaching assignment at the college, made lighter by simply cancelling Origins of Life. Had he wanted to eliminate their course anyway? She decided to keep a low profile while she explored her other options. But she promised to visit us in Teotitlán del Valle in December for the holidays. At the airport, as I started through security to head for the gate, I looked back to wave and saw Mom standing there trying to be strong with tears streaming down both cheeks. So sad.

Juana had locked up the cabin and driven down from Ashcroft to meet me at the airport. She didn't like to drive but did well enough when she had to. I still had some lingering fears of driving so we only used the car when necessary. It occurred to me that we could probably sell it when we left and get another next summer when we returned.

It was so good to see Juana's smile, to touch her body, to hear her voice. Being apart drew us together. It happens, they say.

"The rugs are selling even better now," she said proudly as I was driving to the cabin.

"Word is getting out," I said.

"Word?"

"We are becoming known. They've heard of us," I explained.

"I think that's true. Some people hand me this beautiful little card when they arrive." She pulled one from her purse to show me.

I glanced at it quickly as I was driving. "Elegant. But where did this come from?"

"The customers say they find them in the stores or near the exit at the restaurants where they eat."

"It must be Tor," I said. "He's been doing some marketing for us. This angel has wings and never rests."

"True angels never sleep," Juana replied, in a voice that suggested that she had no doubt that Tor was an actual angel. "Anyway, it's working. I think we will sell all of our rugs and blankets by the end of the summer."

I pulled into our parking spot and we walked on the boardwalk planks and across the bridge over the little stream and up to the cabin, lugging my stuff while trying to hold her hand. It felt wonderful to enter that cabin and know that we would be back together for the rest of the summer. After I unpacked my small suitcase, we took a short walk up the valley on the main road to watch the sunset. I still found it hard to talk about Dad without my voice cracking with grief, but I did tell Juana about Mom's situation and that she would visit us in Oaxaca in December.

"That's a terrific idea. I can't wait to meet her. I will tell my parents and they will make sure that she is welcome."

"I don't know how long she will stay," I said.

"It doesn't matter how long. Let's just make her happy while she is there."

"Yes, the Zapotecs know how to make people feel happy. Look at me."

Juana grinned and said, "Even at this sad time, you do look happy."

"Because of you," I said.

When we returned from our walk, we prepared a little dinner together, and jumped in bed, like a couple of old married dudes.

The next day, my first day back, I drove into Aspen to shop for groceries and pick up the mail at our postal box. I found a notification from the Colorado real estate licensing board and ripped it open. I had passed the exam. Wow! That was good news. Now I could look for an agency to work with so that I could sell one of those fancy homes, or maybe even a ranch in the Roaring Fork Valley. I had my own dreams about what I would do with some of that money.

In a shop window, I noticed a poster about the Aspen Music Festival concert for that coming Sunday with the orchestra playing Tchaikovsky's

Symphony No. 6, the Pathetique. I remembered it from my music appreciation class, and I knew that it would bring a flood of tears, but maybe that would be a good thing for me. Get some of my sadness out. Juana and I could close the rug business a little early and go sit outside the tent to listen to the four o'clock concert on the lawn under the aspen trees.

In the next few days, I talked with Juana about my ancestry, reviewing my journey from being an in vitro baby, to being suspicious about my father's family, to his telling me he wasn't my father, on through to this recent crushing news about the sperm donor. She listened carefully, noting how I must have felt, and acknowledging how painful and confusing it must have been for me all those years. We had a searching discussion of the importance or unimportance of ancestry, and we concluded that for her it might feel a little more comfortable if her ancestry were somewhat less important, while for me I had always envied her clear ancestral ties, maybe giving them too much importance. I had always had a strong desire to know who my ancestors were until I met the sperm donor and wanted nothing to do with the jerk except to forget him. We both agreed that who we are, can be and should be determined by being the person we choose to be, not by our ancestry. For me, I liked trying to be Zapotec and she liked trying to be American, so I told her maybe that's why we were such a good couple. We both laughed at that.

I also told Juana that the more I learned about my father not being my actual biological father, the more it felt to me like he was my father.

"He loved you and he raised you," she said gently. "That's why he felt like your father and you felt like his son."

"Yes, it's true, and lately we had become much closer. That's why I miss him so much. I loved him." I started to cry and tried to hide it by putting my hands up to my eyes.

"Cry, Carl. Go ahead and cry. Zapotec men cry. It's okay."

I needed that because I knew that sitting outside the music tent listening to that symphony live on Sunday would make me bawl like a baby.

I drove into the spacious parking lot for the music festival, and Juana helped me carry all of our stuff over to the tent. We learned that we should arrive early to get a nice grassy spot close to the open vents that kind of serve as windows to the tent. We did that and laid out one of our larger Zapotec rugs to sit on and spread out our picnic. Juana had put together some shrimp and fried onion filling for flour tortillas which we ate with corn chips and homemade guacamole. I surprised her with a bottle of California white wine which we drank from plastic cups.

Slowly, the crowd for the concert gathered to go into the tent while more and more "campers" arrived to sit outside with us, many with small children and dogs, two good reasons why they were sitting outside. We enjoyed observing the elaborate preparations that many of the wealthy Aspenites had made for their picnics, particularly their sets of delicate wine glasses in classy portable cases. Everyone remained calm and cooperative, although occasionally some of the dogs would want to play with other dogs and would need to be jerked back on their leash with a harsh command. We heard the orchestra tuning up and then the applause when the concert master came on stage and the conductor stepped to the podium. I explained everything to Juana in soft whispers. The audience inside and out settled down, including the dogs, each one in its favorite position, head on outstretched paws and snuggled up near their owner's feet.

The concert had two shorter works in the first part, including what I was sure was a Beethoven overture. At the intermission, when the picknickers stirred about to pour a little more wine, I gave Juana an abbreviated course in Music Appreciation, consisting mostly of answers to her sharp questions. I told her about the main instruments and how they made the different sounds she was hearing. I gave her the word theme for a melody that keeps repeating, and variation for the creative changes in the theme. Then I told her that Tchaikovsky was Russian, and that his music was full of singable melodies that could be very emotional.

Although I knew what to expect, because we had studied this symphony in my course, the high emotion that it aroused in me hit me hard, as I heard it live for the first time. Here I was sitting with Juana, listening to Tchaikovsky in a small aspen grove, the leaves quaking in the breeze under the bluest of skies. I was an emotional wreck to begin with, still traumatized with the image of my dead father sitting in his chair, worried about my mother being alone, and hoping I would never lose Juana. The tears came in a flood like spring run-off. As I looked over at Juana, I noticed that she was crying, too, maybe for her grandfather, or out of homesickness for the courtyard, or maybe because that melody in the strings, so sad and beautiful, could make anyone cry. What was it about music that it could do that to us? How could it reach inside us and touch the emotions like that, these mere vibrations of air? And where was it touching me? In the brain, the heart, my bones and muscles? Where were the emotions located? And the music wasn't all sad; some sections of it were very joyous and triumphant, but these parts made me cry, too. When the concert was over, we stood up and stretched, and the people next to us, an older couple with what appeared to be their grandchildren, came over to us to say hello.

"Did you enjoy the concert?" he asked in a husky voice that reminded me of Grandpa Swenson.

"Oh, yes, but that music is really sad," I said.

"But beautiful," his wife said. Then, while the grandchildren were petting someone's Yorkie, she pointed to the rug we had been sitting on and said, "Are you the couple that sells the Mexican rugs out by Ashcroft?"

"We are," Juana said. And then she went into her little sales pitch about how they are made from hand-spun wool and natural dyes.

The woman smiled and looked up at her husband as she asked, "Do you like this beautiful one here, Henry?"

"Well, you'd better ask her if it's for sale, honey," he said.

"Yes, we would sell it," Juana indicated. She bent over and found the price tag we had attached to each rug and glanced at it. "It says six hundred dollars."

Henry started digging in his pants pocket and pulled out a money clip of hundred-dollar bills. "I've only got five hundred here, Lizzy," he said, looking down at her as if he expected Lizzy to have a hundred dollars stuck in her bra.

"Five hundred is okay," Juana said, waving the back of her hand. "How did you know about us at Ashcroft?"

"We're friends with Tor," Lizzy said.

"Well, then of course we want you to have it for five hundred," I said.

Then Lizzy's face lit up as if she were suddenly inspired by a fresh idea. "I know what we can do," she said. "We can't make the concert two weeks from now. "How would you like our tickets?" she said. "They're in the fourth row."

"You mean for inside," Juana said, looking up at her in astonishment.

"It's Rachmaninoff," Henry said. "You know, the famous Piano Concerto Number Two. Only it will probably make you cry again."

"Yes, yes, of course we'd like those tickets," I said enthusiastically and without hesitation.

"I'll have Tor bring them out to you," Lizzy said.

"And thanks again for the discount on the rug." Henry gave me the dollars as Juana shook the rug and folded it neatly, handing it to him.

Wow! I couldn't believe it. The fourth row? Rachmaninoff's piano concerto?

Tor had referred me to a real estate office in downtown Aspen, opening another door for us and putting in a good word on my behalf. They welcomed me and over the past weeks I had been working with a client, a younger couple, but older than I, who had inherited a small, older Victorian house from their grandparents in that nice residential section of Aspen near the music tent. Being from Missouri, they would rather have the money than a second home so far away. So the office thought that I might be a good match for this client, being young myself. It was true, and we hit it off great. Tor spread the word, and in two weeks, we had interested prospects, one of which turned out to be the buyer, an older acquaintance of Tor's from the Valley who wanted to move into town. Done deal. It sold for three million and the company earned ninety thousand off of it, giving me sixty.

I told Juana and she was completely astonished and wild with excitement. We agreed that we could find some good causes to spend it on back in Oaxaca, beginning with the pre-school at the church and Gabriella Gutiérrez, the girl with the brain cancer. Selling real estate seemed to me like an enjoyable way of fighting the plague, especially when I thought of myself as Robin Hood, taking from the rich and giving to the poor.

When Tor came out to the cabin with the concert tickets, I thanked him for all of his work behind the scenes to help us out in so many ways, mentioning each way. Then I invited him to sit down with me at the computer to view my accounting records to see how the business had performed. For the nearly two hundred rugs and blankets, averaging five hundred dollars per sale, some more and some less, we were right around one hundred thousand dollars gross, and by subtracting expenses for shipping and the modest costs of our simple lifestyle, we had a pile of profit to take back to the workers of the weaving community. Tor was delighted; his dream had come true.

"Just what I was hoping," he said, "for my little project to help folks out in Mexico. Of course, you and the families have done all the hard work, but at least you are now receiving fair compensation for that work."

"More than we could get in the so-called boutique shops at fine

Mexican resorts," Juana said. "My family will be very pleased."

"Will you return next summer?"

"Is that an invitation?" I asked.

"Oh, heavens, you don't need an invitation," Tor replied, shaking his head back and forth.

"Well, a lot can happen between now and then," I said with a little hesitation, "but I'm sure Juana's family would like us to return."

"The cabin will be waiting for you. What about your car?"

"I was thinking of selling it," I said.

"Good, because I think I have a buyer for you."

Tor was always one step ahead, always doing something for somebody else. I thought of asking him if he knew about Albert Camus and fighting the plague, because Tor was a perfect example of Doctor Rieux, but then I caught myself and held my lips together tightly. Nobody really needs to know about Albert Camus, I told myself, or Buddha, Confucius, Jesus, or Mohammad, to do good deeds. I enjoyed knowing about them along with Monet, Picasso, Jane Austin, Thomas Hardy, and all of my other intellectual companions, because I lived the "life of the mind" as my professors at LTC called it. But Tor seemed to be a natural Golden Rule guy who just went about caring for those he met. I think a lot of people in Aspen thought of him in that way. Yes, this angel seemed to have hard-wired divine connections.

One unexpected pleasure that came from selling rugs and blankets in Aspen was the opportunity to meet people from all over the world. We were surprised to encounter people from India, Thailand, and the United Arab Emirates, who had found our remote cabin way back in the Ashcroft Valley.

The woman from India, draped in a colorful patterned silk sari and with a red bindi dot on her forehead, bought a sizable tote bag that Cecelia had made by sowing together two small blood-red rugs and putting cloth handles on it. "Now I have a carry-on to take with me on the plane," she said.

"Yes, and you could probably fit a small rug in there," Juana said, showing her one with a pattern of flying birds.

"I'll take it," she said, and then Juana spent time talking with her about the woman's family, her town, and the Hindu temple dedicated to the goddess Durga.

The young man from Thailand, complete with a saffron robe and shaved head, liked a small rug with a Tree of Life pattern. As Juana was explaining it to him, she asked how he liked Aspen.

"The most unusual place I have ever visited," he said. "And so calm and peaceful over here in the valley. A wonderful place to meditate."

"I'm from Mexico," Juana told him, "and I feel like a completely different person here."

"Indeed, you are. The Buddha taught that we have many selves. There is no such thing as a permanent self. Everything changes."

"My friend Carl here has explained to me about Buddha's life, and I love his teachings." She smiled at him with that smile, and I could see the poor monk melting underneath his orange robe.

Two women from the United Arab Emirates, dressed fashionably with gold jewelry, and wearing dark headscarves, became completely fascinated with the rugs and asked Juana several questions about how they were made.

"People from the United States," I observed, "go to the Middle East to shop for Persian rugs."

"Yes, we have many types of hand-woven rugs, those you call Persian, being from Iran, but we have nothing like these." She pointed to some of her favorites.

"I am sure they would sell well in Dubai," the other woman said. "You should consider exporting them to us."

"Yes, we would be happy to work with you," the first woman said as she handed Juana a business card.

Juana delighted in these international contacts and told me on one of our walks at sundown that she still wanted to travel, but felt that she was already traveling as she met these people from other countries. She said that her Zapotec soul was no longer shut up behind the courtyard wall, but was flying all over the world through the people she had met here.

Juana and I arrived early on Sunday afternoon for the concert, having sold our last two rugs that morning. Before the concert, we sat outside on a stone bench enjoying fresh chocolate chip cookies and bottled water sold at a small concession stand near the entrance to the tent. We were fascinated with the fashionable garb of the elderly crowd that slowly gathered by the tent, waiting for the doors to open. When they did, we showed our tickets, and young people, probably students at the music school, handed us programs. We followed the crowd, moving left toward the stairway, and I was surprised as I glanced around at how big the tent was inside. The seats for the orchestra were spread across a large stage, and the seating for the audience curved around in a semicircle of upholstered tiered benches. I took Juana's hand as we made our way down the steep stairs to find Lizzy and Henry's assigned seats in the fourth row.

When we were seated, Juana said, "I can't believe I'm here." She held out an arm and pinched it, as if to check if it were really her own. Look at this place. We are so close. And what's this book they gave us?"

"It has program notes, explanations of the music we will hear. Let me find you the place where it describes Rachmaninoff, and you can read about him."

"How cool that I can do that now."

Juana's English had improved a lot over the summer from talking to people about many different subjects while she was selling them rugs. She had been reading novels in English, too, so I was sure she would get something from the program notes. I let her read to herself for a while.

"Okay, it looks like this guy was very sensitive to criticism. Some critics blasted him, and he got very depressed and stopped composing. Is that it? Juana was checking her understanding of the notes with me.

"That's right, but he had a counselor." I pointed out, remembering Marv.

"Yes, a psychiatrist, it says, who used hypnosis to restore his self-confidence. Then he started composing again."

"And the result was this very concerto we will hear today." I noted.

"When was all this happening?"

"The concerto premiered in October of nineteen one."

"Oh, yeah, I see it here now. Wow! These notes are fantastic. I feel like I know this guy." She looked up as the pianist came on stage and sat down right in front of us.

The conductor appeared, bowed to the audience, and turned toward the orchestra while nodding at the pianist to begin. The music started out with the piano, very softly at first, but growing louder and louder like a church bell ringing, the chord in the right hand changing slightly each time, and the note in the left staying the same—bong, bong, bong, bong—but both getting louder until the full orchestra came in as if to lift us out of our seats and put us right on stage in their midst. So we listened and we watched, completely enthralled, and I noticed Juana's eyes flitting back and forth, looking for the source of every sound she heard. And she observed the pianist closely as his hands moved in a blur up and down the keyboard right in front of her.

I cried at the end, tears of grief for my father, but also tears of joy for the happiness I was having just being able to share this concert with my Zapotec princess. It seemed so natural the way love was just happening to us and growing stronger and stronger each day, like the opening notes of the concerto. I wasn't sure where our lives were going, but Juana had taught me to enjoy the pleasures of the present.

We gathered up our programs and I took Juana's hand as we climbed back up the stairs to the main entrance and stepped out into the clear air and the pinkish orange tones of the sunset to enjoy what was left of our last Sunday evening in Aspen.

15

Building an Authentic Life With My Zapotec Princess

Returning home. Where to sleep? Mom's new friends at the college. How Juana had changed. Grandpa Swenson dies. Mom comes to Mexico. Learning about natural dyes and medicinal plants. A tour of the ruins. A research job offer. COVID is coming. A small wedding and surprise fiesta.

We allowed ourselves one day after that magnificent concert for packing up, closing down the cabin, and saying good-bye to Tor. We caught our flights to Mexico on the following day. It was a tiresome trip with many legs and long wait-times in airport lobbies, which made it seem like we were further from home than we actually were. Home? Was I saying home? It was for sure the only home I had now, with no prospect of returning to Texas to live with my mother in a house she might sell soon.

As we were flying into Oaxaca, I told Juana that I felt like I had no home now, and she said, "Actually you have two homes, one in Aspen and the other in Mexico."

"You're right. And some people work a lifetime to have something like that, warm sunshine in the winter and cool breezes in the summer. We exchanged proud smiles and then I asked, "Do you think it will be all right for me to just live with your family now? Do you think they accept me?"

"Well, you aren't exactly living for free when you have brought so much prosperity to our weaving community. I couldn't have done this by myself, you know."

"But I'm not Zapotec."

"And I'm wondering if I am anymore."

"Of course, you are," I assured her, but I knew what she meant. "I like who you are." Then I gave the conversation a different direction. "By the way," I asked her, "how will we sleep at your place, I mean, where?"

"That could be a problem," Juana said. "I'll have to think about that."

"Well, don't think too long because this plane is on its final approach for landing in Oaxaca." She just grinned.

Francisco picked us up at the airport in the green bean machine. Naturally he wanted to hear everything about the rug business in Aspen, and when Juana told him what we had made, giving the exchange amount in pesos, he nearly drove off the road staring at her as he questioned her over and over—you mean, you mean—to make sure he was hearing her right. Finally, he broke into a big smile and said, "Good for you guys."

"No," I said, "good for all the people who made those rugs and blankets. Now they will earn what they are worth. And thanks for all the work you've done, too, Francisco, to make this a success."

When we arrived, all of the family members were waiting for us in the courtyard at the table, except for Cecelia, who had married Guillermo during the summer and was living with his family. As Francisco shared with them the amount in pesos, we reminded them that each item had been tagged with the name of the weaver, and that a separate price had been established for each item. The task of the next few days would be to distribute the share of income earned, less expenses, to each family that had been part of the sales agreement. Juana told her family about the things Tor had done for us as our guardian angel, and everyone kept smiling as she talked on and on in Zapotec. Obviously, they were glad to have her home, and they smiled at me too when she referred to me, always nodding her head in my direction when she was talking about me. Everyone looked happy and healthy, but Abuela Paulina seemed frail and a little withdrawn. Was she having problems hearing? But she kept smiling at me, like she was proud for having trusted me to take care of Juana in Aspen.

Juana and I slept in our respective rooms that night and the next morning went off together to visit Padre Paulo, who was lining up teachers so that he could open the pre-school in early September. I told him that I wanted to buy some new tables and chairs and more storage bins for materials. He was delighted.

The next day, we went to visit the family of Gabriella Gutiérrez, the young cancer patient for whom the village had raised money to cover the costs of her medication. Juana asked how the fund was lasting and told the mother that if she ever needed more, that I had some money in a special account reserved for her. She said that they were okay for now, but thanked us for making them feel secure about continuing the treatment for Gabriella.

As we walked down Avenida Juárez, people greeted Juna and thanked her for what we were doing for Teotitlán del Valle. Word definitely had spread. The women smiled at me, and the men put an arm on my shoulder and called me Carlos. Everyone was treating us as a couple. How had we suddenly become Juana and Carlos to the residents of this small town? Did Juana's family look at us as a couple and were they telling others?

We settled into our routines in the next two weeks, and I resumed my teaching in the pre-school and at the university, assisting Francisco at the farm on Saturdays, helping him with the new flock of sheep he had purchased. I told him I was sorry about what he had gone through with Brenda. He just shrugged and said "live and learn." I tried to discuss it with him, but I could see he didn't want to. So then I told him that I had some funds we could use for a good down payment on a new van, but he said we should wait until the green bean machine wears out.

Life was fine, but something was missing, and Juana and I both knew what it was. We went over to our bench overlooking the valley at the back of the cemetery to have a little talk.

"I miss sleeping with you," she said, going right to the point.

"I hoped you would bring it up. Me, too."

"What can we do?" she asked.

"Maybe sleep over at Mitla in the moonlight on a cold slab of marble. How does that sound?"

"I hope you are teasing because it sounds terrible," she replied.

"Well, what then?"

"I've been thinking."

"You always are. What did you come up with this time?"

"I have an idea, but we need to be careful, and I want to make sure you approve."

"Well, let's hear it." I was getting a little impatient, thinking about sleeping with her so comfortably back at the cabin in Ashcroft Valley. Now we need a strategy?

"I could offer my parents a choice. One option would be for us to have one room that is ours, and I would explain to them that many young couples, even in Mexico, live together today like that. I won't tell them about Aspen, but they can probably guess that we already did that this summer."

"And the other option?" I asked.

"I can suggest that we could get married instead, but that would put pressure on you to marry me and would break their strong tradition about having their daughter marry a Zapotec man."

"So you are proposing…Sorry, let me chose another word."

"Oh, wow! It does sound like I'm proposing, doesn't it? But that's supposed to be for you to do." She shook her head back and forth repeatedly as she said, "I'm sorry. So sorry. I didn't mean to put you in this situation. It was just an idea."

"Actually, it's a fabulous idea. Don't apologize. Which option do you think they will pick?"

"Well, I think they will agree to let us share a room as a couple and sleep together at night. But we saw what they did to Francisco's marriage proposal to Brenda."

"You've got a good point there," I said. "But if they want us to marry, we need to be ready."

"Yes, we need to think about it and make sure that's what we want to do. We might be spending a lot of time on this bench having serious conversations." She smiled that smile.

"Or maybe not," I said. "Maybe Abuela Paulina will have a hand in writing the next chapter of our story."

It only took Juana two days before she found the courage to approach her parents with the choices she had devised as our strategy. Meanwhile, we continued our serious conversations about marriage. Were we too young to marry? Were we too different? Was I too tall or was she too short? Had we agreed that we didn't want children, at least not any time soon? Did it matter that I wasn't Zapotec, or even worse, that I was American? Did we really want to be married or did we just want to sleep together? We discovered that we were in amazing agreement about our answers.

I reminded Juana that my mother was coming and that we would need a room for her, too. Juana said that her parents would just give her the room that Tor used. "Nice try, but we didn't need to sleep together just to make a place for your mom."

That Sunday night, after Juana's discussion with her parents, we sat in the courtyard at the table so that she could tell me all about it.

"Was Abuela Paulina there, too?" I asked.

"Yes, of course, but not Francisco."

"What did your parents think?"

"They considered both options carefully, and although they had some reservations about our living together, they didn't really object. As for marriage, neither Mom nor Dad objected to the fact that you weren't Zapotec. The issue for Francisco wasn't an issue for me. I reminded them that your mother was coming, and they began to review what rooms would be used for what. After a full discussion of which option would be the better choice, Abuela Paulina asked, 'Why not both?' I asked my grandma, 'What do you mean by both?' Paulina said 'Well, live together now, 'like young people do today, and if that works out well, then get married later, maybe while Carl's mother is visiting. Wouldn't that make sense?' Everyone agreed that it did. And then Abuela Paulina leaned forward and squeezed my forearm with both hands as she whispered, 'Just don't lose that fine young man. Hang on to him tight, Juana, and don't let him get away.'"

When Juana told me that, I had to laugh. "It sounds like she really likes me."

"No. loves you. If she were younger, I would definitely need to be jealous."

"So, it's agreed?" I wanted to be sure.

"Yes, you can propose when you are ready, in a year or two, or tonight." She grinned.

"And when does the living together start?" I asked.

"How about tonight?"

We stared at each other for a second, and then we raced up the stairway to our rooms and spent the rest of the evening consolidating our belongings into one room. Hers.

During the autumn weeks before the holidays, I kept in touch with Mom a little more frequently than usual through email, phone, and text. She had not received the hostile comments she had expected at the college, at least not directly or openly, although she said that it's hard to tell what's being passed around through campus gossip. What she experienced instead, was isolation, a wall of polite neglect: colleagues, students, and friends acting as if nothing had happened, chatting informally with her about almost anything but that grim topic of her husband's death, encased as it was in calculated silence. That was the general pattern, but two colleagues she had not known well previously reached out to her over the wall of silence to talk with her seriously about her pain and her grief.

The first of these was Vanessa Winter, Jolene's mother, and my professor in art history. My experience with her as my teacher was that she cared about people, and I wasn't surprised when she reached out to my mom as a person in need. They talked woman to woman, my mom said, about the medical issues, and it was revealed that Vanessa had visited the fraudulent sperm bank doctor once herself, but just once, before they adopted Jolene. Yes, I had always suspected Jolene had been adopted. The two professors went to Danny's Diner for salads and quickly become good friends. Eventually Doctor Winter told mom about the huge crush Jolene had had on me, and Mom wanted to know if I had known about that. I emailed her back right away to tell her that it was difficult even for one so blind as I was at the time, to be unaware of Jolene's attraction to me, but that I was glad I had dodged her advances. I left it at that.

But then I remember spending the rest of the night thinking about Jolene's being adopted. It made me very agitated, and I couldn't think of anything else as I tried to fall asleep. I had suspected that Jolene had been adopted, but to know it for sure unleashed a flurry of questions in my mind. Did Jolene know that she was adopted? When did her parents tell her? How much detail did they give her? Did she have the same uncertainty about her ancestry that I had? If so, why had we never discussed the obvious problem we had in common?

I had read some things about adoption in my sociology class, and that night I began to recall and apply the information from class to the concrete case of Jolene. She seemed to be of the same background as her parents, but that didn't rule out completely an international adoption. What if she came from Bulgaria or Romania or Croatia? How old was she when she was adopted? Did she have childhood memories of living in an orphanage? Did she know anything about her birth mother and had she tried to find her? I remembered my professor saying that adoption was not so easy on the adoptee as we might think, and that some children seem just fine until some event kicks off a spasm of self-doubt, a questioning of personal worth, a bewilderment about identity. Had that happened as she sat next to me in The Origins of Life?

Okay, so I was perseverating, but I couldn't stop. So I began to think about Jolene's complex personality, how she liked me but said hostile things that put me off. Her serial list of boyfriends, her inability to settle with just one. What was that all about? Were her personal characteristics and tendencies a result of her awareness of being adopted, of being loved by her adoptive parents, but being initially rejected by her birth mother? What were the circumstances of her initial family and their reasons for putting her up for adoption? And what about that year away from college, her drug addiction, and her apparent pregnancy ending in abortion? What a complex person that Jolene was.

As the sleepless night wore on, I couldn't get Jolene off my mind. Had I known for sure about her adoption, maybe we could have talked more about it. As it was, I didn't show much empathy or understanding of her, just holding her at arm's length because she actually frightened me. I felt a lot of regret, wishing that I had somehow been able to be a better friend to Jolene. On the other hand, some people get so messed up, that it's hard to be their friend. I didn't sleep well that night, even with Juana next to me, and I remember her awakening and asking me what was bothering me. I told her it was nothing, knowing that it would be way too complicated to explain. She hugged me, and I finally fell asleep.

The next morning, as I read my mother's email again, I was reminded that the other person to reach out to Mom was my counselor Marv. She told me that one afternoon he had wheeled over from his office, navigating the ramps into the Science Building and making his way through the open door of her office to greet her unexpectedly. She knew who he was because I had told her and Dad how I had received huge amounts of help from Marv. She was amazed, she said, at his ability to make her feel comfortable right away and get right to the point with his questions. How did she feel about being betrayed by Calvin MacGill? What feelings had the suicide left her with and how was she feeling now about still being at the college? She said that Marv told her she would need to become reconciled to the reality of the loss of her husband, but that it would take time. So she asked him if a faculty member could ever visit him regularly by appointment for grief counseling, and he told her, "In your case, yes." Then he asked her how I was doing, and she told him that she was sure I was attaching much less importance to ancestry now, having come to meet the horrible sperm donor in person, but that I was happy at last with the person I had become, with a little help from a Mexican princess. So she made an appointment and went to see Marv the next week.

I want to draw you a clearer picture of Juana now after our having known each other for two years. Yes, it had been that long since my service learning term had begun in Mexico, and I had seen Juana for the first time coming down that stairway to greet me with her now legendary smile. Was it perhaps love at first sight? If so, neither of us understood it at the time, and it took the experience of being together, apart, and then back together again, for us to realize that Cupid had seriously touched our hearts to make us into the couple we had become.

I was certain that Juana had grown more beautiful and that it was not my imagination being hi-jacked by love. She already had the beauty of a Zapotec princess when I met her: the copper-colored skin, braided black hair, and dark eyes. But it seemed to me that her eyes had more sparkle now, perhaps from her keen interest in everything around her. Her hair, no longer braided, was longer and hung gracefully over her shoulders, and it seemed shinier. And that gorgeous smile now had variations for joy, humor, irony, and teasing. Those lips that spoke three languages always seemed to me to be saying 'kiss me.' Her personality had enhanced her already good looks as her petite, light-brown body moved effortlessly and joyfully in her work and leisure.

The greatest changes in Juana, however, were not physical, but intellectual and emotional. She had been a good student in high school, and learned English quickly in her classes with Señor Valdez, but, as we know, she had not been encouraged by her family to go to university. So she begged me to teach her everything I learned at Little Texas College. I warned her that some of it could be disturbing, but she waved that off as no excuse and asked me, whenever we had spare moments together, to teach her some more of what I had learned. That was a tall order, trying to recall the main points of so many courses, but actually, it was a good exercise having to decide what ideas were most important and had influenced me the most. This began when I returned to Mexico after my autumn term graduation and grew more frequent and intense as we lived in Aspen, maybe because we had more free time together then.

For example, I taught her about the Origins of Life course, explaining some of the content and how I had taken it from my parents. I recalled some of the information from their lectures as we hiked on the wilderness trails at the end of Ashcroft Valley. Who could ask for a better classroom than that for discussing how the earth had evolved? We also had wonderful discussions of culture from my anthropology course, using some examples of mores and socially-constructed customs presented in class, which we compared with ancient and present-day Zapotec culture. Juana loved our discussions of the history of Texas, and was fascinated by the way the Texans took advantage of Mexico at a time of weakness to take away half of their country, the part that now makes up the states of the Southwest. I shared with her some things about impressionist art and classical music, as well as some of my favorite works of literature.

When we were comfortable with this informal way of learning together, I ventured into presenting ideas from the world religions to her. I was a little worried about destroying her traditional Catholic faith, but that never happened because her faith was strong, and she took in new ideas comfortably, like a broad-minded Hindu enjoying many gods and delighting in the stories of the early life of Buddha, Confucius, and Mohammed. When we discussed Daoism, she thought she found ideas that were similar to ancient Zapotec traditions about looking to nature to discover the Way. I wasn't always the teacher, because sometimes I asked her to teach me more about Zapotec history, culture, and religion. She shared with me what she knew, and I was impressed with how much that actually was. I also talked with Juana about what I had learned about other cultures from my friends Ken and Alex.

At one point, I began to explain to Juana my personal struggles to find meaning in life, and I told her about the concept of the absurd in the writings of Albert Camus. She said she thought she understood and especially liked the idea of fighting the plague, but after thinking it over for a few days, she told me that calling life absurd was itself absurd, and that nothing could change her belief that life came from God and was to be enjoyed as a gift and used creatively each day to make an impact on the world in some way, particularly in helping others.

As a result of these discussions, her experience in Aspen, and her success in selling rugs for the weaving community, Juana had become more secure with herself, not so restless about having new adventures, and more content just to live every day to the fullest. Her English, which had always been very good, was now fluent, and she was eager to express her ideas and feelings to me in English. She still wanted to travel, to see more of the world, but that desire was not as urgent as before, because she had traveled already and was not sure if she would ever see anything more beautiful than the Ashcroft Valley.

It is not surprising that Juana became a much-needed point of stability in my life by the way she lived her life with enthusiasm, appreciation for the gift of being, and caring for others. I can only think of trite metaphors to describe what she had become to me: the solid rock surrounded by the breaking waves of a churning sea, the North Star in a constantly changing night sky. Juana brought my life to life, and of course, I loved her. I had no doubts about that anymore.

A few days before the Thanksgiving break at the college, Mom emailed me to tell me that she was catching the next flight to Minnesota. Grandpa Swenson was back at Theresa House and it didn't look like he was going to graduate or flunk out this time. The doctor said that he only had a few days to live. No, it wasn't necessary for me to join her.

Then she phoned me three days later to tell me what had happened. Grandpa Swenson had had a serious heart attack and although they revived him at the moment, they couldn't do anything more for him and referred him to hospice care. He died a day after she arrived. Mom and her half-sister Lena worked like beavers to get done the many things that needed to be done so that Mom could return to Texas. Lena would follow up and they would stay in touch. Decisions still had to be made about how to sell the farm, but Mom would eventually inherit a substantial sum from her father. None of this had disrupted her plans to visit me in Oaxaca, she assured me.

Then she told me that she would go to see Marv that afternoon. I wished that I could go see Marv. I loved my grandpa, and now I was grieving for him, too. These were my first experiences with death— two in a row, boom, bam— after years of not thinking about it much at all, except as a "topic" in my religion courses. Juana, after her grandpa's death, had introduced me to the Mexican holiday, the Day of the Dead, for remembering those who had passed on, and I understood the idea that death was a part of life, but now it was a part of my life, and I didn't like it at all. Grandpa Swenson had been full of wisdom, and I knew I would miss him. I didn't know if I would ever adjust to the death of my Father. I thought of him every day and sometimes the smallest, unexpected thing could trigger sadness or sobbing. Now here was the death of my grandpa, too. I found it hard to accept that I wouldn't see either one of them again. So then, I checked each morning with Abuela Paulina to see if she was okay. She had learned to reply in a short sentence that Juana had taught her in English: "I'm doing fine." She always said that to me, even on the days when she wasn't.

~

Francisco borrowed Guillermo's Ford to pick up Mom at the airport, and of course, Juana and I rode along to meet her. On the way back, I sat up front speaking Spanish with Francisco, while Mom and Juana got acquainted in the back. By the time we arrived at the door in the wall, Mom and Juana were bonded like mother and daughter, speaking comfortably with each other like old friends, as Juana took on her tour guide role while Mom asked questions about the landscape, the people, and the history.

Naturally, all of the family members came into the courtyard to meet Mom, except for Cecelia who was gone now, and they smiled and commented in Zapotec as Juana introduced Mom to Magdalena and Sebastian, Francisco, Naxali and Naconda, and eventually to Abuela Paulina, who shuffled along slowly now with a walker.

We didn't know how long Mom would be staying, so we arranged a lot of site-seeing for her in the first few days, taking her to the market, the church, the pre-school, and then to Mitla, saving Monte Albán for later. Because it was the Christmas season, the town was decorated and the market was filled with special holiday treats. A life-size nativity scene was at the entrance of the church and the carol Feliz Navidad seemed to float around everywhere. Of course, there was no snow for a snowman, so the town attached cardboard images of snowmen to the lamp posts.

Mom wanted to learn about the weaving, the treatment of the wool, and the dyes. So, Juana and I took her over to see the man who supplied the red dye, cochineal. I hadn't visited there myself and found it really interesting. We entered what looked like an ordinary greenhouse for raising cactus plants, but it turned out to contain quite a complex breeding operation.

Mom jumped right in asking smart questions, as Juana translated, and I wondered how Mom had become so skillful at that way of drawing out essential information. We discovered that the powder Juana buys for the red dye is composed of ground up dried insects with the scientific name Dactylopius coccus. Mom wrote it down in a little notebook she carried with her as Juana spelled it out. An oval-shaped, soft-bodied scale insect lives as a parasite on prickly pear cactus leaves, taking out the moisture and nutrients it needs. After the insect is ninety days old and has itself reproduced, it is "harvested" by brushing or picking it off the leaf, drying it, and grinding it up for a beautiful crimson dye.

Why is it red? Because the bug produces a red-colored carminic acid that deters predators. Who are its predators? Lady bugs, ants, and of course birds. How long has this insect been used for the color red? It was used by Aztec and Maya peoples in the second century BCE. Later, in the colonial period in Mexico, it was second only to silver as a key export. Where was it used? In the robes of Catholic cardinals and in the uniforms of English soldiers called Red Coats. And is cochineal still used today? Not as widely because there are artificial synthetic dyes, but you might still find it in lipstick. How do you make use of it in weaving? Soak the wool in the dye with a solution of water and calcium salts. If you soak it before the wool is spun, that's called dyed-in-the-wool, but if you soak it after the spinning, then it's called yarn-dyed. Are there other natural dyes? Many. Red cabbage, carrots, hibiscus, marigold flowers, and of course indigo for blues and purples. I had a feeling that Mom had found an interesting application for her training as a scientist. And the way she asked questions, my gosh, it seemed like she could draw out enough information in ten minutes for a chapter in a book.

I shared more with Juana that night about my mother's education and teaching experience and after pondering this information for a moment, combing the back of her fingers through her shiny black hair, Juana said, "Abuela Paulina, knows a curandera, and I'm thinking your mother might like to talk with her about medicinal plants. So we arranged a visit with the town curandera, not a witch at all, Juana assured us, but a very kind and knowledgeable woman known and respected throughout the village for her suggestions about good health and healings for sickness.

We walked down the cobblestone street past Pepe's Taberna and then onto the unpaved dirt road for a short distance, arriving at a modest single-story dwelling with a small veranda, but no walls or courtyard, just a secluded little house with what appeared to be a sizable garden out in back. I was surprised to be greeted not by a wrinkled ancient sage, but a younger woman, probably in her early forties who invited us in graciously. Juana told me that they had almost called on her when I was sick to near death with that high fever during my first visit, but that her mother, Magdalena, wasn't sure that curandera cures would work on an American. As Juana served as interpreter for English and Spanish, I noticed that my mother had been presented as a scientist and professor visiting from the US, a botanist.

After getting acquainted, the questions began to flow, but this time coming from the curandera. "We know that plants have curative properties, but I'm not sure I know why."

Mom was not hesitant to jump in with a scientific explanation. "We call these phytochemicals. Plants synthesize chemical compounds as a defense against insects, fungus, diseases, and herbivorous, excuse me, plant-eating animals. Plants have evolved their defenses for survival—we might say they make their own medicines—and humans can draw on some of their chemicals for cures."

"Then why are so many scientists opposed to herbal medicines?" the curandera asked.

"I think it is because testing herbal medicines for safety is difficult and so is measuring the strength of the phytochemical to know what dose is best, that is, how much to take. We have a lot of problems with false advertising claims and labeling, but that doesn't stop people from taking them. It is an industry of several billion dollars in the US."

"But many curanderas have a very good idea about how much to take of an herbal medicine and what the results will be. My mother and I together have been doing this for many years, and her mother and grandmother before her. We have treated a lot of patients. Why don't scientists study us?"

"Well, that's a good suggestion," Mom replied. "Actually, the United Nations World Health Organization is trying to make a database of the chemical effects of medicinal plants."

At that point, an elderly woman stepped slowly into the room, the wrinkled sage I had been expecting, apparently curious about who had come to visit and why her daughter had mentioned her mother.

After polite introductions, my mom asked them if anyone from the university in Oaxaca had ever come out to study their medicines.

"No. Could you do that?" the daughter asked.

"Well, if the right laboratories were available, I suppose I could learn how. But perhaps you could show me your garden. I assume you are growing the curative herbs there, not just vegetables."

On the way out back into the garden, Mom asked her, "What are your most common cures?"

"Well, let's separate the psychoactive drugs, like cocaine, morphine, and nicotine from our medicines. Those are much too dangerous here in Mexico. We work with Ginko for dementia, Turmeric for inflammatory diseases, Primrose oil for women's conditions, Flax seed for blood pressure, Lavender for headaches, and Chamomile for anxiety and insomnia." We walked down the rows of the garden as she pointed to the various plants they were growing there.

"And do they work?" Mom asked.

"People tell us they do, but we haven't studied it scientifically. We'd like to, but we don't know how to do that."

After that, we went back into the house and the curandera's mother brought us teacups and a beautiful clay pot of chamomile tea. We talked more, enjoying the tea, and on the way home, I asked Mom if she felt any effects from the tea. "I don't know," she said, "but I am so sleepy I think I could lie down right here on these cobblestones and take a nap."

The following week, we took Mom to Monte Albán to see the famous Zapotec ruins, and of course we went on a Tuesday, knowing that Señor Valdez would be our guide. We joined his tour group and when he discovered that this lovely American woman was my mother, he gave her special attention and they became instant friends. Not surprisingly, Mom was blown away by the majesty and age of what she was seeing in these ancient ruins, and she examined everything with great curiosity, including the plants that were still growing there, wondering if some, perhaps, were very ancient species. Juana and I knew the place well, of course, but we learned a lot of new things that day by the way Mom framed her questions to draw out all that Señor Valdez knew, which, as I have pointed out before, was a lot. She was especially interested in the astronomy building placed on an angle to better align with the sun on the solstice. She mentioned how much her husband would have enjoyed seeing it, and triggered a spasm of grief for me as I felt the presence of his absence.

When Mom told Señor Valdez that she had met with the village curandera, he launched into a discussion of Zapotec medicine, and Mom was as impressed with what he knew about that, just as he was also taken with her knowledge of botany. He asked her if he might talk with his colleagues at the university to see what was being done there in the field of herbal medicine, and she told him there was no harm in exploring. Juana and I exchanged smiles because we knew what could happen when Señor Valdez started exploring.

On the next day, Juana received a phone call from Señor Valdez inviting Mom to meet on Friday with faculty from the biological sciences department and the medical school to learn about their cooperative project in alternative medicine studies. That meeting led to another, and soon they were ready to offer her a research position in ethnobotany, pending review of her credentials, to help them identify and quantify healing compounds in plant substances. They recruited her persistently and offered to provide her with an apartment in faculty housing. She could also teach one seminar offered in English on evolution or perhaps heredity. She said she would consider the offer seriously, and when she told Juana and me about it, she seemed very excited. Would this be her new life?

Shortly after Mom had received this generous offer from Universidad Autónoma Benito Juárez de Oaxaca (UABJO), the breaking news arrived in Mexico about a strange virus spreading across the US that they were calling COVID 19. It was already killing people in nursing homes in the US. No one seemed to know how serious it was or how quickly it would spread, but Mom said that this was a killer and nothing to fool around with at all. Would we be "trapped" in Mexico? Neither Mom nor I felt that way because we loved Oaxaca and its surrounding areas, and after some discussion, she agreed to stay. She would accept the offer of the position at the university, and I would continue to teach English and work at the preschool as long as it was safe to do so.

When the holidays were over and the new year was underway, three questions remained, all concerning the same important matter: Would Juana and I get married? When would we get married? How would we get married? We decided to do it soon before the virus came to Mexico. After considerable discussion of my not being Zapotec, I persuaded Juana that it would be best to have a small wedding to which we invite only family members, which included my mom, Juana's parents, Francisco, and Abuela Paulina. I had to explain to Juana the meaning of the English expressions: "Don't make waves," "Don't rock the boat," and "Keep a low profile." We set a date just three weeks away. Thankfully, there would be no honeymoon night with a blood-stained handkerchief.

We made our invitations to the family members, swore them all to secrecy, and made arrangements with Padre Paulo for a quiet wedding at the church. When the day arrived, Juana and I went to the church first, with family trailing behind, all of us dressed in our best clothes, but nothing fancy like a wedding dress or tuxedo to call attention to us as we walked up Avenida Juárez to the church. It was a bit of a trek for Abuela Paulina, so Francisco gave her a lift in the green bean machine.

When the family was assembled at the front of the church, we all gathered close together near the rail, ready to begin the ceremony. Padre Paulo glanced down the aisle and paused. A Catholic Church in a small Mexican town like this is always open for prayer and a few visitors began to enter, genuflect, and come forward part way down the aisle. Those were followed by a few more, and then many more, and soon there was a steady stream of people flowing down the aisle, actually more like the Roaring Fork River at run-off time, than a stream, bringing with them a certain jovial air of excitement and anticipation. I gave Juana a puzzled look.

"I didn't tell anyone, Carl. I swear it wasn't me." Juana said, shaking her head vigorously.

"Then who? For sure I didn't say anything, and I know my mother kept it a secret."

We looked into each other's eyes searching for a clue and finding it at the same instant. I whispered to Juana, "It must have been Abuela Paulina."

"She would only need to tell one or two of her friends," Juana whispered, "for the whole town to know."

"And invite themselves?"

"Well, it is a custom here to attend weddings. No invitation is actually necessary."

"So much for our private wedding," I said, smiling, so she wouldn't think I was upset.

"They like you, Carl. They approve of us as a couple," she said firmly.

"Then I guess they should attend." I shrugged.

"We really have no choice now. We can't send them home, you know," Juana said, breaking into that famous smile.

I don't remember much about the ceremony, just that Padre Paulo said a lot of ecclesiastical things that sounded hard to believe, but harmless enough in Latin and Spanish. But when he asked me that important question about taking Juana as my wife, I answered yes in a strong voice and with sincerity. The ceremony was over in a short time, we kissed, and soon we were headed down the aisle through a sea of smiling faces. Our parents were right behind us, and I could hear Abuela Paulina's walker scraping along the stone surface. When we stepped through the main entrance of the church, we saw a large crowd gathered outside in the plaza.

"It looks like half the town is here," I said.

"At least," Juana replied, with a touch of pride.

Padre Paulo turned to us and smiled as he waved to his flock. "I think you need to go to the refectory now," he said.

"Where I teach?" I asked, a little confused.

"Where some food will be served," Padre Paulo said.

"So you knew about this all along?" I asked him in Spanish.

"There is nothing to know. It's simply the custom when there is a wedding," he replied, holding a shrug, his arms outstretched in innocence.

"There's no way to have a private wedding here?" I asked.

"Not in this town. When two or three are gathered in His Name…"

"There will be a fiesta," Juana said jubilantly, almost shouting, while Padre Paulo looked a little shocked at her unexpected conclusion to his statement about Jesus.

And she was right. The mariachi band, augmented by several guitars and trumpets, was already playing in the plaza as we began to walk over to the refectory to enjoy what I knew would be a great wedding feast. The new small tables I had purchased for the children were pushed aside and their new chairs stacked in a corner. Several long adult-size tables had been set up in their place and were ladened with the assembled cuisine of the Oaxaca Valley, some Spanish dishes, some more traditionally Zapotec, everything inviting and mouth-watering. Many of the women wore their traditional dresses. Francisco was setting up folding chairs for the elderly, and he helped Abuela Paulina get seated and then brought her a plate of food.

Some of my students were there, and the mayor's son, along with his father, the mayor, came up to give us their congratulations in Zapotec, Spanish, and English. Gabriella Gutiérrez, along with her parents, stopped by to wish us well, and I noticed that she herself looked well and very much alive.

As for Juana, she couldn't stop smiling as she greeted all of her friends, neighbors, and relatives with hugs, introducing me proudly as her husband Carlos. Cecelia and Guillermo came up to congratulate us. "I never thought I would live to see this day," she said.

"And I almost didn't," I reminded her.

Magdalena and Sebastian were standing with my mother, and the three of them were beaming at us with happy parental smiles, seeming to watch our every move.

The music from the band was drifting in from the plaza, and the crowd of people, both inside and out, gave off the rising tones of friendly chatter that happy crowds generate.

I drifted away mentally for a moment, a little overwhelmed with the magnitude of what I had just done, but without regret. I pictured my father and grandpa for a moment, and as I remembered them, I swallowed hard to suppress a sob. My search for ancestry had been over for many months, and in this moment with my marriage to Juana, I suddenly realized that my search for identity was complete as well. I decided then and there that if this plague thing became a serious problem, disrupting lives wherever it spread, I would use the next few months to write up my story, now that I knew the ending.

"Where are you, Carlos?" Juana asked, noticing that I seemed to be floating away.

"I'm right here with my bride, the Zapotec princess, and I'm wondering, now that I'm married, if that makes me a Zapotec prince."

"Oh, if only I were an actual princess," she said, shaking her head, "that would be a real storybook ending, wouldn't it?" She looked up into my eyes.

"We are never too old to pretend," I said.

It made her smile and she gave me a kiss on my cheek. Then she said, "Be sure to try the cold rice pudding dessert with cinnamon and raisins. It's delicious."

Encore

Now you know the end of my story, as far as it goes, that is, up to the pandemic. As Abuela Paulina had taught Juana: the same story can have many endings. After we were married, I had realized that each person's unique story, as it unfolds and continues on, has additional endings, each one reaching some tentative closure at a particular point in time in that person's life. But then there are more stories and more endings, perhaps enough for a sequel. Our story ended with a wonderful wedding, yet I knew I had to be ready to turn the page to another chapter and still another ending. And so, I couldn't help but wonder what would happen next in my life, and how I might respond to new challenges and opportunities. Is our destiny simply blind fate, is it in our hands, or is it in the hand of God, as Juana believes it is?

Actually, I was beginning to embrace the idea of "not knowing the future" as a way of life, as I learned to cherish each present moment. I still had an underlying sense of the absurdity of life and estrangement from the culture I grew up in, but I also welcomed the challenge of fighting the plague by doing a little good where I could and using the angel Tor as my model. Now I was also embracing the long-term commitment of making Juana, my new wife and the love of my life, as happy as possible, which I knew, in turn, would make me happy. But how would all of that be affected by an actual killer plague?

No matter how successful I had become at living in the present, my concerns about the future continued to nag me. Even though I was very happy with my life in Aspen and Teotitlán del Valle, proving myself consistently capable of shutting out the rest of the world as irrelevant, I couldn't help wondering, as I emailed back and forth with my former classmates in the Senior Suites, where things might be going in the US, in Mexico, and in the rest of the world. I tried to tell myself that it wasn't important, but I sensed that it was, at least as a matter of interest and awareness. Francisco showed me where to buy the daily newspaper, and I read it carefully each morning in Spanish.

It is for this reason that I want to share with you an amazing discussion about the future that Juana and I had with my mother. Mom had invited us to dinner, perhaps as a belated wedding present, but more likely just as a time to get together for an evening of serious talk, which Mom said she always cherished but seldom found. She asked Juana if she could recommend a nice place to eat in downtown Oaxaca, and Juana did not hesitate for even a moment as she suggested the Hotel Camino Real, where Guillermo had taken her on her first and only date with him. We explained to Mom how it was a converted sixteenth century convent with thick stone walls that kept it cool all day and with an award-winning menu of regional food served in its restaurant at night. So that's where we went for a conversation so memorable that I have to tell you about it. I'm not sure whether my story has brought enough applause to warrant calling this an encore, but here it is anyway and that's what I've called it. It's short.

We met at Camino Real in the early evening and asked Juana to serve as our tour guide as she showed us the old chapel, now a banquet hall, and the landscaped courtyards, complete with a swimming pool. Eventually we were seated at a small round table in a quiet corner of the quaint restaurant. Mom was enchanted with the classy antiquity of the place. The waiter floated quietly into our section and took our orders without writing them down, and I wondered how he could possibly remember them by just listening, since we all ordered something different.

We sipped our wine, asked Mom about her new job, and I shared with her the news from some of my college friends, Jolene, Alex, Rachel, and Brenda, that they were really concerned about how this projected killer pandemic, an actual plague, could negatively impact their future. It must have been an important topic for us as well, because "the future" became our subject for the rest of the evening as we dove into it like scuba divers testing out how deep we could go.

"Yes, we really must deal with this virus," Mom began. "It was discovered, you know, in China, just this past December. The Chinese kept it a secret, claiming it had originated in a seafood market in Wuhan, calling it an unexplained pneumonia. But already in January, just a few weeks ago, cases were discovered in Thailand and Japan, making clear that it was being spread from human to human. But how?" she asked, not expecting us to answer. "Scientists are debating now about whether the virus spreads through large drops or small, the smaller ones being what they are calling aerosol droplets. If it is the former, people need to keep a safe distance and disinfect the hands."

"But if it is the little drops, more like a spray, what then?" I asked.

"Well, widespread use of effective masks will be required." Mom paused to take a sip of her wine. "But the most important response will be to develop an effective vaccine as quickly as possible. Then we need to transfer the technology of production to other countries quickly and persuade people all over the world to get vaccinated. That will take time, and there may be resistance."

"In Texas, I remember people already being opposed to smallpox and polio vaccines," I said.

"Not just Texas. But you are right, the resistance is already there. And don't expect our President to provide much leadership, especially if it involves government mandates to wear masks. His followers don't like to have the government telling them what to do."

"Where did this anti-government attitude come from?" I asked.

"Yes, your father used to say, 'How did we the people become they the government?'"

"Does this mean that we may not be able to go to Aspen this summer?" Juana asked, suddenly seeming to grasp the implications of this contagious virus.

"Will they have to cancel events like the music festival?" I asked Mom.

"Yes, I'm guessing that large-scale events with sizable audiences will be cancelled."

"That will cut out our tourist market," I suggested. "Even if we wore masks, we wouldn't have customers."

"How sad," Juana exclaimed, not able to hide her disappointment, "What will we do with our rugs and blankets?"

"Well, what you have always done with them, but without the good financial return we got this year," I pointed out.

"Maybe we can make a deal with that customer from Dubai," Juana suggested. "I still have her business card."

"The main thing," my mother said, "is to try to stay healthy here in Mexico, listen to the scientists and doctors, and do what they suggest, because this virus will kill people. Maybe millions. It's not a mild flu."

That left us all silent for a few moments, and we were glad to have the food arrive so that we had an excuse for not talking. Naturally, it was delicious and worthy of our full attention for a while. I noticed that Juana had a large oval plate, almost like a serving platter, with bones on it, sliced in half lengthwise with the center exposed. "What did you order?" I asked trying to conceal my shock. "Bones?"

"Baked bone marrow. It's delicious," she said, using her spoon to scrape out a brown substance from the center of the bone that looked to me like dried blood clots. "Would you like a taste?" she asked, offering me her spoon.

"I think I'll pass this time," I said, realizing that I still had a few areas where I was not—to invent a new term—fully Zapotectified.

Mom was laughing at the faces I was making. Then she said, "I'll try some, Juana. Why not?"

I enjoyed my chicken mole. Later, as I watched the waiter remove the platter of bones, I asked Mom, "What do you think will happen to the colleges and universities?"

"Well, we were already learning to develop online courses and there will be more of that to reduce the contact of students with each other and their teachers during the pandemic. It will change the way we teach and students learn, but I don't think we will shut down completely. The more serious threat, which you may be alluding to, is the attack on science and the broader assault on truth. I'm afraid that our academic freedom is coming under attack, and of course that's the very foundation of what we do in colleges and universities. My new colleagues here in Oaxaca know a lot about what's taking place in the US, and they share my concern and respect my observations."

Juana was frowning, and I was sure that it must be difficult for her to understand our conversation, but then she asked, "Attacked how?"

"Not being able to teach evolution without interference," Mom said.

"Or Texas history as it actually happened. It's not just the science fields," I tried to explain. "Dad and I discussed this. You find and examine the relevant information, choose your text, make your syllabus, develop your lectures, and follow the facts to teach the truth."

"Ah, yes, but not too much truth," Mom said, shaking her head from side to side. "The truth can be disturbing, so now we have to warn the students before we speak the truth."

"So people are starting to interfere with your teaching?" Juana asked in disbelief.

The waiter returned to see if we were enjoying our dinners and asked what we were thinking about for our desserts.

"Churros!" Juana told him. Then, turning to my mom, said, "Oh, excuse me, I'm so sorry. Maybe you would like to see the menu."

"No," I said. Mother needs to know churros. Yes, two orders, one with chocolate sauce, one with butterscotch."

"What are these churros?" Mom asked. "They must be delicious."

"Like small sticks of warm donuts, only much, much better," I told her. "And while we are waiting, Juana, I want to ask my mother a few more questions about the future. And, of course, you should ask your questions, too." I turned to Mom then to tell her, "You don't need to give long answers, just your best predictions based on what you already see happening, like a Hebrew prophet."

"A prophet? Well, that's asking a lot from a scientist like me, but I'll try."

"Okay, here we go. What will happen in the election coming up next fall?"

"Assuming there will be one? That the President won't call a state of emergency and suspend it? Depending on the nominee of the opposing party, the President could be defeated. But even if he is, he may claim that there was voter fraud and try to overturn the results."

"Refuse to make the transition? End the democracy?"

"The unthinkable has become possible, Carl."

"Wow!" Juana was shocked. "Could that really happen in the US?" She scratched her head before asking, "Tell me about these mass murders. Is there any hope for passing gun laws, or does everyone already have a gun?"

"Good questions, Juana. There are now more guns than people in the US," Mom said. "Guns are everywhere, including the assault rifles used in school shootings. You have many guns here in Mexico, too. We know this because we sell them to you. The guns come from the United States, where our population consumes the drugs made available by the Mexican cartels. I don't expect to see restrictions on gun ownership anytime soon because so many people make so much money on selling them."

"Some people are saying that there will be another civil war in the United States," I pointed out. "What do you think are the chances for that?"

"Well, I don't think there will be a territorial war as there was between the North and the South. We are a badly divided country right now, but in each state, no matter which party they favor, the population is divided within. Even Texas is a badly divided state. So the civil war, if it is to occur, may be between quarreling factions within each state. Even some families are being torn apart over politics. Maybe large numbers of people will get so angry that they'll just start shooting each other."

"As they do here in Mexico over the drug trade?" Juana asked.

"Yes, that's why some of our leaders say we need guns: to protect ourselves in the next civil war." Mom explained.

Juana leaned over to ask me if it was okay to change the subject and ask another question, and of course I told her to go ahead. "What about climate change?" Juana asked. "You are a botanist, so I guess you know a lot about the environment."

"Yes, I have many colleagues who exchange emails with me on this subject. First, of all, we need to recognize that it may be too late. It is hard to know if we can reverse the damage already being done, resulting in wildfires, rising ocean levels, changing weather patterns, and the extinction of species. We will need to make enormous changes in the way we live, and I'm not sure that will happen soon enough or in a significant enough way to turn things around. I'm not very optimistic about this. Sorry."

"What about war?" I asked, knowing that I didn't want to go out and kill anyone or come back disabled like Marv.

"And what about war with atom bombs?" Juana added, her face squinched up in a frown.

"Oh, my, let's hope we learned our lessons from the last century. War solves nothing and brings enormous devastation and displacement of people fleeing for their lives. But war in the twenty-first century? Will China attack Taiwan? Will Russia invade Ukraine? Can North Korea just start shooting off missiles at South Korea? It seems unlikely, but what I fear is that a conventional war will be initiated, let's call it a ground invasion, and then everyone needs to be really cautious because the invader holds up the threat of nuclear retaliation if anyone resists or aids the country being attacked. Nuclear weapons become the deterrent against justified resistance to an unjustified invasion."

"Oh, wow! I hadn't thought about it that way," I said. "So everyone starts wondering when atomic weapons might actually be used. We just sort of slide into an atomic war from a conventional war?"

"I'm just saying that it is a possibility," Mom replied.

The churros arrived at that moment, and I knew we would be relieved to have a diversion from such a serious conversation. I showed Mom how to break off a piece and dip it in the small bowl of chocolate sauce. "What do you think?" I asked her as she tasted one.

"Well, they are about the best thing I've ever eaten anywhere. Marvelous."

Juana was grinning. "I've never met anyone who didn't like churros. Now try the butterscotch sauce, both of them."

As we enjoyed our churros, I began to think about all that my mom had said, reminding myself that this was actually my mother who had said it. She really was a brilliant woman. And now that I was getting to know her better, it appeared that our views of the world were very similar. And so, I ventured a comment. "You know much more about all of these things than I do, Mom, but I'm thinking that maybe we share a similar philosophy of life now."

"Philosophy? Meaning what?"

"That what goes on in this world, as it is being lived now in these times, is basically absurd. I mean the things we've been discussing seem ridiculous to me. I feel very estranged from the culture of my country. It seems that so much of what is done and said runs counter to my basic beliefs. Yes, I do have some now, and I feel like a complete stranger in this world we live in today. But as I listen to you, Mom, it seems that you must feel estranged, too, and that you and I are quite similar in our outlook on life. Juana and I have talked about this a lot, and although she doesn't like the word absurd, we both feel very estranged from this world you have just described, so much so that we don't want to bring children into it."

"That's interesting. No grandchildren?" She raised her eyebrows at first, but then smiled, nodding with understanding. Perhaps she was recalling that along with her as grandmother, that monster, Calvin MacGill, would also be their grandfather. "Well, yes, I feel estranged, too, and I've noticed that more frequently since my husband Leon took his own life," she said, turning to Juana to explain. "He is the man who helped me raise Carl, and we taught a class together and had an odd sort of love for each other. He had also grown very fond of Carl." Then returning her gaze to me she said, "And I notice that you and I have become grown-up friends. Now you are helping me to see that we share this same sense of estrangement and alienation. It's true, you know, but a little dangerous. I think your father had that outlook, too, so much so that maybe it contributed to his suicide." She was swishing a piece of the churros around and around in the remaining chocolate sauce.

"I also think we have similar values," I said. "I've been thinking about values a lot lately, you know, that basic sense of what's right and wrong, and what's actually important. I'm not sure where that comes from, but I know I have it now."

"From your studies," my mom said. "From the professors you respect."

"From our parents," Juana said. "We absorb it from them without even being aware of it."

"I think that's true, Juana," I told her. "I know I got it from Mom and Dad sort of unconsciously, listening to them as I ate dinner every night. Some things seem right to me now, and other things really disgust me."

"In my tradition," Juana added, "we also believe our deepest values come from God. There's just that little light in all of us that tells us what's right. We may not do it, and some people just about put that little light out, but it's there."

Juana expressed it so beautifully. I squeezed her hand and smiled at her, but then I reached out and took Mom's hand, too, and we just held on to each other like that for a while. Then I said, "Tell me one more thing, Mom, do you have any causes?"

She thought for a moment before she said, "Causes? I think so, but first tell me how to stop eating these churros. I've already had way too many." Then she said, "Your father had a favorite expression. He used to say, "You can either stand up for something or fall for everything."

"Oh, I like that," Juana said. "I think I understand the English. "If I don't have convictions, I will be fooled by everyone. Is that it?"

"Yes, I think that's exactly what it means," I said. "So I'm asking Mom if she has things she likes to stand up for and support."

"I'm interested in protecting threatened species, animals as well as plants." She thought for a moment, and then she said, "Suicidal grief. Everyone talks about suicide prevention, but what about the horrible predicament of those of us who are left behind by someone who has actually done it? We need help, too. Yes, suicide survivors. I'm getting interested in that because it has really been horrible for me. Is this what you mean by causes, Carl?"

"I think that those are good examples, Mom. I guess you are suggesting that a person can be estranged from society and still have causes?'

"It is a little contradictory, isn't it? A bit of a paradox," she observed.

"Like being happy to be alive when you know that life is mostly absurd." I added with a smile.

Mom looked down at her right hand still stirring one of the churros around and around in the chocolate sauce. "Here, please, someone take these away from me." She put the one she was holding onto her plate and pushed the plate and the dish of churros away from her. "Here, Carl, perhaps you can finish them."

"Not me," I said, "but aren't they terrific?"

"To die for?" Juana asked. "Isn't that what you say?

I knew that in the near future I should try to identify something I could die for besides churros.

We thanked Mom for the dinner and conversation. She caught a cab back to her empty apartment where she was living alone near the university. Juana and I drove home in the green bean machine, chattering above the roar of the engine about how happy we were to be alive and to have each other, but how worried we were about the pandemic and our uncertain and precarious future.

I parked the van in the small dirt lot near the side street off of Avenida Juárez where Francisco always kept it, and we walked, holding hands, to the door in the wall where I had first entered and then re-entered more than a year ago. It was quiet in the courtyard. I thought that everyone must have been sleeping soundly. Juana and I sat down at the table to relax a little, to digest the conversation and the churros, and to enjoy the moonlight before going up the tile staircase to our room.

We talked about what Mom had predicted about the plague, and it made us nervous, wondering if and when we would get to go back to Ashcroft to sell our rugs and blankets, to smell the sweet scent of pine and aspen trees, and to hear that glorious music in the tent. I rubbed my tired eyes with both palms before I said to Juana, "I've finally found the way I want to live my life, and now I'm worried that I won't get to do it. I really don't want to miss the opportunity to live, before I die, in the way I have chosen to live, now that I know what that is."

"Just hang on tight, Carlos, she said, calling me by my new name and reaching over to touch my arm. "Be patient. You'll get your chance."

"But when?" I asked.

"Tomorrow morning when you wake up and realize that God has given you another day to live."

Well, I slept soundly that night and woke up the next morning feeling fine, and so did Juana, but as we came down the stairs together, we saw Francisco, Sebastian, and the two boys, Naxeli and Naconda, working together to spread out a bed of sand in the center of the courtyard. Magdalena was arranging the candles and spreading around pink bougainvillea blossoms. Abuela Paulina had died in her sleep that night. We didn't know what the future would bring, but we knew what we had to do that day.

READERS GUIDE

1. Carl is not sure about who he is or where he came from, meaning who his real parents are or their heritage. As it turns out, there are good reasons for Carl to be concerned. Is this a worry that is unique to Carl or are there many people unsure of their roots? How certain are you about your ancestry?

2. Knowing one's heritage and identifying with it is significant to some people while others say it doesn't matter. How important is knowing your heritage to understanding who you are?

3. Some people live life without thinking much about life's meaning. Carl wants answers to the big questions as part of his search for identity. Are you a searcher, like Carl, or do you tend to accept life as it comes along without asking many questions?

4. Carl finds that science describes how, but is not very helpful in explaining why. Are you a person that wants to know why we exist and where we are going, or do you find most of the why questions to be unanswerable anyway?

5. When Carl learns in anthropology about the socially-constructed norms of different cultures, he feels alienated from the society in which he lives. Do you feel comfortable with what appear to be the accepted values of your society or are you, like Carl, somewhat alienated and estranged?

6. After the freak hit-and-run accident involving his roommate Ken, Carl

becomes convinced even more that life is fairly meaningless and absurd. What do you think about the way his counselor Marv Cohen tries to help him cope with his sense of nothingness?

7. During Carl's stay at the Zapotec weaving village in Mexico, he experiences a completely different and satisfying way of life. Have you ever been immersed in a contrasting culture, either at home or overseas? What effect did it have on you?

8. Carl thought he was falling in love with Juana, but he wasn't sure about how it would work out. Is romance more likely to be clear and certain or ambiguous and confusing? If you have had an experience with romance, which way would you describe it, as clear or confusing?

9. How do variations on the gender difference spectrum affect relationships? How did Brenda's uncertainty about her gender identity affect her personal relationships? Have you had friends or relatives who discover things about themselves through successful or unsatisfying relationships?

10. Have you encountered people like Tor, who are so genuinely kind and loving that they appear to be angelic? In today's world, where so much must be questioned and doubted, how do you feel when you find yourself being suspicious of an angel?

www.ingramcontent.com/pod-product-compliance
Lightning Source LLC
Chambersburg PA
CBHW010747310726
48980CB00004B/392

* 9 7 8 1 6 3 2 9 3 7 1 1 7 *